My husband is a wizard, and he wants to buy a specific magical item from you

Gresh considered the stranger for a moment.

He had assumed she wasn't a wizard, from her attitude toward him, toward his shop, and toward her own belt-knife; she did not wear her knife quite the way wizards wore their magic daggers, though Gresh could not have explained the difference coherently. Besides, he knew most of the wizards in Ethshar of the Rocks by sight, if not always by name, and he was sure he had never seen her before.

"Now," Gresh said, returning to the front of the shop, "what was it your husband wanted to buy?"

"A mirror," the witch said. "A very specific mirror, about this big." She held out her hands in a rough circle perhaps five inches in diamete[illegible]

"What's unique [illegible]?" he asked. "Why do you [illegible]

T[illegible] "It's where spriggans [illegible]

Gr[illegible]t. On the face of it, it s[illegible]—but then, a great deal of what w[illegible] was preposterous. She looked calm and sincere, and why in the World would anyone come to him with so absurd a story if it wasn't true?

"Have a seat, my dear," he said, gesturing to the maroon velvet chairs in one corner. "I'll need to hear the whole story, but let me finish with this other customer first."

Other Cosmos Books

No One Noticed the Cat, Anne McCaffrey
Science Fiction: The Best of the Year, edited by Rich Horton
Shadow Kingdoms, by Robert E. Howard
Fantasy: The Best of the Year, edited by Rich Horton
When the Gods Slept, by Allan Cole
Little Fuzzy, by H. Beam Piper
The Door Through Space, by Marion Zimmer Bradley
The Race for God, by Brian Herbert
If Wishes Were Horses, by Anne McCaffrey
Moon of Skulls, by Robert E. Howard
Star Born, by Andre Norton
Wolves of the Gods, by Allan Cole
The Misenchanted Sword, by Lawrence Watt-Evans

THE SPRIGGAN MIRROR

by

LAWRENCE WATT-EVANS

COSMOS BOOKS

THE SPRIGGAN MIRROR
September 2007

Published by

Dorchester Publishing Co., Inc.
200 Madison Avenue
New York, NY 10016

in collaboration with Wildside Press, LLC

Cover design by Garry Nurrish.

Typeset by Swordsmith Productions

ISBN-10: 0-8439-5907-X
ISBN-13: 978-08439-5907-9

Printed in the United States of America.

CHAPTER ONE

Gresh was yawning, still not entirely awake, when the bell jingled and the just-unlocked door of his shop opened behind him, letting in a swirl of cold air. He blinked once more, flexed his shoulders, and started to turn.

"Don't you *ever* sleep?" his eldest sister's voice demanded.

Gresh finished his yawn, finished his stretching, finished his turn, and then replied, "Good morning, Dina. I slept well, thank you—and you?"

"You certainly didn't sleep very *much*," Dina retorted. She was standing in the doorway, hands on her hips, glaring at him. She wore her wizard's robe, which generally meant she was on business. "I was trying to reach you until at least an hour after midnight. Twilfa didn't know where you were, but wherever you were, you were still awake..."

"And having a lovely time, I might add," he interrupted. He smiled broadly at her, then glanced at the shop curtains he had been about to open and decided not to move them just yet. Dina's presence in her robe often implied a commission, and that might well mean traveling. If it required an immediate departure he would just need to close up shop again. He leaned back against his counter.

"I'm sure you were," Dina said. "Are you planning to see her again, whoever she was, or just add her to the long list of pleasant memories?"

"Well, I don't think you'll be acquiring a new sister-in-law in the immediate future—but you didn't come here to inquire about my love life, Dina. I take it you were trying to use the Spell of Invaded Dreams to contact me last night?"

"Yes, of course."

"And it always leaves you in a foul temper when a spell doesn't work, even if it's not your fault. I apologize for the inconvenience. What was it you wanted to tell me?"

"I need the blood of an unborn child," Dina replied. "I *thought* I needed it urgently, since the spell was already started when I discovered I'd run out, but it seems to have dissipated safely after all, since I couldn't *find* you to get more."

"You didn't *check* beforehand?" Gresh asked, shocked. "You didn't make sure you had all the ingredients ready? *Gods*, Dina...!"

"I checked," she protested. "Of course I checked! I had one vial left." She held up two fingers perhaps an inch and a half apart, indicating the size of the vial in question. "Then a spriggan spilled it on the cat."

"Oh." Gresh grimaced as he pushed himself upright and began fishing in his belt-purse for something. "My sympathies. Spriggans *do* get into everything, don't they?"

"Yes, they do. The little monsters are attracted by

magic, you know—especially wizardry. Locks and spells can't keep them out. I *hate* the stupid things!"

"I, for one, don't blame you a bit," Gresh said, pulling out the key he had sought. "They're a nuisance, no doubt about it." He turned to look at the magically-sealed iron door of the vault room that young Twilfa could not open unassisted. "How much did you need? And how were you planning to pay?" Then he paused and looked at Dina. "Blood of an unborn child? Was that for the Greater Spell of Transmutation?"

"Yes. Not that it's any of your business." She stepped into the shop, pushing the door partly closed behind her, then crossed her arms over her chest.

"You're *sure* it dissipated safely? Isn't that a high-order spell?"

"Of course it is," she said, marching forward. "You let me worry about it, Gresh. I'm just here for the blood."

"Yes, well, I have a reputation to maintain..."

"As a supplier of goods and ingredients, not as a confounded babysitter," she said. "I'm ten years older than you and a master wizard; I can take care of myself."

"I don't want anyone thinking I sold you anything that wasn't exactly as described," Gresh protested. "If you turn yourself into a toad, then I don't want a bunch of wizards whispering to each other that it happened because I sold you a bad batch of baby's blood."

"The blood was bad?" a new voice asked, worried, and brother and sister turned to see Twilfa, their youngest sister and Gresh's assistant, emerging from the rear passageway with the freshly filled coal bucket. She set it on the hearth, then looked at Dina. "I thought you said a spriggan spilled it on the cat."

"No, the blood was *not* bad," Gresh said, with a hint of a growl.

"Is the cat all right?" Twilfa asked, as she transferred coal from the bucket to the grate.

"Is anyone...Are you open?" an unfamiliar voice called from the still partially open front door.

Gresh sighed. "Why don't you two discuss it all while I see to my customer?" he asked, dropping the key back into his purse and heading for the door. "Come in, come in!" he called.

"I can't open the vault!" Twilfa called after him. "I can't open the explosive seal."

"I'll be right back," Gresh told her, as he let in the tall, black-haired woman in a red dress. He did not recognize her, and he was quite sure he would not have forgotten a face like hers.

"The door was open, and I heard voices," the new arrival said uncertainly. She spoke with an odd accent, one that struck Gresh as somehow old-fashioned.

"I was just preparing to open the shop, my dear," Gresh said with a bow. "Do come in." He stepped aside and ushered her into the center of the room.

She obeyed and stood on the lush Sardironese carpet, looking around curiously.

Gresh was aware that Dina and Twilfa were both standing by the iron vault, staring silently at the stranger, but he ignored them. "Now, what can I do for you?" he asked.

The stranger tore her gaze away from the endless

shelves of boxes and jars and said, "We want to hire you."

"*Hire* me?" Gresh smiled indulgently. "I'm afraid I'm not for hire, my lady. I sell wizards' supplies; I don't run errands."

"I'm not a lady," the stranger said. "I'm a witch. We were told that if we wanted something hard to find, something magical, something wizardly, then you were the man to see."

Gresh considered her for a moment.

He had assumed she wasn't a wizard, from her attitude toward him, toward his shop, and toward her own belt-knife; she did not wear her knife quite the way wizards wore their magic daggers, though Gresh could not have explained the difference coherently. Besides, he knew most of the wizards in Ethshar of the Rocks by sight, if not always by name, and he was sure he had never seen her before.

It hadn't occurred to him that she might be some other sort of magician. From her appearance and slightly stilted pronunciation, he had assumed she was just another wealthy ninny, perhaps a princess from the Small Kingdoms, looking for something exotic to impress someone, or trying to hire adventurers for some foolish scheme.

But witches were rarely ninnies—and for that matter, rarely wealthy. They were also not ordinarily his customers, but perhaps this person had her reasons for coming here. He decided she could indeed be a witch, and telling the exact truth.

"Who is 'we'?" he asked.

"My husband and I. Really, he's the one who wants to hire you, but he's busy with the baby, so I came instead."

The *husband* was busy with the baby, so the *wife* was running his errands? The beautiful young wife who claimed to be a witch and whose slim figure showed no evidence of having recently borne a child? Gresh glanced at his sisters. He wanted to hear this explained, but he had his business to attend to. "I do not run errands," he said.

"Fine," the woman said calmly. "Then let me put it this way. My husband is a wizard, and he wants to buy a specific magical item from you."

Gresh could hardly deny that that was exactly his line of business. "Could you wait here for a moment, please?" he said.

"Certainly."

He turned and hurried to the vault door, where he fished out the key again, unlocked the lock, then pried a large black wax seal off with a thumbnail, being careful not to mar the rune etched into the wax. He set the seal aside, to be softened over a candle-flame and re-used later, and placed a glass bowl over it to keep it safe from stray fingers. If anyone else touched that seal, anyone but himself, it would explode violently, and Gresh did not particularly want to risk burning down the shop because Twilfa got careless or a customer got curious.

"There," he said, opening the vault. "Twilfa, find her blood for her, would you? I'll help you in a moment. And afterward, I want you to find Tira."

"Tira?" Twilfa looked at the woman in red, then back at her brother. "What do you want *her* for?"

Gresh glared at her silently for a moment, then turned back to his waiting customer without explaining. Twilfa ought to be able to figure it out for herself, and he did not care to say anything that the customer might overhear. An ordinary person wouldn't have heard a whispered explanation at that distance, but a witch would—as Twilfa ought to know. Tira, another of their sisters, was a witch, and Twilfa had certainly had plenty of opportunity to observe just how keen Tira's senses were. One witch could always tell another and could also evaluate the other witch's honesty. Tira might be useful in assessing the customer in the red dress.

Twilfa threw one final curious glance at the stranger, then stepped into the vault, Dina close behind.

"Now," Gresh said, returning to the front of the shop, "what was it your husband wanted to buy?"

"A mirror," the witch said. "A very specific mirror, about this big." She held out her hands in a rough circle perhaps five inches in diameter. "He last saw it in the Small Kingdoms, in the mountains near the border between Dwomor and Aigoa."

"The Small Kingdoms." That was more or less the far side of the World, and explained her accent.

"Yes. In or near Dwomor."

"And is this mirror still there?"

"We don't know."

Gresh suppressed a sigh. "My dear, the Small Kingdoms are almost a hundred leagues from here, and my time..."

"We have a flying carpet to take you there," she interrupted. "And we can pay you well."

Gresh blinked. "A flying carpet?" He glanced at the vault; Dina and Twilfa were out of sight behind the iron door.

"Yes."

Flying carpets required high-order magic; not one wizard in twenty could produce one reliably. And a wizard who *had* one, assuming he had made it himself, could generally find most of the ingredients for his spells without assistance, rather than paying Gresh. Certainly finding a mirror should not be so very difficult for such a wizard.

"What's unique about this mirror?" he asked. "Why do you want me to find it for you?"

The self-proclaimed witch replied, "It's where spriggans come from."

Gresh considered that for a moment. On the face of it, it seemed preposterous—but then, a great deal of what wizards did was preposterous. She looked calm and sincere, and why in the World would anyone come to him with so absurd a story if it wasn't true?

"Have a seat, my dear," he said, gesturing to the maroon velvet chairs in one corner. "I'll need to hear the whole story, but let me finish with this other customer first."

CHAPTER TWO

Once Dina was safely on her way with a fresh bottle of blood, Gresh locked and re-sealed the vault, closed the front door, and settled on the other velvet chair. He watched as Twilfa slipped out the back, then turned to focus on his customer.

"Now, my dear, if you could explain to me what you know of this mirror, I will consider whether or not I can obtain it for you."

"Thank you." The woman nodded an acknowledgment. "My name is Karanissa of the Mountains. About four hundred and seventy years ago, in the course of my military service, I met a powerful wizard named Derithon the Mage, or Derithon of Helde. He was much older than I, but we thought each other to be good company, and before long I found myself living in his castle—a magical castle floating in a void outside the World entirely. Are you familiar with such things?"

"I've heard of them," Gresh said cautiously. He was wondering now whether he was dealing with a witch or with a madwoman. Although nothing she had said was *impossible*, Gresh had never before met anyone other than wizards who claimed to have lived more than a century, and as he understood it, manufactured places outside the World were extremely scarce—not to mention notoriously dangerous to create.

"Well, Derry had made one, which could be reached through a Transporting Tapestry. We lived there happily for a time, but one day Derry was called away, leaving me in the castle, and he never returned. The tapestry leading out of the castle stopped working, stranding me there. I found out later that Derry had died just on the other side of the tapestry, altering the appearance of the room—you know how Transporting Tapestries work?"

"In theory," Gresh said. He had heard them described, and of course he knew what ingredients went into the spell to make one, but had never personally used one. Anyone could simply step into the image on the tapestry and instantly find oneself in the actual place depicted, no matter how far away it was—but the image had to be *exact*, or the tapestry would not work properly, if at all. "I don't quite see how his death would change anything, though." Gresh knew there were spells that would stop working if the wizard who had worked them died, but they were much less common than most people supposed, and he was certain that the Transporting Tapestry wasn't one of them.

Karanissa sighed. "The tapestry came out in a secret room, and Derry died there, and no one found his body. The tapestry didn't work as long as his bones were lying on what was depicted as empty floor."

"Oh, I see." He had not realized the tapestries were that specific, but it made sense.

"The point is," Karanissa continued, "I was stranded in his castle for more than four and a half centuries. I didn't *know* it was that long—he'd put a spell of eternal youth on me, and the castle was magically supplied with food and water. I used my own witchcraft to let me pass the time swiftly, so I lost track of time, and had no idea it had been that long. At last, though, a young wizard named Tobas of Telven happened to find the secret room and the Transporting Tapestry. He found his way into the castle, and eventually he figured out how to get us both out again. While he was looking for a way out, though, he went through Derry's book of spells, studying the situation and learning more magic. One spell he tried, Lugwiler's Haunting Phantasm, went wrong, and instead of producing the phantasm, it produced a spriggan."

Gresh held up a hand. "What do you mean, 'produced'?"

"Do you know how the spell works?"

"I think I've heard of it." He had heard Dina and others describe it, but he wanted to hear his would-be customer's version.

"Well, it requires a mirror, and in this case, instead of creating the phantasm it was supposed to create, the spell enchanted the mirror, and the spriggan climbed out of the mirror as if the glass were a door. A minute or two later another spriggan did the same thing, and a moment after that a third, and they kept coming. That's where *all* the spriggans come from. By the time we got the tapestry working again there were dozens of them running around loose in the castle, and some of them came through to the World with us. They stole the mirror so we couldn't break it and hid it somewhere, and it's been popping out spriggans ever since."

Gresh stared at her, considering this, keeping his face expressionless.

Spriggans had started appearing a few years ago, without explanation; they had just suddenly been there, getting underfoot, poking into everything, babbling nonsense. It was just one or two at first, but they had gradually been growing more common. Divinations had not, so far as he knew, been able to determine their origin, although everyone was fairly certain they were a product of wizardry. He had never before heard anything about spriggans coming from an enchanted mirror. They were, as Dina had said, drawn to magic in general, and wizardry in particular—but, annoyingly, most magic did not work on them.

That was typical of wizardry; other spells almost never worked properly on something that was already enchanted.

And here was this person, claiming that someone named Derry—no, someone named Tobas—had created them accidentally, by miscasting Lugwiler's Haunting Phantasm.

Gresh knew a good deal about how the Phantasm worked. It was his business, as a wizards' supplier, to know as much as possible about *all* wizardry, so he made a point of coaxing as much information as he could from not just Dina, but every other wizard he sold to. He did not think he had actually picked up any Guild secrets yet, but he certainly knew more about wizardry than the vast majority of people.

The Phantasm was an easy spell, one many wizards had learned before they had finished the third year of apprenticeship. Who was this Tobas who had botched it so spectacularly?

But that wasn't entirely fair, he told himself. Dina had told him that if a spell went wrong, there was no way to predict what it would do. It might just do nothing, like her ruined spell of the night before, or it might do a variant of the intended spell, or it might do something completely different, and the effect might be utterly out of proportion. The famous Tower of Flame in the Small Kingdoms had supposedly been created when someone sneezed while performing a simple fire-lighting spell, after all. Perhaps this spriggan-generating mirror was the result of just as innocent a mistake.

"When did this happen?" he asked.

"5221," Karanissa replied. "Some time in Leafcolor, or possibly at the very end of Harvest."

"Six and a half years ago, going on seven." That was well before Gresh had ever heard of spriggans, so that fit the facts. "Why are you only looking for the mirror *now*?"

"We were busy." She turned up an empty palm. "And we thought the spriggans were harmless. And we didn't know the mirror would produce so *many*. At first we didn't think it would produce *any*, once it was out of the castle."

"Just who is 'we'? You and your husband, or are others involved?"

"My husband and his other wife and I."

Other wife? The husband staying with the baby while Karanissa saw to business suddenly made sense. "And your husband is this wizard named Tobas of Telven, then?"

"That's right."

"You hadn't mentioned that he had another wife."

"It wasn't relevant."

"She wasn't involved in creating the mirror?"

"No. She's not a magician."

Gresh nodded and inquired no further about that, although he was curious. Other people's family arrangements were not his business.

Magical objects sometimes were, though. "And you want me to find this spriggan-generating mirror for you."

"Yes. You come highly recommended; Telurinon and Kaligir both spoke well of you."

Once again Gresh found himself staring silently at the woman for a moment before he spoke. Telurinon was one of the most powerful wizards in Ethshar of the Sands and was rumored to be a high official in the Wizards' Guild. He had reportedly supervised the Guild's efforts to remove a usurper from the overlord's throne last year, though of course no one would admit to telling Gresh anything of the sort. And Kaligir, here in Ethshar of the Rocks, was *definitely* a high official in the Guild—when his name and the question of his status came up a year or so back Dina had admitted he was a Guildmaster and had hinted that he was perhaps the city's senior Guildmaster.

"You know them?" he asked.

"We know Telurinon. We helped him dispose of poor Tabaea. We've met Kaligir once or twice; he was the one who directed us here, at Telurinon's suggestion."

The mere fact that this woman knew those two names made it much less likely that she was mad, but her story was more outlandish than ever. She and her husband had helped defeat the self-proclaimed Empress of Ethshar who had briefly taken power in Ethshar of the Sands last year? And it seemed she and her husband got their shopping suggestions from the upper echelons of the Wizards' Guild.

Add that to a magic castle, eternal youth, the accidental creation of the spriggans that plagued the World, and it was a little much to accept.

"How did you come to be asking their advice?"

Karanissa frowned—the first time Gresh had seen her do so. "They weren't advising us as much as *ordering* us," she said.

"Oh?"

"The Wizards' Guild holds my husband responsible for the spriggans," Karanissa explained. "They summoned us to a meeting, back in Snowfall, and told us as much. A good many wizards have been complaining about the silly things and demanding the Guild *do* something. They've caused a lot of trouble. There's a man named Ithanalin who got turned to stone or something when he tripped over a spriggan, and was petrified until his apprentice taught herself enough magic to cure him..."

"Kilisha," Gresh said. "I know Ithanalin and Kilisha." That was a mild exaggeration; he had met them, even sold them a few things, but no more than that. He remembered the fuss about Ithanalin's accident; he hadn't been *petrified*, exactly, but Gresh supposed the exact details didn't matter.

"Yes, well, that was one instance," Karanissa said. "Ithanalin has been very persistent in demanding Kaligir do something about the spriggans. There have been any number of other ruined spells and spilled potions and wasted ingredients..."

Gresh remembered Dina's precious blood, spilled on her cat. "Yes," he said.

"No one's been killed yet, so far as we know, but it seems almost as if it's just a matter of time, and the Guild wants Tobas to do something about the spriggans before it comes to that. He created them, Telurinon says, so it's his responsibility to stop them. And that starts with destroying the mirror—if we don't do that, it'll just make more."

"But first you need to find it."

"Yes. The spriggans hid it, and we need to find it."

"So you came to me."

"When nothing else worked, yes."

Gresh did not like the sound of that—but then, if the Guild had ordered them to do something about the spriggans back in Snowfall of last year, and they had already been working on the problem for five months, then coming to him had clearly not been their first idea. "What else did you try?" he asked.

"Well, since the Guild wanted us to do it, we thought it was only fair to ask them to help us, so we did. We had Mereth of the Golden Door use every divination in her book, and half a dozen other wizards, as well, but none of them could locate the mirror. We consulted three or four theurgists and even a demonologist, to no avail—the gods apparently can't even perceive spriggans, let alone identify their source, no matter how roundabout you make the questions, and there don't seem to be any demons who deal with this sort of thing. Witches don't have the range—I could have told them that, but Tobas talked to a couple of others just to be sure no one had found a way during the four hundred years I was gone. Warlocks had no idea of how to even begin looking, and the scientists and ritual dancers didn't do much better." She sighed wearily at the memory. "So when magic failed us, we decided to try other methods. Lady Sarai can't leave her duties as the overlord's investigator and didn't have any clever ideas, but Telurinon said you were the best in the World at finding hard-to-find things without magic—so here I am."

"Indeed," Gresh said. He leaned back, keeping his eyes on his guest.

This was, at least potentially, a problem—and an opportunity.

He made an excellent living supplying wizards with the ingredients for their spells; he had been doing it since boyhood. He had started out running errands for his older sisters—mostly Dina, since wizards used so many odd ingredients in their spells, but also occasionally Tira and Chira and Shesta. Witches used herbs and other tools; sorcerers sometimes wanted particular metals or gems for their talismans and were always looking for leftover bits of old sorcery; and demonologists sometimes needed specific things to pay demons for their services. His business was never *entirely* for wizards, but wizards certainly made up the bulk of his business.

He had started with his sisters, but then he had begun to fetch things for their friends, and then friends of friends, and then people with no connection he knew of who had heard his name somewhere. Word had spread; by the time he finished his apprenticeship and opened his own shop, he had developed a reputation for being fast, efficient, honest, and discreet.

He had also developed a reputation for being able to get *anything*, given time.

This reputation let him charge high prices—higher, in fact, than any other supplier in the city. Even so, he had never lacked for business. There were always people willing to pay more for the best.

The problem was that he had to *stay* the best. He had to maintain his reputation as the man who could get anything a wizard needed. He could never admit that there was something he couldn't find, or couldn't obtain once it was found.

So far, no such admission had been necessary; sooner or later he had gotten everything he went after, or else had been able to give good, sound reasons why he would not seek certain things. As he explained to anyone who asked: he would not kill or maim anyone to obtain an item; he would not violate Wizards' Guild rules, and he tried to obey the overlords' laws; and some of the things people had attempted to buy simply didn't exist.

Or at least, he said they didn't exist, and no one had ever proved him wrong.

This spriggan mirror, though, apparently *did* exist. If Karanissa was telling the truth, she *knew* it existed. Fetching it would not break any Guild rules; in fact, the Guild *wanted* it found. He wouldn't be stealing it, or breaking any other laws so far as he could see, and he could see no reason anyone would be killed or maimed if he acquired it. By his own rules, therefore, he should have no objection to going after it. Unless he could find a new and convincing excuse, refusing the task would severely damage his reputation.

Finding it, of course, would enhance his reputation. If he could become known as the man who eliminated the nuisance of the spriggans once and for all, he could crank his prices up even higher. He would be a minor hero throughout the Hegemony.

The problem was that if he agreed to get it and failed to do so, his reputation would be not merely damaged, but ruined—and he had no idea how to find the thing! By Karanissa's account, most of his usual methods would not work.

Of course, no one outside the family knew what his usual methods *were*—and he liked it that way. Keeping his trade secrets secret added to his aura of mystery and kept the competition down.

"Will you get it for us?" Karanissa asked, interrupting his train of thought.

He really had no choice. "Of course," he said. "But it may take some time, and it will be very expensive."

"The Guild has agreed to cover the cost," she replied. "We will pay any price."

Gresh blinked at that. *Any* price?

He had thought he might scare her away; given his reputation for charging high prices, he had thought that when *he* said "very expensive" she might reconsider and save him the trouble of actually finding the mirror. But the *Guild* would pay?

When the Wizards' Guild said "any price," that meant rather more than when anyone else said it. The Wizards' Guild had entire *worlds* at their disposal.

But of course, the witch might not have meant it literally. She could not be a member of the Guild herself and might have misinterpreted what the Guildmasters had actually said. There might be limitations of which she was unaware.

Still, to have access to the Guild's own coffers—he would be rich! *Really* rich, not just as well off as he was now. Or perhaps he might be paid with *more* than money...

That assumed, of course, that Karanissa was telling the truth. Twilfa had not yet returned with Tira, so he had no way of verifying the story.

It also assumed he could indeed retrieve the missing mirror, but he had confidence in his own abilities—far more confidence than he had in Karanissa's account of herself.

He considered trying to stall Karanissa, by asking her questions until Tira arrived—after all, he would need more information from her before setting out to find this mirror—but he decided against it. This was probably not going to be a quick and easy errand. He would undoubtedly talk to her a good many times, with and without Tira.

He would probably need to talk to her husband, as well, but first he wanted to do a little preliminary planning.

"It will take me some time to make preparations," he said. "I will need to speak with your husband and to do some research."

"Of course," Karanissa said. "Whatever is necessary." She rose.

"Bring your husband and his other wife here this afternoon, and we will settle the details," Gresh said, rising as well.

She bowed an acknowledgment.

He showed her to the door, then stood in the doorway watching her walk away down the street toward Eastgate Market.

She was a handsome woman, no question about it, and if her story was true, she was a woman with an incredible history. The task she had set him was going to be a challenge—stupendously profitable, he hoped—but a challenge.

In fact, he had no idea at all, as yet, of how he would do it.

That did not worry him. He would find a way. Various possibilities were already stirring in the back of his mind.

CHAPTER THREE

Gresh sat at his kitchen table across from Twilfa and Tira, stroking his short-trimmed beard. "She said they'd tried wizardry, theurgy, demonology, warlockry, science, and ritual dance. She didn't mention witchcraft, but since she's a witch herself I think we can take that for granted."

"Then why did you want me here?" Tira asked.

"To see whether she was telling the truth," Gresh replied. "Whether she's really a witch and really as old as she claims."

"But you let her go!"

"She'll be back this afternoon."

"You want me to stay here all day? Gresh, Dar and I have our own customers to attend to."

Gresh sighed. "Are any of them coming today?"

"I'm not going to tell you my entire schedule."

"I won't keep you, then, but can you please come by this afternoon? Naturally, I will pay you for your time."

Tira frowned.

"Tira, I'm sorry I dragged you over here for nothing, but I didn't know how the conversation was going to go, and this way you'll know what I want when you come back, and I won't need to try to signal you surreptitiously. And you can tell me if you've ever heard of this Karanissa of the Mountains, or her husband Tobas of Telven, or a mirror that makes spriggans."

Tira considered that for a moment, then relented. "Fine, I'll be here this afternoon and will tell you whether they're lying," she said. "And I never heard of Karanissa or Tobas, but didn't you say they were from the Small Kingdoms? I don't know anyone there. The Sisterhood doesn't operate openly there."

"Thank you."

"And you will indeed pay me my full consultation rate this afternoon."

"Of course."

"I don't want you thinking you can get a discount just because you're my brother, or because you're the famous Gresh the Supplier."

"Of course not."

"Good." She pushed back her chair and stood up. "I'll be back this afternoon. If I have a chance, I might talk to a few people about this Karanissa."

"Thank you," Gresh replied. He and Twilfa watched silently as Tira straightened her shawl and marched out the back door. Except for Dina, his sisters almost always used the back door, at his request. He didn't want anyone wondering why all these non-wizards were coming to his shop.

And they did come fairly often. His sisters were his most important trade secret. Oh, he had plenty of other sources and contacts, a network of agents scattered across the western half of the World, but his family was at the heart of his unique ability to acquire the things his customers sought. He had based his entire business on sisterly affection and sibling rivalry—what one sister could not find, another could, and would, because to refuse would be to disappoint their only brother *and* miss a chance to crow.

Gresh was only eight when he first realized he could play off Dina, who was then a freshly accredited journeyman wizard, against Difa, then an apprentice warlock, to his own benefit. He had known all along that Difa had originally intended to be a wizard and had only become a warlock because the possibility was new and exciting and as a warlock she would not be once again following in her older sister's footsteps. Still, it was not until Dina made journeyman that Gresh had discovered he could exploit this rivalry, challenging each sister to show that she could do more with her magic than the other. Warlockry was still relatively new and unfamiliar at the time, which had helped—questions of which sort of magic was better at what had not yet all been settled.

Tira was already in her third year of apprenticeship then, and she, too, had joined the competition quickly enough. Chira and Pyata and Shesta joined in their turn. No two of Keshan the Merchant's daughters chose the same school of magic—that would have been copying—but all were determined to demonstrate that *their* magic was best.

Then Gresh had reached apprenticeship age himself and faced the prospect of learning his own magic. Dina had not yet been ready for master's rank, but she could have found him a place with a wizard somewhere.

Or Difa could have found a master warlock. Tira

could probably have found a witch. The others were still apprentices themselves, but...

But it didn't matter, because Gresh had decided he didn't want to be a magician. It would have meant choosing one sort of magic—and one of his sisters—over all the others. Whichever school of magic he chose, the sister in that school would have deemed it a victory and the others a defeat; factional lines within the family that had always been fluid would become fixed.

He might have chosen a variety of magic that *none* of them had studied, which would have avoided choosing sides by rejecting all of them, but even at twelve he had been able to foresee a lifetime of being told, "You chose *your* magic instead of *mine*, so I can see you won't want my help!" Although finding a magic none of his older sisters had chosen would have worked as far as not choosing sides at first, it ignored the question of what might happen when his younger sisters began choosing *their* apprenticeships.

No, there were too many potential complications with *any* school of magic. Appealing as learning magic might have seemed, he did not want to alienate any of his sisters, or choose one over the others. He liked being able to call on *all* of them.

So he had apprenticed to their father, which had made both their parents happy, and he had learned the merchant's trade, learned bookkeeping and bargaining, buying and bartering—and he had made use of all his twelve sisters in his business, older and younger, from Dina the wizard to Ekava the seamstress, and had eventually taken on Twilfa, the youngest, as his assistant. Because of the family's competitiveness no two had pursued exactly the same occupation, even after their contacts could no longer find new varieties of magic, and he now had available for consultation representatives of eight different schools of magic, as well as a seamstress, a sailor, and a guardswoman.

That didn't include the husbands or children his sisters had acquired over the years—nine of the twelve were married, and three of them had offspring old enough to have begun their apprenticeships. His nephews, nieces, and brothers-in-law were not as usefully diverse as his sisters, but they did add to the mix.

"So do you want to talk to Chira?" Twilfa asked, when Tira was out of sight. Chira was the family sorcerer, and Karanissa had not mentioned trying sorcery.

Gresh considered that, then nodded. "I think that's a good place to start, and she definitely owes me one." He had located several sorcerous items for Chira over the past few years and had been generous in pricing them. Karanissa's omission of sorcery from her list was probably just an oversight, and Gresh did not see how any sorcery he was familiar with might help, but it wouldn't hurt to ask.

"I'll fetch her," Twilfa said, rising.

"And if you see any spriggans on the way, try to catch one," Gresh said.

Twilfa paused. "You want to have one here for Chira to try her talismans on?"

"I want to ask one a few questions," Gresh answered. "For all I know, we may not need *any* magic to find this mirror."

Twilfa blinked. "You think it might just *tell* you where the mirror is?"

Gresh turned up a palm. "Why not?" he asked. "Spriggans are stupid little creatures, and they seem to want to be cooperative—why *wouldn't* it tell me?"

"If it's that easy, wouldn't this Karanissa have already tried that? Or her husband?"

"They're magicians, at least in theory. She's a witch; he's a wizard—they're accustomed to doing things magically. It may have never occurred to them just to ask."

Twilfa started to say something, then stopped and thought for a moment. "You could be right," she admitted.

Gresh smiled at her. "You're learning," he said. "Magicians are just as fallibly human as anyone else."

Twilfa stuck her tongue out at him and turned away.

Gresh watched her go, then leaned back and began planning.

The mirror was probably still somewhere in the Small Kingdoms—why would the spriggans have taken it anywhere else? He could accept Karanissa's offer of transport by flying carpet, but how big a carpet was it? How much could it carry? It might be better to travel on the ground.

Although his customers were nominally buying the mirror, what they really wanted was its destruction; should he bring tools for breaking it? An ordinary mirror could be smashed readily enough, but enchanted items had a tendency to be uncooperative in unexpected ways.

Of course, depending on just what he did to locate it, he didn't necessarily want Tobas and Karanissa to know how he found it; if customers found out how simple some of his methods actually were it could hurt his business.

He needed to talk to a spriggan, no question about it, to find out as much about the mirror as he could. He glanced down the passage toward the shop; naturally, no spriggans were in sight. When he was busy and had no use for the little pests they were everywhere, getting underfoot and making a mess, but now that he *wanted* one, there were none to be found.

Well, Twilfa might have better luck in apprehending one. Or he could stroll down Wizard Street later and listen for outbursts of profanity or the sound of falling crockery.

Then the doorbell jingled, and he rose hurriedly to attend to his customer.

Ordinary trade filled the remainder of the morning. Twilfa returned shortly before lunch with word that Chira was busy at the moment but would be along later and that all the spriggans seemed to be hiding.

"Of course," Gresh said.

They had finished a meal of salt ham and cornbread, and Twilfa was clearing the table when Gresh heard a thump. "What was that?" he said.

"What was what?" Twilfa asked, stacking the pewter plates.

A loud crash sounded from the front of the shop.

"That," Gresh said, as he leapt up and dashed down the passage.

As he had expected, he found a spriggan sitting on the floor below a high shelf, surrounded by broken glass and drying blood. The creature looked up at him as he entered, then sprang to its feet and ran for the door.

Gresh darted in front of it, cutting off its escape. It

stopped dead and looked up at him, crestfallen. Its big pointed ears drooped.

"Sorry sorry sorry," it said, in a high-pitched squeak of a voice.

Gresh smiled. "Of course you are," he said. "I'm sure you didn't mean *any* harm at all, did you?"

The spriggan stared up at him uncertainly, its bulging round eyes fixed on his face.

"You were just *curious* about what was in the bottle, right?"

Hesitantly, the spriggan nodded, never taking its eyes from Gresh's face.

"And you certainly didn't *mean* to spill dragon's blood worth *five rounds of gold* all over my carpet, did you?"

The ears drooped even further. "Sorry," the spriggan said.

"Do you know how much five rounds of gold is?"

The spriggan blinked once, its thin, pale eyelids seeming to appear out of nowhere. "No?"

"It's a very great deal of money. You now *owe* me a very great deal of money."

The creature looked panic-stricken. "Spriggan doesn't *have* money," it squealed.

"I can see that," Gresh said. The spriggan was naked and only about eight inches high; there was nowhere it could hide a purse, or even a single coin.

Gresh had never bothered to take a good hard look at a spriggan. The first few he had encountered had been glimpsed from afar, or in the process of fleeing, and by the time he saw one close up and relatively still he had lost any interest in the little pests. Now, though, he stared down at the creature that crouched before his feet, studying it.

It was roughly human in shape—but it also looked a good bit like a frog, an impression aided by its lipless, oversized mouth and bulging pop-eyes. Its shiny, hairless skin was a dull green—Gresh thought he had seen a few that were more of a brown color, but this one was definitely an ugly shade of drab green. It came no more than halfway up his shin; if it stood straight and stretched its bony arms, those long-fingered little hands could probably reach his knee.

This one apparently had no fingernails; some of them did, though. He remembered hearing that some could use their fingernails to pick locks.

Why did some have nails, and some not? Was there any significance to the different colors? There were plenty of unanswered questions about spriggans. No one knew whether they had one sex or two—or, Gresh supposed, more. No one knew why they all seemed to speak the same sort of broken Ethsharitic, or whether they had names. Not one had ever, so far as Gresh knew, admitted to having any name but "spriggan." They generally spoke of themselves in the third person, but Gresh wasn't sure if that was universal.

One thing he discovered, having one this close, was that they did not seem to have any odor at all. He was fairly sure he would have been able to smell a person at this distance, but all he could smell right now was the spilled dragon's blood.

He was going to need to clean that up, but right now dealing with the spriggan seemed more urgent; the blood and broken glass could wait. He supposed he probably should have kept that in the vault, with the other expensive materials, but wizards used so *much* dragon's blood that he had never bothered—he and Twilfa would have spent half the day locking and unlocking the iron door. It seemed as if half the spells used in Ethshar of the Rocks required dragon's blood.

The stuff had a sharp, metallic odor, and Gresh's nose could detect nothing else. On a whim, he leaned forward and sniffed at the spriggan.

It backed away a step, startled. "*No* money," it said. "You let spriggan go now?"

The creature had no scent at all, so far as Gresh could discern. He could smell the blood and the carpet and a dozen other normal shop odors, but nothing at all that might be the spriggan. That was odd, like so many things about the little pests. "You'll just have to pay me with something *other* than money," he said.

"But spriggan not have *anything*," the spriggan wailed woefully.

"You can pay me with *answers*," Gresh said.

The spriggan calmed down slightly. It blinked up at him, then looked from side to side, as if hoping to see an explanation standing nearby.

Twilfa was standing in the passageway, watching the conversation, but there were no explanations in sight.

"What answers?" it asked warily.

"You owe me five rounds of gold," Gresh said. "That's forty bits. Let's say each answer is worth, oh, two bits—which I'm sure you'll agree is *very* generous of me. Then you owe me twenty answers."

"What *kind* of answers?"

"Answers to my questions."

The spriggan considered that carefully, then brightened visibly, its immense ears straightening. "Yes, yes!" it said. "Answer questions! Then you let spriggan go, yes?"

"Yes," Gresh said.

"Good, good! Have answers, have fun!" It ventured a tentative smile.

"Don't get *too* happy," Gresh warned. "You still have to give me those twenty answers."

"Will! Will! Ask questions!"

"Indeed I will. First off, did you come out of a mirror, as I've heard?"

"Not know what you heard. That one answer." It blinked up at him.

Gresh grimaced. Obviously, he would need to be more careful about his phrasing. "Fair enough," he said. "Did you come out of an enchanted mirror?"

"Yes. That two answers."

"You're counting...Can you even *count* to twenty?"

The spriggan hesitated. "Not sure," it admitted. "Can try. Can count to twelve for sure. Twenty is more than twelve, might not get all the way. Try, though." It smiled happily. "That *three* answers!"

Gresh sighed. "I suppose it is. Now, do you know where the mirror you came from is?"

"No. Not know. That four."

"No, it isn't!" Gresh protested. "That's not an answer!"

"Is, too. 'Not know' is answer. Just isn't *good* answer. You not say *good* answers!"

Gresh put a hand to his forehead. "I'm being outwitted by a spriggan," he said. "I don't believe this."

Then he lowered his hand and said, "Where was the mirror when you last saw it?"

The spriggan turned up empty hands. "Not know," it said. "Five."

"You have to give me *honest* answers, you know."

"Did. Have. Will."

"How can you not know where it was?"

"Not good with places. Not good with names. Not remember well. Six."

"Well, how did you get here from wherever the mirror was?"

"Walked, mostly. Ran some. Got thrown once by pretty woman who found spriggan in her skirt—maybe eight, nine feet? Rolled down slope once. Is seven? Yes, seven."

"Seven down." Gresh sighed again, and rubbed his forehead. "Which direction did you walk?"

"Not know names of directions. Walked away from sun. Not like light in eyes. Eight."

"But the sun moves!"

"Sun moves, yes. Spriggan know that. Spriggan is not *that* stupid."

"But then you'd walk west in the morning, and east in the afternoon, and you'd wind up in the same place—was the mirror here in the city?"

"No, mirror not here! Silly. Walked in mornings, had fun in afternoons—talked to people, played games. Nine."

"So you went west."

"Away from sun in morning."

"That's west."

The spriggan turned up an empty palm. "You say is west; spriggan not argue."

"So you came from the east—which makes sense, since we're on the west coast. You didn't turn aside, go north or south?"

"Went other direction when water got in the way. Ten."

"Water? You mean the ocean?"

"Mean big, *big* water, great big huge water. Is ocean? Ocean's eleven."

"So when you got to the coast you turned aside and walked up the coast to the city."

"Turned aside *twice*. First time long ago, then not so long at all. Twelve."

Gresh struggled to remember his geography. The second time would be when the spriggan reached the west coast, of course, but the first time...

That would have been the Gulf of the East, the water between the Hegemony of the Three Ethshars and the Small Kingdoms.

"The first time you turned aside—you walked around the very big water and crossed a long bridge across more water, and then headed west again?"

"Yes, yes! Long bridge with guards."

"Across the Great River."

"What comes after twelve? Thirty?"

"Thirteen," Gresh said automatically, as he tried to choose his next question.

CHAPTER FOUR

"Thirteen," the spriggan said.

Gresh frowned. He was using up his twenty questions faster than he liked.

He had made progress, though; knowing that the spriggan had turned aside at the Gulf of the East and crossed the toll bridge on the Great River meant that it had, indeed, come from the Small Kingdoms.

But how far had it come? Where in the Small Kingdoms had it started? Gresh couldn't very well search all of the two hundred or more little principalities for one little hand-mirror.

"How long did it take you to walk from the mirror to the first big water? How many mornings?"

The spriggan turned up empty palms. "Don't know," it said. "Didn't count. Is fourteen?"

"Yes," Gresh admitted, annoyed with himself for wasting a question. He *knew* the spriggan couldn't count, and the stupid little thing probably hadn't maintained anything like a steady pace in its journeying.

A thought struck him. *Had* it started in the Small Kingdoms? What if it had started *east* of the Small Kingdoms, in the Great Eastern Desert?

"Have you ever seen a desert?" he asked. "A big sandy place, where no one lives and there are no trees or farms?"

"No," the spriggan said. "Would be no fun, huh?" It hesitated. "Fiveteen?"

"Fifteen."

So the mirror was definitely *in* the Small Kingdoms. He had five questions left to narrow it down.

"Do you know which kingdom the mirror is in?"

"No. Not good with names. Or kingdoms. Sixteen, yes?"

That was no surprise. "Is the mirror in the mountains, or on the plain, or in the forests?"

"Um..." The spriggan was clearly struggling to think. "Yes," it said. "Seventeen. That almost twenty?"

"Getting close," Gresh said. "But you didn't answer the question—which is it, in the mountains or on the plain or in the forest?"

"Mirror is in mountain," the spriggan said. "Eighteen."

"No, that's just seventeen! You didn't answer the question the first time."

"Wasn't same question! *Did* answer!"

"It *was* the same question! You just didn't hear it right the first time."

"Was two questions!"

Gresh glared at the spriggan, and the spriggan glared back. Then something registered.

"Wait a minute," Gresh said. "Did you say the mirror is in a mountain? You mean *inside* a mountain?"

"Yes," the spriggan said, folding its spindly arms across its narrow chest. "Said that, meant that. Nineteen."

"It's in a *cave*?" Gresh said, before realizing that he might have just thrown away his last question.

"Yes. Tenteen."

Gresh caught himself, closed his lips tight, closed his eyes, and did *not* correct the spriggan. Instead he tried to think what else he could ask.

He opened his eyes and glanced at Twilfa, who had obviously been listening and had, just like him, barely caught herself before calling out a correction. He could see her biting her lip as she turned away and hurried down the passageway to the kitchen, out of sight.

Gresh had no idea how many more questions he could get away with; it could be just one, or it could be a dozen before the spriggan caught on. He couldn't afford to waste any.

"What time of day does the sun first shine in the mouth of the cave?" he asked.

The spriggan considered that for a moment, then said, "Middle of morning, maybe? Not sure. Um... eleventeen?"

Then the cave mouth faced more east than west and was probably on the eastern slope of a mountain.

"From the mouth of the cave, what buildings could you see? Castles, towers, farmhouses, villages, anything?"

"Only building was broken one. Castle or tower or something. Don't know names of buildings." The spriggan looked puzzled. "Is eleventeen? Said that before?"

"No, you didn't say it before," Gresh lied as he considered that. "Eleventeen is right."

A ruin. Nothing else. That made sense; if there were

inhabitants in the area they might have noticed the steady stream of spriggans coming down from the cave. Word would have gotten around.

Or *up* from the cave, he reminded himself. Caves could occur at the bottoms of mountains as well as the tops.

This one, wherever it was, was in sight of a ruined fortification in otherwise uninhabited terrain, far enough from civilization that no one had recognized it as the source of spriggans.

Unfortunately, to the best of Gresh's knowledge, that described a good-sized portion of the mountainous central Small Kingdoms, from Zedmor in the northwest to Lumeth of the Towers in the southeast.

Lumeth of the Towers...could the cave be in sight of *those* towers, the gigantic ancient ruins rumored to be older than humanity itself?

But there were three of those, not just one, according to the travelers Gresh had spoken with.

"When you came out of the cave and went west over the mountains, what did you find?"

The spriggan blinked at him. It hesitated.

"Rocks," it said at last. "Trees. Lots of trees. Twelve...twelveteen? Not sound right."

"Twelveteen," Gresh said. "You saw forests." That narrowed down the search; Gresh knew that the southern end of the mountain range extended into open grasslands, and the forests that had once covered the northern end had been cleared for farming. He had had reason to learn such details, since some of the ingredients he sold included forest products—leaves from the topmost branch of a sixty-foot oak, for example, or dew from the underside of a fiddler fern.

Forests—so it wasn't in Lumeth or Calimor, or anywhere north of Vlagmor. What could he ask that would narrow it down further?

"Did you see a lake as you traveled westward through the forest, or cross a river?"

"No. No lake. No rivers in forest, just little streams. Didn't cross big river until the long bridge with the guards. And that...thirteenteen? No, that twenty! Twenty, twenty, twenty! Right, twenty?"

"Twenty," Gresh admitted.

So the mirror was in a cave on the eastern side of a mountain somewhere between Vlagmor and Calimor, and *not* in the central area where the spriggan's westward march would have encountered Ekeroa's lake, or the river that drained the lake and much of the western mountains into the Gulf of the East.

Karanissa had mentioned Dwomor and Aigoa. Gresh was not sure exactly where those were, but he thought they lay somewhere not *too* far from Ekeroa. If the mirror were still in Dwomor, and Dwomor was where Gresh had thought it was, and the spriggan headed west, it should have seen the lake—but it hadn't.

That was interesting, but not necessarily significant. Even if the cave was directly east of the lake, if the creature hadn't headed due west over the mountains it might have missed the water. Depending what time of year it had emerged from the cave, the sun might have risen well to the south of due east, so that it might have headed northwest...

"Go now?" the spriggan asked, interrupting his chain of thought. "Please?"

"Fine," Gresh said. He did not think he was going to

get any more useful information out of the creature. He had used up his questions. He glared at the spilled blood and broken glass, thinking he hadn't gotten much for the price. "You can go—but *don't come back*, ever!" He shook a warning finger at the little creature. "I don't want ever to see you again!"

"Yes, yes. Not come back. Promise."

"Good enough." He stepped aside and even opened the door. The spriggan dashed past him into the street, squeaking wordlessly.

Gresh stood in the door for a moment, watching it flee. He saw his sister Chira approaching, her sorcerer's pack slung on her shoulder. She waved cheerily, and he waved in return. Cleaning up the blood would have to wait—it had probably already spread as far as it was going to and would have soaked into the planking anyway. It might well need magic to remove it. Talking to his sorcerous sister was more important; he tried not to waste anyone's time but his own.

A moment later, after apologizing for the mess, he was ushering her to the chairs in the corner and calling to Twilfa to fetch tea.

"So, little brother, what can I do for you?" Chira asked happily, as she tucked her skirt under her and settled onto the velvet. She gave the broken jar a quick glance, then looked at him expectantly as she slid her bag from her shoulder and lowered it to the floor.

Gresh smiled at being called "little brother." He was over six feet tall, at least six inches taller than Chira, and given his solidly-muscled build and her slim figure, he probably weighed twice what she did. All the same, the four-and-a-half-year difference in their ages ensured that he would always be "little brother" to her.

"I need to find a particular enchanted mirror," he said. "It's in a cave somewhere in the Small Kingdoms, in the central mountains—not the area right around Ekeroa, but somewhere between Vlagmor and Calimor, probably on the eastern slopes. A couple of magicians have tried to find it with various methods and failed, but so far as I know they didn't try sorcery."

"What kind of mirror?"

Gresh held out his hands as Karanissa had. "A hand mirror, roughly this size," he said.

Chira looked down at her pack for a moment, considering. "Nothing comes immediately to mind," she said. "It's in a cave, you said?"

Gresh nodded.

"So I can't follow the sunlight to it. And mirrors don't have any special smell to track. What sort of enchantment is on it?"

Gresh hesitated. "A faulty version of Lugwiler's Haunting Phantasm," he said.

"Wizardry, then?"

"Yes, of course."

"No 'of course' about it," Chira said, reaching for the shoulder strap of her bag. "There are plenty of other kinds of enchantment."

"Well, yes, but...you know I work mostly with wizards. And what other kind of magic would make it so hard to find?"

"Demonology. And some kinds of sorcery—we do work with mirrors sometimes."

"True, true. I'm sorry."

"Oh, don't be sorry." She waved a hand in dismissal.

"You're right, you mostly work with wizards, I know that. And I owe you. We both know that. So tell me about Lugwiler's Haunting Phantasm—is that one that produces smoke?"

"No, that's one...well, it doesn't matter what it ordinarily does..."

"It might," she interrupted.

"...but this mirror produces spriggans."

Chira stopped moving, one hand holding the strap at her knee, the other tucked at her side. She stared at him.

"Spriggans?" she said. She glanced at the pool of dragon's blood. "Like the one I saw running out of here?"

"Yes. Like that one—and yes, that one broke a jar of very expensive blood. Spriggans are a huge nuisance, and this mirror generates them. In fact, it may be the only source."

"Someone knows where the spriggans came from?"

"So they tell me."

"And they've hired you to find it?"

"We're negotiating."

"Why?"

"Why are we negotiating? Because we haven't agreed..."

"Why do they want you to find it?"

"To destroy it, I think."

"They don't know where it is?"

"No. Spriggans carried it off and hid it in a cave, apparently."

"Your customer told you that?"

"That spriggans carried it off, yes. I found out about the cave myself."

"How did...No, never mind. I'm sure it's a trade

secret. Except...if one of our sisters could tell you it was in a cave, why couldn't she tell you where?"

Gresh smiled. Chira did indeed know his methods. "It wasn't anyone in the family," he said. "It was an independent informant. He'd seen the cave, but didn't know the route, or exactly where it was."

Chira shook her head in amazement. "How do you *find* these people?"

Gresh turned up empty palms.

"Well, so someone's hiring you to find this mirror and destroy it. You're sure about that?"

"I'm sure about hiring me."

"But destroying it? Not changing it to make something else, something worse?"

That possibility had not even occurred to Gresh. He wondered if Karanissa's good looks had biased him, and had perhaps kept him from considering potential dangers. "I don't know for certain," he admitted. "But rest assured, now that you've pointed out the risk, I'll make absolutely sure of their intentions before I let anyone else touch the thing. Assuming, of course, that I find it."

Chira snorted. "You'll find it," she said. "You always find what you go after, one way or another. You always have. Remember when Mother hid the candy when we were little? It didn't matter where she put it; you'd always have a piece by bedtime."

Just then Twilfa emerged, carrying a tray bearing a pot and two cups of tea.

"Just two?" Chira asked, as she accepted hers.

"Mine's in the kitchen," Twilfa said.

"You're welcome to listen," Gresh said. "It's all in the family."

"No, that's all right," Twilfa replied. She set the teapot on a nearby shelf, then turned, tray in hand, and retreated toward the kitchen.

Gresh frowned at her departing figure.

"I make her nervous," Chira said quietly, cradling her teacup.

"You're her sister," Gresh protested.

"I'm twice her age," Chira pointed out. "I was halfway through my apprenticeship by the time she could crawl."

"Well, I was about thirteen, and an apprentice myself," Gresh said. "It's not as if we were playmates, either."

"But she works for you. She sees you every day. And you don't carry around a bag of mysterious ancient talismans."

"No, I sit in a shop full of magic! Blood and body parts on every shelf and a vault with explosive seals only I can open!" Then he waved it away. "Whatever. It doesn't matter."

"We've always been a competitive family," Chira said. "You were special, being the only boy, so maybe you didn't..."

"I noticed," Gresh interrupted. "I definitely noticed. But that doesn't mean I like it when Twilfa treats you like a stranger."

"Not a stranger," Chira said.

"Not a sister, either!"

Chira raised her empty hands. "Never mind that. I'm not here to see Twilfa, or to talk about her."

"Fine. At any rate, I want to find the mirror. Can you help? And rest assured, I won't just hand it over to my employer with no questions asked."

"I can't see how I can find the mirror directly," she replied. "It doesn't give off light or sound or odor, so far as you know?"

"No."

"And it was an ordinary mirror before it was enchanted, not made of anything unusual?"

"Just a mirror—polished metal, or glass and silver, I suppose."

"Then I can't think of anything that would find the mirror itself." She hauled her pack up onto her lap as she spoke and began unbuckling the straps. "But I do have something that might be useful."

"Oh?"

She rummaged in the bag as she said, "I have something you can use to find and follow spriggans. Maybe when you get close you can use it to backtrack to the mirror."

Gresh nodded thoughtfully. "That might help," he agreed.

She pulled a talisman from the pack, a dully gleaming metal disk that looked rather like a hand-mirror itself, and held it out. "It isn't specific to spriggans," she said. "But it can tell you when anything is moving within a hundred feet of you and follow the motion, even if you can't see anything yourself. You can tell it to watch one movement and ignore another, or tell it to watch for a particular size or speed."

Gresh accepted the disk warily and looked at its round surface; his reflected gaze looked back at him, far more faintly than from an actual mirror, but still clear enough.

"How does it work?" he said.

CHAPTER FIVE

Operating the sorcerous talisman was not as simple as Gresh would have liked. He was sitting in his front room, once again going over the various gestures and commands it obeyed, making sure he wouldn't forget them, when the front bell jingled. He looked up from the device as Twilfa hurried from the kitchen to answer the door.

He had been practicing with it since Chira left, which had been long enough for Twilfa to clean up the broken jar, wipe up the spilled blood as best she could, and arrange a carpet and a few boxes to hide the bloodstains, which Gresh had promised to have magically removed at the first opportunity. She had scarcely finished that when Tira had arrived at the back door, and Twilfa had barely settled her in the kitchen with a sausage roll and a mug of small beer when the bell rang. Twilfa still reached the front door before Gresh could even slip the talisman into the pouch on his belt. Twilfa was in full bustle this afternoon, rushing around and getting things done with remarkable efficiency. By the time he was upright and had straightened his tunic, she was showing the customers in.

The young man Twilfa ushered into the shop appeared to be in his mid-twenties, but since this was presumably Tobas of Telven, a wizard powerful enough to own a flying carpet, appearances might not mean much in this case. He had dull brown hair and rather pale skin and stood just slightly taller than average. He wore a black tunic trimmed with red and gold, and good leather breeches.

Behind him were two women—the tall, black-haired witch, and a shorter, plumper woman with hair equally black, but curly rather than straight. She had milky-pale skin, whereas Karanissa's was brown, and the other woman held a bundle in her arms—a bundle with tiny fingers and a face.

The baby was wrapped in fine white linen embroidered in blue and green; its mother wore green velvet and yellow silk. The family could obviously afford to dress well, though Gresh did not think much of their taste—no two of them went together well, not even the mother and child.

"Come in, come in," he called, tucking the talisman out of sight as Twilfa ushered the foursome through the door. He rose to greet them—and not incidentally, to impress them with his own height and physique. That little bit of psychological advantage might be useful.

Karanissa stepped forward to make introductions. The man was indeed her husband Tobas, the other woman her co-wife Alorria of Dwomor, and the infant was their daughter Alris, who was still at an age where she did little more than stare, wave her hands aimlessly, and occasionally drool.

"She's named for her grandmother," Alorria said, as

Gresh smiled down at the baby and held out a finger for her to grab. "The queen of Dwomor."

Gresh managed to hide his surprise at that. When he had first heard the baby's name, he had immediately wondered whether it deliberately combined elements of both wives' names, which would have been a remarkable bit of diplomacy. In his admittedly limited experience with polygamists, co-wives tended to treat each other like sisters, which is to say, with a great deal of barely concealed rivalry and an intense interest in maintaining their own place within the family. For a mother to give a baby a name that reflected both women hardly fit that model, so it wasn't surprising that Alris was not, in fact, named in part for Karanissa, nor that Alorria made sure he knew that—but it *was* surprising that Alorria's mother was a queen.

Alorria herself had not been introduced as a princess—but then, she was married to a wizard, and the Wizards' Guild would not allow someone to be both wizard and royal. Alorria had presumably had to give up her title and her place in the succession when she married Tobas.

Gresh wondered what that place had been. If she had been next in line for the throne then her attachment to Tobas must have been quite intense, but if she had half a dozen older brothers then she hadn't really given up much of anything. The Small Kingdoms were awash in surplus princesses, due to the tradition that princesses must marry princes or heroes, but princes could marry anyone they chose—emphasis on any *one*, as multiple marriages complicated the bloodlines and inheritances too much and were therefore not normally permitted for royalty. Which was another reason Alorria's shared marriage seemed odd.

How in the World had this Tobas wound up married to a witch *and* a princess? It wasn't as if it was common for a man to have more than one wife; most women wouldn't stand for it. Gresh had only very rarely managed to keep company with more than one woman at a time, let alone *marry* them. Not that he had married *anyone*, or particularly wanted to.

"Would you like to sit down?" he asked, gesturing toward the velvet chairs.

"There aren't enough chairs," Alorria said.

"I'll be happy to stand," Gresh said. "Let the ladies be seated."

"I'm not a lady," Karanissa murmured.

"*I* am," Alorria said, settling onto one of the chairs and cooing at Alris.

Karanissa started to say something else, then bit it off and took the other chair.

"Your mother was queen of Dwomor?" Gresh asked Alorria as he leaned comfortably against the wall by the hearth.

"She still is," Alorria said. "And my father is King Derneth the Second." The pride in her voice was unmistakable.

That eliminated any possibility that Alorria had been exiled from her homeland and had made the best of her situation by marrying a wizard. Tobas could not be a prince himself—the Guild would never have allowed that.

But in that case, if Alorria had obeyed the rules at all, Tobas must have been a hero.

That was interesting.

Gresh remembered that Karanissa had said that the three of them had helped the Guild deal with Empress Tabaea. The details of exactly what had become of Tabaea had not been made public. Apparently the Wizards' Guild had employed some extremely dangerous magic, and rumor had it that all that had remained of the self-proclaimed empress was her left foot. The overlord's palace in Ethshar of the Sands had reportedly been gutted in the process, as well. Had it been *Tobas* who did that?

Gresh glanced at the wizard, who gave every appearance of being a rather ordinary young man. It was hard to imagine him flinging around that sort of high-powered spell.

Even if it had, though, that couldn't have been what qualified him as a hero in Dwomor. The timing was wrong, as little Alris had certainly been conceived well before Tabaea's downfall.

Karanissa had said that Tobas rescued her from an other-worldly castle and had accidentally created the first spriggans, but neither of those really seemed the sort of thing that Small Kingdoms royalty would consider adequate heroism. If he had rescued *Alorria*, or one of her parents—well, perhaps he had.

Gresh pushed the matter aside; maybe he would find out later. Neither of the women seemed particularly reticent.

"Well, Tobas," Gresh said. "I understand you want me to find a mirror for you."

"That's right." The wizard held up his hands. "About this big. Silvered glass. The sort wizards like to use, but glass, not alloy."

Gresh knew, of course, exactly what he meant—a great many spells required mirrors, so he provided them for his customers. Wizards sometimes preferred to use mirrors that weren't as breakable as glass, but they were willing to pay for something better than polished copper, and silversmiths had long since settled on a standard form for a silver-alloy "wizard's mirror." The exact mix of metals was a trade secret and varied somewhat from one workshop to the next, but the basic design was fairly consistent.

Other wizards, or the same wizards on other occasions, used glass mirrors, breakable or not; sometimes the image quality was more important than fragility, and glass did not need as much polishing.

Gresh stocked both varieties, of course.

"Like this," he said, picking one from a nearby shelf.

Tobas took the mirror and looked at it critically. "Slightly larger," he said. "And with a simple edge, not this beveled fancywork."

Gresh nodded. "And you last saw it somewhere in the mountains near Dwomor," he said.

"I last saw it—well, I last *saw* it in my own hand as I fell through a Transporting Tapestry, but a spriggan snatched it away a few seconds later and ran off with it. I haven't seen it since."

"Yes, of course. Now, I have an idea where it is—the general area, not the exact spot—and I believe I can obtain it for you, but there are certain things we must settle before I agree to get it."

"Anything you want."

"You don't mean that."

Tobas hesitated, looking as if he intended to argue,

then sighed, his shoulders slumping. "You're right, I don't. I mean anything I can give you without utterly ruining myself. Let us hear your terms, then, so we can discuss them."

"Well, first off, your wife said that the Wizards' Guild was financing this and would pay any price. Did she mean that literally?"

"Not *any* price," Tobas said, with a sour glance at Karanissa. "We won't give you Alris, for example, or make you master of the World. But the Guild can be very generous if it means eliminating spriggans."

"Forgive me for being blunt, but I'm a businessman, not a diplomat—how much is that?"

Tobas sighed again. "Name your price, and I'll tell you whether we can meet it."

"All expenses, of course—I don't know just how long it will take me to obtain the mirror, nor what resources I'll need—plus ten percent interest. To start."

"Of course."

"I'll want a deposit of one hundred rounds of gold toward those expenses."

"That shouldn't be a problem."

That brought them to the moment of truth, the moment Gresh had been anticipating and dreading ever since Karanissa's earlier visit. It was a moment that he had dreamed of ever since he first began working as a wizards' supplier; he was in a position to demand *anything he wanted* of the Wizards' Guild.

He could ask for money, for gold by the ton, but that seemed so pedestrian—and besides, if he did, he might well unbalance the local economy, since it was scarcity that gave gold its value. He could ask for, not the

World, but a kingdom—Dwomor, perhaps—but then he would have the responsibility of ruling it, of overseeing the welfare of its inhabitants, and he would have to be careful about using magic, or antagonizing neighboring kingdoms into starting a war. He could ask for his *own* little world, like the castle that Karanissa had been trapped in—but there were risks there; he might become trapped in it, as she had been, or there might be...complications. Wizardry could be a tricky, unreliable thing. He had heard stories about people opening portals into realities that were already inhabited by creatures that did not appreciate the intrusion, or realities that were so distorted, so strange, that they seemed like an endless series of traps, or even some that were not inhabitable by human beings at all—they lacked air or other necessities, or occupied time or space so alien that hearts could not beat and blood could not flow.

He could have made up a whole list of spells he wanted cast for him—love spells, blessings, transformations, animations, Transporting Tapestries, flying carpets, the bloodstone spell, and so on—but that lacked elegance.

But there was something simple that wizards could do for him, something priceless, something that could not go wrong once the spell was cast properly in the first place—though it could be lost through carelessness or by choice. He had dreamed about this since childhood and long ago settled on what he would demand.

"And as my payment I want eternal youth and perfect health," he said. "I won't insist on a specific spell, but it must be *permanent* youth. I do not want to ever be older than I am now."

"Um," Tobas said. He glanced at Karanissa.

"That's my price," Gresh said. He nodded at Karanissa. "If she's told me the truth, exactly such a spell was cast on her centuries ago, so please don't tell me it isn't possible."

"*I* can't do that," Tobas said. "I haven't been able to provide it for myself or Alorria yet, let alone anyone else."

Alorria made an unhappy noise in agreement.

"Someone provided it for *her*," Gresh said with another nod toward Karanissa.

"Derithon the Mage," Tobas said. "He's been dead for centuries. It isn't immortality, you know; Karanissa can still die, just like anyone else. It just won't be of old age."

"I know. That's good enough."

"And there are other loopholes."

"You'll have plenty of time to explain them to me."

Tobas grimaced.

"You said the Guild would pay any price; well, that's my price."

"I'll need to talk to Kaligir."

"You do that, then."

"I'll see him as soon as I can, and we'll get an answer for you. I *think* he'll agree, but I can't promise."

"Well, that's good enough for now. So that's the first point."

"There are others?"

"One more that I know of; others may arise in our discussions."

Tobas sighed yet again. "What is it?"

"I need to know why you want the mirror. I will not be a party to seriously destructive spells."

"We want to *smash* it, of course!" Alorria said before either of the others could reply. "I'm *sick* of these spriggans!"

Gresh nodded. That was what he wanted to hear. He looked at Tobas.

"She's right," he said. "We want to smash it—if that will stop it from producing spriggans. Or destroy it by some other means, or neutralize it somehow. We won't know for certain until I get a good look at it."

"No? Why *wouldn't* you just smash it?"

Tobas grimaced. "Because we don't know what that would do. If every fragment then starts spewing out spriggans, or some new sort of creature, that would be even worse, of course."

"Could that happen?" Gresh asked, startled. He had not thought of that possibility.

"We don't know," Tobas said. "Nobody does. The spell that created the mirror only happened once, by accident, when I made a mistake in Lugwiler's Haunting Phantasm, and I don't know what the mistake was, so we can't analyze it and guess at the spriggan spell's exact nature when we don't have the mirror in hand. Scrying spells can't see it, even the most powerful ones, since it happened outside the World. And they can't find the mirror, or study it. We don't know exactly why, but presumably it's just the nature of the spell."

The project was beginning to sound less appealing again. Being the person who let the spriggan mirror be smashed and unleash some new horror on the World would be *very* bad for his reputation, even worse than not finding the mirror in the first place. "So you don't know *anything* about the spell, except that it makes spriggans?"

"And it was intended to be the Phantasm. That's right. We know that the mirror pops out a spriggan every so often—the intervals vary, but it seems to generate at least a dozen a day, usually far more. The spriggans are not all identical and seem to be changing slightly over time. The first few spriggans never had any claws, for example, but some of them do now. And we know that if you close the mirror in a box the spriggans will appear anyway until they burst the box from inside..."

"*Will* they?"

"Oh, yes. I tried that, before I lost it. Those spriggans were very unhappy by the time they finally broke free. I think that may be why they were so determined to get the mirror away from me, so I couldn't do it again with a stronger box. Spriggans do seem to care about each other, in their own confused fashion, and they seem to want the mirror to keep on making more of them."

"Stupid little creatures," Alorria muttered, as Alris patted a tiny hand against her mother's shoulder.

"They can't help it," Karanissa whispered.

"So if the mirror is smashed—wait, do we know it *can* be smashed? Some magical artifacts are unbreakable."

"We don't know," Tobas admitted. "It was dropped onto a hard floor once or twice after it was enchanted and didn't break, but that was never from a significant height, and its failure to break didn't seem anything out of the ordinary to me at the time."

"I think a spriggan caught it every time it was dropped," Karanissa added.

"That may be so," Tobas admitted.

"We don't know what will happen if it *is* smashed?"

"No."

"So breaking it might mean we have dozens of smaller enchanted mirrors spewing out spriggans, or something worse?"

"It might."

"And if it's broken, what happens to all the spriggans it's *already* produced?"

"We don't know."

"I think we might want to find out before we do anything irrevocable."

Tobas hesitated. "We might," he agreed. "But I have no idea how that would be possible."

"If we brought it to be studied, perhaps?"

"Perhaps, and we may do that—but Gresh, there may be a way to ensure that its destruction won't do anything terrible even if we *can't* do any elaborate analysis."

"Might there? And what would that be?"

Tobas looked at his wives, then back to Gresh. "I can't tell you," he said. "Not here, not now. But if you find the mirror, I'm fairly sure we can dispose of it safely."

"*Are* you?" Gresh frowned. He hated secretive customers. He had plenty of secrets of his own, of course, but he always resented it when *other* people had them, as well, even though he knew it was unreasonable of him. "*I'm* not sure. This thing sounds as unpredictable as the Tower of Flame. I'm afraid I can't just trust you on this."

Tobas frowned back. "What?"

"I am not going to just hand the mirror over to you and trust you to dispose of it. It's too potentially dangerous. If that's the job, then I'm turning it down."

Here was his way out of committing himself to a job he might not be able to do, a way to avoid any risk to his reputation—though it might also cost him the greatest fee he could ever collect.

The others all stared at him. Alorria's mouth fell open. "You'd give up a chance at *eternal life*?" Alorria asked.

"Gresh, I admit the mirror might be dangerous, but you know the Wizards' Guild already has spells far more dangerous," Tobas said. "We used one to kill Tabaea, right in Ederd's palace, and had to use another one to cancel that one out. We have spells that could destroy the entire World, and you're worried about giving us a mirror that spits out spriggans?"

"A mirror *of unknown capabilities* that happens to spit out spriggans."

"Wizards deal with unknown dangers all the time!"

"But I don't always care to help them do it!"

"Sir," Karanissa said quietly. "If I might point something out?"

Gresh turned to her, then glanced toward the passage to the kitchen. He hoped that Twilfa had Tira back there listening, as she was supposed to. "And what would that be?" he asked.

"While it's true we don't know what else the mirror may do in the wrong hands, we know what it *does* do in its current situation," she said. "It produces spriggans, and it seems to do so endlessly. Do you want the whole World flooded with them?"

Gresh blinked at her. "Oh, they're a nuisance, but I'm sure..."

"*No*," Karanissa said, cutting him off. "You don't understand. They're a serious danger."

"Oh, now, really..."

"They have existed for six or seven years now, correct?"

"Well, I didn't see any until much more recently, but it's been a few years..."

"There are over half a million of them in the World now," Karanissa said, interrupting again. "The wizards could determine that much. More are appearing every day, usually dozens or even hundreds more. They've spread everywhere. They get into everything."

"Yes, but..."

"*Have you ever seen one die?*"

Gresh blinked again. "What?"

"Have you ever seen a dead spriggan? Have you ever seen one die? Have you ever seen one injured?"

Gresh stopped to think.

"They break things constantly; they trip people; they play with sharp things and hot things and dangerous things; they're stupid and clumsy, and they're attracted to magic, which we all know is very dangerous stuff. But have you ever seen one die? Seen one bleed? Seen one missing fingers or toes?"

"They feel pain..." Gresh said slowly. He had observed that a few times.

"Yes, they do—if you slap one, it'll wail. And they get hungry, and cold, and all the rest—but they *don't die*. They *can't be killed by natural means*. And that mirror is spitting out more and more of them. If we don't stop it, spriggans will eventually fill up the entire World, packed side by side from Tintallion to Vond—but we won't be around to see it, because we'll all have starved to death long before that, when they've eaten all the food."

Gresh stared at her for a moment. Then he said, "Oh."

There was no need to ask whether anyone had *tried* to kill spriggans; the creatures were so annoying that *of course* people had tried to kill them. He had never really thought about it before, but it was obvious. The witch was absolutely right; he had never seen one injured, never seen a dead one lying in the gutter with the drowned rats after a heavy rain, nor anywhere else. No wizard displayed a stuffed spriggan in his workroom with the snakeskins and dragon skulls and pickled tree squids.

As for disposing of them magically—well, magic didn't work properly on spriggans. Everyone knew that; it was part of the problem. There were undoubtedly ways to kill them, or at least remove them from the World, but whether those ways could be used safely and effectively was less certain.

A world totally flooded with spriggans was still decades or centuries away. Gresh knew he wouldn't live to see it without magic, but the idea of a constantly increasing supply of spriggans, more and more and more of them every year...

The risk to his reputation suddenly seemed less important.

"I'll want to know more about how you plan to dispose of the mirror," he said. "If not here and now, then when the time is right. I won't turn it over until I'm satisfied with your plans."

"Agreed," Tobas said.

"You'll provide transportation."

"Of course."

"You'll show me where all your adventures with the mirror happened, if I ask."

"Gladly."

Gresh nodded. "Then get Kaligir to agree to a payment of a hundred and ten percent of all my expenses and eternal youth, a contract with no trickery or ways of weaseling out of it, and we have a deal."

Tobas and both his wives smiled at him.

CHAPTER SIX

"My little brother is going to save the World," Tira said, as Gresh and two of his sisters seated themselves at the kitchen table.

"I might," Gresh said.

"And get *eternal youth* in exchange!" Twilfa said.

"That's the plan, yes."

"Jealous?" Tira asked.

Twilfa turned to glare at her. "Aren't you?"

"Oh, maybe a little—but death is a natural part of life, and if everyone lived forever the World would fill up with people instead of spriggans."

Twilfa did not reply to that, but Gresh did not need even a witch's limited ability to hear other people's thoughts to know she thought Tira was mouthing foolish platitudes. "I'll probably trip and break my neck a sixnight after they perform the spell," he grumbled. Then he turned to Tira. "I take it you heard everything."

"Yes."

"And they're telling the truth?"

"Well, the witch is; I'm not absolutely sure about the wizard. You know reading wizards is tricky. And the other woman, the mother, is so caught up in her own concerns I couldn't tell you a thing about what she actually believes."

"She didn't say much, in any case," Gresh said. "But the witch was telling the truth? Spriggans don't die?"

"She certainly believes it. Whether it's a fact I can't be sure."

"And Tobas?"

"He *seemed* to be telling the truth. He felt surprisingly forthright for a wizard. Usually they're so bound up with worrying about keeping all the Guild's secrets that they can hardly be honest about anything even when they try. This one, though—I think it may be because he's still young, and he's been lucky, and that's made him over-confident, but so far as I could tell he wasn't trying to mislead you at all. The only time he held anything back, he told you."

"Maybe it's because he really, *really* wants that mirror," Twilfa suggested.

"That could be it, actually. He might have been so focused on getting the mirror that he wasn't worrying about anything else."

Gresh frowned. "Do you think Kaligir will agree to my terms?" he asked Tira.

"How should *I* know?"

"Did *they* think he would?"

"Yes—but I don't think they know him very well."

"Hmm."

"So how will you find the mirror?" Twilfa asked. "That spriggan you talked to didn't know where it is."

"That's not the only spriggan in the World."

"That's sort of the point," Tira remarked.

"You know, there *must* be some way to kill them," Twilfa said. "Maybe not a natural one, but magic can do almost anything. Couldn't a demon eat one, or a warlock's magic squash one?"

"Maybe," Gresh said. "And there may well be wizardry that can destroy them—but the cure might be worse than the disease. Maybe that spell that killed Empress Tabaea could kill spriggans, but from what I've heard the spell could have destroyed the *World* if it hadn't been stopped. Even if we knew how to kill them, if they don't die naturally and that confounded mirror keeps spitting out more... I want to find the mirror and put an end to it, so we don't wind up in the middle of an everlasting war against the little pests."

Twilfa shuddered.

"So when you find the mirror, what are you going to do with it?" Tira asked.

"I don't know," Gresh admitted.

"Will you give it to Tobas?" Twilfa asked.

"I told you, I don't know. I barely know the man."

"Does Dina? Being a wizard and all."

"I don't know—and I want to talk to Dina, in any case. I need to know more about the magic involved. Maybe she can give me some idea what Tobas has in mind. Twilfa, could you..."

"I'll go," Tira said.

Gresh looked at her in surprise. "I thought you and Dar had business this afternoon."

"It can wait."

"Well, that's...that's very generous of you. I can certainly use Twilfa here at the shop. I'm going to assume that Kaligir will agree to my terms. I'll start my preparations for a trip to the Small Kingdoms."

"Is there anyone else I should find for you?"

Gresh took a moment to think. He saw no obvious use for a warlock or a demonologist, so there was no reason to call on Difa or Shesta. He had already spoken to Chira. Pyata was the family theurgist; Karanissa had mentioned the odd fact that the gods couldn't perceive spriggans at all, just as they sometimes couldn't see warlocks or demons. Pyata had once said the same, so she wouldn't be any help in dealing with the little nuisances, but she might be able to advise him about travel plans—the gods were usually reliable at predicting the weather, for example, and this time of year he wasn't sure what temperatures to expect in the mountains.

That was hardly urgent, though, and besides, Tira's husband Dar was a theurgist, as well, and could handle such simple matters.

He didn't need any new clothes, nor any sort of expertise with fabrics or sewing, so there was no reason to talk to Ekava. Neva was at sea somewhere, not due back for a sixnight. The city guard had no business in the Small Kingdoms, so Deka would be no help. He would probably be bringing some healing herbs and perhaps a few interesting intoxicants along, but he would need to check his own stocks before troubling Setta, the herbalist. Her husband Neran the ship chandler might have some useful supplies if Gresh needed to climb around in the mountains, but that could wait until his plans were a little more advanced.

That left Akka, the ritual dancer, four years younger than Gresh.

"Don't go out of your way, but if you see Akka or her husband, you could tell her I could use a dance of good fortune."

"If I see Akka, maybe. If I talk to Tresen he'll want to know what you're planning and whether he can help."

"Good point. Don't tell Tresen anything, then, but if you see Akka..."

"Right. Anything else?"

"You might ask Dar about the weather in Dwomor for the next few sixnights when you get home."

"I'd be happy to. It's off to Wizard Street, then. Take care, little brother." She rose from the table, and with a wave over her shoulder she headed for the back door.

Gresh and Twilfa watched her go. Once the door was closed, Twilfa leaned over and asked, "Why is she being so helpful? She wasn't this morning."

"Didn't you hear her? I'm going to save the World. I think she likes the idea. You know what witches are like, always looking for ways to do good and insisting they don't care about money. Here's a chance for her to help her greedy brother do something really *useful*, instead of just fetching oddities for wizards." He grimaced. "Not to mention that even witches are getting fed up with the spriggans."

"Oh. Oh, I suppose so." Twilfa glanced at the door just as the front bell jingled. She hopped up to answer it.

Gresh did not rise. Twilfa could handle ordinary business, and she would call him if he was needed. Right now he wanted to think about what he should bring to Dwomor.

He had already decided that Dwomor would be the first stop; that seemed to be where everything had started. He intended to travel by flying carpet, if the one Tobas had was large enough; that would be much faster than anything else available. If it *wasn't* large enough, well—he would deal with that if it became necessary. That meant he could not bring very many bags, and it also meant he couldn't travel alone. Tobas would, of necessity, be coming with him, since Gresh did not know how to operate a flying carpet and could hardly expect Tobas to trust him with it in any case. That was not a problem; Tobas would probably be useful, and it shouldn't be very hard to distract him on any occasion Gresh did not want company.

He would not bring anything wizardly, then—that would be Tobas's responsibility. He would want to discuss that with him and make sure the wizard had all the ingredients he needed for any spells he knew that might be helpful.

He would have Chira's talisman to help him spot movement. Now, were there any other sorcerous devices he might bring? He had a handful in the shop, but half of them were not functioning. After some thought he decided that the other half didn't have any obvious applications for this expedition.

He would need to bring money and his usual assortment of tools, and since he was undoubtedly going to be dealing with spriggans, he thought some snares would be useful. He would also bring a bag of candy—he had heard that spriggans liked honey-drops.

He had a set of snares and nets intended for catching

rabbits or hawks, but they should serve well enough for spriggans.

Were there any particular trade goods that might be useful in mountainous country? Nothing came immediately to mind.

He mulled over possibilities for several minutes, until Twilfa called him to help a customer whose needs were somewhat esoteric, and who did not trust a teenaged assistant to meet them.

Trade was brisk for the next hour or so, and he became so involved in conducting his normal business that Dina's arrival caught him by surprise. "What can I get for you?" he asked, before he remembered that he had sent for her.

"A less troublesome brother," she replied.

He smiled crookedly and gestured for her to follow him to the chairs by the fire. "Well, I'm afraid the supply is limited, and we'll just have to see if we can modify the one you have, rather than replace him. I'm sorry, Dina; thank you for coming. I hope the transmutation spell went well?"

"I haven't done it," she said. "It takes eight hours, so I have to do it at night, when I won't be interrupted. I don't have an apprentice to stand guard, not since Inria made journeyman."

"Oh, of course. I hope it *will* go well, then." He gestured for her to sit.

She remained standing. "What did you want me for, Gresh?"

Gresh glanced around. Twilfa was making change for the last of the other customers over at the far side of the shop. The vault was standing open, and the fire was burning low, but otherwise everything was in order. No one appeared to be listening in—though of course someone might be using a scrying spell on them. The shop was warded against such spells, but no ward was perfect.

"Have a seat, please, Dina; I have some questions I need to ask you."

"What sort of questions?"

"To begin with, tell me everything you know about Lugwiler's Haunting Phantasm."

"Lugwiler's...? You know the basics, don't you? It's a third-order invocation requiring a mirror, black sand, spider's ichor, a rat's eyeball, three crow feathers, the long outside bone from a bat's left wing, and the wizard's own saliva." She made a surreptitious gesture indicating that there was another ingredient she was not listing, which did not surprise Gresh. He knew that most spells used the wizard's dagger somehow, and that for some reason this was not ordinarily mentioned. She settled into the chair, still speaking. "It's generally used as a minor curse and has no obvious other use, though it's always possible someone might think of one. It's handy in that it doesn't require anything from the intended victim, not even a true name, though in normal usage it won't take effect until a line of sight is established between the victim and the enchanted mirror. It can be triggered by a command from the wizard when he sees that connection, or set as a booby-trap for the next person who happens into the mirror's effective area. Why are you asking me this?"

"Because I've been asked to retrieve a mirror that was used in a failed attempt at it," he said, taking the other chair. "Are there known ways it can fail?"

"Well, yes, of course—it can dissipate harmlessly, or attach the curse to the wizard instead of the intended victim, or detonate the mirror, which wouldn't leave anything to retrieve."

"Detonate?"

"Explode. Shards of glass or metal everywhere. One of Dabran's apprentices did that once and almost took out her own eye, not to mention smashing assorted jars and a good lamp and scaring Dabran's cat half to death."

Gresh nodded. "It's supposed to produce a phantasm, right? A monstrous little creature that only the victim can see?"

"Well, an image, anyway. No one's entirely sure just what the phantasm itself truly is—whether it's a living creature or a malign spirit or a minor demon or an illusion or what, or whether it's really where the victim sees it, assuming he's seeing something real to begin with. One theory is that what the spell actually does is affect the victim's vision so that he's catching glimpses of another reality, one inhabited by these hideous little things. Another is that the creatures, whatever they are, are all around us all the time, and what the spell does is to let the victim see things that are normally invisible to us. Mostly, though, we assume it's just an illusion, that the spell plays tricks on the victim's mind."

"What do the phantasms look like?"

"How should I know?"

"You've never seen one?"

"No one's ever had a reason to put a curse on me, thank you very much, dear brother."

"But you learned the spell as an apprentice, didn't you?"

She glared at him. "As it happens, no, I didn't. Have I ever bought rat's eyeballs from you? I've read about it, and I got the formula in a trade with Sensella of the Isle, but I've never tried it—Dabran's apprentice, whatever her name was, made me wary. And even if I had, if I did it properly *I* wouldn't see the phantasm."

That was mildly inconvenient. Gresh had hoped to get every detail of the spell, perhaps see it performed, in order to give him more background, and it appeared Dina couldn't readily provide that. She did have the formula, but trying a new spell always carried some risk. He was sure she wouldn't do it unless he paid for it.

Of course, he could count that as a research expense and charge Tobas and the Guild for it. He might resort to that.

"So it can dissipate, or explode, or hit the wrong target," he said. "Has it ever produced something other than the expected phantasm, that you know of?"

"Well, now, who knows what the expected phantasm is? For all we know, every victim might be seeing something different. Most of the victims don't compare notes, and the descriptions usually boil down to, 'Oh, ick!' They mostly involve hair and claws and eyes, but don't get into a lot of specifics—for one thing, the victim usually only sees the phantasm from the corner of her eye, and it's gone when she looks for it."

"Someone could try it twice and see whether they get the same image."

"They could. Maybe someone has. *I* haven't, and no one's ever mentioned it to me. This isn't a spell that gets a great deal of attention, Gresh."

"Well, perhaps it should. It appears that on one

occasion it *did* produce something else, instead of a phantasm."

"And they want you to recover that particular mirror to see if they can do it again?"

"Something like that."

"It probably won't work—that spell has half a dozen deliberate variables in it, depending on exactly how you want the curse to operate, as well as all the usual ways to mess it up. The mirror probably isn't what mattered."

Gresh hesitated, debating whether to explain in more detail what he was after, but then decided against it, at least for the moment. Instead he asked, "How do you get rid of Lugwiler's Phantasm?"

"It depends how you set it up in the first place. If you had any sense, you made it conditional—it would work until the victim did something, such as apologize, and then it would end by itself. Or it would only work so long as the victim stayed in a particular area, or carried a specific object—then you wouldn't *need* a countercharm."

"But suppose it wasn't conditional."

Dina sighed. "Let me think. Casting Javan's Restorative on the victim should work."

"Would the victim need to cooperate for that?"

"To the extent of being present and not interfering in the preparation, yes—though it *might* be possible to use his true name instead." She frowned. "I wouldn't want to try it that way, though; it's a seventh- or eighth-order spell, and I don't like improvising at that level. It can be put in a potion or talisman, though, and if the victim drinks the potion or invokes the talisman..."

"I don't think that will work in this case, Dina. Are there any other countercharms?"

"*I* don't know. A Spell of Reversal might do it. They say that works on almost anything."

"Spell of Reversal? I don't think I know that one."

"That's because the only difficult ingredient in the usual version is hair from a stillborn child; everything else is simple, basic stuff like candles and water and shiny stones that nobody would bother to pay your prices for. Besides, it must be tenth-order or worse; *I* can't do it, and not many wizards can."

"So how does it work?"

"It reverses a process or undoes a spell, so if you're quick enough and a good enough wizard you can undo some of your worst mistakes. There are rumors it's even been able to raise the dead if the timing's just right. You can make a broken jar unbreak itself, a knife unrust, blood flow back into a wound, or a river run uphill. But it doesn't reverse it permanently—after half an hour or so it wears off and the natural flow is restored. If you've reversed it back to before the process started you can try to prevent it happening again—put the jar somewhere safe, keep the knife dry, bandage the wound—but the natural order returns, and that river's going to run downhill again, the wound is going to bleed, and you can't stop it."

"So how would that work on Lugwiler's Haunting Phantasm?"

"I'm not sure it would—but if it did, and you used it quickly enough, you might be able to undo the spell, reverse the process to before the mirror was enchanted, and make it as if it was never cast. Or at least make the victim not have looked at the mirror, or whatever."

Gresh nodded thoughtfully; that sounded like a stupendously useful spell. The ability to reverse anything? That could have a thousand applications.

Tenth-order, though—and it probably took hours to prepare...

"Can it be put in a potion or talisman?"

"Not a potion; you cast it on a *process*, not a person, so a potion wouldn't work. Maybe it would work in a talisman or a powder; I don't know."

Gresh was about to ask who might know more when the doorbell jingled. He glanced over toward Twilfa, who was opening the door, and her expression prevented him from continuing the conversation. He rose.

"Tell your master that Kaligir of the New Quarter is here to see him," said the new arrival, as he stepped across the threshold.

CHAPTER SEVEN

Gresh arranged his features into his most welcoming smile as he crossed the front room to greet the thin man in elaborate robes. The wizard was almost as tall as he was, even without counting the shiny black cap he wore.

"Master Kaligir!" he said. "What a pleasure!"

The wizard looked at him, then cocked his head to one side and said, "I was going to question that, but on further consideration it probably *is* a pleasure for you—my presence means we haven't rejected your terms out of hand." He glanced around, and nodded at Twilfa. "Your assistant?"

"Yes—my sister, Twilfa of Ethshar." That was the name he used for her when talking to patrons. At home or in other contexts, she had always been Twilfa the Helpful.

"And is that Dina the Wizard? One of your customers?"

"Another of my sisters, Master."

Dina rose and bowed. "I can go if you would prefer, Guildmaster."

"Stay. Sit. We may need a neutral party."

Dina sat. Gresh kept smiling, but did not like the sound of Kaligir's words.

"Shall I go?" Twilfa asked, gesturing toward the passage to the kitchen and looking back and forth between the two men.

Gresh looked questioningly at Kaligir.

"It's your house," the wizard said. "I'm sure you have a way for her to listen in, and of course you might just tell her everything afterward, so please yourself."

"He brought others with him, Gresh," Twilfa said. "Several others."

"They're waiting in the street," Kaligir confirmed. "I didn't see any need to crowd everyone in, and if I can't intimidate you without them, then you're clearly mad."

"Twilfa," Gresh said. "Would you see if any of our guest's escort would care for a mug of beer while they wait?"

Twilfa dropped a quick curtsey, and said, "Or I can make tea."

"Beer will do for now."

She nodded, then hurried to the kitchen to find a tray and fill a pitcher.

Kaligir watched her depart, then turned back to Gresh. "I am not sure," he said, "that you understand the situation."

"I think I do," Gresh replied. "You want me to retrieve the mirror that Tobas of Telven lost six and a half years ago. The mirror has a botched form of Lugwiler's Haunting Phantasm on it—one that was botched in a completely new way, unlike any previous casting of the spell. It's the source of all the spriggans in the World, and you want to put an end to the production of spriggans before they become a real danger. They're already a serious nuisance, and the Guild has realized that they don't die of natural causes and that their number is increasing steadily. Do I have that much correct?"

"You do."

"You have come to me because all previous attempts to locate the mirror have failed, and I have a reputation for being able to find anything."

"Not exactly. *Tobas and his wives* came to you because of this; the Guild did not, and I did not. We merely ordered Tobas to deal with the problem and agreed to fund his efforts."

"And he dealt with it by coming to me, for the reasons I stated."

"Yes."

"And because of this, because I appear to be your last hope to find the mirror without sending hundreds of treasure-hunters searching through the Small Kingdoms for it and possibly making matters even worse, you told Tobas that you would pay any fee I might ask, but when I asked for eternal youth, you balked."

"No."

Gresh blinked. "No?"

"No. We did not balk. However, the price you set has changed the situation. We agreed to provide Tobas with *funding*, not unlimited magic, and your price is not mere money. Tobas cannot pay it. While he has a suitable spell in his book of spells, he is not yet capable of casting it and won't be for years. It's far too complex for him."

"Very well, then, *Tobas* balked, not you."

"No, Tobas did not. He came to me, in my role as the Guild's representative in Ethshar of the Rocks, and explained the situation and asked if the Guild could pay the fee you had set, since we had said we would finance him."

"And the Guild declined to do so?"

"No. The Guild has agreed. Your fee will be a successful casting of Enral's Eternal Youth, to be paid as soon as we are convinced that the mirror will never again produce spriggans. You may need to provide the ingredients for the spell, however—some of them are difficult."

"Of course," Gresh said, unable to repress a smile. "I'm sure I can do that."

"If not, your reputation is undeserved," Kaligir said dryly.

"But if you agree to my terms—why are you here? Why not just send Tobas back with a contract?"

"Because you are not going to be acting for Tobas. We have decided, given your terms, that if you accept this commission you will indeed be acting for the Wizards' Guild itself. That alters matters. We've agreed to your fee, but that doesn't mean everything is settled."

"It doesn't? I'm in the business of selling things to wizards that they need in their spells. Tobas wanted this particular item, and I agreed to sell it to him, on certain conditions, and set my price. He may have turned his end of the agreement over to the Guild, but I don't see how that changes anything. What else needs to be settled?"

"Several things. The Wizards' Guild does not tolerate any sort of deception or insubordination in our hirelings."

The last trace of Gresh's smile vanished. "I'm not deceiving anyone, and I'm not subordinate to anyone, either."

"You are now. You're dealing with the Guild itself now, not an individual wizard—the Guild that sets rules kings and overlords obey if they wish to live, rules that every magician of every school of magic in the World must heed. We take a direct interest in anyone with a magically extended lifespan, just as we do rulers or magicians, since such people have the time to have a disproportionate influence on the World. By setting the price you have you have drawn our interest, and the Guild's authority, once invoked, cannot be resisted."

Gresh did not like the sound of that at all. "I'm just selling you a mirror; we've agreed on a price. What else does the Guild care about?"

"Times, for one thing. Penalties for non-performance, for another."

"I'm not sure I understand. Perhaps you would like to sit down, so that we can discuss this?"

"I'll stand, thank you," Kaligir said. "What I believe you may have missed is the *urgency* of this task. The Wizards' Guild is notoriously slow to act on many issues, but when we *do* act, we want immediate results."

"Of course."

"It has occurred to us that you might well agree to fetch the mirror and then find excuses to put it off—that one reason you demanded a youth spell is that you expect to spend a significant part of a human lifetime in planning and preparation. The possibility was also mentioned that once you have the mirror in your possession—if you ever do—you might decide to alter your price and demand more than a youth spell. I am here to make absolutely certain you understand that nothing of this sort will be acceptable."

Gresh stared silently at the wizard. He had honestly not known he could still be so deeply offended by...well, *anyone*.

"Sir," he said at last. "I am an honest tradesman, with a reputation to uphold. I will have your mirror for you as quickly as I can and at the agreed-upon price—eternal youth and payment in gold equal to a hundred and ten percent of my expenses, with one hundred rounds of gold as a down-payment. Not an iron bit more or less than that and with delivery as prompt as I can make it."

"How prompt is that?"

"I can't possibly know. I know it's in a cave on the eastern slope of a mountain somewhere between Calimor and Vlagmor, within sight of a ruin, but that leaves a great deal of territory to search. I might find it the first day, or not for months."

Kaligir blinked, and then it was his turn to stare silently. The silence was interrupted by Twilfa passing through the room with a tray of mugs and a pitcher of beer. The wizard watched her slip out the front door, then turned back to Gresh.

"You know that, do you?" His tone was much more conciliatory now. He had gotten rather strident in the course of the conversation, and that stridency had abruptly vanished.

"Yes, I do," Gresh replied. "And that information cost me goods valued at five rounds of gold, which will be included in my bill for expenses, though of course the down payment will more than cover it. Did you think I wouldn't have begun my investigation?"

Kaligir hesitated, then admitted, "To be honest, yes, I did. I suspected, in fact, that you had set your price on the assumption we wouldn't meet it and that you had no intention of finding the mirror."

"I believe you owe me an apology, then."

"Yes, I believe I do, and you have it. I have apparently misjudged you; I apologize."

"Thank you." Gresh's own voice, which had also crept up in volume, lowered a little.

"Nonetheless, I still need to explain the terms further."

Gresh frowned. "Why?"

"Because I am speaking for the Wizards' Guild as a whole. We agreed on terms in council, and I have no authority to modify them. Resentment of the spriggans has reached a remarkable level of ferocity, and it was impressed on me that despite our own years of dawdling, we want results quickly. We have therefore settled upon...well, I now wish we hadn't, that we had trusted in your good faith, but alas, we did not. Your reputation for greed exceeded your reputation for honesty."

This was sounding worse and worse; Gresh had begun to wish he had simply told Karanissa the shop was closed the other morning, and refused to get involved with any of this. "And?" he said.

"And the Wizards' Guild has declared your shop and

your services to be forbidden to all wizards until such time as you find the mirror. You will sell not so much as a drop of virgin's blood until the mirror has been dealt with."

"By all the gods who hear! That's outrageous!"

Kaligir turned up a palm. "Think of it as incentive."

"It's insulting."

"Yes, I suppose it is. I'm sorry. On the other hand, there is a reason I brought half a dozen other master wizards with me today."

"Oh?"

"To speed you on your way and make certain of your success, we are volunteering, on behalf of the Guild, to equip your expedition with magic you may think would be useful—potions, powders, perhaps the loan of an enchanted jewel or dagger. Within reasonable limits, of course."

That sounded like a bit of good news, finally, but Gresh was wary. "I had assumed that Tobas would accompany me and provide me with spells as needed," he said.

"And he will, if you want—but Tobas's apprenticeship had certain...irregularities, and his training is spotty. While he has access to a great many spells, many of them unique and remarkably powerful, he can't always perform them reliably, and he hasn't learned certain commonplace spells. Furthermore, as you know, some spells take hours or days, and we thought it might be useful to have them in more immediately accessible form."

Gresh remembered his interrupted conversation with Dina. "It would indeed," he said.

"Well, we are here to supply that—each wizard here, myself included, knows how to prepare powders and potions. Choose what spells you want—given your line of work I'm sure you know much of what we have available—and we'll prepare them for you."

That *was* good news—though the bit about Tobas being improperly trained wasn't, and there were still some things that needed explanation. "Ah...why so many wizards? Why not just one good one?"

"Because each spell takes time, and we will be preparing them simultaneously, one per wizard. Depending just what you request, having one wizard do them all might take sixnights, or even months. Besides, we are unpaid volunteers, doing this on the Guild's behalf for the general good, and no one of us is *that* generous with his time and energy. We're all eager to get back to our own concerns."

That made sense. Gresh nodded. "You said powders and potions, or loans? What about making talismans for me?"

Kaligir frowned. "Don't ask *too* much, Gresh," he said. "Tolnor's Forging is not undertaken lightly and takes a sixnight or more for every spell—the slightest slip, and a day's work has to be repeated until it's perfect. You can't stop partway through. There have been wizards who spent *years* trying to get a single enchantment right, having to snatch naps when they could, being fed quick bites by their apprentices or families because they couldn't leave the work area. No one is volunteering for that; most of us aren't even capable of it."

"Oh." Gresh had never actually known just what

was involved in creating enchanted objects that carried reusable spells, but given the rarity of such artifacts it made sense that the spell would be difficult and expensive. He just hadn't realized *how* difficult and expensive.

"And as soon as you have the magical preparations, we trust you and Tobas will depart for the Small Kingdoms."

"Indeed." He glanced at Dina. "And might one wizard answer questions for me, instead? A wizard who is very familiar with Lugwiler's Haunting Phantasm?"

"An excellent suggestion. Then you agree to our terms?"

"Do I really have a choice?"

"No. The Guild has decided you don't. You will find the enchanted mirror and deliver it promptly to Tobas or another representative of the Wizards' Guild, and the Guild will pay you the agreed-upon price. Now, have you given any thought to the spells you want to have available?"

"A little." He glanced at Dina again. "The Spell of Reversal would be useful, and Javan's Restorative..."

An hour later all the volunteers but one had been sent home to their workshops to begin work on spells Gresh had requested—using ingredients he had provided, of course; their altruism was not unlimited. One, a plump middle-aged woman named Heshka, had stayed to advise Gresh on the workings of Lugwiler's Haunting Phantasm, flying carpets, Transporting Tapestries, and other relevant wizardry, as well as what little was known about spriggans themselves.

Gresh worded his questions carefully, never asking

certain things outright, and concluded that his initial guess had been right—the wizards had tried divinations of every sort, but had never thought to seriously interrogate the spriggans themselves about where they came from, or backtrack them to the mirror. That was typical of wizards, especially city-bred ones—such ordinary, non-magical methods simply never occurred to most of them. A few had at least *asked* the spriggans about where they came from and had almost always gotten, "Don't know. Don't remember," as the answer.

Gresh began to wonder whether that was actually true. Everyone always assumed that spriggans were too stupid to lie effectively, but Gresh had started to wonder whether they might not be quite as idiotic as they appeared.

As for the spell that created them, Gresh learned more of the mechanics, but Dina's description had covered most of what he wanted, and Heshka confirmed Dina's account. The Haunting Phantasm manifested a hideous little creature that only the chosen victim could see, but no one really knew whether the spell created an illusion, created a real creature, or summoned a pre-existing creature from somewhere.

"Illusions don't trip people or knock bottles off shelves, so spriggans aren't illusions," Gresh said.

"They don't look anything like the phantasm, either," Heshka pointed out. "No fangs or fur. We have no idea just how wrong the spell went; it may not have resembled the Phantasm at all by the time Tobas finished it. For one thing, he performed it in a castle outside the World. How do we know *that* didn't completely alter its nature? No one else has ever tried that. He may not even have made any mistakes other than choosing the wrong place to perform it!"

"Ordinarily, when the spell is complete, and the phantasm is haunting the chosen victim, how is the mirror involved? Does breaking it break the spell?"

Heshka looked startled. "No, of course not. Once the spell is done, it's just an ordinary mirror; it has nothing to do with the phantasm. I told you, the spriggan mirror is *different.*"

"So I see," Gresh said, stroking his beard. "And do you think that might be because the spell was never actually *finished*? Might it stop making spriggans if the curse were directed at its original intended target?"

"I don't *think* so," Heshka said. "It *was* directed at its original intended target—didn't Tobas tell you? The target even held the mirror at one point. If that didn't complete it, what would?"

"The trigger word?"

"I don't think he was doing that version—though you might ask him."

"I take it you've spoken with Tobas about this. Who *was* the original intended target?"

"Well, *that* might be why it went wrong, too. We're fairly sure it was an Invisible Servitor. Something artificial, anyway, that Derithon had left running loose in his castle. You *really* aren't supposed to cast the curse on anything but humans, but Tobas didn't know that. He should have known he was in a magically created void because he had already found corridors that behaved unnaturally. Using the spell to curse a magical creature, something that's effectively a spell incarnate, while you're in an enchanted castle in a magically created void where space isn't the same shape was foolish. It's amazing the spell didn't do something even worse than a plague of spriggans. I think we can all be grateful that the Haunting Phantasm is a simple, low-order spell."

"I see," Gresh said thoughtfully.

The Wizards' Guild generally tended to be very conservative, and cases like this were a major reason why. Wizardry was absurdly powerful, dangerous stuff that tapped into the raw chaos that underlay ordinary reality. Even simple spells could go spectacularly wrong. That was why wizards screened their apprentices carefully and imposed draconian rules on each other. Mistakes that would be harmless in any sane enterprise could be fatal to everyone in the area when wizardry was involved. It was theoretically possible for a single wizard to destroy the entire World, and while a portion of the Guild might actually survive that, no one cared to put it to the test. The Guild and individual wizards therefore did everything they could to prevent the careless use of wizardry.

This was often a self-solving problem, actually—sloppy or untalented apprentices didn't survive to become journeymen. The death rate wasn't as discouraging as it was for demonologists, but it wasn't zero, either. Even non-fatal mistakes might leave an apprentice with four legs and fur, or trapped in an unbreakable bottle, or otherwise incapacitated.

Tobas appeared to be that rare and fortunate thing, a wizard who had done something very stupid when he was young and survived it unscathed. Gresh would want to watch him very closely. Tobas *should* have learned from his mistakes, but that didn't mean he *had*, and someone who did something stupendously stupid once might well do something stupid again.

At last he could think of no more questions to ask. He thanked Heshka and Dina and sent them both home, noticing as he did that the sun was down and the lamps were lit. Weary, he stretched, and headed to the kitchen, where he discovered that Twilfa had found Akka, the family's ritual dancer, as he had asked, and had brought her back to the shop. The sisters were chatting over empty plates while a third plate, holding a supper of cold salt ham and honeyed pears, waited for him.

He sat down to eat, but before he could pick up his fork Akka turned and asked, "What sort of dance do you need?"

"A blessing on travelers, I think," he said, as he cut a bite of ham. "I'm going to the Small Kingdoms on an errand." He popped the ham in his mouth. "And if you can do anything to make spriggans more cooperative, that would help."

"And I suppose you're too busy to actually *watch* the dance, let alone participate."

"You suppose correctly."

"It would be much more effective if you joined in."

"I don't work magic, Akka," Gresh said. "You know that. I'll use *other* people's magic happily; I do it all the time. But I don't make my own magic, ever."

"You could at least stand in the center of the pattern."

Gresh considered that for a moment. The wizards had said it would take two days to get the powders and potions ready. He estimated he would need half a day for his own preparations. That left a day and a half. He had thought he might to use the time for further research and to handle the normal course of business, but now he remembered that the Guild had ordered his customers not to buy from him until he brought back the mirror, so there wouldn't *be* any normal business. He wasn't really sure just what research remained to be done. He might try to catch and talk to a few more spriggans, and he might have more questions for Tobas and his wives, but beyond that, what would he do with his time?

"When will your troupe be ready?" he asked.

CHAPTER EIGHT

Gresh eyed the carpet critically. "Will that thing really hold us?" he asked.

"Oh, yes," Tobas assured him. "It's quite safe."

"No, it isn't," Alorria said.

"Ali..."

"It isn't! It's amazing none of us have ever fallen off, and we've gotten hit by birds and gotten bugs in our eyes..."

"Shut up, Ali," Karanissa said. "We *haven't* fallen off, and we aren't going to, because part of the spell on the carpet is to adjust its shape to hold us upright and to adjust its path through the air to keep us on it."

"It's *hard* to fall off a flying carpet," Tobas said.

"But it can be done," Alorria insisted. "And we *do* run into birds and bugs, and there's no protection from wind or rain..."

"I'm sure Gresh can handle riding it," Karanissa replied.

"I'm sure I can," Gresh agreed, but he had some doubts. The carpet was only about six feet wide and nine or ten feet long, and it was a long way to the Small Kingdoms, well over a hundred leagues. He and Tobas would presumably want to sleep on the way. Put the two of them on that carpet, along with their baggage and supplies, and...well, it would be cozy.

He had asked Tobas to bring it over so he could see how much room he would have for supplies, and he was not happy with what he saw. The carpet was nicely patterned in blues and reds and hovered steadily a foot off the hard-packed earth of East Road, but it really was small and didn't look very sturdy. Gresh tended to think Alorria was right about its safety.

"The four of us flew here from Ethshar of the Sands on it," Tobas said. "It wasn't bad."

"It was crowded," Alorria said. "I was frightened the whole time that I was going to drop the baby."

"But you didn't," Tobas said. "Really, it wasn't bad."

From Ethshar of the Sands to Ethshar of the Rocks was about fifty leagues. "How long did that take?" Gresh asked.

"Oh, half a day."

Gresh threw Tobas a sideways glance. "Half a day?"

"About that."

"That's fast!"

"That's the *point*," Tobas said.

"Well, yes," Gresh acknowledged.

"It's going to be crowded," Alorria said. "It was bad enough with four of us."

Gresh looked at her, startled. "What?"

"I said it would be crowded," Alorria said.

"But *you* aren't coming!"

"Oh, yes, I am! You think I'm going to miss a chance to show our daughter to her grandparents? They haven't seen her yet, you know. And I am not about to let Tobas strand me and the baby here with a bunch of strangers. I don't know anyone in this city! We've been staying at an inn near Eastgate, and I am *not* going to stay in a place like that without my husband to protect me. Not to mention that caring for a baby is a lot of work, and I expect Tobas to do his share of it, and he can't if he's in Dwomor and Alris is here, can he? I am *definitely* coming, Gresh the Supplier, and don't you think you can prevent it!"

"We may be able to leave her and the baby with her parents in Dwomor while we're out in the wilderness," Tobas said apologetically. "Or if the trip is *too* strenuous, perhaps in our home in Ethshar of the Sands."

"Or our *other* home," Alorria said.

"As far as anyone in this World can tell, that *is* in Ethshar of the Sands," Karanissa said.

Gresh was not at all sure what homes they were talking about, but the details didn't really matter. "So we're going to crowd all four of us and our baggage onto..."

"Five," Karanissa said.

Gresh turned to glower at her.

"I'm afraid my wives don't like it if I travel with only *one* of them," Tobas said.

Karanissa glared silently at him, while Alorria said, "No, I *don't* like it if you try to go off alone with her, and I don't mind saying so! I know you married her first, and you're both magicians, but you're my husband, all the same, and I'm not going to let you run around with another woman, even if she *is* your wife! Especially not now that I have the baby."

Gresh closed his eyes wearily.

"It's going to be crowded," he said.

"We can hang the luggage from the sides," Tobas said. "It won't be that bad."

"I'll need to re-pack my things," Gresh said.

"Honestly, it can lift several tons," Tobas said. "You'd be amazed. We moved half our household from Dwomor to Ethshar on it, in a single load. Secure everything with a few ropes, and we'll be fine."

"All the same, I prefer to rearrange," Gresh said. He did not say so, but what he now intended to do was to stuff everything into the magical bottomless bag Dina had made for him years ago, as much to keep Tobas's wives from poking into his belongings as because he was concerned about the carpet's capacity. It would make unpacking much more of a job, since everything had to be removed from the bag one item at a time in the exact reverse of the order it went in, but he would feel more secure.

He really hoped Akka's dance did some good. Her group had gathered the other night and danced until they were dripping with sweat, and Gresh hoped the effort hadn't been wasted. It had certainly *felt* invigorating, as if the dancers were pouring energy into him, so presumably it had done *something*.

"Can you be ready to leave in an hour and a half?" he asked.

"We're ready to leave *now*," Alorria said.

"No, we aren't," Karanissa retorted. "Our belongings are still at the inn, and we haven't paid the bill or told Kaligir we're leaving."

"But everything's *packed up*, Kara," Alorria said.

"We can be ready in an hour," Tobas said. "We'll be in Ethshar of the Sands by nightfall."

"But we're going to Dwomor," Gresh said.

"Not today," Tobas said. "We'll spend the night at my home in Grandgate, and *tomorrow* we'll head for Dwomor. It's a long day's flight from Ethshar of the Sands to Dwomor. We'll want to start bright and early. It's not much fun flying in the dark."

That, Gresh was forced to admit to himself, made sense, probably far more sense than trying to sleep on a grossly overcrowded carpet. "An hour, then," he said.

"We'll be here." With that, Tobas and his wives climbed aboard the carpet and settled down cross-legged on the worn wool: Tobas at the front, Karanissa at the rear, and Alorria in the center with Alris clutched in her arms. From the smooth efficiency with which they took their places, Gresh judged they had done this several times before.

The wizard made a sound and a gesture, and the carpet rose smoothly upward, to rooftop level, before turning and heading east down the street.

Gresh watched it go, then sighed and went back into the shop, wondering whether he could stuff his other luggage directly into the bottomless bag, or whether he would need to unpack it and shove everything in piece by piece.

When it came time to try, most of his bags fit just as they were, but the single largest had to be unpacked and fed in piecemeal. Gresh was glad that he had asked Dina to make sure his bottomless bag had a good wide mouth and wished it had been just a *little* bit larger—that big bag, containing a bedroll and pillow and his formal robes, among other things, had *almost* fit.

He would need to take all that stuff back out, item by item, before he could retrieve the bag of tools and snares, or the precious box of powders and potions, or the bag of magical ingredients, or the sack of non-perishable food, or the case of wine, or all his other clothing and toiletries. He thought he might want to take the time to arrange things in a better order at some point on the journey, but for now he would make do. The important thing was that he had packed all the supplies he wanted to bring into the one magical bag, the apparent size of a very large watermelon, and the apparent weight of the heaviest single item in it. He was not entirely sure what that item was, though; he just knew how the spell operated and that when he hefted the bag it seemed to weigh fifteen or twenty pounds.

That was quite manageable. He could easily sling the bag over one shoulder and carry it for as far as necessary.

When Tobas's carpet once again swooped down from the rooftops to hover in front of the shop, Gresh was ready, the bottomless bag at his heel, and five of his sisters—Twilfa, Dina, Chira, Tira, and Akka—standing beside him to say their farewells.

The carpet looked rather different now; instead of a simple flat cloth surface it had taken on the appearance of a miniature caravan, laden with baggage. On either side hung an assortment of bags, valises, traveling cases, and other luggage, suspended from a network of ropes and cords that crisscrossed the carpet itself. These bags didn't seem to interfere with the carpet's ability to fly, and the ropes barely indented the carpet's surface at all—in fact, some appeared to be stretched *above* the fabric, between edges that curled slightly upward. The passengers were once again seated cross-legged in a row down the center, with the two women crowded together to create a cramped fourth space, carefully kept open, between Tobas and Alorria. Gresh noticed that Alorria now wore a slender gold coronet, and Karanissa had her hair tightly bound into a long, thick braid.

The carpet fluttered in from the east and wheeled just above head-height, setting the dangling luggage swinging, then settled down toward Tobas's door, stopping the instant the lowest-hanging bundle brushed the dirt of the street. This meant the carpet stayed a good three feet up, perhaps four, rather than the single foot it had managed on the previous visit.

"*Hai!* Gresh!" Tobas called from his position at the front of the rug, waving. "Are you ready?"

"Yes," Gresh said, picking up his bag with one hand and giving Twilfa a quick final hug with the other. He stepped forward.

"Just the one bag?" Tobas asked.

"It's bottomless," Gresh explained, carefully not expressing his surprise that Tobas had apparently not used anything of the sort himself.

"Hallin's spell?" Tobas turned up a palm. "I have the instructions for that one, but I could never make it work. Half a day or more!"

"But you have a flying carpet," Dina said, startled. "Varrin's Lesser Propulsion takes a day and a half and is at least an order or two higher than Hallin's Bottomless Bag!"

"Oh, I didn't *make* this," Tobas said. "I bought it. We used to need to do a lot of traveling around

Dwomor, so I had some friends find me one I could just barely afford. It must be about a century old—it's about thirty years into its eighty-year cycle."

"What?" Gresh said, suddenly worried about the carpet's reliability. He much preferred dealing with wizards who used their own magic, rather than borrowed or bought devices. They knew how to fix it if something went wrong.

"Varrin's Lesser Propulsion needs to be renewed every so often," Dina explained. "When it's first cast it only lasts for one cycle of the greater moon, from one full moon to the next. But every time the spell is renewed it lasts twice as long, so after a few cycles it's good for years at a time. What he calls the eighty-year cycle is...let me see...the tenth renewal. It's really a little less than seventy-nine years."

"Is that good?" Gresh asked.

"Well, if he's right, you won't need to worry about renewing the spell—old flying carpets are worth more than new, because of that; by the tenth renewal they last longer than most owners will live. The thing is, each renewal is more difficult—you need to use certain elements of the original spell, and they tend to get lost after a few cycles."

"One reason I could afford this carpet," Tobas said, "is that the original maker's heirs have mislaid one of the seven white stones, so the spell can't be renewed forty or fifty years from now."

"But you're *sure* it's good for years yet?" Gresh asked.

"Mereth of the Golden Door says it is. Do you know a better diviner?"

Gresh looked at Dina.

"She's not local, but I've heard of Mereth," Dina admitted.

"She lives in Ethshar of the Sands," Tobas said. "Near the palace."

"She's supposed to be good," Dina acknowledged. She turned back to Tobas. "You can't do Hallin's Bottomless Bag?"

"I wouldn't say '*can't*,'" Tobas replied. "Let's just say I *haven't* done Hallin's spell."

"The Bottomless Bag," Dina corrected him. "Hallin invented more than one spell, you know."

Tobas blinked at her. "He did?"

"Yes, he did! The other important one is Hallin's Transporting Fissure. Seventh- or eighth-order. You never heard of it?"

"Um...no," Tobas admitted. "I haven't. But I probably couldn't use it in any case—I can't work seventh-order spells with any sort of reliability at all. And I've always just heard the Bottomless Bag referred to as Hallin's spell—after all, it works on things besides bags."

"I'm sure this is all very interesting for you wizards," Alorria interrupted. "But some of us would like to get home before dark. If Gresh has all his things in that one little bag, so much the better. He can climb on the carpet, and we can go."

"Yes, of course." Gresh handed his bag to Tobas. "Hold this for a moment, would you?"

Tobas accepted it warily. "It won't explode, away from its true owner, or anything?"

"No, of course not!" Dina said. "I made that bag properly!"

Tobas turned, startled. "*You* made it?"

Gresh was trying to judge the best way to mount the carpet, whether to climb up the dangling luggage or simply vault onto the carpet. He decided on the vault; he grabbed two of the ropes and jumped.

"Yes, *I* made it! Did you think *Gresh* did it? He's no wizard..."

The carpet felt rather like an oversized feather bed, Gresh discovered as he landed. He rolled forward awkwardly as his eldest sister shouted angrily at Tobas. "Dina," he said, as he tried to untangle himself from the cords and hoist himself into a sitting position. "Could you please not argue with my other customers?" He put out a hand to right himself and found he was leaning on Alorria's knee. He quickly snatched his hand away and murmured, "My apologies, lady."

"Be careful, Gresh!" Twilfa called.

Gresh finally managed to right himself, and smiled. He called back, "Why? If I get myself killed you inherit the business!"

"I'd rather not just yet, thank you," Twilfa retorted.

"Be careful, Gresh," Dina said, with a significant glance at Tobas.

"I will, Dina."

"Good luck, brother," Akka said. "We'll dance for you every sixnight."

"Thank you."

"Take care," Tira said.

"Good fortune and a swift return!" Chira called. She waved, and as she did Tobas did something with the fingers of his right hand, and the carpet began to rise, rotating very slowly.

Then all five women on the ground were waving, and Gresh was clinging to a rope with one hand and waving back with the other, ignoring Tobas's attempt to hand him his bag. He turned his head to keep watching his sisters and saw that Alorria was holding up one of Alris's chubby little hands and waving that, as well.

Then the rotation was complete, the carpet pointing east. It began to rise again, and to move forward, gaining speed as it went. In a moment Gresh could no longer see any of his sisters. He turned around to face forward and finally accepted the bag Tobas had been trying to hand him. "Thank you," he said.

"You're welcome," Tobas replied. He glanced back past Gresh's shoulder. "And people say *I'm* mad, to have *two* wives! I heard the one on the end call you brother, and the young one's your assistant, but that still leaves three."

"They aren't my wives," Gresh protested, as he watched the buildings flash by on either side. The carpet was still rising, so they were now even with third-floor windows or the rooftops and gutters of the lower structures.

"They're still three women."

Gresh hesitated, then admitted, "They're *all* my sisters." He looked forward, past Tobas, and saw the towers of Eastgate approaching with frightening speed.

"What, all four of them?"

"All *five* of them. My assistant Twilfa is the baby of the family." They were passing over the broad hexagon of New Eastgate Market; the merchants and shoppers were looking up in surprise as the carpet's shadow swept over them. The wind of their passage whipped at

Gresh's hair, and just as Alorria had warned, an insect of some sort bounced off his cheek.

"The wizard, too?" Tobas asked.

"Dina's the oldest." They were past the market and soaring along far enough above East Road that it no longer mattered whether they actually stayed above the street—they would clear most of the rooftops in any case. Gresh had to shout to be heard over the rush of wind. He realized they were passing over the intersection with Wizard Street, and he pointed to the north. "Her shop's over there."

When he turned his gaze forward again, Gresh saw that the towers ahead were...well, they were straight ahead, and the carpet was rushing directly at them.

Then they zoomed over Old Eastgate Market, and *between* the two towers of the gates, clearing the city wall by four or five feet, and they were outside Ethshar of the Rocks and flying east at a phenomenal speed, on their way to Ethshar of the Sands.

CHAPTER NINE

"My home village of Telven is somewhere over that way, on the coast," Tobas shouted over his shoulder, waving his right arm vaguely.

Gresh glanced to the south, then frowned. "Isn't that still the Pirate Towns?" he asked.

"That's right," Tobas said. "The Free Lands of the Coasts, they call themselves. I grew up there. My father was a pirate, Dabran the Pirate, captain of *Retribution*. A demonologist out of Ethshar of the Spices sent the whole ship to the bottom, with all hands, when I was fifteen."

Gresh nodded but did not reply. He was unsure whether Tobas was serious or not, and besides, conversation was difficult over the constant roar of the wind as the carpet sped through the air.

They were about four hours out of Ethshar of the Rocks, and Gresh had discovered that while riding the carpet didn't seem particularly dangerous, Alorria had been right that it wasn't exactly fun. There *were* frequently bugs splattering against their chests and faces, at least at lower altitudes; the luggage piled around Tobas was speckled with their remains. Birds hadn't been a problem, but the unrelenting wind of their passage was tiring and annoying and made it impossible to talk comfortably. Gresh also now understood why Alorria wore a coronet and why Karanissa had gone to the trouble to braid her waist-length locks. His own hair was long enough to whip about uncomfortably, flicking across his eyes at inopportune moments. He was sure he looked positively dreadful, with his hair awry and dead gnats smeared everywhere.

The worst part of flying was that it was *boring*. A day earlier Gresh would not have believed that soaring through the air at fantastic speeds on a magic carpet could become tedious so quickly, but it had. They had passed over a hundred miles of farms and fields and forests. After the first hour or so they all looked very much the same.

If he had been able to talk freely with his companions it might not have been bad, but the wind prevented that—the wind, and his uncertainty as to how much he could believe of what Tobas and Alorria told him. Alorria had said that Tobas slew a dragon to win her hand and that he had served for a time as the court wizard to her father, Derneth II, king of Dwomor. However, Tobas had already been married to Karanissa at the time and had been spending most of his time in another world, so it had been complicated. Tobas claimed to have inherited Derithon the Mage's book of spells, rather than compiling his own, which was undoubtedly a violation of custom and probably of Wizards' Guild rules but which explained why his training was so uneven. Tobas had served only a partial apprenticeship under a senile and dying master, but the old book allowed him to teach himself much more.

Now Tobas claimed to be a pirate captain's son. How would a pirate's son have wound up apprenticed to a wizard at all? Gresh was beginning to think he wouldn't have believed any of this if Kaligir hadn't shown up with those other wizards to provide him with magic. Pirates and princesses, dragons and castles and centuries-old witches and all, sounded like far too much adventure to have jammed into Tobas's one short lifetime. Good honest magic Gresh understood, and spells gone wrong, so the flying carpet and the spriggan mirror were easy to accept, but the rest of it...

But four-hundred-year-old Karanissa was there behind him on the carpet, and Tira had said she spoke the truth. Alorria, princess of Dwomor, was there, as well, and no one back in the city had expressed any reservations about her claimed heritage. Kaligir had believed enough of Tobas's story to agree to pay Gresh's fee, and to provide him with all those lovely vials and jars, safely tucked away in Gresh's bag.

Gresh hoped he had chosen those prepared spells wisely. He had equipped himself with powders that were good for a dozen castings each of Lirrim's Rectification, Javan's Restorative, Javan's Geas, the Spell of Reversal, and as the result of a fit of originality, the Spell of the Revealed Power, as well as seven doses apiece of potions that would provide Varrin's Protective Bubble or the Spell of Retarded Time. The five magical powders had all turned out different colors, which several wizards had assured him was normal. They were all carefully tucked away in clearly labeled glass jars in a well-padded wooden box, along with labeled vials of the two crystal-clear potions.

Those spells were all the help Kaligir's little committee would provide, so Gresh hoped that his heavy emphasis on counter-spells would prove appropriate. He had decided against any levitations; the flying carpet should serve well enough. He had also considered and dismissed a variety of communication spells, illusions, invisibilities, and other simple magic on the assumption that even Tobas ought to be able to provide those. Having those other spells as potions might have been faster, but he hadn't had that many wizards available to produce them and had preferred to use his limited resources for the most difficult or important spells. His options had not been unlimited; he had had to choose preparations that six wizards could produce in less than three days. It had taken some argument even to get a second potion, since that had required one wizard to perform the spell for Tracel's Adaptable Potion twice in quick succession.

With his sisters' help, he had equipped himself with a few of his usual devices, as well as Kaligir's contributions; the Spell of the Spinning Coin would keep Twilfa informed of his general state of health, the amulet strapped to his left wrist held a rune that would protect him from most hostile magic, he had a bloodstone tucked away that could be used for the Spell of Sustenance if food ran short, and Dina and Chira had provided half a dozen other talismans of various sorts. He felt reasonably well prepared.

The one thing he regretted was that he hadn't managed to include any decent divinations in his supplies—but since the Guild had already tried every known divination in previous attempts to locate the mirror, he had reluctantly chosen to skip those, even though they might have been useful in less direct applications.

Right now he thought a divination to tell him whether Tobas was embellishing his personal history might have been welcome, but he didn't have one available.

"Is that where we gave that man a boat?" Alorria called, pointing.

"Yes," Tobas called back.

Gresh decided not to even ask about that. He did peer off to the south, though, and glimpsed the ocean in the distance, glinting in the afternoon sun.

They must be past the peninsula that held the Pirate Towns. Tobas's alleged home must have been near the eastern boundary. That meant it was only another fifteen leagues or so to Ethshar of the Sands, perhaps even less.

Gresh had been to both the other Ethshars before, in the course of his business, but by ship, rather than flying carpet. Carpet was definitely faster, but all in all, he thought he preferred to take a few days to go by ship.

And the journey to Ethshar of the Spices, and then across the Gulf of the East to the Small Kingdoms, was almost twice as far.

While they were in Ethshar of the Sands, Gresh decided, he would unpack enough to get out a book to read. He had brought a few histories, written by various court scholars in the Small Kingdoms, in hopes that by balancing out the various patriotic lies he could glean some useful information about the region's past. He had on occasion traveled the Great Highway across the northern end of the Small Kingdoms to Shan on the Desert, and he had taken ship up the river to Ekeroa, but he had never before actually set foot in Dwomor or any of its immediate neighbors. The existing maps and reports invariably reflected their makers' biases as much as any physical reality.

He had originally thought he would be reading his books in bed by candlelight, but now he thought otherwise. It had not occurred to him when he was packing that riding a carpet would be a good time to read, but now he could not think of a better use of his travel time.

At least the sun was behind them now; for the start of the flight it had been in their eyes.

Behind him Alris started crying again—all in all she was a well-behaved baby, but four hours of wind would be wearing on anyone, and of course every baby cried sometimes. Gresh glanced over his shoulder.

"Give her to me!" Alorria said, turning. Karanissa had been holding the baby, giving Alorria's arms a rest, but quickly handed her back to her mother. Gresh suspected that she was perfectly happy to unload the squalling little nuisance.

Alorria bounced the child for a moment, cuddling her, then said unnecessarily, "She's hungry!"

Gresh had figured that much out from Alris's gestures and expression, and he knew very little about infants—he had handled his youngest sisters and a few of his nieces and nephews on occasion, but never taken a great interest in them. He politely turned his gaze forward again as Alorria unbuttoned her tunic to take care of the situation.

"What do you plan to do when we reach Dwomor?" Tobas asked him, shouting over the wind.

"Find the mirror," Gresh said.

"Yes, of course, but how?"

"That's my business."

"Well, yes, but..."

"Tobas," Gresh interrupted, "I'll find it. Leave the details to me."

Had they been safely on the ground he might have been less abrupt, but the truth was Gresh didn't *know* exactly how he was going to find the mirror. He would improvise, as he usually did. Telling a customer that would be bad business, though.

He glanced over to the right; the ocean was plainly visible now, and the coastline was sandy beaches. It couldn't be terribly much farther to Ethshar of the Sands. He peered forward, into the distance, hoping to glimpse the Great Lighthouse or the towers of Grandgate, but as yet he could see no sign of them.

He shifted in his seat, adjusting his legs to keep them from getting stiff; the carpet soared smoothly onward, undisturbed by his movement. A small boat or spring-mounted wagon would have rocked, but whatever magic kept the carpet in the air was not bothered by such things.

He wondered why carpets were the traditional way to use Varrin's Lesser Propulsion. It would make more sense to use boats or wagons, which already had seats and sides, and would be harder to fall off. Why not build things specifically *designed* to fly through the air, with solid sides, and perhaps a transparent panel of some sort at the front to block the wind and keep the bugs off the luggage? Admittedly, you wouldn't be able to roll those up and store them in a closet, but was that really so important? Even just enchanting a sofa instead of a carpet would be more comfortable, and that could be used on the ground readily enough; it wouldn't need any special storage.

But no, wizards always used carpets. It was traditional. It was what people expected, so it was what wizards did. Wizards were very fond of tradition.

Of course, one reason for that, he had to admit, was that the traditional ways of doing things were known to be relatively safe. Carpets *worked*; they didn't explode or run away or eat people or argue with their owners. There was a lot to be said for that. It might just be that when Varrin invented the spell, hundreds of years ago, he had first cast it on a carpet, and everyone had used it on carpets ever since simply because that was known to work.

Not that terribly many people used it at all; it wasn't a simple spell. Gresh doubted there were more than a hundred functioning flying carpets in the World, and some of them, like the one he was on, were decades old.

Still, you'd think some eager young wizard would experiment a little. Maybe he would ask Dina about it when he got home, suggest that there might be good money in making flying craft a little more sensible than carpets. He had a momentary vision of swarms of skyboats zipping around above the city, or flying caravans replacing merchants' ships...

The Wizards' Guild might not like that. The merchants and shipwrights and ship chandlers might have reservations about it, too. And homeowners might be a bit wary about large heavy objects overhead, for that matter. He vaguely recalled hearing something about how Varrin's *Greater* Propulsion, which in bygone days had lifted entire castles and ships and kept them aloft indefinitely, was considered too dangerous to be used by anyone without special Guild approval exactly because sometimes the things *did* fall, with very unfortunate effects on whatever happened to be underneath.

So any plans for marketing sky-craft would require caution—but still, it shouldn't be impossible to sell a few.

Behind him he heard Alorria cooing, and then a surprisingly loud belch from Alris. He resisted the temptation to look back, and instead stared ahead over Tobas's shoulder, looking for Ethshar of the Sands.

There, at last, he could see the conical turret atop the Great Lighthouse, and then the crenellations around the lamp itself, peeping above the horizon, still tiny in the distance. A little to the left was an almost imperceptible flicker of red that was the banner atop Grandgate. Gresh smiled.

The remainder of the journey went much more quickly. Having their eventual goal in sight helped immensely, even when Tobas insisted on taking a small detour to the north instead of flying over the central portion of the city. He refused to explain why beyond saying, "It's not safe to fly over the palace anymore."

Gresh didn't think a direct path would have brought them within half a mile of the palace dome in any case, but it didn't really matter. He watched with pleasure as they skimmed along twenty feet above the top of the city wall, looping aside to miss the guard tower at Northgate, then swinging out over the Wall Street Field and the rooftops of Northangle, before finally descending onto a street he did not recognize, a few blocks from Grandgate's north tower.

The carpet came to a stop a yard in the air, just as it had in front of Gresh's own shop in Ethshar of the Rocks, and Tobas half-jumped, half-tumbled off the front, then turned and stood, looking uncertainly at Gresh.

Gresh realized quickly that the young wizard was in the habit of helping his wives down from the carpet, but was unsure whether Gresh would welcome assistance. Gresh solved his problem by rising to his feet and offering Alorria a hand, then ushering her to her husband's waiting arms. He held the baby long enough for Alorria to reach the ground, then passed her back to her mother.

Karanissa followed, and before Tobas could release his hold on her, Gresh leapt to the street unaided—where he stumbled and almost fell. His long ride had stiffened him more than he had realized.

He caught himself, though, and looked around with interest.

The houses and shops in this city were much as he remembered them from his three previous visits—unlike the taller and often narrow homes of Ethshar of the Rocks, nearly all the buildings here stood just two stories in height, or at most three, often with a steeply sloping tile roof coming down almost to the ground-floor ceilings. The limited height, despite the shortage of land within the city walls, was due to the inability of the sandy soil to support tall buildings without serious engineering; the steep roofs were to shed the heavy spring rains, as there was little snow this far south.

Wood and plaster were common here, and stone was scarce—neither wood nor stone was easy to obtain locally, given the terrain, but wood was cheaper to ship in.

To the east the immense towers of Grandgate loomed high above the rooftops, shining in the afternoon sun. The street itself was packed sand, lighter in color than the dark and stony streets of his home city, and lined with houses built wall-to-wall; perhaps one in three had a shop window and signboard to indicate that it held a business as well as a home. Gresh spotted a baker, a vintner, a tinker—the typical things one would see in any residential neighborhood.

They had stopped in front of perhaps the smallest house on the entire street, a tiny, half-timbered structure with no sign or shop-window.

"I rather expected you to live on Wizard Street," Gresh remarked. "It's nearby, isn't it?"

"A block and a half west," Tobas said. "But I couldn't really afford it. There weren't any vacant properties, so I would have had to buy out an existing business, and those aren't cheap. Besides, I don't really want to run a shop—I was never trained for it."

"He's a court wizard, not a shopkeeper!" Alorria said, as she collected various baby supplies from the carpet.

"Except we don't live in Dwomor anymore," Karanissa said. "The Guild ruined the Transporting Tapestry that came out near there. Which makes it difficult to be their court wizard."

"Well, if you didn't insist on keeping close to the castle..." Alorria began.

"It's my home!"

"And Dwomor is mine!"

"And neither of them...oh, never mind," Tobas said. "Be quiet, both of you, and let's get the carpet and luggage inside." He drew his belt-knife and cut one of the cords holding the baggage and handed Karanissa a valise.

"You need to open the door," Alorria said, as she waited with the baby on her hip.

Gresh got his own bag and one other, then followed and waited as Tobas peeled a black wax seal off the door-latch—a seal very much like the one he used on his own vault back in Ethshar of the Rocks. That answered any questions Gresh might have had about how Tobas kept his home secure in his absence; the rune on the wax would explode and cripple or kill anyone else who tried to open the door. Presumably there were similar seals, or other magical protections, on the other doors and windows.

The door swung open, and Tobas held it back while both his wives entered the house; Gresh was close on their heels, and a moment later Tobas followed, with two more bags. He, Gresh, and Karanissa proceeded to fetch the rest of the luggage in, while Alorria tended to the baby's needs and got her dressed in a fresh gown, until finally Tobas was able to roll up the carpet and bring that, too, inside, closing the door behind him.

The party and their belongings were now clustered into a small, sparsely furnished parlor; a dusty hearth filled one end of the room, while a few chairs and a small table were scattered about elsewhere. The plank floor was bare; Gresh suspected that the flying carpet currently tucked under Tobas's arm usually lay on it. Two doors led to back rooms, and a steep staircase led to the upper story—Gresh could see the slanting ceilings that reduced that second floor to a fraction of the size of the already-tiny ground floor.

The place was considerably smaller than his own home and business; it did not look like the house of a wealthy wizard, to say the least. Even Akka and her useless husband had a more luxurious home, though it was in worse repair, and Gresh suspected they had gone far into debt to pay for it.

"Welcome to my home," Tobas said. "You can sleep here tonight, if you like, or take a room at an inn on Grand Street, whichever you prefer. I think Karanissa can provide us with some supper, or there are the inns for that, too, as you please."

Gresh looked around at the utter lack of a couch or any likely place a guest room might be hidden away and concluded that staying here would probably mean sharing a bedroom with three adults and a baby. The adults weren't a real problem unless one of them snored, but the baby...

"You'll have the place to yourself, if you stay here," Karanissa said, as if reading his thoughts. As a witch, she very well *might* be reading them. "We'll be sleeping elsewhere."

"Where?" he asked, startled.

"I'll show you," the witch said. "Come on."

Gresh followed as Karanissa led him up the stairs, which emerged, as he had expected, into a single good-sized attic room. Sunlight spilled in through windows on either end, and for most of its length the two long sides slanted in. Three beds and several bureaus and nightstands were arranged between the stairs and the rear wall. The front area, above the parlor, was almost empty, with just a pair of velvet-upholstered chairs at one side.

The portion above the parlor hearth was somewhat different from the rest; here the side wall was vertical, closing in the chimney, rather than sloping, and a pair of heavy gray drapes hung on it. As Gresh reached the top of the stair, Karanissa strode to these drapes and pulled a cord, drawing them back to reveal a tapestry.

"There," she said, pointing. "That's where we'll be."

CHAPTER TEN

Gresh stared at the tapestry in astonishment. He had never seen anything quite like it; the realism, the attention to detail, was amazing. Neither stitch nor brushstroke was visible at first glance—if not for the slight billowing as it moved in the breeze created by the opening drapes, and the neatly sewn silk binding at the hem, he might almost have taken it for a painting, or even a window.

The image on the tapestry was also unlike anything he had seen before. It was a single scene, a picture of a castle—but it was a castle out of a nightmare, a weird structure of black and gray stone standing on a rocky crag, framed against a red-and-purple sky, approachable only by a narrow rope bridge across an abyss. Faces and figures of demons were carved into the structure at every opportunity; the battlements were lined with gargoyles, and monstrous stone visages peered around corners, from niches, and from the top of every window. A dozen towers and turrets jutted up at odd angles, some topped with rings of black iron spikes, others with conical roofs carved to resemble folded batwings. Even the one visible door was surrounded by a portico carved to resemble a great fanged mouth.

"Don't touch it," Karanissa warned.

"I won't," Gresh assured her, as he realized what he was looking at. "That's a Transporting Tapestry, isn't it? One that goes out of the World completely?"

"Yes. And it leads to our real home, more or less."

"The castle? You live in *that*?"

"Most of the time—at least, since Tabaea's death. Before that we spent most of our time in Dwomor Keep, where Tobas was the court wizard for Alorria's father."

Gresh remembered the story Karanissa had told him when she first came to his shop—that she had spent four hundred years trapped in a wizard's castle, and Tobas had rescued her. *That* was presumably the castle he had saved her from. And she had later said that the Guild had ruined the tapestry that had been the only exit from the castle.

"How do you get out of it?" he asked. "I mean, if you're planning to sleep there tonight..."

"We have another Transporting Tapestry in the castle," Karanissa explained. "When the Guild ruined our old one while they were trying to stop Tabaea, they replaced it with another that comes out near here. That's why we bought this house and relocated to Ethshar of the Sands—it's where we can get out of the castle." She sighed. "At first I thought I'd like that—I never really felt very welcome in Dwomor Keep, after all, since it's Alorria's home."

Gresh started to ask a question about the relationship between the two women, then caught himself. He did not want to pry into their personal lives uninvited. "It hasn't worked out?" he asked instead.

"We don't really *belong* here," she said. "Tobas is from a little village in the Pirate Towns, Alorria is a princess from the Small Kingdoms, I'm from the distant past—none of us really *fits* in a city like this. When I was here as a girl it wasn't a city at all; it was General Torran's staging area for the western campaign—they were still dredging the ship channel and drawing up plans for the city wall, and Grandgate was one tower called Grand Castle because there wasn't a wall yet to put a gate *in*. There wasn't any palace or city, just tents and wooden sheds."

Gresh glanced out the window at the street and tried to imagine that; he failed.

"Now there are more people in the Grandgate district alone than in all of Dwomor, so Alorria is as lost here as I am," Karanissa continued. "The Guild brought Tobas here because he'd been doing research in countercharms, trying to fix some of the things that had gone wrong back in the mountains, so someone thought he was some sort of expert and called him in to help against Tabaea's magic Black Dagger, and he didn't argue—he thought it would be fun, and that he might know something useful. He *does* have the formulas for plenty of spells, including some that had been lost for centuries, but all the same, he's not really *that* good a wizard—more than good enough for Dwomor, or anywhere in the Small Kingdoms or outlying lands, but here in the three Ethshars he's only up to journeyman level, really. He doesn't know anyone except Telurinon and a few other wizards..." She let her voice trail off, and sighed.

"He seems to have the Guild's respect," Gresh said.

"Yes, he does, and he earned it," she agreed. "He was the one who finally stopped Telurinon's stupid miscalculation from destroying the whole city. They showed their respect by ordering him to find and stop the spriggan mirror—typical of them. If you do one impossible thing your reward is to be asked to do another."

"But he made the mirror in the first place?"

"Which is why we didn't argue when they told him to stop it. He does feel responsible. So he's been running around the city talking to magicians and conferring with Lady Sarai and so on, until finally someone suggested we talk to you, and here we are. But when this is all done, we're going to have to hold a family conference and decide just where and how we want to live." She looked at the tapestry. "We may have to give that castle up—or at least, spend much less time there."

Gresh glanced at the image and shuddered; he could not think of giving up that horror as a real loss.

Then Karanissa shook herself. "That's all for later, though. Tonight we'll be sleeping in the castle, so that Tobas can collect some things he needs from the workshop there, and you can have this place to yourself. We'll be back out first thing in the morning and off to Dwomor."

Gresh started to nod, then stopped. "Wait a minute," he said. "Is that the workshop where the mirror was first enchanted?"

Karanissa looked at him. "Yes. Why?"

"There might be evidence..."

"No." Karanissa held up a hand. "We checked, very carefully."

"You're absolutely certain the mirror isn't still in there somewhere?"

"Oh, yes. We saw it go through the tapestry to the mountains. Besides, we haven't seen any new spriggans in the castle in years—there are still about half a dozen that never left, but we only see those same ones, never any others."

"Hmm." He was not absolutely convinced. He had seen people lose things in plain sight often enough to have no faith at all in the human ability to see what was actually in front of them, and after his twenty questions a few days before he had far more respect for how deceptive spriggans could be. But Karanissa was a witch and probably knew what she was talking about.

Even a spriggan would know a castle was not a cave—or could there be a cave somewhere in that stone mass the castle sat upon?

"Are there any ruins in that...that place?" he asked.

"What place?" Karanissa glanced from him to the tapestry. "The void? No, there are the two stones—the little one at this end of the bridge, and the big one holding the castle. That's all. There's nothing a ruin could stand on, nowhere it could be."

Then at any rate, the mirror had not been in there when that particular spriggan emerged from it, and it wasn't likely it had gotten there since.

"Thank you." Gresh gave the tapestry a final look, then turned away and headed back down the stairs to rejoin the others. Karanissa came close behind.

Alorria looked up from playing with Alris's fingers. "Showing off the castle, Kara?"

"Just explaining where we're going tonight, Ali."

Alorria made a face. "The baby and I may just wait out here," she said. "I hate crossing that bridge."

Tobas exchanged glances with Karanissa, and Gresh thought that the two of them were not entirely displeased by Alorria's words. "I thought you didn't want to be alone," Tobas said.

"I won't be—I'll have Gresh to protect me."

That prompted an awkward silence that was finally broken by Alorria saying, "I assume we can trust him well enough. He doesn't want to antagonize the Guild, after all. He won't let anything happen to us."

"Of course I won't," Gresh said.

"And I can manage the baby by myself for one night, Tobas."

"Of course you can," Tobas agreed.

"It's not as if we're in any danger of being eaten by a dragon or attacked by Vondish assassins here in the city."

"You aren't in any danger from them back in Dwomor, either," Karanissa said.

"Well, you never know," Alorria said.

It was plain from Karanissa's expression that she thought you *did* know, but she didn't say anything further on the subject.

"You can always change your mind, Ali," Tobas said. "We'll leave the door unlocked."

"I'll be fine here with Gresh."

"All right, then. Let us see about finding some supper, shall we? Kara? I'd rather not deal with a crowded inn, if we have any food here."

"We have wine and cheese in the kitchen and half a salted ham, but there's no bread."

"I saw a baker just across the street," Gresh offered. "I could buy a loaf."

"And bill the Guild for it, I suppose," Tobas said.

"Of course!"

"I'll see what I can do, then," Karanissa said, heading for one of the two doors at the back.

Half an hour later the four adults sat down around the little table in the kitchen, where Karanissa had set out a simple but satisfactory meal. Gresh had purchased a few sweet cakes, as well as a loaf of good bread; Karanissa had boiled generous slices of ham; and Tobas had found the butter, cheese, and wine. During supper's preparation the conversation had been casual and fragmented, but now Gresh turned to Tobas and said, "Tell me how you came to enchant the mirror in the first place, in as much detail as you can. You never know what information might turn out to be useful, and I'd like to have the story *now*, just to be sure that I don't need to look around inside that haunted castle of yours before we go on to Dwomor."

Tobas tore off a chunk of bread and buttered it thoughtfully, then began his story. "I grew up in the village of Telven, near the eastern end of what you'd call the Pirate Towns, and I didn't bother with an apprenticeship when I was twelve because I was my father's only acknowledged child, and I expected to inherit his ship, *Retribution*. When a demonologist sank it and left me orphaned at the age of fifteen, I had to change my plans, but of course by then I was too old for any respectable apprenticeship."

He took a bite of bread, then continued. "Fortunately for me, there was an old wizard named

Roggit who lived in the marshes just outside of Telven. I used to think he was too senile to see that I was obviously too old, but now I'm fairly sure he took pity on me. Either way, he took me on despite my age. Unfortunately, he wasn't much of a wizard, and he was even less of a teacher, and his health was terrible. I lived with him for a year and a half, or maybe it was closer to two years, and while he did get through all the essential initiations in that time, by the time he died peacefully in his sleep he had only taught me one useful spell—Thrindle's Combustion."

"Unfortunate," Gresh said. "But presumably you inherited his business, as his apprentice at the time of his death—did his family contest that because of your age?"

"He didn't *have* any family, any more than I did," Tobas said. "But as for his business, such as it was, he had put an explosive seal on his book of spells, and I didn't know any better than to open it. The whole house burned to the ground, book and all, and I was left with nothing." He took another bite. "So I set out to seek my fortune—not that I had much choice, after losing two separate inheritances."

He went on to describe making his way to Ethshar of the Spices, where he had discovered no one had any use for a wizard who hadn't finished his apprenticeship and knew just one spell. In desperation he had signed up to slay a dragon in the Small Kingdoms, more or less accidentally, as much to stay out of the hands of slavers as because he thought it was a good idea. He told Gresh about his first visit to Dwomor, sparing no details, to Alorria's dismay. She tried to defend her homeland, but Tobas refused to retract his negative comments. He explained about the terms on which the dragon-hunters had been hired and how they had been divided up into teams.

By the time he finished his account of wandering in the hills northeast of Dwomor Keep, finding Derithon's fallen flying castle, salvaging the Transporting Tapestry, and stumbling through it to join Karanissa in her captivity, supper had been eaten, a bottle of wine had been drunk, the daylight had faded away, and the candles had been lit.

Tobas explained how he had begun working his way through Derithon's massive collection of spells, trying as many of the easy ones as he could to gain enough practice that he might have a chance of surviving attempts to use higher-order wizardry to get Karanissa and himself out of the castle and back to the World. He described every detail he could remember of his failed attempt at Lugwiler's Haunting Phantasm.

Gresh listened closely and had him review several portions before permitting him to continue the story.

The spriggans had stolen the mirror just as he carried it through the revitalized Transporting Tapestry, back out in the World, and he had not seen it since. He had married Karanissa, and then more or less accidentally slain the dragon after all. In order to collect the promised reward he had been required to marry Alorria, as well—which, he was quick to note, was no hardship. He had never *planned* on having two wives, but he certainly didn't *mind*.

He glanced from one woman to the other at that point, but no one else commented.

There were parts of the story that did not seem to

make sense, Gresh thought—the account of removing the Transporting Tapestry from the fallen flying castle, for example. How and why had Tobas removed it without going through it?

And for that matter, why had the castle fallen in the first place? Presumably Varrin's Greater Propulsion had failed, but why? A wizard of Derithon's obvious accomplishments wouldn't have been careless with something so important as the enchantment holding up his home. Was there some inherent flaw in the spell?

And there was the way Tobas had simply let the spriggans run off with the mirror without pursuing them, and how it had been years before spriggans started turning up in any numbers.

There was something Tobas wasn't telling him. Gresh suspected that it was related to the wizard's plans for disposing of the mirror.

"We should go," Karanissa said, as Gresh asked a few more leading questions, hoping for some further hint. "We have a long day ahead of us tomorrow, and you need to pack up things from your workshop."

"A long day, but not a strenuous one," Gresh pointed out. "You'll just be sitting on a carpet all day."

"That's tiring enough for *me*," Karanissa said.

"But you haven't said a word yet about how you helped Lady Sarai defeat Empress Tabaea," Gresh protested.

"That has nothing to do with the mirror or the spriggans," Tobas said. "And it *is* getting late." He rose.

Gresh glanced at Alorria, hoping that she would insist her husband brag about his part in defeating the mad magician-thief who had somehow temporarily overthrown the overlord of Ethshar of the Sands, but she was dozing off, and the baby in her arms was sound asleep. He sighed.

He would be traveling with these people for days, perhaps months. There would be time to worm the truth out of them.

"I suppose it is," he conceded.

Karanissa rose and leaned over to touch Alorria's shoulder. "Ali," she said. "Time for bed."

"Uh?" Alorria started; Alris stirred but did not wake. Then Alorria nodded. "Oh, yes. Bed. Yes." She rose, as well.

"I'll clean up," Gresh said, but as he looked around he realized that while he and Tobas had been talking, Karanissa had already cleared away most of the dishes and other evidence of their supper.

"We'll see you in the morning," Karanissa said.

"Come on upstairs, Ali," Tobas said. "We'll get you and the baby tucked in." The family headed for the stairs.

Gresh watched them go, while brushing the last crumbs from the table and taking the empty wineglasses to the scullery tub.

Something in the mountains of the Small Kingdoms had downed a flying castle, centuries ago. Something in that same area had apparently interfered with two Transporting Tapestries. Tobas had apparently thought the spriggans would not be a problem there, even though he *had* considered them a hazard in his other-worldly castle. Something associated with Tobas had defeated an incredibly powerful rogue magician, allegedly gutting the interior of the overlord's palace in the process and leaving nothing of Tabaea but her left foot, when the Guild's ordinary efforts had failed. And if Karanissa was to be believed, the Guild's failed attempts had endangered the entire city. And a Transporting Tapestry had been permanently ruined somewhere in the process.

On top of all that, Tobas was reputed to be an expert on countercharms—though Karanissa denied that he deserved that reputation.

Gresh frowned.

He could think of one explanation for everything, though it might not be the right one. It fit with a few other rumors that he had heard about Tabaea's demise, as well. All of this could be explained if Tobas had stumbled upon an all-powerful countercharm of some sort, presumably one created long ago, perhaps as a weapon in the Great War. Such a charm might have brought down the flying castle, rendered the tapestries and the mirror temporarily inert, eventually destroyed one tapestry permanently, and erased both Tabaea's magic and whatever magic the Guild had used unsuccessfully against her.

That would also account for the secrecy; the Wizards' Guild would not want it widely known that so powerful a defense against their magic existed. It would account for why they were sending Tobas to deal with the mirror, rather than a more experienced wizard. He probably had the charm, if it existed, in his possession and was not willing, or perhaps not *able,* to loan it to anyone else.

Gresh had not noticed any jewels or amulets or other obvious magical devices on Tobas anywhere; he carried a knife and pouch on his belt, like most people, but wore no rings or brooches or pendants, so far as Gresh could see.

The charm might not be anything so obvious, of course; it could be a rune burned into Tobas's flesh, or a pebble in his pocket, or...well, almost anything. If it existed at all.

Presumably, Tobas intended to use it on the mirror and make sure the effect was permanent this time. That would be a very satisfactory conclusion to the whole business.

A general-purpose countercharm like that would be very useful and very valuable—but Gresh told himself not to get greedy or do anything stupid; it wasn't his, it almost certainly wasn't for sale, and he was getting paid quite enough for the mirror as it was. Trying to obtain or duplicate this theoretical charm would almost certainly annoy the Wizards' Guild, and that could ruin his business and get him killed.

No, he would leave it alone. He would find the mirror, collect his reward, and go on to live a very, very long and prosperous life without it.

It really *was* late now, and he was tired. Perhaps in the morning he would think of another explanation for the holes in Tobas's story and realize that such a countercharm probably didn't exist at all. He picked up one candle, blew out the other two, and headed for the stair.

He did make one small detour, though, peering through the other door off the little front parlor. As he had expected, it led to a wizard's workshop, but a very small and poorly stocked one; the crude workbench was dusty and bare, the four shelves above it half-empty. If the parlor, kitchen, and attic had not already made it obvious, this workshop demonstrated that the little house really wasn't much of a home to Tobas and his family—at least, not yet.

He closed the door carefully and climbed the steps.

Alorria and Alris were sound asleep on the nearest bed; Tobas and Karanissa were nowhere to be seen, but the tapestry shimmered eerily in the candlelight. Cautiously, Gresh set down the candle and closed the drapes over it. He did not want to wake up in the middle of the night and see that ghastly image, or worse, stumble into it while looking for a chamber pot or something.

He then made his way to the farthest bed, so as to have as much space as possible between Alorria and himself. There he pulled off his boots, peeled off his socks, blew out the candle, and then fell back onto the down-filled mattress.

His last waking thought was the realization that he could tell by the faint scent lingering on the pillow that this was Karanissa's bed.

CHAPTER ELEVEN

Gresh awoke in the darkness to the sudden unpleasant and loud discovery that Alris was not yet sleeping through the night. He pushed himself up on one elbow and squinted into the gloom, determined that Alorria was moving, and then, as the baby quieted, he lay back down and tried to get back to sleep.

He dozed off quickly enough that time, but the second time the baby's crying woke him, the first faint light of dawn was seeping in the windows, and he had to debate briefly with himself whether to rise or not. He decided not, but getting back to sleep was more difficult, and it scarcely seemed as if he had managed it when he heard Tobas calling his name.

"Mrph," he said. Then he rolled over and realized that the windows were bright with full daylight. He raised his head and called, "I'll be right there!"

Five minutes later he ambled downstairs to find the parlor empty—the carpet and baggage had all been carried out to the street and reassembled, with two new bags added. Tobas was securing the last few knots as Gresh peered out the door. Both women were standing nearby, looking over the arrangements.

"You missed breakfast," Tobas told him, looking up from his labors. "But we saved you bread and cheese to eat on the way."

"Try not to get crumbs everywhere," Alorria added, as Karanissa smiled apologetically.

"We thought it would be best to let you sleep," the witch explained. "We didn't know how late you had stayed up."

"Not very late," Gresh said, with a meaningful glance at the baby Alorria was holding to her shoulder. "But I didn't sleep very well, so I appreciate it."

Alris let out a belch, and white goo dribbled onto a rag Alorria had draped on her shoulder. The baby goggled at Gresh. Gresh smiled back.

Babies were cute, he thought, but he was very glad he didn't usually live with one. They were noisy and smelly and needed constant attention, mostly in the form of cleaning up things he preferred not to deal with.

"Forty leagues this morning," Tobas said, straightening up. "Stop in Ethshar of the Spices for luncheon, and then across the Gulf of the East this afternoon, and another forty leagues or so takes us to Dwomor Keep. We'll stay there tonight, and then head out to look for the mirror as soon as you're ready—perhaps even tomorrow?"

"I hope so," Gresh said.

"You have your bag?"

Gresh did indeed, and displayed it.

"Good! Then climb aboard, Ali, and Kara, and we'll get airborne."

Gresh noticed there was no mention of possibly leaving anyone behind, either in Ethshar of the Sands or the castle in the tapestry. He supposed it had been discussed before he awoke and didn't bother to inquire into the matter. Instead he watched as the women boarded the carpet, then climbed on in his turn, squeezing into his allotted space.

The route out of Ethshar of the Sands took them between Grandgate's main towers, leading Gresh to suspect that Tobas simply *liked* flying between pairs of towers. They passed well over the half-dozen smaller towers between the big ones, however, and over all three layers of walls and gates, missing several opportunities to show off the rug's maneuverability.

Once outside the city the main road headed east by northeast, while their own route was almost due east, so they gradually diverged, the coastal highway angling off to the left while they flew over beaches and sand dunes, with the shining Southern Sea on their right. They had been flying less than half an hour, and Gresh had only just brushed off the last breakfast crumbs, when the beaches, too, curved away to the north, and they found themselves flying over open ocean.

Gresh found that slightly worrisome at first; if the spell failed and the carpet fell, they might all drown. He quickly realized, though, that he was being ridiculous. They were high enough up that the fall would almost certainly kill them in any case. Besides, he had known the route included a leg across the Gulf of the East; the Southern Sea wasn't any worse.

By the time they were an hour and a half from Grandgate they were out of sight of land; the faint line on the northern horizon had finally vanished in the distance. It didn't reappear for some time, and when it did,

Gresh had noticed something else that distracted him.

"Why is the water a different color ahead?" he asked, pointing. The ocean behind them was a dark gray-blue; ahead it lightened to a slightly greenish shade.

"Shoals," Tobas said. "There's shallow water from here to the western edge of the peninsula, and it looks different because you can sort of see the bottom."

"It's good fishing grounds," Karanissa called from behind.

Indeed, Gresh could see boats ahead, a dozen or more spaced out across the water. Earlier he had thought he might have glimpsed sails off to the south, but they were not flying over the shipping lanes, so none had been close enough to identify with any certainty; here, though, the boats were working close in, and there could be no mistaking them. He shifted over closer to the edge of the carpet for a better look.

"Don't fall off!" Alorria called.

"I won't," Gresh assured her, but he stopped creeping sideways and sat where he was, leaning over a leather case as he watched the fishing boats. They were casting and hauling in nets; the nets fell into the water dark and empty, but came up full of gleaming silver fish, twinkling in the sun.

"This whole stretch of coast is lined with fishing villages," Tobas remarked. "And each one has a magician or two who knows a preserving spell of some sort—usually wizards with Enral's Preservation, but sometimes witches or even theurgists. Half those fish will wind up in the markets in Ethshar of the Spices, three or four days old, but looking and smelling fresh-caught."

"Enral..." Gresh knew that name.

"Yes, the same one who discovered the eternal youth spell you've been promised," Tobas said. "Preventing decay was his specialty, it seems."

That seemed to tarnish the glamour of it, somehow, to learn that his eternal youth spell was related to the magic that kept fish fresh on their way to market—but he was being silly, Gresh told himself. What did it matter how the spell had been developed, so long as it worked?

They flew over the pale waters of the shoals for almost an hour before finally reaching the coast, where they did, indeed, pass directly over a busy fishing village, where long wooden piers stretched out across the mud and sand to reach water deep enough for the boats. Inland was initially a tangle of salt marshes, sand dunes, and scrubland. There was no ground here worth farming, no path firm and stable enough to be called a road.

That changed gradually; the ground rose, smoothed out, and dried out. Scattered farmhouses appeared, and the paths winding between them grew broader. The farms remained small, though—these were not the big grain farms of the plain, but herb farms, growing the plants that herbalists and wizards and witches used in their magic, as well as the spices that gave Ethshar of the Spices its name and distinctive odor.

People were working in the fields and walking on the roads; most glanced up when they saw the carpet whizzing overhead. Tobas waved to them occasionally; the others, further back on the rug, were not really in a position to do so.

The herb farms and spice plantations began to give way to orchards and vegetable farms, and then Gresh glimpsed sunlight on water, red tile roofs, and brightly colored sails in the distance.

"Do you have any friends or favorite places in Ethshar of the Spices?" Tobas asked over his shoulder. "Somewhere we might stop for lunch?"

"I know a few people here, but only as people I do business with," Gresh shouted back. "I wouldn't call them *friends*, exactly. I wouldn't stop in without letting them know I was coming."

"That's more than *we* know," Alorria said, looking up from the baby at her breast. "We always just stop at an inn."

"The Dragon's Tail, near Westgate, is pleasant enough," Gresh remarked. "That's where I generally go."

"We usually stay at the Clumsy Juggler," Alorria said.

"I like the name," Tobas added.

"I hear it's a good sound inn, but perhaps a little overpriced," Gresh replied. Then he remembered that he always got discount rates at the Dragon's Tail because of his occupation—the proprietor had made a specialty of hosting wizards' suppliers because that drew in wizards, who could be ruthlessly overcharged. Dragging Tobas and his wives there might not be a kindness; the Guild might be paying his expenses, but he had no idea what the family finances were like otherwise. "But on the other hand, we might try somewhere new." There were half a dozen inns lining the eastern side of Westgate Market, so they would hardly need to explore any unfamiliar part of the city. Besides the Dragon's Tail and the Clumsy Juggler there were the Blue Lantern, the Gatehouse Inn, the Market House, and the Pink Rose, or a score of others in the few blocks around the corner on High Street.

They could avoid the city entirely. "What about the Inn at the Bridge?" Gresh asked, pointing north.

"That's an hour out of our way!" Tobas said.

"Oh." Gresh had no experience judging speeds and distances from the carpet and had to take the wizard's word for it.

It seemed reasonable, actually. Valder's inn was a day's travel from Ethshar of the Spices on foot. And they were descending now, swooping down toward the city wall.

The towers of Westgate seemed puny, insignificant things after the overblown fortifications of Grandgate back at Ethshar of the Sands. Tobas did not even bother guiding the rug between them, but swooped around the north side of the gate before descending into the market square.

Westgate Market was crowded, unsurprisingly—it was the middle of a lovely day in the month of Greengrowth, and after the tedium of winter and the spring rains most people were eager to be out in the sun. There was no room to land the carpet initially, and Tobas brought it to a halt about ten feet up, the dangling luggage hanging a foot or so above the tallest heads.

Naturally, several people stared, pointed, and laughed. The people directly below it moved aside, to get a better view, and Tobas let it sink slowly downward.

"Well, there they are," he said, waving a hand at the inns. "Pick one."

Gresh looked back at the women, but Alorria was

busy with the baby, and Karanissa turned up a palm.

They probably *all* cheated wizards, Gresh told himself. "The Dragon's Tail, then," he said, pointing to the one second from the corner of High Street, with its crude sign of a green zigzag on a background so stylized that Gresh would never have known it was meant to represent sand and sea if the inn's owner hadn't told him.

The carpet glided toward the inn's door, descending as it went; the watching townsfolk scattered before it. Tobas curved the route around a stall stacked with jars of honey and maneuvered in close beneath the sign.

There he dismounted and beckoned for Gresh to do the same, as Alorria gathered up the assorted bags and cloths she needed to tend the baby. Karanissa waited patiently at the rear.

"What about your luggage?" Gresh asked, bringing his own one bag. "Will you be casting spells to protect it?"

"Don't worry about it," Tobas said, as Gresh dropped to the earth.

"Listen, I know only a madman would try to rob a wizard, but this city *has* its share of madmen—I've met a few."

"We'll take care of it." He accepted Alris, then stepped aside while Alorria slid off the carpet. She turned back for her collection of baby gear.

Gresh noticed that Karanissa hadn't moved. "Are you leaving her on guard?" he asked.

"Not exactly," Tobas said.

"I'm ready," Alorria said, as she stepped back with her arms full.

"Good." With that, Tobas gestured, and the carpet began to rise. It stopped at a height of perhaps a dozen feet, well out of reach.

Gresh watched, puzzled. Yes, leaving it in mid-air would keep it safe from ordinary thieves, but what was Karanissa doing on it?

Then as he watched, she stood up and casually walked off the carpet—but instead of falling she spread her arms and drifted gracefully to earth.

Witchcraft, of course; Gresh had forgotten that some witches could levitate, since most could not, and even those who could were so limited in what they could do that they rarely bothered. Getting off the ground was apparently very, very difficult—but slowing a fall was relatively easy.

"It won't rise without anyone on it," Tobas explained, as he caught Karanissa and lowered her the last foot or two. "It hovers just fine, but it won't *go* anywhere unless someone's on it."

Gresh nodded.

"Come on, let's eat," Alorria said, heading into the inn. The others followed.

There were no empty tables, but half the inn's staff recognized Gresh, and so a space was cleared for his party by asking a couple and two unaccompanied diners to move, rearranging the available seating. Alorria's obvious annoyance at how the servers deferred to Gresh was mollified when one barmaid went into ecstasies of cooing over Alris, and they ate a fine meal with minimal displays of ill temper. Gresh pointed out the skin of an actual dragon's tail pinned to one wall, but none of the others were particularly impressed.

An hour later they emerged to find four boys throwing rocks and other small objects, trying to land them on the hovering carpet. When Tobas cleared his throat, the four took one look at him, then turned and ran.

No one pursued them, though Alorria looked as if she wanted to. Instead Tobas picked Karanissa up by the waist and tossed her upward, as lightly as if she were a mere toy rather than a grown woman—witchcraft again, obviously.

She caught the edge of the carpet and pulled herself up. A moment later a shower of pebbles, sticks, half-eaten candies, and bits of string tumbled down. Gresh grinned at the sight; Alorria frowned furiously. Apparently those boys had been at it for some time and had been fairly successful at their game.

"Is anything damaged or missing?" Tobas called up, gesturing as he did so.

"No."

And with that, the carpet began descending. When it was low enough, Tobas lifted Alorria and Alris into place, and then the men clambered aboard. When everyone was settled in their accustomed places Tobas waved a hand, and they soared up and out of the market.

Their route now took them east across the city, from the crowded streets of Westgate to the elegant shops of the New Merchants' Quarter, then over the rooftops of the mansions of New City. Gresh watched the overlord's palace slip past on the left and tried to make sense of the tangled streets of the Old City, but they were no more comprehensible from up here than they were on the ground.

Then they sailed over Allston and Hempfield and Eastgate and out over the city wall into the sandy expanse of the eastern peninsula. No one farmed here, but a few homes were scattered about, and along the beaches to the left Gresh could see children digging for clams.

The coastline curved away to the north, and the wasteland below grew more deserted, until an hour after they had left the city the coastline reappeared ahead of them. They had reached the Gulf of the East and headed out over open water.

Before long the land was lost behind them, and only water was in sight in all directions. Save for an occasional glimpse of a merchant ship's sails in the distance, the monotony of the crossing was unbroken until the coast of the Small Kingdoms appeared, rushing toward them.

This land was no flat oversized sandbar like the peninsula, but was rolling green hills behind a line of crumbling brown cliffs. Tobas adjusted the carpet's altitude, taking it higher to be sure of clearing all obstructions; it had descended a little while crossing the Gulf.

As they soared over the white line of surf breaking against the steep slopes below, Tobas pointed out the forbidding stone fortress that clung to a rocky stretch of shoreline just to the south. "Imryllirion," he said.

Farms and meadows flashed past, and mere moments later they passed almost directly over another castle, a few miles inland. Tobas announced, "Chatna."

He continued to tell Gresh, unasked, the name of each kingdom they passed over—Hsinorium, Strivura, a corner of Nebhala, Torthon, Danua, Ekeroa, and

Vectamon, though they did not pass within sight of towns or castles in Hsinorium or Nebhala or Ekeroa, and Castle Torthon was merely a speck on the horizon. The trees hid most of Vectamon Castle, as well.

They crossed the river in Ekeroa, and the land began to rise, farms giving way to woodland. The sun was low in the sky behind them, mountains were looming ahead of them, and the carpet was rising, when Tobas said, "Lumeth of the Forest claims that land to the right." He gestured at what looked to Gresh like just another stretch of unbroken forest on rolling hills. "But Vectamon and Dwomor don't recognize the claim."

"It's Dwomoritic land," Alorria said.

"The Vectamons don't think so, any more than the Lumethans do," Tobas retorted.

Alorria replied in a language Gresh had never heard.

"She's fluent in Vectamonic," Tobas said. "But she mostly uses it to insult them."

Gresh decided that was a hint that he should not ask for a translation.

Then they were descending to treetop level and heading directly for a sprawling castle that appeared to be in a state of mild disrepair, and Gresh forgot the conversation and focused his attention on Dwomor Keep.

CHAPTER TWELVE

Dwomor Keep had obviously not been built quickly or recently. It occupied the center of a small plateau, surrounded by a double handful of thatched cottages that presumably constituted the capital city, but the castle itself was quite large—easily as large as the Fortress back in Ethshar of the Rocks, at least if measured by any surface dimension. The interior volume of the solidly compact Fortress might well exceed the space enclosed within the keep's sprawling tangle of wings, towers, and turrets, though.

Every wing or tower of Dwomor Keep seemed to have been constructed in a different architectural style. Some walls were smooth, unadorned stone, while others were rough, or decorated with elaborate carvings. Windows ranged from narrow arrow-slits to grand mullioned or tracery affairs with hundreds of leaded panes, and were made variously of clear glass, stained glass, and wooden shutters over unglazed openings.

There were two unifying features, however—every exterior wall was constructed of the same gray-brown stone, and every roof, whether tile, thatch, or slate, seemed to need repair.

As they approached close enough to see into the courtyards, Gresh discovered the inner structures to be even more varied than the outside, as these walls did not need to be good defensible stone. Some were brick, or wood, or half-timbered plaster, or even wattle-and-daub, while others were that same gray-brown stone.

The courtyards themselves all appeared to be mud, though, untroubled by any pavement or boardwalk.

The carpet swept down toward this castle, and Tobas and both his wives began to shout and wave. People appeared in windows and on battlements, waving in response. The carpet flew a long loop around the castle so its passengers could greet everyone, but finally came soaring in toward a railed wooden platform that looked newer than any of the other structures. It stood atop an old slate roof, next to a tower where a new door appeared to have been cut into an old wall, and had no recognizable purpose for any ordinary castle.

It was, however, just the right size for landing this particular flying carpet.

The rug settled gently onto the platform, stopping when the luggage first lightly touched the wooden surface. Tobas then climbed off the front of the carpet, then stepped around the side to help his wives and child off. Gresh was left to his own devices and clambered awkwardly off, pulling his bag up and heaving it over one shoulder.

A moment later Tobas had the door open, and the entire party stepped into the tower, into a good-sized sitting room. Faded tapestries hung on several walls, and a few rather worn settees were arranged below them. Assorted tables, chairs, and cushions were scattered about, and three rugs covered portions of the plank floor, leaving a good-sized bare area in the center—one that Gresh recognized as a convenient place for the flying carpet. A spiral stair rose in one corner, and in the far wall two carved wooden doors stood solidly shut.

Gresh had barely had time to look around at the chamber within when a knock sounded on one of the carved doors. "Come in!" Tobas called.

The door swung inward, and a thin old man in an elaborately embroidered tunic leaned in. "Lord Tobas?" he asked.

"Yes. All of us, and a guest."

"His Majesty the king wishes to invite you all to dine with him tonight."

"Convey my best wishes to His Majesty, and we would be delighted."

"Is there anything we can do for you in the meanwhile?"

"If you could give us a hand with the luggage, it would be welcome."

"Of course. I'll send footmen." Then the door closed again.

"It's good to be home!" Alorria said, smiling broadly and looking around happily, gently bouncing the baby in her arms.

"It *is* good to be back," Karanissa agreed. "Home or not."

"They seem to have kept it clean," Tobas said. "I hope no one's disturbed my workshop."

"I thought you took everything dangerous with you," Alorria said.

"I did. I still hope no one disturbed it—I want to be able to find things."

"I didn't think you left anything worth finding," Karanissa said.

"This is your home?" Gresh asked.

All three of the other adults tried to answer simultaneously, Alorria saying "Yes," Karanissa saying "No," and Tobas saying, "When we're in Dwomor." The two women exchanged looks, and Karanissa added, "It used to be, before we bought the house in Ethshar of the Sands."

"It still is," Alorria said, with happy assurance. "We just don't live here all the time."

"It will be again," Tobas said. "If we find the spriggan mirror and deal with it successfully."

That sounded interesting. "Oh?" Gresh said.

Tobas grimaced. "I'm not as smart as you, Gresh—when the Wizards' Guild ordered me to stop the spriggans, I demanded payment, and they agreed, but I didn't think of asking for eternal youth. I asked for another Transporting Tapestry, one that comes out here in Dwomor Keep, so we could come back here permanently. I *like* being my father-in-law's court wizard and don't really want to live in a big city. They agreed to make one for us—though of course it will take a year or so, and no one's even started on it yet. There aren't very many wizards who can make one, and most of them aren't willing to put in the time."

"But when it's made, you'll live here again."

"Yes." Tobas sighed. "Eternal youth for Alorria and myself would have been clever, but I just didn't think of it. I'll just have to hope I can work my way up to doing it myself eventually."

"I'm sure you'll manage it," Karanissa said.

"Plenty of wizards don't," Tobas said.

For a moment silence fell, as no one knew quite what to say, but then Alris awoke and began crying, and Alorria, cooing and rocking, carried her up the spiral staircase.

"We have the entire tower," Tobas said. "The bedrooms are the next floor up, and my workshop above that."

Gresh nodded. "Do you get many spriggans here?"

Tobas blinked foolishly at him for a moment. "What?"

"Are there many spriggans in Dwomor? Does your magic attract them to this tower?"

Tobas glanced upward. "It ought to, oughtn't it?"

"*Does* it?"

"Not that I've noticed," Tobas admitted.

"I've seen a few here and there in Dwomor," Karanissa said. "But they're no worse here than in the Hegemony of the Three Ethshars—perhaps not as bad."

"But the mirror isn't terribly far from here."

"Well, we don't *know* that..." Tobas began.

"*I* do," Gresh interrupted. He was not ready to believe the spriggan he had interrogated had fooled him as completely as that.

"All right, then," Tobas said, clearly nettled. "I don't know why there aren't more of them here; there just aren't."

Before Gresh could reply there was a knock at the door. Karanissa reached over to open it, revealing half a dozen young men in green-and-white uniforms.

There were several minutes of bustle and confusion as the footmen brought the luggage in from the landing platform and stowed it where Tobas and his wives directed them. Gresh tried to stay out of the way.

"I'm going to dress for dinner," Alorria announced from the stairs, where she was blocking a footman's way. He was balanced precariously, holding an immense leather trunk he had been carrying upstairs.

"Good," Tobas said. "So will I."

A moment later, when the luggage had all been dealt with, the six footmen brought in the carpet itself and spread it on the floor, exactly where Gresh had thought it should go. Then one of them bowed to Tobas and asked, "Will there be anything else?"

"No, thank you," Tobas said. "Very good work, all of you."

The footman bowed again, and the entire half-dozen quickly exited the suite.

"Pardon me a moment, Gresh," Tobas said. Karanissa was already climbing the spiral stair, and Tobas followed her, leaving Gresh alone in the sitting room.

He glanced around, then shrugged and sank onto one of the settees. He had no intention of trying to unpack anything here; his most appropriate change of clothing for dining with a king was well down the bottomless bag. His Majesty Derneth II would just have to put up with a guest in traveling clothes.

He looked around the room again, but saw nothing of particular interest. No spriggans were in sight.

That was curious, really. If the mirror was generating spriggans somewhere within a few leagues, and the spriggans just wandered randomly, then their population density here should be several times what it was anywhere in the Hegemony, and it plainly wasn't.

That meant that their wanderings *weren't* random. It wasn't simply an attraction to wizardry that motivated them, because if it were, then Tobas's workshop would have been overrun with them when he was working as Dwomor's court wizard.

Gresh wondered just what was really going on. Were spriggans more organized and more intelligent than they appeared? Was there some pattern to their behavior over the past few years? He felt a slight chill at the thought. What if they were not just an infestation, but an actual deliberate invasion? Was it *really* just a botched casting of Lugwiler's Haunting Phantasm that had brought them into the World?

Then Karanissa came back down the stairs in a white silk gown that made Gresh forget about spriggans and mirrors and spells, not to mention the inconvenient fact that she was married to someone else. He rose quickly and bowed to her.

"You know, after so long in your company on the carpet, I can hear your thoughts," she said, pausing at the foot of the stair. "Especially when they're as clear as they are just now."

For an instant Gresh hesitated. He did not want to offend a wizard's wife.

On the other hand, Karanissa could have easily ignored his reaction. She had chosen not to, and that gave Gresh some latitude.

"Then you know there's nothing I can do to control them," he replied with a smile.

"I know you aren't even trying. Really, do you feel no shame at all at lusting so blatantly for another man's wife?"

"None," Gresh replied. "For three reasons."

"Oh?"

"Yes. First, you call it blatant, but you're a witch—would an ordinary woman know what I am thinking? Look at my face, rather than the thoughts behind it, and I think you'll see my expression is well within the bounds of mere polite admiration."

"Ah. You're right—and you do have a dozen years of practice, don't you? And the advice of your sisters, as well."

"Indeed. Second, lust is a natural and healthy response to a sight such as the one before me now. While it is the custom to disguise it in polite company, I know that it is the disguise that is unnatural, not the desire."

"Most men are not as certain of that as you are."

He nodded an acknowledgment. "You would know that better than I."

"And your third reason?"

This was the one that had convinced him to be honest. "With all due respect, lady, you would not have put that dress on if you did not want to provoke lust. The angled neckline, the fit at the hips—that dress is *designed* to inflame men's hearts, and as a witch you surely know it and chose it for that purpose."

"Ah, one of your sisters is a seamstress, isn't she? I hadn't known that."

"Ekava, the next-to-youngest," Gresh agreed. "Still a journeyman, but she knows her profession well enough."

Karanissa glanced upward and stepped away from the stairs as Tobas appeared, hurrying down the spiral. He wore a loose black robe and a pointed velvet cap, looking every inch a wizard save for the fact that he held a sleeping baby in his arms. "Alorria will be down in a moment," he said, shifting Alris from one elbow to the other and straightening the lush crimson blanket that now wrapped her.

Until now Gresh had always seen Alris bundled in white or gray or yellow, if one didn't count the usual stains and discolorations. It appeared that tonight even she was dressed up for their dinner with the king. Gresh looked down at his own brown wool tunic and black leather breeches and decided they would do well enough—he was a traveler, after all, and could not be blamed if he looked the part. If they stayed in Dwomor for any length of time, and royal suppers were the norm, he might eventually take the time to dress up, but not tonight.

The three of them stood silently for an awkward moment; then Tobas said, "I'll see what's keeping Alorria." He handed Alris to Karanissa, then hurried back up the stairs.

Karanissa watched him go, then looked down at the baby and smiled. She glanced at Gresh.

"She'll be down soon enough, once she realizes I'm holding her child," Karanissa said. "You look fine just as you are; don't worry about it."

"*You* look...well, 'fine' isn't strong enough," Gresh replied.

"Thank you."

Gresh started to form a question, but Karanissa answered before he started to speak.

"Ali is a princess here," she said. "Alris is the king's grandchild. I prefer not to fade completely into the background. I hope this dress will work to compete with the two of them."

"I can't imagine *you* fading into the background anywhere," Gresh replied.

She smiled at him, much as she had at the baby a moment before. "Many men consider me too tall and thin and dark; they prefer their women a little fairer and more rounded, like Ali."

Gresh's immediate thought would never, ever have been spoken aloud, but Karanissa was a witch; it didn't need to be audible.

"Tobas has no fixed preference," she said softly. "He tries very hard not to favor one of us over the other. Anything beyond that is none of your business; I say this much only so that I will not be troubled by your curious thoughts any further."

"I'm sorry," Gresh said. "If I could have prevented *that* thought, I would have."

"Of course. And if I could have avoided hearing it—well, actually, I could have and should have; I was careless." She sighed. "I was trying to hurry the conversation, so...Ah! There they are!"

Gresh looked up to see Tobas leading a smiling Alorria down the stairs. Tobas was still in his robe and cap; Alorria wore a green-and-white dress elaborately embroidered in green, black, and gold. Where Karanissa's white silk was unadorned and simple, clearly designed to draw attention to its wearer rather than itself, Alorria's gown seemed intended as an exercise in ostentation, with fancywork at collar and cuffs, intricate lace ruffles across the bodice and around the hem, velvet puffs at the shoulders, and gold-edged slashes in either upper sleeve. Her hair had been brushed out and arranged so that the sides were swept back into two wings, then secured with the familiar golden coronet.

To Gresh, she looked old-fashioned and faintly ridiculous—no one would wear such a dress in present-day Ethshar—but he knew that this was the semi-formal attire of a princess in the Small Kingdoms. Whatever her garb, she was an attractive young woman, and judging by her expression very pleased with her appearance, so he tried to look appropriately admiring.

He wondered whether Karanissa was still listening to his thoughts and detecting his faint scorn for Alorria. He risked a glance at her and thought he saw a faint nod.

"Shall we go?" Alorria said, flouncing cheerfully off the bottom stair and snatching the baby from Karanissa's arms.

Gresh made no comment as he was led through a veritable maze of corridors and stairwells; he was trying to take in as much of his surroundings as possible. He was also keeping an eye out for lurking spriggans. There *ought* to be some around here. Why didn't he see any?

He accompanied the wizard's family into a good-sized dining hall where a few dozen people were milling about; places were set at the long table, but no one had been seated yet.

His party was greeted with shouts of greeting and

much shaking of hands and slapping of backs, but Gresh could not follow any of the happy conversation—it was all in an unfamiliar language he took to be Dwomoritic. Alorria was smiling and laughing, clearly in her element. Gresh thought he understood now what Tobas saw in her beyond a pretty face.

He heard his own name spoken a few times, and then suddenly he was shaking hands with a young man with silky white hair, red eyes, and unnaturally pale skin.

"A pleasure to meet you, Gresh," he said, in perfect Ethsharitic. "I am Peren the White—Lord Peren the Dragonslayer, they call me here, but that's just Small Kingdoms pomposity."

"Dragon slayer?" Gresh said, as he eyed the man's strange hair.

"I didn't slay it, of course," Peren said. "Tobas did. He blew its head off with a single spell. But I was there, trying to help, and before that I was the one who got him out of his castle when he was trapped there, so he's always shared the credit with me, and I got a share of the reward." He pulled forward a young woman who was unmistakably related to Alorria, and who wore a green dress that was also clearly akin to Alorria's. "This is my wife, Her Highness Princess Tinira of Dwomor—she and her dowry were my share."

"I am honored to meet you," the princess said with a curtsey. Her Ethsharitic was heavily accented, but intelligible.

"The honor is mine," Gresh said with a bow, thinking as he did how odd it was that princesses, nominally people of high rank, were treated as mere property, to be handed out as rewards for heroism. He knew the reasoning behind it—princesses were too good to marry mere ordinary men, but at the same time the Small Kingdoms produced a surplus that had to be dealt with somehow—but it still seemed slightly perverse.

"I know you have met my sister Alorria," Tinira said. "Have you met any of my other siblings?"

Gresh turned up an empty palm. "I have only just arrived..."

"I will fetch them! Wait here!" She turned and bustled away, leaving Gresh and Peren together.

"A lovely young woman," Gresh remarked.

"I'm a lucky man," Peren agreed, watching his wife.

"You are an *unusual* man," Gresh said. "If you will pardon my impertinence, might you be interested in selling some of your hair?"

"What?" His gaze whipped back to Gresh.

"Your hair. I believe it might be quite valuable in my business."

Peren frowned. "Aren't you...well, some sort of adventurer? How would my hair be of any value?"

"No, no," Gresh said. "I'm not an adventurer; I'm a wizards' supplier. I sell the wizards of Ethshar of the Rocks their dragon's blood and virgin's tears—and if I'm not mistaken, pure white hair such as yours is useful in certain obscure spells. I've never found a reliable source. Fortunately, demand has been so slight that I haven't *needed* a source, but it's best to be prepared."

"You're...a supplier? A merchant?"

"Yes, exactly. A merchant, like my father before me, save that he trades in more ordinary goods—exotic woods, perfumes, that sort of thing." As he said that, it occurred to Gresh to wonder whether his father had ever done any business here; he mostly traded with Tintallion and the other northern lands, but there had been a few expeditions to the Small Kingdoms...

"And you have a market for albino hair?" Peren asked.

"I believe so, yes. Not a huge quantity of it, but I could certainly use a few locks."

Peren stared at him for a moment, then said, "I have two questions, and I'm not sure which to ask first."

"If one of them is 'How much will you pay?,' I'll need to..."

"No," Peren interrupted. "That's later. The first one is, if you're just a merchant, why has Tobas brought you halfway across the World?"

"Oh—has he told you why *he's* here?"

Peren grimaced. "He has half a dozen reasons to be here, beginning with showing his daughter off to her grandparents, but I assume you mean that he's running some mysterious errand for the Wizards' Guild. He said you were helping him with it, but not the nature of it."

"Then I shan't say too much either, but I will say that I have a reputation back home as a man who can always find what his customers want, if the price is right. I have agreed to obtain a certain object for Tobas and the Guild, and I believe it to be somewhere in the mountains to the northeast of this castle. It's not adventuring; it's just a hunting expedition. Just business."

"Not a dragon?"

"No."

"Fair enough."

"And your other question?"

"Simple enough. I've dealt with wizards' suppliers

before—I was the one who sold off the blood and scales and teeth and all the rest of it when we killed the dragon seven years ago. I've sold them a few other things since then—as I'm sure you know, there are certain spells that call for ingredients that are best obtained by someone with an intimate relationship with a royal family."

"Yes, I know. Your question?"

"Why is it that in all these seven years, none of those suppliers ever asked about my hair?"

Gresh smiled and turned up a palm.

"Amateurs," he said. "You were dealing with amateurs. *I*, Lord Peren, am a professional."

CHAPTER THIRTEEN

By the time dinner was served Gresh had made the acquaintance of a significant portion of the royal family of Dwomor—King Derneth II, Queen Alris, the king's brother Prince Debrel, the king's unmarried sisters Princess Sadra and Princess Shasha, and half a dozen of the king's nine children, the others having been married off to the royal families of other kingdoms. Three grandchildren were also present, counting little Alris—known here, understandably, as Alris the Younger. One prince had a wife, recently brought from Yorbethon, and still clearly not entirely adjusted to her new surroundings.

Two of the absent daughters also reportedly had children, but those children, like their mothers, were elsewhere.

If nothing else, it was clear that there was no danger that the current dynasty would run out of heirs any time soon.

Unfortunately, only about half the royal family and a handful of retainers spoke any Ethsharitic, and not all of them were anything close to fluent, leaving Gresh unable to communicate with most of the company. He still tried to make the best impression he could, especially when he was presented to the king and queen.

He had to explain repeatedly that he was not a wizard nor an adventurer, merely a businessman.

All in all, he did not consider the evening a great social success; his unfamiliarity with the language put a damper on any attempt to strike up an intimate acquaintance with one of the local women, since he was not stupid enough to attempt to seduce a princess or anyone with a husband in evidence, and his other conversations all seemed to follow the same route while going nowhere.

The food was excellent, though—plentiful servings of well-seasoned roast beef, cabbage soup, stewed apples, and cherry compote. The wine was astonishingly good; when he remarked on it he was informed that Dwomor prided itself on its vineyards, and the only reason they weren't better known was that they didn't produce enough of a surplus for significant exports.

He did manage to conduct some business, after a fashion; he added Peren to his permanent list of suppliers and talked to several people about spriggan sightings in the area. He was surprised how few people had ever seen the little pests; a few even professed not to believe in the creatures at all.

That seemed very odd, given that the mirror was in the area. Rather than being attracted by Tobas's magic, the spriggans seemed to be deliberately *avoiding* Dwomor Keep. There was clearly something going on here that he didn't understand, and he wondered whether it was related to whatever secrets Tobas was keeping. If there really was a powerful countercharm of some sort in Tobas's possession, such as Gresh had previously theorized, perhaps the spriggans feared it.

He had no hard evidence, though, and no one he spoke to seemed to know anything about it, so at last he dropped the subject.

When the meal was over the Lord Chamberlain, who turned out to be the thin old man who had first knocked on the sitting room door, took him aside. "We have arranged accommodations for you, sir; if you would follow me, I will show you to your rooms."

At that Gresh realized just how tired he was. He had started the day in Ethshar of the Sands, spent more than half the day on the flying carpet, visited Ethshar of the Spices, arrived in Dwomor, and survived a royal supper, all of it after a rather poor night's sleep. He was happy to follow the chamberlain to a pleasant apartment on the second floor.

All his luggage was still in the bottomless bag in Tobas's sitting room, though. He mentioned as much to the chamberlain.

"I will see to it, sir."

Gresh settled into a chair, planning to just rest his feet for a moment; he was awakened by a knock at the door, where he found a footman holding his bag. He accepted it with a polite remark that the man obviously didn't understand, but the two of them exchanged bows, and then the footman went about his business, leaving Gresh alone.

Gresh considered his situation for perhaps two or three minutes. Then he made his way into the bedchamber, dropped the bag, pulled off his boots, blew out the candle, and fell into bed.

No crying infants disturbed him; no woman's lingering scent troubled his dreams. He slept well and awoke refreshed and was not surprised to see, upon looking out a window at the angle of the sun, that he had slept long. The morning was well advanced, the sun high in the east.

He was hungry, but not ravenous, and decided that he would prefer not to eat breakfast in the same clothes he had worn to bed. He began emptying his bag. He was unsure how long he would be staying in Dwomor Keep, but he thought he might as well unpack thoroughly.

He had pulled out perhaps half the contents when a knock sounded at the apartment door. He answered it and found Tobas.

"Good morning," the wizard said. "I hope I'm not disturbing you."

"Not at all; I was just unpacking a little," Gresh said.

"I see. I was wondering what your plans are for today. Will you be heading out to look for the mirror?"

"Actually, I would very much like to get a look at where the mirror first entered the World, and I was hoping you could fly me there this afternoon. I assume it won't take very long to reach the area?"

Tobas hesitated. "The carpet can't take you all the way," he said. "I can get you to the general area and point out a few things—it's perhaps an hour's flight—but it isn't a safe place to fly."

Gresh stared at him. "Why *not*?" he asked, baffled. He remembered now that Tobas had said the center of Ethshar of the Sands wasn't a safe place to fly, either. That part of the city was where the usurper Tabaea died. And this place in the wilderness was where

Derithon's flying castle had crashed. The all-purpose countercharm, if that's what it was, was presumably involved.

"I can't tell you that."

Gresh glared for a moment, then said, "Fine. Get me as close as you can. Shall we meet at midday?"

"I'll come find you," Tobas said.

"Fine."

Tobas bowed, and turned away. Gresh watched him go, then closed the door of the apartment.

Whatever the secret was Tobas was hiding—well, first off, he wasn't hiding it very well. Second—it appeared that whatever had been done in the mountains and in the overlord's palace had after-effects. That was interesting—and did it have anything to do with the spriggans' mirror?

He would probably find out that afternoon. He returned to unpacking his bag.

A few hours later he had sorted out his belongings, changed his clothes, stuffed a few carefully selected items in a small shoulder-pack, stuffed several others back in the bottomless bag, and had gotten lost wandering the castle corridors looking for a bite to eat. The servants he encountered did not include anyone who could make sense of his Ethsharitic or his gestures, but he eventually found himself directed to the Lord Chamberlain, who sent him back to his apartments with assurances that a tray would be sent up forthwith.

The tray did arrive—bread, cheese, wine, figs, and dried apricots—and he was licking the last of the sticky residue of the figs from his fingers when Tobas knocked on the door again.

After admitting the wizard, Gresh finished his glass of wine and re-corked the bottle, then grabbed his little pack. He took a moment to reassure himself that the bottomless bag was tucked out of sight; then he followed Tobas upstairs.

Ten minutes later the carpet rose from the platform outside Tobas's apartments with the two men on it—and no women or children, nor any luggage but Gresh's pack.

It seemed much roomier that way.

About forty minutes later they came swooping down over a forested valley, and Tobas said, "There it is." He pointed at an impressive cliff ahead.

Gresh followed the pointing finger and saw the ruins at the foot of the cliff, barely visible among the trees. He blinked, and said, "Fly level, please."

"We *are* flying level," Tobas replied. "It's the castle that's crooked." Then the carpet veered off, swooping up to the right.

Gresh turned his head to keep the castle in sight.

It was still some distance away, so he could not make out all the details, but he could see the tops of five towers and one gable end protruding above the treetops. As Tobas had said, the castle was crooked; the trees made that obvious, now that he was paying attention. The entire structure was tilted at a ridiculous angle; it was a wonder that any of the towers still stood.

The roofs were red tile, though streaked dark with dirt and moss; the walls were smooth stone, either off-white or a very pale yellow. Gresh was not sure which. It appeared to be a very simple structure, with no ornamentation or elaboration.

The carpet came around in a full circle, and Gresh realized they were descending into a clearing in the forest. "Are we landing?" he asked.

"Yes."

"Can't we get closer than this?"

"Not safely, no."

"Wait a minute, then," Gresh said. He unslung the pack from his shoulder and loosened the drawstring, then began rummaging in it.

The carpet slowed and descended further, making another loop. The trees now hid the castle completely.

Gresh pulled Chira's talisman from the pack and gestured over it, setting it to detect anything between a foot and half a foot in height, and taller than it was long. That, he thought, should limit it to spriggans. Squirrels and other such creatures should be longer than they were tall, at least when moving. He spoke the command that activated the device.

Nothing happened; the surface did not glow, and no markings appeared.

He reset it for all small creatures, as a test, and promptly located what appeared to be several mice, squirrels, chipmunks, and other animals. He switched the settings back, and it went dead again.

"What is that?" Tobas asked, staring.

Gresh looked up, startled. He had been so involved in working the talisman that he had not consciously noticed that the carpet was now on the ground, and Tobas was standing on it and looking down at him.

"Sorcery," he said.

"You're a sorcerer?"

"I know a sorcerer."

Tobas did not seem entirely satisfied by that response, but before he could say anything more, Gresh said, "Can we get any closer to the castle?"

"On foot, certainly—we can walk right up to it. But it's not safe to fly the carpet any closer."

Gresh considered that for a moment, staring into the forest toward the castle, then shook his head. "Get us airborne again and move us around to the..." He glanced up at the sun, then at the disk in his hand. "...the east," he said.

"Why?"

"Because the mirror isn't in this area."

Tobas started to ask another question, then stopped. He sat down and waved a hand, and the carpet rose. "You know, it's only an hour's walk to the castle from here," he said. "We could visit it, if you want."

"Why would I want to?" Gresh said. "Do you think the mirror might be in there?"

"No," Tobas said. "In fact, I'm sure it isn't."

"Because the same thing that makes it unsafe to fly there would make the mirror...well, it would do something to the mirror?"

"Yes," Tobas admitted reluctantly. "It wouldn't work there. That was why I let the spriggans take it in the first place—I never thought they'd get it out of the...out of...away from the castle."

"You have some kind of powerful countercharm there?"

"What? No, I...Not exactly."

"But there's something there that interferes with certain spells. And you used the same thing against Tabaea in the overlord's palace in Ethshar of the Sands."

"Not just...Well, after a fashion."

"Do you know which spells it stops? How certain are you it affects the mirror?"

"It prevents *all* wizardry," Tobas said. "*All* of it. It doesn't cancel out anything, or counter it, or reverse it—it's just that no magical effects happen there."

"So it didn't break the enchantment on the mirror, when it was in the castle?"

"No. It just...*suspended* it, I suppose. And the Transporting Tapestry, and everything else. The carpet can't fly there—it's just a carpet. For that matter, I suppose Karanissa ages any time she's in there—but the instant the mirror was somewhere normal, spriggans must have started popping out again. And the tapestry still works, the carpet flies, and Karanissa doesn't age, as long as they're somewhere normal. If I use the Spell of the Spinning Coin and then I go in there, the coin still spins—but I can't spin one when I'm there, even if I immediately leave for someplace else. You do understand that this is a Guild secret and to reveal it may carry a death sentence?"

"*You're* revealing it to *me*."

"We're on Guild business, and you'd already figured part of it out, and I can't see any way to *not* tell you if you're going to look for the mirror around here. I don't think Kaligir would appreciate it if you wasted all his powders and potions by trying to use them in there."

Gresh grimaced. "That's a good point. Or even just wasting time searching the area, if you're really sure the mirror can't be in there."

"I'm sure, believe me. No wizardry has worked there in four hundred years. There's an entire town up on the cliff that had to be abandoned as a result."

"Four hundred years?"

"I shouldn't have said that."

"So that castle—that was Derithon's? And Varrin's Greater Propulsion shut down when it came too close to whatever it is, and the tapestry stopped working, and that was how Karanissa was trapped in there?"

Tobas sighed. "Yes."

"Does witchcraft still work there? Or sorcery?"

"Witchcraft definitely does; I can't be entirely certain about sorcery, as I haven't tested it, but I believe it does."

"Karanissa might be useful to have along, then."

"If we were going to the castle, maybe, but you just said we didn't need to."

"True. A good point." Gresh stroked his beard thoughtfully, then glanced down at the talisman he still held. "Take us around...what do you call it? Is there a whole area here where wizardry doesn't work?"

Reluctantly, Tobas admitted, "Yes."

"What shape is it? Is it a line, or...?"

"Spherical. We mapped it out years ago; it's a sphere close to two miles in diameter, centered on top of the cliff. That must be where he stood..." He stopped.

"What? Who?"

"Never mind. It's a sphere, centered on top of the cliff."

Gresh nodded thoughtfully. "Two miles. And in Ethshar of the Sands...?"

"None of your business. Much smaller."

"Of course. And your plan for disposing of the mirror, the one you wouldn't tell me—is to take it into that sphere and smash it?"

"Yes," Tobas admitted. "And now that you've learned my secret, where did you want to go?"

"Oh, yes. Around to the east, along the edge of the...the sphere." He looked down at the talisman. "Low and slow, please."

He did not expect to find the mirror in the woods, of course; unless the spriggan had completely fooled him it was in a cave, not a forest, and in a mountain, not a valley. He did, however, want to find a spriggan or two. He hoped to backtrack some to the mirror, and he was also trying to figure out why so few ever reached Dwomor Keep. It might turn out to be important.

Or it might not matter at all. Now that he knew a little more about it, he had to admit that Tobas's plan of taking the mirror into the no-wizardry area and smashing it sounded feasible. It was simple and direct, and he couldn't see anything obvious that might go wrong.

They still had to find the mirror, though. He knew it was in a cave, in sight of a ruin, probably facing east, and at one time it had been in that ruined castle over there, so it seemed very likely that it was somewhere in the mountains just to the west—why would the spriggans have taken it any farther than they had to?

But you never knew, with spriggans. It might be twenty leagues away in Vlagmor; that might explain why so few spriggans troubled Dwomor.

For the moment, though, he intended to start with the area around the castle. He peered intently at the sorcerous talisman in his hand as the carpet sailed gracefully along, skimming the treetops.

CHAPTER FOURTEEN

They had made roughly a quarter-circle around the fallen castle when Gresh finally spotted a spriggan. "Down!" he barked.

Tobas gestured, and the carpet dove to the ground. Gresh vaulted off, talisman in hand. He left Tobas standing on the carpet, blinking foolishly, as he dashed into the bushes. Mindless of the thorns and branches tearing at his sleeves, he reached forward to where the talisman indicated a small moving object.

"Help help help help help!" a squeaky voice shrieked. "A crazy man is grabbing for me!"

"Come out where I can see you!" Gresh shouted.

"No! You're grabbing!"

Gresh stopped and straightened up as best he could in the middle of the thicket. "No grabbing," he said. "Just talk."

"No grabbing?"

"If you stay in the bushes I'll grab you, all right," Gresh growled, as he looked at the disk in his hand. The spriggan was about four feet in front of him, in the thickest and thorniest part of the bushes. If he dove for it he would have just one chance. If he missed, he wouldn't be able to disentangle himself before the spriggan had put a hundred feet between them. "If you come out and talk, no grabbing."

"Promise?"

The spriggan wasn't moving. "I promise."

"You first."

"All right, then. I'm going to step back out of the bushes, and then you'll come out, and we'll talk. No grabbing—as long as you talk. If you try to run away, you'll make me very angry, and you wouldn't like that."

"You first."

Carefully, with much snapping and scratching, Gresh backed out of the bushes until he stood in an open patch beside the carpet. He waited, hands on his hips.

A moment later a small green face peered out at him. "No grabbing?" it squeaked.

"No grabbing," Gresh agreed.

"Talk?"

"Talk."

"What talk?"

"I want you to tell me a few things."

"Fun things?"

"Maybe."

"What things?"

"Where did you come from?"

The spriggan blinked up at him. "Mirror," it said.

That was exactly what Gresh wanted to hear. "Where is that mirror?" he asked.

The spriggan hesitated, looking around the clearing; then it stuck an arm out and pointed to the northwest. "That way."

"How far?"

Spriggans might not be human, but there was no misunderstanding the expression on the creature's face as it said, "Don't know." It obviously thought Gresh was an idiot for asking.

"How long ago did you come out of the mirror? Today? Yesterday? A sixnight ago? Longer?"

"Not today."

"Yesterday?"

"No. How much more talk?"

"We're almost done; I just want to find the mirror."

"Why?"

"I promised I would."

"Stupid promise."

"Maybe," Gresh admitted. "But I made it anyway."

"You no fun."

"I know. No fun at all. Where's the mirror?"

"That way." It pointed again. "Maybe four days ago."

"In a cave?"

The spriggan frowned. "How you know that?"

"It's still in the cave?" Gresh persisted.

"Done talking." And with that, the spriggan ducked back into the bush and vanished.

Gresh reached for his talisman, then stopped. There was no point in harassing one particular spriggan. There would be more of them out there. Instead he brushed off the worst of the twigs and bits of leaf, then turned and marched back to his waiting companion.

"I heard that," Tobas said.

"Yes, I would assume so," Gresh said, as he settled cross-legged onto the carpet. "I didn't think you were deaf."

"You were interrogating that spriggan."

"Well, yes. And you're stating the obvious."

"Is that how you plan to find the mirror? Is that how you know more or less where it is?"

"I questioned a spriggan back in Ethshar of the Rocks, yes."

"But anyone could do that!"

Gresh looked at him. "But *did* anyone do it?" he asked. "I'm the one who actually thought of it and tried it, so it doesn't really matter whether anyone else *could* have."

"But that's...You're charging the Guild Enral's Eternal Youth for *that*?"

"You and Karanissa told me the Guild would pay almost any price for the mirror. You never said anything about using esoteric methods to find it. Simple methods often work just as well."

"But...just *asking*?"

"Do you have a better idea? You tried scrying spells and oracular deities and all the other possibilities offered by modern magic, and they didn't work, as I recall. My method has at least gotten us close."

"By *asking spriggans*."

"Yes. After all, they're the ones who know where the mirror is."

"But you just... just *asking*..."

"Yes. You'd be surprised how often asking questions gets answers. Very few people—or creatures—are as obsessed with secrecy as you wizards are."

Tobas stared at him for a moment, then said, "I was right. You *are* smarter than I am. It's good common sense, and I didn't think of it—though now I feel as if I should have. With wits like that, why didn't you become a magician, or go to work for the overlord?"

"Because I didn't want to; I didn't like all the rules they have to worry about. I chose to be a merchant, like my father before me—and I'm glad I did. I'm good at it. Now, can we continue the search and still be back at Dwomor Keep before dark?"

Tobas glanced at the position of the sun, then nodded. "We have about an hour, I'd say."

"Then let's get this carpet moving."

Tobas made a gesture, and the carpet rose gently. "Where to?" he asked.

Gresh pointed northwest, the same direction the spriggan had. "That way." He grimaced. "I just wish I knew how far a spriggan wanders in four days."

"Well, it's about a three-day hike from here to Dwomor Keep for a human, if you aren't particularly rushing." The carpet started drifting forward, as well as up.

"Somehow I doubt a spriggan would get anywhere near that far."

"So do I."

Gresh looked around as the carpet reached treetop level, then protested, "I said *that* way!"

"We can't," Tobas replied. "That would take us through an edge of the dead place. The sphere."

Gresh bit back a retort; he supposed the wizard had a point. The detour would make it that much harder to follow the spriggan's direction, though.

But then, how sure was he that the spriggan had been right? It undoubtedly knew which way it had been walking when it reached that thicket, but it had probably wandered back and forth during those four days; the direction was at best an approximation. With a sigh, he picked up Chira's talisman and began searching for more spriggans.

A pair skittered by briefly, at the edges of the device's range—but then the carpet swooped around into a loop, spiraling upward to top a cliff and get over a rocky peak that intruded on their course, and Gresh lost contact with them.

They soared over the mountaintop and began descending the much gentler western slope. Suddenly the talisman sparkled and buzzed with the presence of spriggans ahead—but only briefly and unevenly.

"Slow down!" Gresh called.

Tobas gestured, and the rug slowed. "What is it?"

Gresh did not answer; instead he studied the talisman, trying to make sense of its responses. It took him a moment to remember that it did not detect spriggans as such; it detected *motion*. The creatures ahead had been moving, then stopped, but every so often one would shift position, and the talisman would flicker.

They were hiding, obviously.

Or perhaps the local squirrels sometimes sat up on their hind legs and looked around; that would probably show up in just the same manner. He sighed. "Keep going," he said. "But not too fast."

Tobas obeyed.

Gresh kept a close watch on the talisman, but looked up every so often to scan the surrounding countryside for caves. The spriggan he had questioned had said the mirror was inside a mountain, so the cave was in a mountainside, not down in the valley below. There were plenty of mountainsides in sight, but none had any obvious openings in them.

He had hoped that the cave would be the obvious place, in the cliff right next to the fallen castle, but if Tobas was right that was impossible—that was inside the dead-to-wizardry zone.

At least, unless the cave stretched back far enough into the mountain to reach beyond the sphere...

"Are you sure the dead area is a sphere?" he asked.

"Yes," Tobas said.

Gresh was slightly startled that the wizard did not hesitate or qualify his response in any way, but gave a quick flat affirmative that left no room for argument. "What if there were a tunnel going back into the cliff?" he asked. "How far would it have to go to get out of the area?"

Tobas looked off to the left, toward the cliff and the castle's towers showing above the trees, and considered the question carefully.

"About three-fourths of a mile, I'd say. A little less if it sloped steeply downward."

"Oh." A cave that long was not out of the question, but it seemed unlikely that the spriggans would have carried the mirror so deep into the earth.

On the other hand, the spriggan had not originally said it emerged in a cave. It had said it was inside a mountain. Three-quarters of a mile would definitely be well inside.

He needed to capture another spriggan for questioning; that was all there was to it.

Then he looked at the talisman and saw the golden trace of a moving spriggan ahead. "That way," he said, pointing.

Tobas obeyed.

A second spriggan's trail appeared, and a third, all three moving west to east.

That was interesting, that they were all going in the same direction. They might be heading away from the cave, looking for somewhere they could have more fun. Instead of directing Tobas toward the three of them, therefore, Gresh decided to backtrack them. "West," he said.

The carpet sailed on, just above the treetops, down one slope and up the next, as Gresh studied the talisman. He spotted more spriggans in the forest below—and all of them seemed to be moving east.

Then their numbers began to increase; the talisman sparkled with their trails, and now some were veering north or south.

But none were going west, even now.

Gresh looked up. The carpet was rising steeply. They were rounding the northern end of the cliff now, moving out of sight of the fallen castle, and the spriggans were still scattering out from somewhere to the west.

But hadn't the spriggan said the castle was in sight of the cave mouth?

No. It had said that a ruin was, but it had never really said *what* ruin. Gresh had just *assumed* it was the crooked castle.

"Are there any other ruins around here?" he asked.

Tobas glanced back at him. "There's an entire abandoned town up on that mountainside," he said, pointing up at the top of the cliff.

"It's in the dead area?"

"Oh, yes. That was where we first found out that wizardry didn't work."

"Ah."

They swept up over the top of the slope, and Gresh could see the ruined town. That, he decided, might well be the ruins the spriggan had meant—yes, it had said it saw a castle or a tower, but it had admitted it knew nothing of architecture. "That way," he said, pointing. "As close as you can get without going in the sphere."

They flew on for several more minutes while Gresh tried to locate more spriggans and determine which direction they were moving, but they had become scarce again. Finally Tobas said, "We need to head back soon."

Gresh hesitated, looking up at the sun. It was almost brushing the mountaintops ahead.

"All right," he said. "We'll come back tomorrow."

"If you like."

"I do," Gresh said. "I'm sure the mirror is around here somewhere. We just need to find it."

"That *is* the general idea," Tobas agreed. He gestured, and the carpet swooped upward and headed toward Dwomor Keep.

CHAPTER FIFTEEN

For their second day of searching Gresh insisted on an earlier start and told Tobas to start just to the west of the ruined town. He also stuck a long-handled net through his belt before departure and added a few snares to the items already in his little shoulder-pack.

They spent an hour or so exploring from the air, and Gresh was able to locate what appeared to be a point of origin from which spriggans were radiating to the north and east—but not to the south, because that would have led them through the no-wizardry area, and very few to the west, directly over the mountains. That neatly explained why so few found their way to Dwomor, which lay to the southwest.

Gresh had Tobas circle over the area, looking for a cave.

The area was a mountainside facing east, and much of it did indeed have a view of the ruined town on the western slope of the next mountain over. The fallen castle lay beyond that, at the foot of the cliff east of the town. A trail led off to the southwest, and Tobas assured him that that led, by a somewhat circuitous route, back to Dwomor, but it passed through the no-wizardry bubble, so the spriggans presumably avoided it.

The forest did not completely cover this particular mountain; several areas were bare brown rock. There were grassy and mossy patches, as well, and brush-covered areas where the slope was too steep or the soil too thin for trees. Gresh scanned these carefully, looking for a cave-mouth, but he saw none.

Chira's talisman was sparkling and sizzling with spriggans as they circled, and here they were moving in every direction, so that no exact center could be found, no spot from which they all radiated. There were dozens, perhaps hundreds of spriggans in the bushes and trees below. Gresh saw a few running across open country, as well.

It was obvious that some of them did not immediately leave the area once they had emerged from the mirror. Gresh wondered what they found to eat; some of the bushes had apparently been nibbled on, but that would hardly feed the numbers the talisman was reporting. The wizards had assured him that spriggans didn't *need* to eat, that they were incapable of starving to death, but they certainly *liked* to eat and felt hungry when they didn't. There couldn't possibly be enough food for the spriggans below unless they were eating tree bark and dry grass, or just dirt.

In fact, the number of spriggans below was rather intimidating. Somehow Gresh had assumed that as soon as they came out of the mirror they all promptly marched off looking for people to annoy, but apparently that was not exactly the case. Karanissa had said there were half a million of the little pests in the World, and Gresh had pictured them being fairly evenly spread over the entirety of it, from Vond to Tintallion, but now he was beginning to wonder whether a significant portion hadn't stayed right here. Chira's talisman was glittering as if a wizard had cast some sort of glamour on it.

For the first time it occurred to Gresh that he might not be able to simply walk into the cave and pick up the mirror. If there really were hundreds of spriggans down there, and they wanted to defend it, he might face a real challenge.

Even after a dozen circles he could not see a cave anywhere. He had to conclude that it was under the trees somewhere. He didn't want to go over the whole mountainside on foot, but it didn't seem he was going to spot it from the air.

"Land," he told Tobas.

"Anywhere in particular?" the wizard asked.

"No. Wherever is convenient."

Tobas nodded and sent the carpet downward, landing it on a relatively level patch of meadow well up the mountain. Spriggans fled squealing as its shadow swept over them, and the carpet came to rest, crushing a few square yards of delicate yellow wildflowers.

Gresh stood up and looked around. Downslope to the east the meadow ended in a rocky outcropping and a sudden drop-off, and below that was a patch of forest—mostly birch and aspen, from what Gresh could see. To the north was a stretch of broken ground and tangled brush. Westward the meadow rose gradually for perhaps fifty yards, then suddenly gave way to steep bare stone jutting upward toward the peak. To the south the meadow dropped away at the shoulder of the mountain, providing a spectacular view of forested hills rolling away into the distance.

Gresh pulled the net from his belt, holding it halfway along the handle, and looked about. He had seen dozens of spriggans as the carpet descended, but they had all apparently taken cover. "*Hai!*" he called. "Anyone here?"

"They were all over the place a moment ago," Tobas said.

"They still are," Gresh said. He had spotted several of the silly creatures, crouching down to blend in with the tall grass, weeds, and flowers. It appeared there was a reason they were green. "Anyone want to talk to me a little?" he called.

"We have fun?" someone ventured warily.

"We might," Gresh said.

"You put down net?"

"If one of you comes out to talk to me, I'll put down the net."

Several squeaky voices whispered to one another; then one spriggan stood up. "Spriggan talk," it said.

"Good!" Gresh tossed the net onto the carpet, then knelt down in the grass. "Come and talk."

The spriggan approached cautiously. "You want what?"

"I want to know where the mirror is that you came out of," Gresh said. "I know it's in a cave somewhere on this mountain, but I don't know exactly where. Can you show me?"

The spriggan considered that for a moment, then said, "That not sound like fun."

"Could you show me anyway?"

"Promise no net?"

"If you show me, I won't net you. I promise."

The creature hesitated, clearly thinking hard.

"No tell!" another spriggan called.

"Not think it good idea..."

"I'll give you candy," Gresh said, before the spriggan could complete a firm refusal. He reached back and unslung the pack from his shoulder. He had thought he might need to bribe the little pests at some point, and his pack held a pound of honey-drops.

A pound might not be enough for the occasion, though—he glanced around and realized there were *hundreds* of spriggans surrounding the carpet. They were not bothering to hide very carefully anymore. He had never seen anything remotely close to this many at once before.

"Candy?" the spriggan said brightly. Several other little green heads popped up here and there.

"First show me where the mirror is."

"Um. Not sure..."

"Well, whoever shows me gets the candy." He opened his pack, found the bag of candy, and pulled a golden honey-drop the size of his thumb out of the paper sack. He held it up for the spriggans to see. It occurred to him that a candy that a human could pop in his mouth and suck down to nothing in a couple of minutes would be the size of a whole meal to one of the little creatures.

"*Oooooh!*"

"Show! Show!"

"I show you!"

Half a dozen eager spriggans jumped out of the tall

grass, reaching for the candy he held high above their heads.

"Show me, and I'll give you the candy," he called.

"This way! This way!" shouted a dozen spriggans, even as a dozen others tried to shush them. Gresh had trouble keeping track of any individual in the tall grass, but he could plainly see the general movement toward the west, toward the exposed stone of the upper slope. He followed, holding the candy high in one hand, the open pack again slung on his shoulder and held in place with the other hand.

"Gresh?" Tobas called.

"Stay with the carpet," Gresh told him. "In fact, you might want to get airborne, in case we need to make a quick escape."

"Yes, of course," Tobas called. The grass rustled as the carpet rose a foot or so. Gresh did not look back, but kept his attention focused on the spriggans as he followed them toward the rocks.

As he walked he studied the stony slope ahead, but he still did not see a cave mouth; it must, he thought, be hidden somehow. Could someone have cast an illusion spell, perhaps? Spriggans seemed to have some magical abilities, such as their talent at opening locks, but surely *they* couldn't have done such a thing. Had some wizard done them a favor, for some reason? If not, then the spriggans had been either very lucky or very clever to have found such a well-concealed refuge. There were a few cracks and crevices in the rocks, but no cave...

Then one of the spriggans hopped up on a rock and thrust its hand into one of the cracks. "Here! Here!" it called. "Cave here!"

Several others quickly joined it, squeaking and pointing. Gresh's heart sank as he broke into a trot.

He began cursing himself for a fool as he approached the rocks. He had been thinking of the cave as one a grown man could fit in, but that was stupid. Why in the World would spriggans want one that big? They would undoubtedly feel much safer with their precious mirror tucked into a cave a human couldn't fit in—an opening an eight-inch spriggan could slip through would be just a useless crack to a six-foot man!

He strode up to the rocks and peered into the crack the spriggans were pointing to; sure enough, he could see no back to it. Instead of ending, it seemed to open out into darkness inside the stony wall. The crack ran about four feet across the slope, between two stone slabs, and when he thrust in his arm he could not feel anything but cool air.

But the opening was no more than six inches high at its widest point.

He turned and looked at the opposite slope and discovered that the trees hid most of the ruined town from here, but one moderately large stone structure happened to be plainly visible. It was not a castle or tower, but to a spriggan it might well look like one—it was round on one end, and roofless.

That was obviously what his informant had seen. Everything fit. He turned back to the horizontal slit in the rocks.

"The mirror is in there?" he asked.

The shrill chorus of "Yes, yes, yes!" was deafening.

"Candy now!" a spriggan said. The chorus began chanting, "Candy, candy, candy!"

"You promised!" shrilled one voice.

"Can you bring the mirror out, so I can see it?" Gresh asked.

The hundred voices were suddenly stilled. For a moment the only sounds were rustling leaves and the wind in the grass.

Then one shocked voice said, "Not allowed!"

"Mirror stays in cave," another added.

"Spriggans could *die*," said a third.

"Promised candy if we showed cave," someone said. "Didn't say fetch mirror."

"How do I know it's really in there?" Gresh countered.

The spriggans looked at one another; then a large brownish one said, "Wait." With surprising agility, it hopped up to the crack in the rocks and trotted into the opening—it barely had to duck at all

Gresh ducked his head, though, to peer into the cave after the spriggan. He shaded his eyes and tried to follow the creature's movement.

It was sliding down a slope; Gresh could see its brown back as it slipped into the gloom of the interior. The crack *did* open out, and the spriggan vanished into the darkness.

"Bring light!" the spriggan called.

Gresh blinked, then looked around. He pulled up a clump of dead weeds and twisted them into a makeshift torch, then called to Tobas, "Do you have a tinderbox?"

"Something better," Tobas called back, as he fumbled at his belt-pouch. "Hold that thing up."

Gresh obeyed, and a moment later Tobas did something with his dagger and a bit of orange powder, and one end of the bundle of weeds burst into vigorous flame—so vigorous, in fact, that Gresh had to move hastily to avoid being burned. He flung the flaming stalks into the cave.

Then he stooped and peered in after them and saw the brownish spriggan dragging the burning twist of weeds. The flame illuminated the cave's interior quite well.

Gresh was astonished by what he saw; once past the impossibly narrow entrance the cave was really quite good-sized. It extended at least fifteen or twenty feet back into the mountain, and much of it was high enough that a man could stand upright. It seemed to extend across the full width of the rock face, at least fifty feet from end to end—it was hard to be sure, with only the central portion lit. This whole section of slope, it appeared, was hollow. It looked as if a chunk of the mountainside had folded down upon itself, long ago—as if a cliff or ledge had collapsed and wedged itself across the top of what had been a small gully, covering it completely but not filling it in.

There were dozens of spriggans in there, shielding their eyes against the sudden glare, as the brownish one stood in the center of the cave holding his improvised torch near a small shining disk. As Gresh watched, a pair of scrawny green arms rose up out of the disk's surface, as if it were the surface of a tiny pool, and then a spriggan pulled itself up with those arms, hopping out of what could only be the infamous mirror.

"There!" the brownish one called. "See? See?"

"I see," Gresh acknowledged. "Come on up and get your candy, then."

"Me, too!" shrieked one of the others, and a wild chorus of squeals erupted.

The brownish spriggan left the torch in the cave as it scampered back up to the opening, and out into the sunlight; Gresh waited until it emerged, then handed it the large honey-drop.

The spriggan promptly stuffed the candy in its mouth and smiled stickily at Gresh.

A hundred others shrieked, and two hundred hands stretched out hungrily. Gresh quickly began distributing the candy, making sure no one got more than one piece.

The bag emptied very quickly, and he handed it to a spriggan while saying apologetically, "All gone."

"*Nooooo!*" wailed a score of high-pitched voices, as the one with the bag turned the sack inside out and began desperately licking the last bits of sweet from it. Gresh held out his empty hands and retreated away from the cave mouth.

"Tobas," he said in a conversational tone. "I think we should go now." He glanced back over his shoulder.

The carpet had risen to perhaps three feet above the ground, and Tobas was watching uneasily as spriggans jumped up and down around it, trying to leap up onto it.

"Tobas?"

The carpet drifted higher, but no closer.

"*Tobas!*"

The wizard finally looked up and noticed Gresh moving away from the cave. He wiggled his fingers, and the carpet came swooping across the meadow. Gresh turned and ran for it, leaping onto it as Tobas brought it past.

A moment later the two men were seated safely on the carpet, Tobas at the front and Gresh near the back, sailing some twenty feet above the ground. The meadow below them seemed to be covered in spriggans shrieking for candy or shouting about mirrors and promises.

"It's in there," Gresh said grimly.

"What is?" Tobas asked.

"The *mirror*, of course. It's in the cave there."

"What cave? I saw you poking at the rocks, but I didn't see a cave."

Gresh let his breath out in an exasperated sigh. "There's a cave," he said. "But the entrance is much too narrow for humans. The spriggans can climb in and out easily, but *we* can't."

"Oh. And the mirror's inside? You're sure?"

"I saw it," Gresh said. "I saw a spriggan climb out of it."

"So it's really there? It's not a fake?"

"Unless someone is casting some rather sophisticated illusions, it's really in there."

"We have to get in there, then."

"Yes, of course," Gresh agreed. "I had figured that much out myself. We need to get in there, or get the mirror out somehow. The question is, *how*? The spriggans don't want to bring it out; they seem to have some sort of agreement among themselves that it must stay in there."

"Why?"

"How should I know? One of them said that if it was brought out they could die, but I don't have any idea why."

"So we can't just bribe them to fetch it? I saw how much they liked that candy of yours."

"I don't think so—not unless we bring enough candy for the entire half-million of the little pests, and I'm not sure even that would do it."

"Then how can we get it out?"

Gresh grimaced. "You're the wizard," he said. "I was hoping *you* might have an idea."

"You're supposed to be the expert on fetching things."

"And I can find a way, don't you ever doubt it—but I hoped you might have a nice easy one."

Tobas considered that for a moment, looking down at the rocks and the seething mass of spriggans. "Ordinarily I might suggest using Riyal's Transformation to shrink down to mouse size, but somehow I don't think I want to go down there while I'm smaller than a spriggan," he said.

"We might keep that as a last resort," Gresh said.

"The Cloak of Ethereality would let me walk through the stone," Tobas said. "But it only works on the wizard casting the spell, so I'd need to go in alone, and I couldn't carry anything while ethereal, so I'd need to stay in the cave until it wore off and then hand the mirror out to someone."

"That might work."

"Then I'd need to use it *again* to get out. It takes eight hours to wear off—there's no known way to reduce the time."

"It still might work."

"I'm not thrilled by the idea," Tobas said. "Are there spriggans in the cave? Because they might not be very happy to see me in there, ethereal or not. And whoever I pass the mirror to...well, I wouldn't be able to help much if anything happened before the eight hours were up."

"Is there some way you could levitate the mirror out?"

Tobas considered that for a moment, then turned up an empty hand. "Varen's Levitation would work if I could touch the mirror, and if wizardry will work on it—if it's magic-resistant, like spriggans..."

"You need to touch it?" Gresh interrupted.

"Yes."

"That won't work, then, unless you get into the cave; it's much too far back to reach from outside."

"Oh."

That exchange reminded Gresh of something, though. "Could your wife levitate it out?"

"Who, Alorria? She's not a wizard..."

"No, your *other* wife. Karanissa. She's a witch, and she can levitate. I saw her do it in Ethshar of the Spices."

"Oh! Oh, of course. I don't know—she probably could. But I don't know if that's a good idea."

"Well, you have some time to think of a better one on the flight back to the castle."

Tobas considered that, looked down at the meadow, then asked, "What if the spriggans move the mirror again, now that they know we're looking for it? What if they hide it somewhere even worse?"

"If we're quick we can be back here by mid-afternoon. I don't think they're organized enough to move it that fast. Besides, where would they find a better hiding place than that cave?"

"You're probably right," Tobas agreed. He looked up at the sun, only just past its zenith, then down at the meadow, where there were no signs of organized activity of any kind, but merely dozens of silly little creatures running about aimlessly. "You're right. If we're quick."

"And...?"

"And we should go." He gestured, and the carpet surged forward, picking up speed. As the wind whipped Gresh's hair back, the carpet curved its path to the southwest, toward Dwomor Keep, leaving the spriggans, the meadow, the cave, and the mirror behind.

CHAPTER SIXTEEN

"You are not going anywhere with her without us," Alorria said, sitting herself down on the carpet, Alris the Younger in her arms. She was wearing a white tunic and green skirt that did not go well with the rich reds and blues of the carpet, and the baby was wrapped in white bunting and a green blanket.

"Ali, you're being silly," Tobas said, hands on his hips. "This is magician business, and we'll have Gresh with us..."

"You two are *not* going *anywhere* without us!" Alorria insisted.

"There are *three* of us, and we need Karanissa because she's a *witch*, not because she's my wife! We'll be back by nightfall..."

"Find another witch, then."

"There isn't time!"

"Then take Alris and me along!"

"It isn't *safe* for a baby!"

"It's safe enough for the three of you."

"We're not babies!"

"I'm not, either, and I can look after Alris while you two do your magic!"

"Ali, get off the carpet."

"No. Before you try to force me, remember who my father is and where *we* are."

"I am not likely to ever forget," Tobas said.

"Tobas, let her come," Gresh said. "What are the spriggans going to do? They wouldn't hurt a baby. We're wasting time arguing."

"Kara?" Tobas turned to his other wife, who was standing ready in a simple red dress, holding a bag she had hastily filled with things she thought might be useful in dealing with the spriggans and their enchanted mirror.

"*I* don't care, so long as she stays out of the way when I'm working," the witch replied.

"*Fine*, then," Tobas said. "We'll all go, and Ali and Alris can play with the spriggans while we steal their most precious possession and destroy it."

"That might actually be a useful distraction," Gresh said mildly.

"Oh, get on the carpet."

Moments later all four of the adults were seated, each holding one bag nearby—Gresh had his powders and potions and tools in his small shoulder-pack, Tobas had his grimoire and the ingredients for various spells in a leather valise, Karanissa had assorted herbs and crystals to aid her witchcraft, and Alorria had a large collection of diapers, rags, and other baby supplies, and of course Alris was in her arms. At Tobas's command the carpet rose smoothly into the air and sailed northeastward from Dwomor Keep.

"We need to do something about these bugs," Alorria said, as she sheltered her daughter from a swarm of gnats.

"Ali, it's a flying carpet," Tobas said, exasperated. "We'll be above them soon enough."

Gresh resisted the temptation to say something. He agreed with Alorria, actually, that it wouldn't be unreasonable to add some sort of protective cover, but he did not want to take sides in a marital squabble—at least, no more than he already had in advising Tobas to let Alorria accompany them. Besides, he did not want to antagonize the wizard who was supposed to be helping him, nor his nominal employer, nor the representative of the Wizards' Guild, and Tobas happened to be all three of those things.

Finally, he didn't want to suggest anything because he saw a marketing opportunity and did not want to throw it away. It should be easy to make money selling enclosed flying machines that would be safer and more comfortable than carpets, and he wanted to keep that money in his family. He would build the craft, or maybe hire Akka's husband Tresen to do it, and then have Dina cast Varrin's Lesser Propulsion on them. He didn't want to involve Tobas, as either partner or competitor.

That would all have to wait, though. First they had to get the mirror out of the cave, then smash it. They might need to take it to the no-wizardry area around the ruined village and fallen castle to break it, but that shouldn't be difficult—it was just across a narrow valley.

So he kept silent and watched the countryside flashing by below them as they swept through the mountains, covering a three-day hike in less than an hour.

Despite the delays caused by gathering Karanissa

and her supplies and by Alorria's insistence on coming, it was not much past mid-afternoon when the carpet settled back onto the grass in the mountain meadow beside the peculiar little cave where the spriggans had hidden the mirror.

Tobas had set it down in the exact spot it had rested in before; the grass was still pressed down from the previous visit. Gresh frowned slightly, as he saw no reason not to have landed right next to the cave, but decided it wasn't worth arguing about, not with the entire family along. He was afraid that Alorria and Karanissa might take offense at criticism of their husband, or find an excuse to start bickering.

Dozens of spriggans were visible from where Gresh sat, scattered around the meadow and the surrounding terrain, but most were making at least a pretense of hiding, and none made any threatening moves or showed any signs of approaching the carpet.

"It's over there," Gresh told Karanissa, pointing, as he got to his feet and slung his pack on his shoulder. "Come on, I'll show you."

"We'll wait here," Tobas said, staying seated cross-legged where he was. "To watch the carpet."

Gresh glanced at Alorria, who smiled up at him without moving. "You two go ahead," she said.

Gresh had thought that Alorria would stay with Tobas—after all, the wizard was the prize for whom the two women were competing. He was reassured to see that he was right and had not misjudged the situation. "As you please," he said, nodding his head in a faint intimation of a bow. He beckoned to Karanissa. "If you would, please?"

"Of course." She was already on her feet and followed gracefully as Gresh crossed the meadow.

The two did not hurry; they still had hours before sunset. Gresh was conserving his energy and making contingency plans, while Karanissa was enjoying the gentle breeze and the scattering of wildflowers.

The crack in the rock wall was half-hidden by shadows, and Gresh was not sure he would have found it again immediately if not for the trampled weeds in front of the opening. As it was, he had no trouble in locating it, but he quickly realized that the torch inside had long since burned out, leaving the interior dark and the mirror invisible; all that was left was a faint whiff of smoke.

"It's in there," he said. "I can make a light and throw it in..."

"That won't be necessary," Karanissa said.

"What you do?" a spriggan squeaked up at them, as Karanissa raised a hand to the opening in the stones. Gresh turned, intending to shoo the creature away, but then saw that it was not alone—a few dozen spriggans had gathered around and were looking up at the two humans worriedly.

"Nothing terrible," Gresh said. "We just wanted a look at the mirror in the cave."

"Leave mirror alone!" shrieked a spriggan, one that was an unusually bright shade of green and had noticeable fingernails.

"We won't..."

"You don't take mirror!" squeaked another.

"Listen, we don't..."

"Not touch mirror!"

Gresh looked to Karanissa for aid, but the witch was staring intently into the crevice. Gresh realized something inside was glowing and turned to see what was happening.

A faint pale glow was coming from the mirror itself; as Gresh watched, it started to rise into the air.

But then several spriggans leapt onto it, dragging it back down, and as Gresh watched dozens more piled on, until the glass disk was completely hidden beneath a pile of squirming little green-brown creatures.

The glow vanished, plunging cave, mirror, and spriggans into utter blackness, and Karanissa gasped, then slumped, catching herself against the rocks.

"Are you all right?" Gresh asked her, worried. He glanced at her, then turned his attention to the spriggans.

They had formed a half-ring around the witch and himself, about three feet away and about four spriggans deep, and more were peering down from atop the rocks above the cave opening. So far they weren't moving, but just standing, watching the two humans intently.

It occurred to Gresh that where one spriggan was harmless, a few hundred of them would not be; in fact, they might be unstoppable. If they just kept flinging themselves at a person, they could probably smother him to death, or crush him under their weight—and if Karanissa was right about their indestructibility, they wouldn't be hurt in the process.

This errand, fetching the mirror, might be far more dangerous than he had thought.

"Karanissa?" Gresh asked.

"I'm all right," she whispered. "Just tired. All those

spriggans—I kept trying, I thought I might be able to snatch it out from under them, and they must have weighed a hundred pounds at the very least..."

"I understand," Gresh said.

He knew that unlike most magicks, witchcraft drew all its energy from the user's own body. What Karanissa had done had tired her just as much as if she had reached that far into the cave with her hand and tried to lift the mirror with all those spriggans on it, not to mention the energy used in creating that faint light. That must have taken a good bit of strength, and she was a slender woman. Naturally, she would need to catch her breath after such an exertion.

He looked out over the ring of spriggans, across the meadow, at the carpet fifty yards away. Tobas and Alorria were seated on the little rug, facing each other and bent over, heads almost colliding, as they played with the baby. Gresh could see a pudgy hand waving in the air. Several spriggans were watching the baby, as well, but all from a respectful distance of several feet. They had not formed the sort of encirclement that he and Karanissa faced.

And why would they? The baby and her parents weren't doing anything, weren't trying to steal their precious mirror.

Even a baby not yet half a year old was far larger than a spriggan—but there was only one baby, and there were hundreds of spriggans.

Gresh debated calling out to Tobas, asking for help, but so far the spriggans crowding around were not doing anything aggressive or making any demands, and he did not want the wizard to over-react and start throwing spells around carelessly. He also did not want to do anything that might prompt the spriggans to attack.

Besides, he and Karanissa still hadn't retrieved the mirror, and if they didn't get it out of the cave soon, the spriggans would almost certainly carry it off and hide it somewhere else, now that they knew that Gresh and his comrades were trying to take it.

This was all very annoying, and Gresh was irritated with himself for not having prepared for this situation. When he had thought about how they would retrieve the mirror he had somehow not expected to find this great horde of spriggans guarding the confounded thing, and in retrospect he wondered *why* he hadn't considered the possibility. He supposed it was because he hadn't thought of the little nuisances as intelligent enough to do anything so organized, but he now saw that this had been foolish of him. They could talk, they could use tools, and even a family of birds can organize well enough to guard a nest. Spriggans were stupid, but they weren't *that* stupid.

Right now a hundred or so were watching him intently.

"Did you want something?" he asked the encircling spriggans.

"You go away!"

"Leave mirror alone!"

"Not touch!"

"Why?" Gresh asked. "It seems like an interesting thing. Why shouldn't I look at it?"

"Might break!"

"Spriggans *need* it!"

"Could *die!*"

"Well, if it's *that* important," Gresh asked, "why do you have it out here in a dirty old cave, where some animal might get in and break it, instead of safely locked away in a castle somewhere?"

Too many tried to reply simultaneously for Gresh to make any sense of the response to his question. He held up both hands in a calming gesture.

"Now, now," he said. "There's no need to shout." He pointed to one especially excited-looking spriggan. "Can *you* explain it to me?"

"Not *trust* castles," the spriggan said. "Full of people. Some people not *like* spriggans, might break mirror on purpose!"

"Well, what about a deserted castle?" He did not actually point at the mountain to the east, but there could be no question of what he meant.

"Not safe! Mirror not *work* there!"

"Well, how safe is it here? What if a wolf got into that cave?"

"Mirror *works* here, and spriggans guard cave, keep animals out."

"You guard it? Is that why you're all here?"

"Yes, yes! Not like it here, but guard mirror, keep safe!"

"You don't like it here?"

"No! But spriggans stay and guard."

"*Some* spriggans didn't stay, though—I've seen them all the way on the far side of the World, in Ethshar of the Rocks."

"Spriggans take turns. Enough stay here to fill cave, and others go, then come back."

Enough to fill the cave? Gresh glanced into the darkness of the opening and tried to guess how many that actually was. A great many, certainly. There was another obvious question. "They come back?" he asked.

The spriggan looked uncertain and glanced at its companions.

"Someday, maybe," one squeaked.

"That the idea," added another.

"So they're out having fun, while you're stuck here guarding the mirror. That doesn't seem very fair."

"Life not fair," a spriggan agreed.

"Must guard mirror," said another.

That didn't seem to be getting anywhere; Gresh glanced at Karanissa, who seemed to be largely but not completely recovered. He decided he needed to keep the conversation going a little longer. "Why is the mirror so very important?" he asked. "Aren't there already enough spriggans in the World?"

"Oh, yes," one spriggan said brightly.

"Maybe."

"Not know."

"Not matter."

"You go now," said a larger-than-average one.

Karanissa leaned over and whispered into his ear, "Some of them don't much like that question—I could feel their dismay when you asked it."

That was the closest Karanissa had yet come to him, and Gresh tried not to be distracted by the scent of her, or her hair brushing his shoulder. He concentrated on her words.

They didn't want to tell him why the mirror was

important—but it apparently was *not* for making more spriggans; that was interesting and unexpected. Why *did* they care about it, then? He had taken it for granted that they wanted to reproduce, like any living creature, and that the mirror was important to them for that reason, but perhaps that was not the case at all. Magical creatures did not always follow the usual rules.

But what *else* did the spriggan mirror do?

If he could get it to a properly equipped wizard's laboratory back in the Hegemony of the Three Ethshars, the Guild's experts might be able to figure that out, but out here on the mountainside, with a few feet of rock between him and the mirror, the only way to determine it seemed to be to ask the questions the spriggans didn't want asked and to coax honest answers out of the little pests.

"What does the mirror do that's so important?" he asked.

"You go now," the big spriggan said. "No more questions."

"But I..."

"You *go* now." The threat was now unmistakable, despite the creature's squeaky, high-pitched voice.

Gresh looked around and saw that the ring of spriggans had thickened and solidified as new arrivals filled in gaps and pushed their comrades closer together. Spriggans were now peering out at him from the mouth of the cave, as well. There were hundreds, perhaps thousands, of them in all.

Enough to fill the cave, that one had said—and none of them were smiling. They didn't look worried or confused anymore; they looked determined.

"If we go now..." he began, then stopped. He had been planning to ask whether they would move the mirror, but he did not want to give them any ideas that hadn't yet occurred to them. He turned to Karanissa and said, "Can you...?"

"No," she interrupted. "Don't even ask. With all of them in there?"

"We need to get into the cave somehow."

"*No! You stay out of cave!*" shrieked a spriggan.

"What we need is to chase them away," Karanissa said.

"Any ideas on that?"

She turned up an empty palm. "Nothing comes to mind."

"No witchcraft you can use?"

"Not with so many."

"No chase spriggans! *You* go!"

"Go away! Go away!"

"Maybe a spell? Wizardry, or some sorcery from your pack?"

Gresh looked at the couple on the carpet, still happily playing with the baby, oblivious to what was happening to their companions. He tried to think what spells might be useful, and how he might get Tobas's attention. Why didn't the wizard look up? Was that baby of his *that* fascinating? He was supposed to be helping Gresh get the mirror, not counting his daughter's toes for the hundredth time.

Or there were the powders and potions in his own pack; would any of those help? He reviewed what he had brought.

Lirrim's Rectification and Javan's Restorative were

counterspells and would be of no use here—though they might be very important once he had the mirror. Javan's Geas would force someone *not* to do something; if it worked on spriggans he could command at least a dozen of them not to interfere with him and Karanissa while they retrieved the mirror, but he didn't have anywhere near enough powder to affect a mob of this size.

And that assumed it worked on spriggans at all, which was by no means a certainty.

The Spell of Reversal had no obvious application, and its exact effects could sometimes be hard to predict.

The Protective Bubble would shield them from any attacks by the spriggans, but they would not be able to reach the mirror through it; magic *could* pass through it, in theory, but only in severely weakened form, so Karanissa's witchcraft, which had already proven inadequate for pulling the mirror out of the cave past the spriggans, would not be much use. The Spell of Retarded Time could slow down everything except the person drinking the potion, and he could use that to escape if things turned nasty, or to give himself time to prepare something, but he could not see just how to apply that effectively in the present situation. And Karanissa would need a dose, as well; his supply was not unlimited.

That left the Spell of the Revealed Power.

"What's the biggest thing you've ever defeated?" he asked Karanissa quietly, hoping the spriggans wouldn't overhear, despite their big pointed ears.

"What? Why?"

"What's the biggest thing you've ever defeated?" Gresh repeated. "Or mastered somehow? Have you ever killed a wolf, perhaps? You did say you'd spent time in these mountains."

She lowered her voice still further. "Yes, but I never encountered a wolf, and even if I had, I wouldn't have killed it. I'm a witch; I can soothe animals. I can hear you even if you don't talk aloud at all—just shape the words in your mind."

Gresh was not entirely sure how to do that, but he could and did reduce his voice to an inaudible murmur. "Soothing a wolf would count as defeating it; have you ever done that? Even a tame one?"

"No."

"Do you have anything in your bag that's been used to defeat a large beast, or a monster of some sort?"

"Gresh, what are you talking about?" He barely saw her lips move, but the words seemed very clear—obviously, she could use her witchcraft to speak as well as hear. "I'm a witch, not a hunter. Why would I have fought monsters?"

"I was just looking for some way to use this spell I brought."

"*What* spell?"

"The Spell of the Revealed Power," he whispered. "It's a transformation. It turns anyone or anything into an exact replica of the most powerful thing it's ever built, defeated, destroyed, mastered, or otherwise demonstrated power over. A knife that's killed a wolf becomes the wolf, a hammer that's smashed a wall—or built one—becomes a wall, and so on. Have you had any children? As I understand it, a mother of five would become five grown people—she would disappear as herself until the spell is reversed, but she would be all five of her children in the prime of their lives. But I'm not sure. She might just become the strongest of the five."

"I've never had any children," Karanissa said, and Gresh thought she sounded annoyed at the question. "Just what are you planning to *do* with this spell? Why are you asking?"

"I'm trying to think of some way to use it to chase away the spriggans so we can get that mirror out of the cave."

"Oh." She frowned. "Well, *I* don't have any triumphs or conquests that would be any use, so far as I can recall, but of course Tobas killed a dragon once. Would that help?"

Gresh blinked and looked at her. Then he turned and looked at Tobas, who had finally looked up from the baby to see what was taking so long.

"How big a dragon?" he asked silently.

CHAPTER SEVENTEEN

"All right, we'll go back to our flying carpet," Gresh announced. "Just make way, and we'll go."

The spriggans looked at one another and squeaked a few questions back and forth, but then a path gradually opened. Gresh took Karanissa's hand and led her through the gap and across the meadow, toward the carpet.

Her fingers were warm and delicate; he was careful not to squeeze them.

They were soon clear of the main mass of spriggans. Even so, others were scattered along their route, forming loose lines along either side. Gresh was aware of dozens of bulging little eyes watching him as he released the witch's hand, unslung his pack, and loosened the drawstring.

Karanissa said nothing. She did not need to ask any questions about his intentions; he was sure she was still sensing his thoughts, even if he was no longer trying to put them into words.

"What happened?" Tobas called, getting to his feet as they neared the carpet. "Did you get the mirror?"

"No," Gresh said, pulling the box of prepared powders from his pack. "The spriggans don't want it moved, and in case you haven't noticed, there are hundreds of them guarding it."

"Oh. Then what do...what are you doing?"

Gresh had slung his pack back on his shoulder and opened the box and was pulling out a jar of sparkling blue powder. "You killed a dragon once, didn't you?"

"Yes, but what does that have to do with anything? I doubt the spriggans are going to be impressed by my adventures."

Gresh pulled the cork from the jar. "*You* did it, right? All by yourself? There isn't a magic sword or anything involved?"

"Yes, I did it, with a spell, but I still don't...oh, no. What's that powder?"

"The Spell of the Revealed Power," Gresh said, spilling powder into the palm of one hand. "I think you should step away from the carpet." He managed to push the cork back in place without spilling the powder from his hand.

Tobas did more than step away; he turned and ran, eastward across the meadow toward the drop-off into the trees. Spriggans scattered from his path, squealing in fright.

With a muttered curse, Gresh closed his fist around the precious powder and called, "Come back here!" He dropped the jar back into the box, hastily closed it up, and thrust it back into his pack, all while continuing toward the fleeing wizard.

Tobas stopped and turned. "Gresh, I really don't think this is a good idea."

"Do you have a better one? A dragon can chase

away the spriggans, and then Karanissa and I can get the mirror out of the cave, and we can get this over with."

A few spriggans yelped and shrieked, as if in confirmation, and Gresh wished he had been a little more circumspect. He had just removed any doubt the spriggans might have had about his intentions.

That made it all the more urgent to get this done *quickly*. They really didn't have time for a long argument, or a careful discussion of every option. There might already be spriggans hauling that mirror out of the cave, and if they did get it away, it would probably not be so easy to find next time. The spriggans would know he wanted to take it from them and wouldn't answer his questions. They already had the idea of hiding it in a hole humans wouldn't fit in; the next one might be *completely* inaccessible. He had to act immediately.

"But just to start, I don't *want* to be a dragon," Tobas said. "Isn't there something else you can transform? One of your tools? A knife? Or what would it do to *you*? Haven't you ever defeated anything powerful?"

"I have no idea what it would do to me," Gresh admitted, ambling casually across the carpet, past Alorria and toward Tobas. He could understand why someone would be reluctant to be transformed, but he saw no other option. Really, they were fabulously lucky to have someone or something here that could be transformed into something as powerful as a dragon! They needed to take advantage of that good fortune. "That's exactly why I won't be trying it on myself. But *you* defeated a dragon! That's perfect, Tobas, and I have Javan's Restorative right here—you know that's the standard counterspell, don't you? There's nothing to worry about. If anything goes wrong, I can change you back in a few seconds!"

"That's not what worries me—well, yes, it is, but it's not *all* that worries me..."

Gresh sighed. They didn't have *time* for this. "Tobas, the Guild sent us here to get that mirror. They won't like it if they find out you refused to help me. Think what they're paying us! A Transporting Tapestry of your home in Dwomor—isn't that worth spending a little time under a harmless enchantment?"

"I suppose it is," Tobas admitted. "But it's the 'harmless' part that worries me. All those spells like the Spell of the Revealed Power where some mysterious magical mechanism we don't understand decides what the spell will actually do are tricky, untrustworthy things—you can't be sure just *what* they're going to do until you use them."

"Well, this one should change you into a dragon, shouldn't it? If we don't get a dragon, or if there's something else terribly wrong, I'll reverse the spell," Gresh said. "I've got the Restorative, and the Spell of Reversal, and Lirrim's Rectification—I can undo just about *anything*."

"I don't know, Gresh," Tobas said warily, as the merchant approached. "There's something we didn't tell you."

"'We'?" Gresh glanced back at the two women on the carpet, Karanissa standing and Alorria seated, both of them watching the two men.

"Yes—they know about it, but I guess Karanissa didn't think of it. I don't think that spell will..."

He was interrupted in mid-sentence by a faceful of powder, as Gresh got close enough to fling the glittering blue dust.

There was no point in arguing endlessly; this was their best chance, and Gresh intended to take it.

"*Esku!*" Gresh shouted the trigger word for the spell as the powder settled on Tobas's face and shoulders, and a golden glow spread swiftly over the wizard's entire body. Tobas began to enlarge rapidly, as if he were somehow being inflated, and to elongate. He bent forward at the waist.

Spriggans scattered, screaming like a flock of maddened birds.

"*Gresh, you fool!*" Tobas bellowed, in a voice that grew louder as he spoke. "The dragon *wasn't* the most powerful thing I've defeated! I stopped the Seething Death in Ethshar of the Sands!"

The glow brightened, making it impossible to see exactly what was happening to Tobas; Gresh heard fabric tear. The thing that had been the young wizard was on all fours now and still expanding; a tail had thrust out behind it, and wings were unfurling from its back. Gresh had to retreat rapidly to avoid being crushed. Whatever Tobas was becoming was very large, and from the bits Gresh could glimpse through the shimmering glow, bluish-green in color.

Alorria screamed, wordlessly at first, her voice mingling with the shrieks of the spriggans. Finally she cried, "*What did you do to my husband?!*"

Then the glow abruptly vanished, and Gresh found himself face-to-face with an angry dragon—a very *large* angry dragon, a good sixty feet from snout to tail-tip, and with a wingspan almost twice that, standing over the torn and shredded remnants of Tobas's clothes.

Gresh had seen dragons at fairly close quarters before, but never unchained, uncaged, and *this* close, and so extremely large. He stepped back.

"*Gresh!*" the monster bellowed, spewing a cloud of sparks and black smoke.

"You can talk!" Gresh said, startled, brushing a spark from his sleeve. He had expected Tobas to lose his voice.

"Of *course* I can...Oh." The dragon blinked his immense red eyes, and his voice dropped from a roar like a thunderstorm to a deep rumble. "So I can."

"*Tobas!*" Alorria shrieked, clutching the baby to her breast. Alris promptly began to cry hysterically, adding to the cacophony. Dozens of spriggans were still squealing and screaming.

"I'm fine, Ali," the dragon said, raising his head to look over Gresh at the women on the carpet.

"*Fine?* You call that *fine?*"

"Yes, Ali, I do," the dragon replied. "I've been turned into a dragon, but I'm still me. I can talk, I'm healthy and strong. I'd call that fine, given some of the alternatives." Then he looked down at Gresh again. "You, though, have *no* idea how dangerous that was! Casting a spell on an unwilling wizard—what did you think you were doing? You're very, *very* lucky that you were right, and I turned into a dragon."

"Well, what else could you have become?" Gresh asked. "What's more powerful than a dragon?"

"I told you," the dragon rumbled. "The Seething Death."

"I don't know what that is," Gresh replied. "I never heard of it. It's more powerful than a dragon?"

"It's a pool of raw chaos that expands indefinitely, destroying and absorbing everything it touches. The Guild's masters think it would destroy the entire World if left unchecked, and *counterspells don't work on it*!"

Gresh frowned, remembering what Kaligir had said about Tobas's uneven training. "You *defeated* it?"

"Yes. I did." The dragon glared at him.

Gresh started to ask just *how* Tobas had defeated it, then thought better of it. "The Spell of the Revealed Power doesn't seem to think so," he pointed out.

"I should eat you. I really should," Tobas growled. He ran an immense forked tongue over his lower lip, and Gresh took another involuntary step back.

"Tobas," Karanissa called. "You're starting to think like a dragon."

The dragon looked at his elder wife, then down at Gresh again. He folded his wings. "I think she's right," he said. "I'll need to watch that. But all the same, as I understand it, the Spell of the Revealed Power should have turned me into a bubbling mass of complete destruction instead of a dragon, and if it *had*, we might all be doomed. You were taking a huge risk, Gresh! You *really* should have heard me out and not cast the spell."

"You may be right," Gresh admitted. He was somewhat embarrassed by his actions. Earlier he had been thinking of Tobas as a dangerous fool for meddling with magic too powerful for him in circumstances where the results might be unpredictable, and here he had gone ahead and done much the same thing himself. It had never occurred to him that Tobas might have mastered anything more powerful than a dragon. He hadn't really thought there *was* anything in physical form more powerful than a dragon. Even so, he really should have considered the possibility. "My apologies," he said. "Apparently whatever guides the spell either considers the dragon more powerful than the Seething Death, or doesn't think you defeated it."

"*I* suspect," Karanissa called from behind him, "that the spell doesn't consider the Seething Death a *thing* at all, and doesn't it turn the subject into the most powerful *thing* he's mastered?"

The man and the dragon both turned to look at her.

"That's probably it," the dragon said. "Because I definitely defeated the Seething Death, and it's definitely powerful enough to destroy the World—but its very nature is that it's a contagious *lack* of thingness. Interesting." He glared down at Gresh. "And very fortunate for us all."

That made sense to Gresh; after all, it sounded as if this Seething Death was a *spell*, rather than an object or entity, and despite its name, the Spell of the Revealed Power never revealed anything intangible or evanescent, but only solid things.

But even if it had somehow turned Tobas into the Seething Death, that might not have been so very dreadful. "I still think Javan's Restorative would have worked," Gresh said.

"I don't," Tobas the dragon replied. "But it should turn me back from *this* shape readily enough."

"When we're safely done with the mirror, yes."

"Oh. Yes. But you should get on with it. I suspect that the longer I stay in this form the more dragonlike

I'll become, and that could be unfortunate if it goes too far. I can feel it already, I think. You look more and more like food every minute."

"Yes, of course, I'll hurry, but if you don't mind, I must ask—what does it *feel* like, being a dragon?"

Tobas snorted another shower of sparks. "Tell me, Gresh, have you ever asked a woman what it felt like to be female?"

In fact he had, more or less, and the answers had never been any use. He saw what Tobas meant about the impossibility of conveying such an experience. Still, he could not resist pointing out, "She had never *not* been female; you haven't always been a dragon."

"That's true, but about all I can tell you is that I feel big and strong and impatient. I believe I can fly if I try, and breathe flame, but I can't begin to explain how I would do it."

Gresh grimaced. "Big—yes, indeed! I've never seen a dragon so large! I wasn't expecting it, even after what Karanissa told me. I'd thought she was exaggerating."

Tobas snorted a little smoke. "Never saw one so large? How many wild dragons have you seen, then?"

"Wild ones? Well, I..." Gresh hesitated, on the verge of giving away one of his trade secrets, then just said, "None, really."

"Well, no one lets them get this large in captivity, of course." The dragon looked down at himself, then turned his head to look over his wings and tail. He cocked his head to one side, trying to judge his own dimensions against the trees and flowers. "This does look about the size of the one I killed."

"It could talk?"

"What? No, it couldn't. It hadn't had anyone around to teach it, I suppose, but I've always heard that big dragons can learn to talk."

"Who taught *you*, then?"

"Oh, don't be stupid," Tobas roared. "My father did, of course. I may have the shape of the dragon I slew, but I'm still Tobas of Telven. Now, can we get the mirror?"

"Right, right," Gresh said, taking a final look up at the dragon before turning his attention back to the cave. "If you can chase away the spriggans, Karanissa and I ought to be able to get the mirror out." He started walking and called back over his shoulder, "Don't touch the carpet, you might tear it."

"Good point," the dragon said, detouring around the carpet and Alorria and Alris as he followed Gresh. Karanissa, too, marched after Gresh, back toward the cave.

The spriggans had gradually quieted during Gresh's conversation with the dragon, many of them fleeing the area, but now that the dragon was moving they began to squeal and babble.

"Tobas!" Alorria called, as the dragon circled around the carpet. "Are you really in there?"

"I'm *fine*, Ali," Tobas replied. "We'll turn me back as soon as we have the mirror."

That elicited a fresh chorus of yelps and shrieks from the spriggans still scattered across the meadow. "*No take mirror!*"

"Dragon no take mirror!"

"Not break mirror!

"Not eat mirror!"

"Oh, shut up, all of you," Tobas growled, a wisp of smoke emerging with his words as he stalked across the meadow. "It's *my* mirror, after all—you spriggans stole it from me, and I'll take it back if I want to!"

That evoked wails and lamentations.

"Tobas?" Alorria called.

The dragon turned his head.

"Shall I get your clothes and try to repair them?" she asked.

Gresh and the dragon exchanged glances.

"That would be helpful, yes," Tobas called.

"We can use Lirrim's Rectification on them if she can't fix them," Gresh murmured.

"Just get on with it," the dragon rumbled in reply.

Gresh hurried on across the meadow. About halfway he glanced back over his shoulder, and up, at the dragon. The size of the beast was astonishing. Equally astonishing was the fact that many of the spriggans still hadn't fled. Oh, they were hurrying to stay out of the dragon's path and giving it a respectful berth, but they were not all abandoning the area completely, as Gresh had hoped they would. The annoying little creatures were braver—or stupider—than he had expected.

Then he reached the rocks and waited for Karanissa to join him.

"Gresh," she said, as she stepped up beside him. "I don't really see how Tobas being a dragon is going to help us. Yes, he's scared away some of the spriggans, but he can't very well scare them out of the cave, and that's where the mirror is. If anything, more of them will hide in there to get away from the dragon. They'll still weigh the mirror down so that I can't levitate it."

Gresh did not answer her immediately. He had hoped the mere presence of a dragon would send every spriggan in the vicinity fleeing over the horizon, but now that that had failed to happen she had a point.

Gresh was not about to let that stop him, though. He had a dragon helping him, and in the present situation that was almost certainly an improvement over a wizard. "Tobas," he called, "can you breathe a little fire into that cave there? Not too much—I don't think we want to melt the mirror at this point, not until we've had a look at it."

"I don't know if I *can* melt it," Tobas said, as he lowered his head until his scaled cheek was just inches from Gresh's own. He had to crane his eight-foot neck awkwardly to bring his eyes down that far. "Dragonfire isn't really as hot as you might think." He looked at the rocks, then asked, "What cave?"

"Here," Gresh said, pointing. "It's too small for a human—that's why I can't just climb in and get the mirror. Spriggans pop in and out easily, but *we* can't."

"I can barely..." Tobas began, but he didn't finish the sentence. Instead he cocked one eye toward the opening. "Oh, I see it." He lifted his head a little. "Stand back."

Gresh and Karanissa quickly stepped back.

The dragon spat a gout of flame into the crack in the rocks. Spriggans screamed wildly from the cave. Gresh shied away from the heat, but tried to see into the opening before the glow faded.

Bits of dried grass and other debris had caught fire. He bent down to the opening and shaded his eyes, peering in.

The mirror still lay unharmed on the cave floor, and dozens of spriggans were still scattered about, many of them staring back at him. A few were sooty, but none appeared to have been harmed by the flames.

Well, after all, they were reportedly invulnerable; why would dragonfire hurt them?

"It didn't work," Gresh reported.

"Well, here," Tobas said. "If the problem is that you can't get into that little cave, I can fix *that*!" He stalked forward again, but this time kept his head up and raised a foreclaw, and curled it into a fist the size of a boulder. Then he flexed it and formed the claws into a flat plane.

"Oh, I don't..." Gresh began, as he backed away.

Tobas thrust forward, driving his claw into the crack in the stone as if it were a wedge.

The entire mountainside seemed to shake with the impact; rocks shattered and tumbled. Then the dragon curled his talons, dug them into the stone, and heaved.

The entire front of the cave tore out; Gresh was knocked off his feet by flying rocks and clumps of earth and blinded by clouds of dust. He fell back coughing on the grass of the meadow.

Spriggans were squealing and screaming, of course, and rocks were clattering against one another, as Gresh sat up and tried to wipe his eyes. His hands were as dusty as his face, so it took a moment before he could see again.

When he could he found himself face-to-face with a satisfied dragon. Tobas smiled down at him, baring ten-inch fangs and that forked tongue longer than a man's arm.

"There," he said. "The cave is open. *I* still can't fit in, but now *you* can."

Gresh looked and saw that the transformed wizard was right. He had ripped out several slabs of rock, creating an opening perhaps five feet high and eight feet wide, revealing the interior of the cave. A score or so of spriggans were still perched here and there in the cave, blinking out at the sunlit meadow in surprise.

Gresh got slowly and carefully back to his feet, brushing himself off as best he could, then turned to give the fallen Karanissa a hand up.

"Tobas, are you all right?" Alorria called from the distant carpet.

"I'm fine," Tobas bellowed back. "Just helping Gresh here."

"Is the mirror still in there?" Karanissa asked Gresh.

"It must be," he replied. He stepped forward, staring through the new entrance into the cave. "It ought to be right..."

And that was as far as he got before the cave roof fell in.

CHAPTER EIGHTEEN

"Oh," the dragon that had once been an ordinary wizard named Tobas of Telven said. "Perhaps I misjudged."

"Perhaps you did," Gresh agreed, looking at the rubble and silently thanking whatever gods might be listening that he had not yet stepped into the cave when the roof collapsed. The dust was clearing, and he could see now that most of the cave was still intact; a section of roof perhaps ten feet wide had fallen in, but that left a good twenty feet of cave on either side.

He tried to judge exactly where he had seen the mirror in there. With the whole area so utterly transformed, it was not an easy calculation to make, but he estimated that the mirror should be just under the left edge of the wreckage.

"It's there," Karanissa said from beside him, pointing to roughly the same spot he had been estimating.

"*No touch mirror!*" shrieked a spriggan from inside the remaining cave.

"*Shut up!*" the dragon bellowed in reply, spraying sparks.

"No no no no no!" the spriggan insisted, jumping up and down.

The dragon did not argue further, but instead, moving with amazing speed for so large a beast, reached in with one huge talon and flicked the spriggan far back into the depths of the cave. Then he withdrew the claw and turned to Gresh. "Get the mirror, and let's get out of here."

"Right," Gresh said, hurrying into the cave.

The sun was getting low in the west, behind the mountaintop, so even with a big piece of the wall and ceiling removed, the interior of the cave was shadowy and somewhat dim. Gresh knelt by the edge of the pile of debris, looking for the mirror.

"It's over there a little farther," Karanissa said. She had followed him in and was pointing at a small mound of rubble.

"If the ceiling fell on it, it's probably smashed," Gresh said. "That would be an end to the matter right there!"

"It isn't smashed," Karanissa said. "I can sense it."

"I knew it couldn't be that easy," Gresh grumbled. He pushed aside a few rocks where Karanissa had pointed, and sure enough, there was the mirror, dusty but intact.

"*No no no no no!*" shrieked a spriggan, leaping on his hand and startling him so badly he fell backward onto the hard-packed dirt of the cave floor.

"Get away!" Karanissa shouted, diving toward the spriggan. It sprang aside, and she snatched up the mirror.

Half a dozen other spriggans seemed to appear from

nowhere, jumping and squeaking and trying to grab the mirror away from the witch. She ignored them as she straightened up. Then she looked down at them, lifted the mirror high above her head, and shouted, "Get back, or I'll smash it on the rocks here and now!"

The spriggans immediately stopped leaping at her skirts and backed away, whimpering. For a moment no one moved or spoke—then the silence was broken by the squealing of several voices out on the meadow, squealing that continued and grew in volume.

Gresh sat up, brushing himself off, and stared up at the mirror gleaming in the witch's hand. He paid no attention to the shrieking and babbling outside the cave. He could not see how the spriggans could stop them now, no matter how upset they were. The dragon should be able to shoo them away well enough. "We have it," he said.

"*I* have it," Karanissa said. "Now what do we do with it?"

"We get it out of here," Gresh told her. He got to his feet and turned toward the opening.

Then he stopped dead, as Tobas said loudly, "Gresh? We may have a problem here." He sounded worried.

Gresh had not known a dragon *could* sound worried, but Tobas unquestionably did—and looking out through the hole in the hillside, Gresh could understand why.

Tobas's right wing blocked much of his view, but by leaning a bit Gresh could see out, and he did not like what he saw. Save for the area immediately around the dragon, the meadow was completely covered in spriggans—and that included the flying carpet. Spriggans were climbing on Alorria's lap, tugging at her hair, and poking at Alris, who was, quite understandably, crying.

Alorria had been screaming for some time, Gresh realized, but her high-pitched voice had been lost in the noise the spriggans made.

"I can't chase them away," Tobas said. "I might hurt Ali or the baby. Or the carpet. There are so *many* of them!"

"So I see," Gresh said.

Like Gresh, Karanissa had turned to see what was happening outside the cave, but she had continued to hold the mirror up above her head, well away from any spriggans—except now Gresh saw movement from the corner of his eye and turned to see a spriggan climbing out of the mirror onto Karanissa's wrist.

"Augh!" she shrieked. "It tickles!"

The spriggan itself looked confused and clambered awkwardly down her arm to her shoulder, then slid down her dress to the ground, where it said, "What happening?"

Several other spriggans started to reply, but Gresh shouted, "*Get away from her!!*"

The newborn spriggan squealed and scampered away, but the other spriggans nearby—there were at least a dozen in the cave with the two humans—stood their ground.

Alorria, out there on the spriggan-swarmed carpet, was still screaming, and a glance upward showed Gresh that Tobas was becoming seriously agitated.

Gresh did not want to be around a panicking dragon.

"Calm down, everyone!" he shouted. "Just calm down a moment!"

"*And then what?*" Tobas demanded.

"You tell them what I say, so they can all hear," Gresh said.

"Tell them *what*?"

"First off, tell them we have their precious mirror, and if they don't get off Alorria right now, we'll smash it on the rocks!"

"*Yes!* You hear that, spriggans?" The dragon's roar seemed to shake the mountainside, and a few loose stones tumbled from the broken edges of the cave roof. "*Get off my wife and daughter*, or we'll smash the mirror! *Now!*"

The spriggans hurried to get off Alorria and Alris—but they did not, Gresh noticed, get off the carpet.

"*Give back mirror!*" a spriggan shrieked from somewhere in the mob.

"Why is it so important to them?" Karanissa asked.

"I don't know," Gresh admitted.

"What should I do with it?"

Gresh considered that for a moment before replying.

They did not know whether they actually *could* smash the mirror; the only way to find out would be to try. The spriggans seemed to utterly dread that possibility; might it be that the mirror's destruction would mean they, too, would perish? More than one had said they *might* die if the mirror was destroyed; did they even *know* what would happen, any more than the humans did?

He had come here to see that the mirror *was* destroyed; why not try to do it? Yes, wizardry could have unforeseen effects, but really, how likely was it that smashing it would be any worse than leaving it alone?

It would upset the spriggans—if it didn't make them vanish—and that was bad, but he and the women had a *dragon* on their side. Surely, they could fight their way through a horde of toothless eight-inch pests. After all, the spriggans would no longer have anything to fight for, and they had never struck him as vindictive or vengeful creatures. Despite their numbers, they had not yet actually harmed anyone.

He and his companions had come here to dispose of this magic mirror, and now was as good a time as any to see if they could simply do it in the most obvious way.

But still, he hesitated. He had been reckless in using the Spell of the Revealed Power on Tobas, and he did not want to make it a habit. Carelessness with magic would sooner or later get him killed, or at least turned into something unpleasant.

Another spriggan began to emerge from the mirror as Karanissa held it, startling him. Without really meaning to, more thinking aloud than giving instructions, he said, "Break it."

A chorus of horrified squeals arose from every spriggan close enough to have heard his words, and Karanissa did not try to speak over the cacophony. Instead she nodded and looked down.

Spriggans were rushing toward her, to catch the mirror if she threw it against the rocks at her feet. Instead she swung around, arm outstretched, flinging the newly arrived spriggan aside and then slapping the mirror broadside against the stone of the cave wall.

Gresh almost reached out to stop her, but not in time. Glass cracked loudly, and the mirror fell from her hand in four jagged pieces. Countless spriggans screamed—and so did the dragon, with a deafening sound like nothing Gresh had ever heard before. Gresh looked up, startled.

"What did you *do*?" Tobas roared, spewing flame into the sky.

"What?" Gresh had had his attention focused entirely on Karanissa's hand, but now he looked around.

There were more spriggans than ever; they certainly hadn't vanished. In fact, there were *many* more. They were no longer just a mob, but covered the meadow at least two layers deep. The carpet had completely vanished, and several were spilling onto a screaming Alorria—not deliberately, but because they could find no other footing.

"Oh, *blast*!" Karanissa said. Gresh turned to see her staring down at the four chunks of mirrored glass that lay at her feet.

Four identical spriggans were squeezing themselves up from the four separate pieces. It took longer than previous emergences, since all four were full-sized but the fragments of mirror were not.

Gresh looked around and realized that all the existing spriggans had also been multiplied by four. Obviously, the link between the mirror and the spriggans was stronger than he had realized, and the breaking of the mirror had to be undone immediately.

That called for magic.

"Oh, gods and demons!" he muttered, as he snatched the pack from his shoulder and hauled out the box of powders. As he did he was imagining all those poor innocent people throughout the World who had been being harassed by spriggans, and who suddenly found each of the little monsters transformed into a quartet. Something had to be done *now*.

Well, that was why he had brought all these counter-charms. He popped open a jar of sparkling orange powder and strode over to the broken mirror, kicking aside four spriggans that happened to be in the way, then unceremoniously dumped a pinch of the powder over the four shards and barked, "*Esku!*"

The powder vanished in a golden flash, and the four pieces snapped together as if drawn by magnets, then healed back into a single mirror, which Gresh quickly snatched up before a spriggan could get it. A quick glance out at the meadow showed that the immense mass of spriggans had been reduced by three-fourths, restored to its original still-alarming size. The cave's population was similarly reduced. Even the four that had emerged from the broken mirror appeared to have merged into one.

"What spell was that?" Karanissa asked, as Gresh struggled to get the cork safely back into the mouth of the jar without dropping the mirror.

"Javan's Restorative," Gresh told her.

"Don't waste that!" Tobas said, peering in from above. "We need that to turn me back."

"There's plenty left," Gresh assured him. "I'm not going to waste it. Besides, wouldn't Lirrim's Rectification or the Spell of Reversal work?"

"I don't know," Tobas rumbled. "The Rectification turns things into what they *ought* to be, not necessarily what they were, and for all I know the spell might decide I *should* be a dragon. The Spell of Reversal only reverses things so far—if I stay a dragon more than half an hour or so, it won't do the job."

"It hasn't been half an hour yet," Gresh pointed out. Despite all that had happened since Tobas was transformed, it hadn't really been very long at all. "I doubt it's been a quarter of one."

A spriggan—*one* spriggan—began to climb out of the mirror and found Gresh's palm in the way. Gresh quickly turned the disk over and lowered his hand so that the creature could escape.

"So we have the mirror," he said. "And smashing it isn't a good idea—if we'd broken it into a hundred pieces we'd probably all have smothered to death." He glanced up at the dragon. "Well, all but Tobas, anyway."

"No smash," a spriggan said timidly. "Please?"

Gresh looked down at the little creature, which blinked up at him from a niche in the cave wall. "No smash," he agreed.

For a moment he wondered why the spriggan didn't want the mirror broken. After all, it only seemed to produce more spriggans. Perhaps the little creature didn't like crowds, or recognized that the World didn't have *room* for all those spriggans?

Though that made the creatures' unwillingness to give up the mirror that much more mysterious. If they didn't want more spriggans, why were they so determined to protect the mirror?

"Then what *do* we do with it?" Karanissa asked, interrupting his thoughts.

"Well, it seems to me that our first goal here is to prevent it from making any more spriggans," Gresh said.

"Isn't it? The Guild's worried that the whole World might fill up with spriggans, so if we can stop the mirror from making more, that's a good start. Dealing with the spriggans we already have is a separate issue, as is destroying it permanently. The first thing we want is to stop it from producing *more.*"

"How do you propose to do that, if we can't just smash it?" Karanissa asked.

"We could take it to the dead area..." Tobas began, but the resulting squeals and screams from the spriggans deterred even a dragon from finishing the sentence.

"Give back mirror," a spriggan called from atop a nearby rock. "You give back, spriggans take it and go away, and give back flying rug and lady and baby. No give mirror, no lady, no baby, no rug."

"And we'd be back where we started," Gresh said. "No, I don't think we'll do that."

"I don't know, Gresh," Karanissa said. "What about Ali and the baby?"

"They aren't trying to hurt them," Gresh said, though not as confidently as he would have liked.

"If we tried to take the mirror to the no-wizardry area they probably would."

"True enough," Gresh admitted. "If we can't take the mirror to the dead zone..." He looked up at Tobas. "You made that no-spell place, didn't you?"

"The one over there?" Tobas said, waving his head toward the opposite slope. "No. That's been there for centuries. A wizard named Seth Thorun's son did it."

"What about the one in Ethshar of the Sands?"

"I made that, yes."

"Could you do it again, here?"

Several spriggans squeaked in protest at this suggestion. The dragon ignored them, as he snorted smoke and said, "Not in *this* shape. Not to mention that it's forbidden—the Guild outlawed the spell long ago. They gave me a special dispensation for what I did before, but I don't have any dispensation to do it *again*. On top of *that*, I didn't bring the ingredients, since it *is* forbidden, and I never expected to have a use for it."

"Well, what ingredients do you need?"

"Oh, no—I'm not telling you that. It's *forbidden*. Using it carries the death penalty. Besides, I can't do it as a dragon, and if you turned me back now, how long do you think it would be before all these spriggans swarmed over us and took the mirror away from us? Not to mention that they'd interrupt the spell—it takes several minutes."

"Swarm...?" Gresh looked out and realized that Tobas was right. The dragon had interposed himself between the cave and the horde filling the meadow. A few spriggans were indeed in the cave, but the main body was out there, apparently kept away only by Tobas's presence.

So Tobas would have to remain a dragon for now, and that meant they had no wizardry available except for the powders and potions in Gresh's box.

Well, he had chosen those spells for exactly this purpose. None of these were intended to destroy the mirror outright, but he hoped one of them might break the enchantment on it and turn it into a harmless disk of silvered glass.

He would have preferred to try them under more

controlled circumstances, but that didn't appear to be an option. He had to do *something* to end this stand-off without giving the mirror back to the spriggans, and he had brought all this prepared magic, with the Guild's blessing. He might as well see whether any of it would do the job.

"Karanissa, could you keep the spriggans away for a moment?" he asked, as he seated himself cross-legged on the cave floor. He set the mirror on his lap, then pulled over the box of spells.

He wanted to be as cautious as possible, starting out with the spells least likely to have unforeseen effects. That made his first choice fairly simple. Javan's Geas could be used to command anyone *not* to do something, and it lasted indefinitely—but no one ever used it on inanimate objects, for obvious reasons. The mirror might be something more than a mere inanimate object, though, so Gresh pulled out the appropriate jar and sprinkled a pinch of dark red powder on the mirror.

This was exciting, using magic himself. He had certainly seen plenty of magic, but he had rarely gotten to use it himself. Turning Tobas into a dragon might have been reckless, even frightening, but it had also been *fun*. It had given him a sensation of power. This experiment with the mirror was far less likely to produce spectacular results, but it was still a bit of a thrill.

He could hear spriggans protesting, but none interrupted him. Apparently Karanissa's witchcraft was up to the task of keeping them away. "Make no more spriggans—by this spell I charge you," he proclaimed. "*Esku.*"

The powder flashed into non-existence, but the mirror appeared unchanged.

"Make no more spriggans," Gresh repeated, just in case he had misremembered and the command was supposed to come *after* the invocation.

"How do we know it worked?" Karanissa asked, looking down at the mirror. She was panting slightly from the effort of keeping the spriggans back.

"We just wait and see whether any more spriggans appear," Gresh answered, as he closed the jar and slid it back into its place in the box. "After all, they've been popping out often enough! No wonder there are half a million of the little pests, if they appear this...Oh, drat."

A spriggan was heaving itself up out of the mirror.

"It didn't work," Karanissa said.

"It didn't work," Gresh agreed. He reached for the box.

The glittering white powder of Lirrim's Rectification flashed silver instead of gold, but had no visible effect at all, and after a five-minute wait the mirror produced another spriggan, demonstrating that the original spell was still working. The spriggan appeared just the same as the others. If the Rectification had had any effect at all, it wasn't obvious.

"I'd hoped that would turn it into Lugwiler's Haunting Phantasm," Gresh said. "I'm not sure why it didn't—after all, that's what the spell was originally intended to be."

"Maybe wizardry just doesn't *work* on the mirror," Karanissa said, as she slumped against the cave wall, exhausted.

"That's possible," Gresh admitted. "But I really hope that's not the case."

"Maybe it's been too long since the original spell,"

Tobas said, peering down through the opening where the cave roof used to be.

"That doesn't seem likely," Gresh said. "From what I'm told, wizardry usually isn't time-limited that way—I mean, you can *always* reverse Fendel's Superior Petrifaction, even if the victim's been stone for centuries." He glanced around. "It might be because there are half a million spriggans out there who think this version of the mirror is exactly what it *should* be."

"That could be," Tobas said.

Gresh tried Javan's Restorative next, over the dragon's objections. Tobas pointed out that they had already used the Restorative on the mirror once without removing the enchantment and argued that they really shouldn't waste another portion of their very limited supply of a very precious spell.

Gresh ignored him and cast the spell, which did absolutely nothing. Spriggans continued to emerge from the mirror at irregular intervals.

The horde of spriggans in the meadow continued to hold Alorria, Alris, and the flying carpet hostage. They bickered and squeaked among themselves, but made no attempt to charge past the dragon. Every so often one would try to sneak past alone, but Tobas spotted most of these and chased them away.

"What does that leave?" Tobas asked, as he brushed a few unusually courageous spriggans back with his tail. "What else have you got in that box?"

"The potions obviously won't help," Gresh said. "The mirror can't drink them. The two powders we haven't tried are the Spell of the Revealed Power and the Spell of Reversal."

"The mirror's been enchanted for years, so I don't know what the Spell of Reversal could do," Tobas remarked.

"Make the mirror suck spriggans back in, perhaps?" Karanissa suggested.

Gresh and Tobas exchanged glances, man to dragon.

"I suppose it *might*," Gresh said.

"Well, what would the Spell of the Revealed Power do?"

"Who knows?" Gresh replied. "It might show us why the spriggans are so determined to protect this thing, when they say they don't care whether any more appear out of it."

"It may be bringing the spriggans from somewhere else," Tobas suggested. "Instead of creating them, I mean. The Spell of the Revealed Power might transform it into an actual doorway into that realm, whatever and wherever it may be."

"And if it did..." Gresh blinked. "If it did, maybe we could send all the spriggans back where they came from! Maybe *that's* what they actually want it for!"

"And maybe it's not," Karanissa said. "Maybe instead it'll dump another half-million spriggans on us all at once!"

"I'll have Javan's Restorative handy," Gresh said.

"The Spell of Reversal," Tobas grumbled. "Use *that*, and save the Restorative!"

"Maybe I will," Gresh said, as he pulled the jar of blue powder from the box. "Let's just see what it does..."

"I don't know if this is a good idea," Karanissa said, backing away.

"She may have a point," Tobas said. "What if it releases an *infinite* quantity of spriggans, and we're smothered to death before you can use a counterspell?"

"That would be unfortunate," Gresh said, as he sprinkled blue powder on the mirror. He had come this far, and did not want to give up. Besides, he had just cast three high-order spells that had done exactly nothing, and was beginning to think wizardry simply didn't work on the mirror. He wanted to find *something* that would affect the glass.

"It would be unfortunate," he repeated. "But I don't think it'll happen. Why would it? What power would that reveal? *Esku!*"

CHAPTER NINETEEN

There was a golden flash, and the man, woman, and dragon stared down at the little mirror.

It remained a mirror, a round piece of silvered glass about the size of a man's hand. It did not transform into a gateway, portal, dragon, spriggan, or monster of any sort.

"It would appear," Karanissa said, staring at it, "that it has never mastered anything more powerful than itself."

"How annoying," Gresh said.

A spriggan suddenly popped up out of the mirror, jumped to a nearby rock, teetered on its edge for a moment, then scampered away. It looked just like any number of the other spriggans. The Spell of the Revealed Power had apparently not changed a thing.

"How *very* annoying," Gresh said.

"You know," Tobas said, "you'd make a terrible wizard, Gresh—assuming you survived your apprenticeship. You have a habit of throwing magic around *much* too carelessly. That spell really *might* have killed us all. Turning me into a dragon, and all the rest—you really ought to use a little more caution."

This admonishment, especially coming from Tobas, whose carelessness with magic had created the spriggan mirror in the first place, stung more than Gresh cared to admit—but he could not completely deny that there was some justice in it. "I take some risks, yes," he said. "I don't think they're excessive. I have a box of counter-spells right here, after all, and this is what the Guild *gave* me these spells for. I brought them here to use."

"But none of them have done anything useful to the mirror," Karanissa said.

"I know. But there's one more to try," Gresh replied.

"The Spell of Reversal? What can *that* do?" Tobas asked.

"Maybe Karanissa's right, and it really *will* suck spriggans back in," Gresh said.

"Even if it does, it will only work for half an hour," Tobas pointed out.

"That's surely better than nothing," Gresh said. "Perhaps we can find a way to keep on casting it, over and over?" He looked up, and even on a dragon's face the dubious expression Tobas wore was easy to recognize.

"Well, let's see what it does," Gresh said, stubbornly. "We might as well."

"I admit I don't see what harm that one can do," Tobas said. "Unless it breaks the mirror into four pieces again."

"I hadn't thought of that," Gresh said, with a tug at his beard. "It might, mightn't it?"

"We could wait until it's more than half an hour since the mirror was repaired," Karanissa suggested.

Gresh looked out across the meadow, past Tobas in

the draconic form he did not want to keep, at Alorria, who was sitting on the carpet, holding Alris in one arm and tugging at Tobas's ruined clothes with the other. He looked at the hordes of spriggans milling about, some of them clearly looking for ways to get at the mirror.

"I don't think we should wait," he said. "I have the Restorative, or I could even just use the Spell of Reversal again." He pulled the final unopened jar from his box, wiggled the cork free, then sprinkled a little purple powder over the mirror, and said, "*Esku!*"

The flash was bluish this time, but after it had faded away the mirror lay on the cave floor just as before and still in one piece. Relieved that it was intact and disappointed that it was not doing anything obvious to reduce the spriggan population, Gresh leaned over and looked into it. He saw only his own reflection looking back at him.

"Nothing," he said.

Karanissa suddenly reached out and grabbed a spriggan before it had time to react. She held it with one hand around its legs, the other pinning one arm to its body.

The other arm waved wildly about as it squealed, "No no! No hurt! No hurt!"

"I'm not going to hurt you," Karanissa told it. "I'm going to see if I can send you back where you belong." She tossed the creature onto the mirror.

It landed on the glass with a soggy thump, got up, brushed itself off, and scampered away unhurt, giggling hysterically.

"I'd say it isn't exactly sucking them back in," Gresh remarked.

Karanissa leaned over and peered down into the mirror, holding her long hair back out of the way with one hand. "It would seem not," she agreed.

"So that didn't work, and we have no other spells to try, so we're back to trying to figure out some way to get it out of here and across the valley to the no-wizardry zone," Gresh said.

"Maybe," Karanissa said, still staring into the mirror. "Or maybe not."

Gresh looked at her. "Maybe not?" He looked down at the mirror. "Why maybe not?"

"Well, look at it," the witch said. "Maybe the spriggan didn't get sucked in, but have you seen anything come *out* of it since you cast that spell?"

Gresh blinked. He stared at the mirror. No spriggans were climbing out of it—but it had only been a couple of minutes. He felt a twinge of hope, but quickly suppressed it.

"Not yet," he said. "But that may not mean anything."

"It *feels* different," Karanissa said. "It's still magical, still enchanted, it hasn't gotten any weaker or stronger, but it feels *different*."

"Can you tell how?"

Karanissa turned up an empty palm. "No," she said.

"*Tobas?*" a distant voice called.

"Ali?" The dragon had been watching the events in the cave with interest, but now he lifted his scaly head and turned to look at Alorria. Gresh, too, glanced in her direction.

"What's going on?" Alorria asked, the words barely intelligible over the intervening distance. "How long are these spriggans going to keep us here? The sun's going down. Are we going to be stuck here all night?"

The dragon's head swung back to the cave for a moment. "Excuse me," Tobas said, "but I've been neglecting Ali." He started to turn away—this time not just by bending his neck, but by turning his entire body.

"Wait a moment," Gresh called. "If you leave, we'll be overrun by spriggans, and they'll take the mirror."

"If you get too close to the carpet you may panic them into doing something unfortunate," Karanissa said. "Or *you* may do something unfortunate, without meaning to."

The dragon hesitated, then said, "I'll just turn around and talk to Ali from a safe distance."

Karanissa and Gresh exchanged glances. "That should work," Gresh acknowledged.

"Good." With that, and with much scraping of scale on rock and rustling of gigantic wings, the dragon turned around, sending spriggans running in various directions squeaking madly, until at last the very tip of his tail slithered across the rocks he had ripped out of the mountainside and curled into the mouth of the cave.

"She's right that the sun's setting," Karanissa said, once the dragon had completed his rotation.

Gresh's reply was drowned out by the dragon roaring across the meadow to Alorria, reassuring her that everything was fine, and that the other two were just experimenting with the mirror to see if they could remove the enchantment.

Alorria called back, but Gresh and Karanissa could not make out her words. After a moment, by mutual consent, they decided to ignore the conversation between the princess and the dragon and turn their attention back to the mirror. Ordinarily making themselves heard over the dragon's bellowing might have been difficult, but Karanissa's witchcraft took care of that.

"There still haven't been any more spriggans," Karanissa said. "It really does feel different. Before it felt as if it were directed *away*, somehow, and now it seems directed *here*."

"Well, the Spell of Reversal..." Gresh began; then he stopped. "Wait," he said. "It was directed *away* before?"

"Yes," Karanissa said. "Definitely."

"Away where?"

Karanissa hesitated, then turned up a palm. "I don't know," she said. "Not anywhere in the World."

"So it was pulling the spriggans from another world into ours?"

"I don't know."

"But you said now it's aimed here."

"Yes."

"But it didn't suck that spriggan into another world. And we looked into it, and it didn't suck *us* in."

"I know. I never said I understood it. I'm a witch, not a wizard."

"Oh, I doubt a wizard would do any better," Gresh assured her. "They rarely really know what they're doing—it's all rote formulas and instinct. They don't actually *understand* their magic."

"I know most of them don't; Tobas certainly doesn't. Some of them seem to do a little better. I thought Derithon had a better grasp of what he was doing than most, but I was very young then, and that might have been my own naivete."

"Derithon was your first husband, four centuries ago?"

"Well, we weren't formally married. I was his mistress. Or technically, a lieutenant assigned special duties under his command."

Gresh blinked. "Lieutenant?"

"In the military of Old Ethshar. The Great War was in progress, after all. I was serving in reconnaissance, using my witchcraft to locate enemy magicians, when we met."

"Of course."

Somehow, despite knowing she was four hundred years old, he had never connected her with the Great War that had ended more than two hundred years ago—but of course she had grown up during the War, and like all magicians of the time would have been conscripted into the military.

The World had been so utterly different then—no wonder Karanissa had said she felt out of place now!

Gresh wondered whether he, too, would feel out of place four hundred years from now, if he completed the job he had come here to do and received the payment he had been promised. That was an odd thought. Was that why so few openly ancient people were around? After all, wizards had been using eternal youth spells for centuries, and even if only a few in each generation ever managed to work them, undying wizards ought to be accumulating, but Gresh hadn't met more than a handful, at most. Did they withdraw from human society because it was no longer familiar, because it was too different from what they had known when young?

That didn't really seem reasonable. Karanissa didn't

fit in well because she had spent four hundred years trapped in a castle, but she didn't seem to want to give up human company, by any means. Most people would have lived through the changes as they happened and could have adapted.

No, there must be some other explanation for the scarcity of ancients.

Scarce or not, he had one here to advise him. "You think they understood wizardry better back then?" he asked.

"Maybe. At least I think Derry did—but he was a couple of centuries old."

"Oh." There it was again, the idea of living for hundreds of years and watching the World change around you—but Derithon hadn't withdrawn from humanity.

Or had he? He had kept his mistress in that weird castle in the tapestry and had flown around the World in another castle, rather than living among ordinary people.

But he had met Karanissa and seduced her. He hadn't been a hermit.

Or had *she* seduced *him*, perhaps? Gresh suddenly wondered whether the Spell of the Revealed Power might turn Karanissa into the likeness of the long-dead Derithon the Mage and whether that might be useful.

He was not about to test out that theory without some careful planning; he had had enough of throwing spells around recklessly. Tobas had been right to criticize him.

"Still no new spriggans," Karanissa said, interrupting his thoughts.

Gresh glanced down at the mirror, and as he did he

caught a glimpse of a pair of pop-eyes watching him from a corner of the cave. The spriggans did not seem upset by whatever the Spell of Reversal had done. There was no ongoing barrage of squeals, nor were there any wild dashes toward the mirror to protect it.

It might be time to ask them a few questions, while waiting to see whether any spriggans emerged before the Spell of Reversal wore off—or after, for that matter. After all, interrogating spriggans had been more obviously useful than wizardry so far.

"Karanissa, would you..." he began.

He did not need to finish the request; she had heard his thoughts. Her hand flashed out and closed on the spriggan's legs, and a moment later it was hanging upside-down from her fist, squealing. Several other spriggans were calling protests from elsewhere in the cave.

"Shut up!" Gresh ordered.

The captured spriggan's complaints died down to terrified whimpering, and the others fell completely silent.

"We aren't going to hurt you," Gresh told it. "If you answer all my questions truthfully for the next half-hour, we'll let you go."

"Not fun," the spriggan whined.

"Sometimes life isn't fun," Gresh told it.

It nodded desperately.

"Good. Karanissa, why don't you turn our guest the other way up, so it can talk more easily?"

Karanissa righted the creature, but did not loosen her grip.

"Now, my little friend, what do you know about this mirror?" Gresh asked, pointing.

The spriggan looked down and gulped. "That where spriggans come from," it said. "That what gives spriggans magic, protects spriggans from harm."

"It does?" Gresh's gaze fell to the mirror for a moment, then flicked back to their captive. "How does it protect you?"

"Not tell!" another spriggan called from a dozen feet away. Gresh threw a pebble at it, and it fled with a squeal.

The captive saw its companion flee, then said, "Just does." It tried to shrug, but the gesture was not entirely successful with Karanissa's hand restricting its movement.

"It didn't protect you from being captured just now," Gresh pointed out.

"No, no. Doesn't protect spriggan from *everything*. But spriggan can't be *killed*, not while mirror is magic."

"What?" Gresh glanced down at the mirror; was that the source of the spriggans' invulnerability? He knew that there was a powerful link between the mirror and the spriggans, or there could have been no fourfold population surge when the mirror was broken, but he had not connected the mirror with the creatures' reported inability to die from any natural cause.

The spriggan did not try to explain; it just looked unhappy and confused. Karanissa interjected a question. "How do you *know* it protects you?"

"*Didn't* always," the spriggan said.

"Explain!" Gresh demanded.

The spriggan looked more miserable than ever. "When mirror first make spriggans, mirror was in big stone house in purple sky." It pointed at Karanissa. "She was there."

"We know where you mean," Gresh said, noting silently that the spriggan seemed very sure the mirror *made* spriggans, rather than bringing them from somewhere else, even though Karanissa had sensed that the mirror was directed somewhere else. "What does that have to do with anything?"

"When mirror was in purple sky place, spriggans had magic, couldn't be hurt—but wizard tried to lock up mirror, didn't like spriggans, so spriggans took mirror to other place."

That accorded with what Gresh had been told by Tobas and his wives. "Yes. That was seven years ago."

"In dark other place, mirror had no magic, so spriggans had no magic. Some spriggans didn't care, went wandering around, got in trouble, made people angry, and people *cut* spriggans! With big scary knives! Sharp ones! Spriggans *died*!"

A chorus of dismayed squeaks came from other spriggans in earshot; the humans ignored them. "They died?" Gresh looked at Karanissa. "I thought you said they couldn't be killed by natural means."

"They can't," Karanissa said.

"Spriggans can't," the spriggan agreed. "Can't *now*, because *smart* spriggans figured out mirror might be magic again someplace else and took mirror from dark stone house to cave—this cave! And mirror had magic again, and *spriggans* had magic again, and spriggans not die anymore, ever—well, unless spriggans go where no magic is; spriggans can be killed there. But only stupid spriggans go there; spriggans can *feel* magic and stay away from bad places."

Comprehension swept over Gresh. Tobas had not bothered retrieving the mirror originally because he had thought it would be harmless in the no-wizardry zone, and it *was*—but the spriggans had eventually hauled it out of the dead area, not because they wanted more spriggans loose in the World, but because of the magical link between themselves and the mirror that made them unkillable.

That the spriggans had figured out that the link existed proved that spriggans weren't as stupid as they looked. The connection certainly hadn't been obvious to *him*. He supposed that hundreds of them had discussed the situation at length, and they had somehow worked it out collectively, but it was still impressive.

The link might provide some of the other magical abilities the spriggans displayed, as well, such as their uncanny ability to open any lock—but it wasobviously the invulnerability that mattered most to them. "So *that's* why you want to keep it safe?" he asked.

The spriggan nodded wildly.

"You were keeping this secret—why?"

"Not want spriggan-killers to know how to kill spriggans! Not want spell broken, or mirror taken to no-magic place again."

That was reasonable. Furthermore, Gresh thought, in all likelihood, no one had ever *asked* them about any of this until he had begun his own investigations. The usual reaction to spriggans wasn't to try to reason with them or determine their origins; it was simply to shoo them away as quickly as possible.

But they *could* be reasoned with; Gresh saw that now. They wanted the mirror to preserve their indestructibility. "And you don't care that it keeps making more spriggans?" he asked.

"Not care much," the spriggan agreed. "Enough spriggans now. *Crowded* here, with so many. We send extras off to find wizards—spriggans like magic. And have fun. But keep enough here to guard mirror."

"You send the extras away, on purpose?" Gresh demanded. "They don't just wander off?"

"Send them away, yes," the spriggan said, nodding again. "That way, on easy old road." It pointed to the north. "Some go off other ways, but most use road."

And that, it seemed, explained why so few wound up in Dwomor—the road the captive indicated led the opposite direction, north and west toward Ethshar, where most of the world's wizards were.

"Why didn't one of you just *tell* us all this, instead of mobbing poor Alorria and making everything difficult?" Gresh asked. "We can work something out!"

"Didn't know you weren't spriggan-killer, maybe?"

"But I said we didn't want to hurt you, didn't I?" He looked at Karanissa.

"I'm not sure," she said. "*Did* you?"

"I think maybe we were too busy with other things," Gresh admitted. "I suppose the way we kept trying to get at the mirror couldn't have looked very friendly." Then he turned his attention back to the spriggan. "So right now, is the magic still working? We changed the spell on the mirror—does that matter?"

"Still works," the spriggan said. "No problem."

"So if we somehow made this change permanent, you spriggans would be happy?"

"Would depend on other things. Not happy when it rains, or when spriggans all get really hungry. Hungry now—you have food?"

"No," Gresh lied. He had a few things to eat in his pack, but he had no intention of giving them to the spriggans. "I meant, you wouldn't mind the change in the spell?"

"Not mind. Magic still working."

Gresh nodded.

That really seemed to explain everything. He tried to think of other things to ask the spriggan before releasing it, and nothing came to mind.

Taking the mirror into the no-wizardry area and destroying it would put an end to the spriggans' indestructibility. If the link was as strong as the quadrupling of the spriggan population when they broke the mirror implied, destroying it might destroy the spriggans, as well, wiping them from existence.

He hadn't really thought that was likely a few hours ago, but the population explosion had changed his mind, and the news about spriggan invulnerability also being connected to the mirror—well, there was clearly a *very* strong link. So destroying the mirror might destroy them all.

Or it might not. They hadn't ceased to exist when the mirror was in the no-wizardry zone before; they had merely lost their magic.

Either way, the spriggans hated the idea of letting the mirror be destroyed or taken into the no-wizardry area and would fight furiously to prevent it. They had no objection to things that merely prevented the mirror from producing *more* spriggans. If there were some way to make the Spell of Reversal permanent...

But Gresh was fairly certain there wasn't. Besides, he had agreed to sell the mirror to Tobas and the Guild, he had not contracted to merely stop the production of spriggans.

"Do you think the Guild would be satisfied if we just prevented the mirror from making more of them?" he asked Karanissa.

"I have no idea," she replied. "I've never known what to expect of the Wizards' Guild. They might be."

"I had thought that anything that would stop it from producing spriggans would break the spell on it, or completely change it, but that doesn't seem to be what happened here, with the Spell of Reversal. Not that I really know what *did* happen. You said it feels different; can you add anything? Has it changed any further?"

"No."

Gresh sighed. This was all getting very complicated, whereas his original plan had seemed simple. "If we could just get it across the valley to the ruins, we could destroy it—smash it to powder, maybe."

"The spriggans would do everything they could to stop us."

"I know." He grimaced. "But we do have a good-sized dragon on our side. Maybe Tobas could clear us a path."

"What about Alorria and the baby?"

Gresh sighed. "I don't know," he said. "I don't know whether the spriggans would really hurt them or not."

Karanissa glanced around at the dozens of little eyes watching them from various corners of the cave. "They would try," she said. "I'm not sure what they could do, but they would try."

He did not doubt her; after all, she was a witch. "What if we took the mirror back to Ethshar? That wouldn't block the magic they want. What would they do then?"

"You know they want to keep it under their own control," Karanissa said. "I don't think they'd be as desperate as if we were heading to the ruins, but they'd still try to stop us. And how could we do it? They're all over the flying carpet, and it would take months to get back to Ethshar on foot, and during those months they'd be constantly trying to steal the mirror back. Every time we slept, the spriggans would grab it."

"What if we got the carpet off the ground with all of us and a few hundred spriggans on it, then dumped all the spriggans off?"

"This would be after you turned Tobas back to a human? How would we get to the carpet through that mob?" She pointed out at the meadow, still swarming with spriggans. "They might also fling so many of themselves on the carpet it couldn't get off the ground."

Gresh sighed.

"All we need to do," he said, "is to get the mirror back to Ethshar and give it to the Guild—then it's *their* problem. We don't need to deal with it permanently ourselves."

"Well, *you* don't," Karanissa agreed. "Tobas and I—well, we made some promises. *Our* agreement with the Guild is to put an end to the problem of spriggans, not just to deliver the mirror."

"Just...put an end to the problem?" Gresh considered that. "So if we *did* make the Spell of Reversal permanent, would that be enough?"

"It *might* be," Karanissa said. "I'm not sure. There would still be half a million spriggans running around loose."

"But there would never be any *more* than that."

"That's why it might be enough."

Gresh looked down at the mirror. "Stupid thing," he said. Then he reached for the box of powders—the temptation to play with magic was still strong, and after all, this was what these spells were *for*.

"I think I'll try a few things," he said.

CHAPTER TWENTY

"Don't turn back—*esku*!" Gresh shouted, as he sprinkled red powder on the mirror.

It flashed gold.

"How will you know whether that worked?" Karanissa asked.

"The half-hour will be up in a few minutes," Gresh said. "You should be able to sense whether the spell reverts, shouldn't you?"

"Probably," the witch admitted.

"If you can't, we'll know when spriggans start appearing, or when we've gone an hour or two without any."

"I suppose so."

The two of them stood staring down at the mirror. In addition to Javan's Geas, Gresh had also tried Lirrim's Rectification again, to see whether it did anything, but there was no discernible effect.

The sun was definitely behind the mountaintop now, and the Spell of Reversal was due to expire at any moment. Tobas was still standing guard in front of the cave, roaring reassurances to Alorria. The flying carpet was still partially buried in spriggans and quite thoroughly surrounded by them, but none were touching mother or daughter.

A sudden thump startled Gresh; he turned to see Tobas staring down at one of his front feet, which was planted firmly on the ground. Then the dragon's face contorted, his neck twisted oddly, and he began making a very odd noise.

"What is *that*?" Gresh asked, startled. "Is he all right?"

"He's...he's laughing," Karanissa said. "I never heard a dragon laugh before."

"I didn't know dragons *could* laugh!" Gresh exclaimed.

Then Tobas lifted the taloned foot, saying, "That tickles!" A spriggan squirmed up out of the spot where the dragon's foot had been and scampered away.

Gresh called, "What was that about?"

Tobas turned to look at him. "Oh, nothing much," the dragon explained. "That spriggan tried to slip by me, so I stepped on it. It didn't squash, though, and it just kept wriggling around under my foot; it tickled dreadfully."

"Oh," Gresh said. The dragon put his claw back on the ground and turned his attention back to Alorria, calling new reassurances to her.

Gresh turned to Karanissa. "I guess they really *can't* be seriously harmed," he said. "If being stamped on by a dragon doesn't hurt them, what will?"

"Nothing," Karanissa said. "I told you. That's the problem."

"I know, I've been thinking about it, and our little hostage explained it, but still, seeing it demonstrated like that..." He turned up an empty palm.

"It *is* strange," Karanissa agreed. "It's strange seeing my husband in the shape of a dragon, too—especially since he's taken it so calmly, once the actual transformation was complete."

"He's a wizard," Gresh said. "He's supposed to be accustomed to magic."

"Getting turned into a dragon is hardly normal even for a wizard."

"I suppose not." Gresh glanced at the dragon's tail, then back at the witch. "But you and he have been involved in some odd adventures before this—trapped in a magic castle, slaying a dragon, defeating the false empress..."

"I know." She shuddered slightly.

"Even just being married to someone with another wife must be a bit awkward at times."

"Oh, yes." She sighed. "I told Tobas before he married Alorria that I wasn't the jealous type, and I've tried not to be. I knew Derry had other women sometimes, and that didn't bother me, so I thought I could handle it. Ali knew what she was getting into, too—I was married to Tobas first, after all. She wanted to marry *someone*, certainly. She had five sisters. Her parents weren't going to find princes for everyone, and that meant a hero, so she didn't have a great many choices. Really, she didn't have *any* choice; her parents gave her to Tobas as his reward for killing the dragon, bribing him with her dowry. But she did like him and admire him. She can be very sweet. We all thought it would work out."

"Well, it *has* worked out, hasn't it?"

"Mostly—but I must admit, Ali is not who I would have chosen to live with for the rest of my life. I've tried not to be jealous of her, but she hasn't always done the same for me."

"I've noticed."

"She feels outmatched. I'm a witch, so I *know* she does, I'm not just guessing. She sees that I'm a fellow magician for Tobas and four hundred years older than she is, with vastly more experience. *She* also thinks I'm more beautiful, though Tobas doesn't, nor most of the other men we meet."

"I think I'd agree with Alorria on that one."

"Well, thank you, but most men don't. They think I'm too skinny, too flat-chested, too dark, too aloof, too tall, too intimidating—whatever. Ali's just as pretty in the face and anything but flat-chested, not to mention nicely rounded elsewhere. Men may admire me, but they lust after her—not that she believes it. And Tobas—I don't know how he does it, but most of the time he really *doesn't* prefer one of us over the other. It's amazing. Not that Ali believes that, either, even though we've both told her it's true. Even though she agrees we should be equal partners, she's always demanding attention, trying to compensate for the advantages she imagines I have." She sighed. "She's been especially sensitive ever since she got pregnant with Alris. Sometimes I think I should get pregnant, as well, just to stay even."

Gresh knew that ordinarily female witches could control whether or not they conceived; he wondered whether Karanissa had actively avoided bearing children, or merely let nature take its course.

And really, she wasn't an ordinary witch; she was four hundred years old. Even with an eternal youth spell, was she still fertile? Did she know?

It wasn't any of his business; she had already told him far more than he had any business knowing, and far more than he would have asked, though he had not been surprised when his remark elicited so detailed a response. He had been fairly certain that she would be happy to find receptive ears. Many men professed to find women incomprehensible, but after growing up with his numerous sisters, Gresh thought he had a reasonably good understanding of the female mind. He had provided a sympathetic and non-threatening audience, and Karanissa had taken advantage of his presence to say things she could not tell her husband, her co-wife, or anyone in Dwomor. He understood that perfectly. He had, in fact, planned it. He liked Karanissa, more than he liked Tobas or Alorria, and had welcomed the opportunity to create a bond.

It was probably a foolish thing to do, though. She was a happily married woman, even if she was not completely satisfied with her co-wife. Once their business with the mirror was done, he would never see her again.

She threw him a sharp glance, and he realized neither of them had spoken for several seconds. He wondered how much of his thoughts she had heard. "Nothing to say about the wisdom of giving my husband another child?" she said.

Apparently she had not heard everything he had thought; she had probably been too caught up in her own concerns. "It's not any of *my* business," he said. "I would think that your situation is complicated enough, though. And you have plenty of time, with your eternal youth spell; no need to hurry."

"*Tobas* doesn't have an eternal youth spell."

"I hardly think that's an issue at this point. He's a young man."

"So are you, but you're concerning yourself with eternal youth."

"I'm not as young as he is, and I know I won't *always* be young unless I do something about it."

"Tobas didn't think of that."

"Or didn't want to deal with it. I'm sure your marriage is complicated for him, too, and obtaining eternal youth just for himself would surely make it worse, while getting it for both Alorria and himself—well, he may not feel ready to extend the current situation for hundreds of years."

Karanissa stared at him. "Do you believe that's it? I didn't intrude, and I believed him when he said he just didn't think of it."

"You're a witch, and you know him far better than I do."

Karanissa continued to stare at him, and Gresh thought he read speculation in her gaze. Was she, perhaps, thinking that Tobas and Alorria might never find a youth spell, and that someday, fifty or sixty years from now, she would be a widow—and if Gresh was successful in his errand for the Wizards' Guild, he would still be around and still be young?

Or was he just flattering himself?

Her intense gaze became uncomfortable, and he looked down at the mirror. "The half-hour must be almost done," he said.

Her gaze dropped, as well. "It is; it's changing right now. I can feel..."

She didn't finish the sentence; instead she stared silently at the mirror.

So did Gresh. The glass had gone black, and then something began to thrust itself upward out of the mirror—but it was no spriggan. It was neither green nor brown, but glossy black—covered with lush black hair, Gresh realized.

It was *larger* than the mirror. Some of the fatter spriggans might have had to squeeze a little, but this creature, whatever it was, was somehow forcing itself through an opening much smaller than its own dimensions.

The hair parted on one side as the thing continued to rise up out of the mirror, revealing a brown forehead. Gresh realized that a human head was emerging from the spriggan mirror. The face was turned away from him, toward Karanissa, who was staring at it in shocked horror.

More hair, a pair of ears, a nose—definitely human.

Then came the neck—that was relatively quick, as it did not need to be magically squeezed as much—and then a pair of shoulders, shoulders clad in red fabric...

"Oh, no," Gresh murmured. "Let me..." He stepped around the mirror and stood beside Karanissa, where he could see the face as the creature continued to force its way up out of the far-too-small mirror.

It was a woman's face, a dark-skinned oval. Gresh recognized it immediately. After all, he had been looking at it for the past half-hour and more.

It was Karanissa.

Gresh looked up and saw the original Karanissa still standing there, looking down at her duplicate. This *wasn't* Karanissa, then; it was a copy.

And the copy had her hands free of the impossibly

small glass now and was pushing herself up, just as the spriggans had, except that she was somehow emerging from the mirror despite being much larger than it. Even the slim Karanissa was far more than five inches across.

The mirror was doing something strange to space, obviously.

Then the imitation Karanissa sat back on the stone and pulled her legs from the little glass circle. She was entirely free, and the mirror once again looked like an ordinary mirror.

This Karanissa, at least initially, appeared indistinguishable from the original. She wore an identical red dress, and her hair was styled just like the original's.

"Well, so much for using Javan's Geas on the mirror," Gresh muttered. "But we must have done something that altered the nature of the spell. Are we going to get a plague of Karanissas now, instead of spriggans?" He found himself thinking that that would certainly be an improvement.

The original Karanissa ignored him as she knelt by the rather dazed-looking copy and asked, "Who are you?"

The copy looked up, obviously confused, and said, "I'm a person."

"I didn't ask *what* you are," Karanissa said gently. "I asked *who* you are."

"I'm...I'm a person," the other said. "That's all I know."

"Where did you come from?"

The imitation looked down at her feet, then pointed. "The mirror," she said.

"Are you a witch?" Karanissa asked.

The copy blinked, then frowned. "I'm not sure," she said.

"Can't you tell?" Gresh asked the original.

"No, I can't," Karanissa admitted. "Which is puzzling, to say the least." She looked up at Gresh. "This...this *person* isn't all here, exactly."

"She isn't...well, you?" Gresh asked. "Could it be that you're being confused because her identity isn't entirely distinct from your own?"

Karanissa reached out and put a hand on her imitation's shoulder; the imitation started slightly, glanced at the hand, then looked up at Gresh. "Do I look like her?" she asked.

"Very much," Gresh said, startled by the question.

"She's pretty."

"So are you."

The copy lowered her gaze. "Thank you," she said.

"You know," Karanissa said, looking up at Gresh, "until I touched her, I wasn't sure she was really there. I thought she might just be an illusion, especially given how she squeezed through the mirror when she obviously couldn't have fit."

Gresh nodded. He was thinking furiously. He did not understand why this duplicate of Karanissa should have emerged from the mirror, but he intended to figure it out. It would almost certainly explain a great deal about how the mirror's magic worked, and that might well help them end the plague of spriggans forever—if they had not already somehow altered the spell permanently.

He glanced down at the mirror to see whether anything else was climbing out of it; nothing was.

This woman, this copy of Karanissa, was solid, but Karanissa said she did not seem real...

"Lady," he said, "do you remember *anything* from before you emerged from the mirror?"

The copy looked up at him again. "Of course not," she said. "I didn't *exist* before I climbed out of the mirror, did I?"

"We don't *know*," Gresh said. "That's why I'm asking."

"Well, as far as I know, I didn't exist until a couple of minutes ago."

Gresh looked at the original. "You say she doesn't seem entirely human?"

"She doesn't seem entirely *real*," Karanissa corrected him.

"Do spriggans? Could she be a spriggan in human form?"

"I'm a person," the duplicate interjected. "I do know that much."

"She..." Karanissa tilted her head and studied the copy. "She's not a spriggan, but there *is* a similarity. I never noticed it before, but you're right, spriggans aren't all there, either. If I hadn't had real humans to compare her to, I probably wouldn't have noticed anything wrong with her."

"There isn't anything wrong with me!" the duplicate protested.

"Stand up and let me look at you," Gresh suggested. "Let's see if you really are an exact duplicate of Karanissa."

The two women exchanged glances, then rose and turned to face Gresh, standing side-by-side in the fading daylight.

"Oh," Gresh said. He blinked, rubbed his eyes, and looked again.

The two were identical in appearance in every detail

except for one. The dresses were the same fabric, the same cut, belted identically, with the same knot at the same place; the hair was the same length and luster, with every lock and curl matching; the eyes were identical in color and shape; the teeth matched; the nose and mouth were indistinguishable—except for one thing.

The copy was *smaller* than the original.

She was proportioned exactly like the real Karanissa, but she was about two inches shorter, a shade thinner, and not quite as wide at shoulders, bust, waist, or hips. Her fingers were slightly shorter; her eyes and mouth were slightly smaller. She was the exact image of Karanissa, but somehow shrunken.

Image, he thought. *Mirror* image.

Gresh looked down at the mirror, then back at the two women.

"Oh," he said. "*Oh*."

He felt simultaneously brilliant and foolish—brilliant because he now was certain of exactly how the mirror's magic worked, and foolish because it had taken him so long to guess the truth.

It probably explained how Lugwiler's Haunting Phantasm worked, too.

It explained why spriggans were indestructible while the mirror's magic was working, but not when it wasn't. It explained why none of them had names when they emerged, why they sometimes varied in appearance but were sometimes identical, why they didn't feel entirely real to witches, and why they had no odor. It explained why they emerged at apparently random intervals, and why the mirror had kept working when broken, but multiplied everything by four.

"Oh, what?" Karanissa asked, visibly annoyed.

"They're *images*," Gresh explained. "Mirror images. They aren't really here in the World at all; they're in the mirror." He leaned forward and sniffed at the smaller woman, and as he had expected, smelled nothing at all—no scent of woman whatsoever.

She looked puzzled at his action, but did not shy away, or make any comment.

"Images? What?" the original Karanissa asked. "*What* are images?"

"Spriggans. The ones we see and talk to aren't *real* spriggans; they're just mirror images. The *real* spriggans are in another world somewhere, a world that has a mirror in it that's magically connected to this one. I wonder whether the reason Tobas's spell went wrong in the first place is because he was doing it in that purple void, instead of here in the World. Instead of linking to the world of the Haunting Phantasm, he linked this mirror to the world of spriggans, which is related to the void the same way the phantasm world is related to *this* one."

"But the Haunting Phantasm doesn't keep spewing out pests."

"The worlds are *different*, of course, so the rules are different, and the magic is different. Wizardry is like that." He turned up an empty palm. "Or maybe he just made a mistake; wizardry is like *that*, too."

Karanissa shuddered. "Sometimes I hate wizardry."

The reduced copy—the image, as Gresh now thought of it—looked from one of them to the other, then said, "I don't understand what you're talking about."

"*Spriggan* understand," a squeaky voice said from behind Gresh's right shoulder.

CHAPTER TWENTY-ONE

Gresh turned to look at the spriggan that had crept up behind him. "Then I'm right?" he asked.

The spriggan turned up an empty hand. "Not know," it said. "But *sounds* right."

"So you're just an image of a spriggan that looked in a mirror in another world?"

"Think so, yes."

"That's why the Restorative and the Rectification didn't do anything," Gresh said, as he continued to work out the details in his own mind. "Because the spell *didn't* go *wrong*, it just went *differently*, so there wasn't anything to restore or rectify. There's no intelligence involved, just an enchanted object, so Javan's Geas can't do anything—nobody is *making* our spriggans, they just *happen* whenever a real spriggan looks at the mirror in the other world."

"I'm still not sure I understand," Karanissa said. "How did you figure this out? Why is this copy of *me* here?"

"She's what gave it away," Gresh said. "When I saw she was smaller than you. The reflections in a mirror are smaller than the originals because of perspective—

they're reduced in size, the amount depending on how far from the mirror the original is. She's smaller than you because she's a reflection—or really, a reflection of a reflection. It's that second step that's why she isn't reversed."

Karanissa stared at him in annoyance, while the imitation appeared politely interested. "Gresh, what are you talking about?" the original demanded.

He sighed; it was all so obvious to him now he didn't see why Karanissa hadn't grasped it. "When I used the Spell of Reversal," he said, "the direction of the spell reversed. Instead of creating solid images of creatures from the spriggans' world in *our* World, the magic began creating solid images from *our* World in the *spriggans'* world. Every living thing that looked in *our* mirror during that half-hour or so had a mirror-image copy climb out of the *other* mirror, the mirror in the spriggans' world. I looked in the mirror, you looked in it, that spriggan we tried to toss back in—copies of us all must have climbed out in the spriggans' world. A copy of *you* was still there in the spriggans' world when the reversal wore off, and it looked in the mirror, so a copy of the copy climbed out here." He pointed at the duplicate Karanissa. "That's her—a mirror image of a mirror image. She doesn't have a name or any memory because she really *didn't* exist until the mirror reflected her into being. She and the spriggans have no odor because smells don't reflect." He considered for a moment, then said, "I'm a little surprised that there's no image of *me* appearing. I must have been reflected into the other world, too. Maybe my duplicate—or duplicates, since I looked in the mirror more than once while it was reversed..." He stopped, and looked down at the mirror, but nothing was trying to climb out of it; that was a relief. He had been momentarily concerned that half a dozen copies of Karanissa and himself might appear.

According to his theory, in some alien world where spriggans were apparently the dominant form of life, images of Karanissa and himself *had* climbed out of a mirror. He wondered what was happening to those images, what they were doing, what the *real* spriggans thought of them. Would they be pests, the way the spriggan images were? They were almost certainly indestructible, like spriggans—after all, you can't hurt an image; it isn't really there, it's in the mirror, and only *appears* to be anywhere else. Spriggans were indestructible because a reflection can't be harmed by striking the reflection itself. A reflection is destroyed when the mirror it's in is destroyed. That's why the spriggans thought they would die if the mirror was destroyed. The mirror's enchantment somehow made the reflections seem solid and able to interact with the real world when the original was no longer looking in the mirror, but they were still just images.

When the spell had been suspended but not broken, when the mirror had been in the sphere where wizardry didn't work, that had changed, and the reflected spriggans had somehow had their own independent and vulnerable existence. That was one part of the spell that Gresh didn't entirely understand, but then, wizardry was a chaotic and complex thing. In any case, the magic was working properly now, and the mirror's creations, whether spriggan or human, were all part of the mirror itself, and therefore couldn't be harmed as long as the mirror wasn't harmed.

That would make those reflected people in the other world harder to manage.

The reflections of Karanissa and himself were presumably much *larger* than spriggans, unless there were some weird factor he hadn't thought of involved. Even if they weren't playfully troublesome, like spriggans—and the Karanissa-image standing a few feet away didn't seem to be—they must be a nuisance just because of their size. It seemed that he and Karanissa had inadvertently unleashed a brief plague of giants on that unsuspecting other world.

That mirror in the other world was presumably indoors somewhere—mirrors generally were, and if it had been out in the open, wouldn't they have occasionally had creatures other than spriggans climbing out of it, during these past few years? The rooms and corridors would have been built with spriggans in mind. Real spriggans were presumably somewhat larger than their Ethsharitic images, but not *that* much larger. Those duplicates of Karanissa and himself must have been jammed into spaces far too small for them, much as the spriggans had been when Tobas shut the mirror up in a box.

The spriggans had eventually burst that box. Those reflected Greshes and Karanissas had probably exploded an entire building. The real spriggans were probably pretty upset about that.

The reason only one Karanissa had been reflected back might be that she was still wedged against the mirror somehow; she hadn't yet climbed out of the wreckage and was blocking the others.

That would also explain why no more spriggans had emerged yet.

Assuming, of course, that his theory was right, and he wasn't just building up nonsense. Maybe what had really happened was that throwing all those spells at the mirror had finally changed the nature of the enchantment completely, into something unrelated to spriggans.

"Karanissa," he said. "You said you can sense changes in the spell?"

"Sometimes," she said.

"Is it back to its original form now?"

"As far as I can tell, yes."

That fit with his theory—but he could still be wrong. He didn't think he was, but he had to keep the possibility in mind.

If he was right, he still had to figure out what to do about it. The Wizards' Guild wanted the mirror destroyed, but the spriggans didn't. It appeared that destroying the mirror wasn't as simple as he might have hoped. Breaking it into pieces made matters worse, and dragonfire hadn't harmed it, but at least it wasn't as indestructible as the images it created.

If it were smashed to the point that it ceased to function as a mirror and no longer reflected anything, that would probably do the job—grinding it to dust might to be sufficient, and if they could get it to the wizardry-dead area and grind it to dust *there*, that would almost *certainly* do it. *Getting* it to the dead area was the challenge, with thousands of spriggans determined to prevent it.

Grinding it to dust anywhere *other* than the dead area did not seem like a good idea; there would inevitably be intermediate stages when the spriggans would be multiplied, and he could not ignore the hideous possibility that every single glittering grain might still serve as a functional mirror as far as the spell was concerned.

If they ground it to dust in the dead area, what was to prevent spriggans or other creatures from someday bringing out those still-enchanted specks, *each* of which might function as a mirror? That was a nightmarish possibility. Tracking down a particle of dust and dealing with it would be far more difficult than locating an intact hand-mirror.

And they wouldn't *know* whether the destruction was adequate and permanent; there would be no way to test it in the dead area, or to reverse it there if it somehow made matters worse.

Melting the thing down so that it was no longer a mirror might put an end to the enchantment. Gresh tried to think how else one could destroy a mirror, besides smashing and melting.

Nothing came immediately to mind.

There was the question of whether *this* mirror was really the one they wanted destroyed. If he was right, and it was linked to another mirror in another world, then wouldn't it be better to destroy *that* mirror, so that it could no longer cast reflections into *this* World?

How could he do that? He had no way to transport himself to that other reality, wherever and whatever it might be.

If he *could* somehow get to that other world, he wouldn't even need to destroy the other mirror. If it were merely covered, so that no one could look into it, that would be enough to prevent any more spriggans or imitation Karanissas from appearing.

That wouldn't do anything to the reflected spriggans that already existed, but somehow, Gresh did not find that such a terrible thought. He looked around the gloomy interior of the cave at the dozens of pop-eyes watching him from the various nooks and crannies.

The spriggans weren't really so very bad. Yes, they got into things and made trouble, but they didn't mean any harm. They just wanted to survive—and to have fun. Since they really were just solidified reflections, destroying the mirror might very well destroy them all.

Slaughtering half a million well-intentioned little creatures and wiping them from existence did not appeal to Gresh. As mere reflections the poor little things presumably had no souls—it took a specific sort of enchantment to make a mirror that captured souls, and he did not think Lugwiler's Haunting Phantasm, no matter how altered, would do it. If they were killed, they would be gone utterly, with no chance at any sort of afterlife—there would be no spriggan ghosts, no spriggans in Heaven or the Nethervoid. Spriggans weren't human, but they were bright enough to talk and to have figured out that the mirror was essential to their survival.

He didn't *want* to kill them all, he realized. Send them somewhere else, perhaps, but not kill them.

He *did* want to stop the mirror from generating any more. If he could just cover the mirror in the real spriggans' world, perhaps seal it away in a box...

Sealing away the *receiving* mirror hadn't done any good, of course, but sealing away the *sending* mirror, so that there were no reflections to send, should work.

He could use the Spell of Reversal to send images of himself into the spriggans' world, but judging by the pseudo-Karanissa they would arrive with no memory of who they were. The copy of Karanissa didn't even know whether or not she was a witch. Gresh-images wouldn't remember that the mirror had to be covered up or hidden away.

If there were some way to get a message to the spriggans themselves, surely they would cooperate—the reflected humans must have done a great deal of damage, and they wouldn't want a repetition. He couldn't send a reflected spriggan or human with instructions, since the new arrival would have no memory.

Well, he thought, looking at the imitation Karanissa, he couldn't send *spoken* instructions that way. Karanissa's dress had reflected, though...

"*Hai*," he called. "Can any of you spriggans read?"

No one answered. He looked at the copy of Karanissa. "Can *you* read?" he asked.

"I don't know," she replied. "I think so."

Gresh frowned, then reached into the box of magical powders and pulled out a jar. "Read that label," he said.

The reflection of Karanissa looked at the original, then at the jar. She peered at the label. "It says 'Lirrim's Rectification,'" she told Gresh.

"So you *can* read."

"Yes, I apparently can," she agreed.

That meant it was possible for a reflected image to have the ability to read. Gresh hesitated, however, at the thought of setting another immortal giant loose among the real spriggans just to send them a message.

But then he realized he didn't need to send another; the giants who were already there, however many there were, could undoubtedly read just fine—after all, this copy of Karanissa was a reflection of a reflection, not of the original. If *she* could read, then so could the copies already there.

But could spriggans?

"What's going on in there?" asked a deep rumble. Gresh looked up to see the dragon that had been Tobas of Telven looking down at him. "How much longer are we going to be here? The sun is down, and even if you turn me human again, and we take off right now, it'll probably be dark by the time we reach the keep. Why aren't we *doing*... Who is *that*?"

The final question was spoken in an earth-shaking bellow, as the dragon noticed the presence of a second Karanissa. Spriggans squealed in terror.

"What did you *do*?" the dragon roared. "Where did it come from?"

"We were experimenting with the mirror," Gresh said calmly. "I've figured out how it works and how to make it stop producing spriggans."

As if to contradict his statement, a spriggan popped out of the mirror just then—the first one since he had first cast the Spell of Reversal. That fit his theory well enough; some brave spriggan had presumably finally ventured into the neighborhood of the other mirror. The new arrival looked up at the man, the two women, and the dragon, then shrieked and ran away into the darkness of the cave's depths. Gresh heard other spriggans calling comfortingly to it.

"You have?" the dragon asked suspiciously. "What was that I just saw, then?"

"I said I know *how* to stop them, not that I've done it yet," Gresh said.

"Of course. You did say that. There's something else you haven't done yet—you haven't explained why there are two of my wife there."

"That was an accident," Gresh said. He pointed. "That's Karanissa." His finger moved. "And that's a magical image of her that doesn't have a name yet."

"An image?" The dragon cocked his head and glared at the reflection with one baleful red eye. "Is it solid, or just an illusion?"

"I'm solid enough," the image replied.

"It talks."

"Oh, yes," Gresh said. "In fact, it's indestructible, just like a spriggan. I told you, we found out how the mirror works, and we did it by accidentally creating...well, her."

"It's *permanent*?"

"Very much so, yes."

"Kara, what's going on? What *is* that thing?"

Before the real Karanissa could reply, the copy shouted, "I'm a *person*! Stop calling me 'it' and talking about me as if I weren't here!"

This outburst startled Gresh; until now the reflection had been calm and quiet and cooperative. Like Tobas, he hadn't been thinking of it as entirely human—he had just been more tactful than the dragon. It seemed there was more to it than he had thought, though.

The dragon stared at the image for a moment; she stared angrily back. Gresh and Karanissa waited.

Finally the dragon said, "I'm sorry, whoever you are. I didn't realize you were, well, *real*."

"That's better," the reflection said, crossing her arms over her chest.

The dragon peered at her for a few seconds more, then asked, "But can someone explain to me what's going on? Do we have the mirror? Can we take it with us and get out of here before it gets dark? How much longer do I need to be a dragon? Ali is getting upset."

Gresh thought Alorria had been upset for quite some time now, but was not stupid enough to say so.

"I'm not sure what the situation is myself," Karanissa answered.

"I don't know what's going on at all," the reflection said.

"I *do* know what's going on, but I'm not sure how to explain it," Gresh said. "I know that in, oh, an hour or so I ought to be able to put an end to the production of new spriggans. I don't know *any* safe way to destroy the mirror, though, and I'm not sure there *is* one, or that we should use it if there is."

That was more or less a lie; Gresh was quite sure there were several ways to destroy the mirror. At least one of them was probably safe. There were spells that could do virtually anything, after all. The problem was that he doubted *anyone* knew which ones were safe, and he suspected the Guild might try a few that weren't.

Simply destroying it, given enough magic, couldn't really be that hard. The trick was to not leave any residue at all, and there were definitely spells that could do that, even if Gresh didn't know what they were.

He suspected that Tobas didn't know any of them,

either. After all, Tobas might be a wizard, but Gresh was a wizards' supplier; they were both familiar, at least in theory, with all the common spells. If Gresh couldn't think of a safe way to destroy the mirror, he doubted Tobas could, either.

There were a few methods that *might* work—throwing it through a Transporting Tapestry to a place outside the World, letting a warlock destroy it, stuffing it face-down into a bottomless bag, feeding it to a demon. Gresh was not going to suggest any of those. It was all too likely that there were unforeseen flaws in them all.

"If there's a safe way to destroy it, why shouldn't we use it?" Tobas demanded.

Gresh's real reason was simply that he decided he did not want to wipe out half a million semi-intelligent beings, but he did not think Tobas would accept that immediately—especially not when he was in dragon form. The wizard had already acknowledged that his shape was influencing his thoughts and behavior. Gresh doubted a *real* dragon would hesitate for a second before exterminating the spriggans.

Instead of admitting his unwillingness to play exterminator, Gresh said, "Because it might wipe all the spriggans out of existence, or it might turn them mortal, *or* it might *multiply them infinitely*—remember when we multiplied them by four? Destroying the mirror might do the same thing a hundred times over—or a thousand."

The dragon stared at him for a moment, then said, "That would be bad."

"I think so, yes," Gresh agreed.

"So what are we going to *do*, then, if we can't destroy the mirror safely?"

"Well, what *I* intend to do is ensure that the mirror won't produce any more spriggans. Next, if possible—and I'm not entirely sure about this part—I'll give it to you, with the understanding that you will not attempt to destroy it. I think I can convince the spriggans to allow that. What I contracted to do was to deliver the mirror to you, the Guild's representative, so after that I've done *my* job—*more* than my job, since preventing it from generating new spriggans wasn't anything I'd promised. If you like I'll be happy, as yet another bonus, to try to help you convince the Guild that this is an adequate solution to the spriggan problem. I think that's more than fair."

"But the Guild..." The dragon hesitated.

"Oh, and I'm perfectly willing to leave you in either human or dragon form, if you think one might be more useful in negotiating with Kaligir and his friends."

Tobas snorted sparks. "Don't be ridiculous. You'll turn me human. I can't accept the mirror in this form; I'd probably break it into a dozen pieces and smother you all in spriggans."

"Good point. Well, you can deliver the mirror to the Guild, if you like—with the appropriate warnings—and let *them* worry about it."

"I can, can't I?" The dragon cocked his head thoughtfully.

"Personally, I'd much rather you just sealed it away in a box somewhere and didn't let them meddle with it," Gresh said. "This all assumes that we can actually get it out of this cave, and I'm not entirely certain of that part yet. I do have some ideas."

"How long is this going to take?"

"Putting an end to new spriggans should take maybe an hour, I'd say. Giving you the mirror and leaving here safely could take five minutes or it could take days, if I can do it at all."

"It'll be dark in an hour."

"I know."

"Ali won't like that."

"I know."

"*I* don't like the idea of flying in the dark."

"I don't blame you. And I may not be done until well into the night. I just don't know. If I do have everything settled fairly quickly, I think I can convince the spriggans to go away and let us leave, and I can turn you human again. If we can't fly safely, we'll just take shelter in the cave until morning. You and Alorria are welcome to join the rest of us here, of course."

"You think we'll be here all night?"

"I'm afraid it's likely, yes."

"Ali won't like that. Ali's *parents* won't like that."

"She insisted on coming along; it wasn't *our* idea."

"I don't think that's going to make any difference."

Gresh turned up a palm. "I know it won't—so lie. Tell her I messed up a spell and can't turn you human until the sun rises again, if you like."

"That might do. There's no food, though, and she's a nursing mother."

"I have a few things in my pack—not much, but a little. We should be able to go back at first light, I think."

"I suppose." The dragon looked at the two women. "Will you be all right, Kara?"

"I'm fine," the witch replied.

"And what about you?"

"I don't know," the reflection said. "I've never seen night before."

The dragon stared at her for a moment, then turned back to Gresh. "What are we going to do with her?" he asked.

"I don't know," Gresh said. "I'm not sure we need to do *anything* with her. She's a grown woman, and effectively immortal. Even if she doesn't know anything about the World, she can probably take care of herself. The spriggans have done all right here."

"But she looks like my wife."

"What of it?"

The dragon stared at him for a moment, as Gresh tried to decide whether those huge red eyes actually glowed, or merely caught the waning light.

"Nothing, I suppose," the dragon said at last. "Get started on whatever mysterious thing you're doing, then, and I'll try to keep Ali from getting hysterical." The huge scaly head withdrew from the hole in the cave roof.

"I hope you know what you're doing," Karanissa said.

"I hope so, too," Gresh said, as he looked around in the fading light, trying to spot some suitable spriggans.

"Excuse me," the reflection said.

Gresh turned to her, startled. "Yes?"

"That was a dragon, wasn't it?"

Gresh glanced up at the darkening sky. "That? Yes, that's a dragon. His name is Tobas."

"Are many of your friends dragons? Is that common, talking to dragons?"

Gresh blinked. That was a very sensible question, but this really did not seem like the right time to address it. "I'll explain later," he said. "Right now, though, I have work to do."

"Oh, of course." She stepped back, with a glance at Karanissa.

Gresh considered the reflection for a second. Despite what he had said to Tobas, he supposed they *would* need to do something about her—after all, they were responsible for bringing her into existence.

That could wait, however. Right now, he had the spriggans to deal with.

CHAPTER TWENTY-TWO

It only took a few minutes to collect several half-burned bits of grass and twig from the floor of the cave and to gather a few reasonably cooperative spriggans—one of them freshly emerged from the mirror.

"Now," Gresh told the spriggans, "we are going to try a few things. If they work, then I want to make an offer to you and *all* the spriggans in the World that I think is very fair, and which I very much hope you'll accept."

"Can't speak for *all* spriggans," one of the larger spriggans said.

"Well, we'll see what we can do," Gresh said. "Now, first off, can any of you read?"

The spriggans exchanged glances. "No?" one of them ventured.

"Let's just see," Gresh said. He pulled out a jar and showed them the label. "Karanissa, could you provide a little extra light? It's getting dim in here."

The witch obliged by holding up a glowing hand. Her imitation stared up at this in obvious amazement, then began studying her own hand.

"Now, look at the jar," Gresh said to the spriggans.

"Can any of you tell me what that label says?"

No one replied. Some stared at the jar; some exchanged glances with one another, but none admitted to having any idea what the label said.

Gresh sighed and lowered the jar. "So you can't read. I was afraid of that. Can *any* spriggans read?"

"Don't think so," the big one said.

"Well, we'll just have to hope the human reflections cooperate, or that your originals can figure out pictograms," Gresh said, as he slid the jar back into its place in the box. "Now, I need a volunteer to go first."

"What first?" a brighter-green-than-usual spriggan asked warily.

"I'll show you, as soon as one of you volunteers. It won't hurt." He certainly *hoped* it wouldn't hurt. He didn't see any reason it should.

"Fun?" asked a nondescript spriggan.

Gresh smiled, hoping he looked sincere. "Yes, I think it'll be fun."

"Have fun, then." It stepped forward.

"Thank you!" Gresh picked up one of his improvised charcoals, caught up the spriggan in his other hand, and quickly began drawing on the spriggan's bare belly.

A few of the other spriggans gasped in horror at Gresh's apparent treachery. Some stepped back as the captive shrieked. A couple of them fled, vanishing into the shadows at the far end of the cave.

"Ack! Tickles!" the spriggan in Gresh's hand squealed, as it began squirming.

"Just...hold still for a moment," Gresh said, as he struggled to complete the sketch he was drawing.

The spriggan began giggling uncontrollably and

thrashing its arms and legs and ears wildly, but Gresh refused to be distracted or release his hold until he had completed the job. Finally, though, he set the little creature down on a rock and released it.

It stood there gasping, hands waving, laughter gradually subsiding into panting. Then it smiled broadly up at him. "*Lots* of fun!" it squeaked. "Do it *again*?"

Gresh smiled back. "No, let someone else have a turn—and don't smear the drawing! Don't touch it! Not yet!" He looked around. "Who's next?" he asked.

This time no one hesitated. "Next! Next!" shrieked another spriggan, beating its comrades in the rush to Gresh's knee. Gresh picked it up with one hand while he reached for another bit of charcoal with the other.

As he worked on this second spriggan—who was less ticklish than the first, but still enjoyed the experience—he kept glancing at the first, to make sure the quick charcoal sketch wasn't being ruined. Before starting the third, he set Karanissa and her reflection to guarding the finished ones, making certain they didn't let anything disturb his crude drawings.

Finally, after decorating six spriggans, he felt he had done the best he could. He set the two women to stand guard over them while he pulled out the jar of purple powder. He sprinkled it over the mirror, then told everyone, "Stand back! Don't look in the mirror!"

Both Karanissas stepped back, and the spriggans scampered after them.

"*Esku!*" Gresh shouted.

The powder flared up and was gone.

"Now, the first spriggan," he called. "The first one I drew on—run forward and look in the mirror, just once!"

After a moment of confused hesitation, the creature obeyed.

"Next!" Gresh called.

One by one, he sent all six to look into the mirror; then, satisfied, he carefully laid his pack over the mirror so that no one else could look in it before the Spell of Reversal wore off.

"Tickle again?" a spriggan asked, sidling up to him.

Gresh looked down at the creature. It was smiling up at him, trying to look endearing—and it was succeeding.

Besides, the thing had helped him with his scheme and deserved some reward. "All right," he said. He picked it up and began tickling.

After all, he had nothing more urgent to do. There was no need to draw any more pictures. He had sent his message.

Or at least, he *hoped* he had; success all depended on the assumption that his guess about the mirror's nature was right. If he was wrong about how it worked, he had just wasted a spell and a good bit of time and effort.

If his theory was correct, though, he had just created six spriggan images in the real spriggans' world, each of the first five with a picture drawn on its belly, and the sixth with a message in Ethsharitic runes.

The pictures were each numbered in the upper left corner—not with numerals, but with tally marks from I to IIIII. The drawings, stick figures done in scratchy charcoal, were intended to convey instructions to the inhabitants of that other world.

The first drawing showed two huge scary people threatening a crowd of spriggans; one of the two giants was still in the process of emerging from an oval intended to represent a mirror.

The second showed two spriggans carrying the mirror between them.

The third showed them placing the mirror in an open box.

The fourth showed them closing the box.

The fifth drawing was the most complicated, showing two scenes—at the top two scary giants coming out of a mirror were heavily crossed out with a big black X that had sent the canvas-spriggan into hysterical screams of laughter, while below that four happy, smiling spriggans stood around the safely closed box. He had had trouble with that one; fitting all of it on a single spriggan had been difficult, and he had used his finest bit of charcoal-tipped twig for the job.

Those five were intended to convey his message to illiterate spriggans, but he hoped they wouldn't be needed. The sixth spriggan's belly had a message written on it: "SHUT THE MIRROR IN A SOLID BOX, AND NOTHING ELSE WILL COME OUT OF IT."

That hadn't been easy to fit, either. He had debated whether to write the runes forward or backward and had settled on forward—yes, they would probably be reversed on arrival, but so would the images of Karanissa and himself.

Now, if the message got through, and someone in the other world heeded it, then that should solve the spriggan population problem—if the other mirror was safely sealed away where no true spriggans could look in it, then no spriggan images would emerge in the World.

Assuming, of course, that he had correctly deduced the spell's workings.

The only way to test it was to wait and see. If anything else came out of the mirror, then he would need to try something else.

Even if it all worked perfectly, that only solved half the problem. The other half was that he had promised he would deliver the mirror to Tobas, and right now there were several thousand spriggans who did not want him removing the mirror from this cave. He was fairly certain that there was no magic he could use to force them—if a sixty-foot dragon wasn't enough to chase them away, then he had no idea what would do the job.

But he might not need to use force.

When he had spent several minutes tickling spriggans, reducing half a dozen of them to helpless laughter, he set the last one on the ground and said, "All you spriggans! Every one who can hear me! Come here—I need to talk to you."

Two or three dozen more emerged from the shadows.

"Karanissa," he said. "Would you go tell your husband to let some spriggans through, to talk to me? Perhaps a hundred or so?"

Karanissa frowned at him, then turned up a hand. "As you say," she replied. She clambered out through the hole in the cave wall, out onto the meadow beside the dragon's tail.

He glanced down at his pack, covering the mirror. That seemed secure enough for the moment, but he put a foot on a corner of the pack, just in case. Then he waited.

A moment later a good-sized group of spriggans

came swarming into the cave, and Gresh found himself surrounded by several dozen pop-eyed little creatures, all staring at him in the gathering gloom. None of them seemed inclined to charge him, or to try to grab the mirror—he had half-expected such a maneuver, and had been ready for it.

When the crowd had quieted he looked around. "Oh, good," he said. "You look as if you're ready to listen."

"Yes, yes."

"Listen."

"Spriggans listen."

Gresh nodded. "Here's the situation, then. Under my pack there is the enchanted mirror you all came from, and that protects you from harm. If it's broken into pieces, each of you is multiplied into however many pieces there are, and there may be other connections, as well. Most of you know about that—maybe all of you. You don't want it to be harmed, or to be taken into the places where wizardry doesn't work, and you hid it away in this cave to prevent anything like that from happening. You're all still here, instead of out in the World having fun, because you're guarding the mirror. Am I right?"

"Right!"

"Yes yes yes!"

"That right."

"We got in here anyway, Karanissa and me, and meddled with the mirror, and our dragon kept you from stopping us—but *you* kept us from taking the mirror away by getting between us and our flying carpet, where the dragon couldn't chase you away safely for fear he might harm either the carpet, or the woman and baby sitting on it. So we have something of a stand-off."

"Right!"

"Yes!"

"You're hoping we'll give up and go away eventually—but that isn't going to work. First off, I'm as stubborn as you are. Second, if we *do* give up, that isn't the end of it—the Wizards' Guild sent us to get the mirror, and if we don't bring it back they'll send someone else, and then someone else, until they *do* get the mirror away from you. They have *lots* of magic, and they'll use it. They want the mirror destroyed, and sooner or later they'll find a way to get it."

"No!"

"Bad wizards!"

"No no no no!"

"Yes, that's how it is." Even in the gathering gloom, Gresh could see the concern and dismay on all those inhuman little faces and the puzzled interest on the reflected Karanissa's visage. He also saw the real Karanissa climbing back into the cave; he sensed that she was listening carefully, both with her ears and her witchcraft. "But I've been studying the mirror, trying spells on it, and I think I've figured out how it works. I've decided that *I* don't want it destroyed, either. If I leave it here with you, though, sooner or later the Wizards' Guild is going to find it and destroy it. So what I want to do is give it to the wizards, *but* make sure that instead of destroying it, they lock it away somewhere safe. If I can do that, it won't be destroyed, and you don't need to stay on this mountain to guard it anymore—you can go out in the World and have *fun*, like the other spriggans! What about *that* idea?"

Several spriggans began cheering and applauding, but others were calling protests and questions, obviously not convinced. Gresh held up his hands for silence, and with a little help from Karanissa's witchcraft, silence descended once again over the unruly mob.

"How you do that?" a large spriggan called.

"Not trust you!" said another.

"Of course, of course," Gresh said consolingly. "Why *should* you trust me? I'm just another big nasty human. But here's what I'll do, to prove I'm serious. I have here a box of magic powders that the wizards gave me to help me fetch the mirror. The red powder casts a spell called Javan's Geas—do you know what a geas is?"

"No." Several spriggans shook their heads or otherwise expressed ignorance.

"It's a compulsion. What Javan's Geas does is keep someone from doing something. It can't make someone do something they don't want to—it's not that kind of geas. But it can prevent them from doing something they *do* want to. You understand?"

That elicited a mixed chorus of "yes" and "no" responses.

"*What are you doing?*" Karanissa's voice said inside his head. He glanced at her and saw her frowning. She had not spoken aloud.

"*Bear with me,*" he told her silently.

"If I put a spell on someone with Javan's Geas," he told the spriggans, "and order him not to break the mirror, then he *can't* break the mirror—the spell won't let him. You see?"

"Yes yes!"

"No!"

"Spriggan see!"

"Spriggan not understand."

Gresh sighed.

"What I'm going to do," he said, "is turn the dragon back into a human wizard and give him the mirror. You understand *that* part?"

"Not let you!" one large spriggan squealed.

"What I *want* to do," Gresh corrected himself, "is turn the dragon back into a human wizard and give him the mirror. Is that clear?"

The responses were a mix of affirmatives and mild puzzlement. Gresh pressed on.

"Then, when he *has* the mirror, I'm going to cast Javan's Geas on him three times. The first time I will command him not to ever give the mirror to anyone else, at any price. The *second* time I will command him not to ever try to damage or destroy the mirror. And the *third* time I will command him not to ever take the mirror into any of the places where wizards' magic doesn't work. After *that*, he'll want to keep the mirror safe. He'll take it back to his castle and lock it up safely, where no one can ever harm it—and *you* won't need to stay and guard it anymore; the wizard will guard it *for* you. You see?"

The spriggans considered that for a moment, while Karanissa silently asked him, "*Have you gone completely mad?*"

"*Notice,*" he told her mentally, "*that I never said anything about not allowing* other *wizards* to take *the mirror from him, should they decide it to be necessary.*"

"If you agree to this," Gresh called to the spriggans, "then just say so. I'll work the magic, and we can all go have fun—no more guarding caves!"

"You not hurt mirror?" a spriggan asked hesitantly.

"I swear to you, by my true name and all the gods, that I do not intend to damage the mirror."

"*Wizard* not hurt mirror?"

"I swear to you, by my true name and all the gods, that if you let us take the mirror away, I will enchant the wizard Tobas of Telven with Javan's Geas so that he cannot damage the mirror."

For a moment, then, the cave was utterly silent, as Gresh looked out over the crowd of spriggans and they stared back.

Then one voice somewhere in the back said, "Fun!"

With that a chorus of squeaking and squealing erupted. Gresh could not make out most of what was being said, but after a moment he got the definite impression that he had convinced a majority of his listeners and that they were attempting to persuade the rest.

"*What if* Tobas *doesn't agree to go along with this?*" Karanissa asked silently.

"*I wasn't planning to give him a choice*," Gresh replied.

With that he reached down and pulled two jars out of the battered wooden box, one of bright orange powder and the other of dark red. Then he asked Karanissa, "Is the magic still reversed?"

"Yes."

"Then we'll have to wait a few more minutes." He sat down on a convenient rock, the two jars cradled in his lap.

CHAPTER TWENTY-THREE

While they waited, Gresh thought over the situation.

It seemed to him that they were reaching a satisfactory conclusion to matters. With any luck his message had been received and understood in the world from which spriggans were reflected, and the mirror would be shut away in a box somewhere, ending the supply of spriggans. That removed it as any serious threat to the World. The half-million spriggans already in existence might be a nuisance, but they could be accepted; he did not want to aid in exterminating them. Ending the existence of half a million beings bright enough to talk, answer questions, and do all the other things that spriggans did struck him as a horrible idea, an unnecessary and unfair slaughter—after all, a good many of the spriggans had never bothered anyone, but had stayed here in the mountains guarding the mirror. That was almost noble, in a way.

As long as the mirror produced no more, Gresh considered the problem to be adequately solved.

His actual agreement with the Wizards' Guild had been to deliver the mirror to Tobas, and he had every intention of doing that, so there was no problem *there*—except for the usual one of getting the Guild to live up to its end of the agreement. Tobas would undoubtedly tell them how he had not used any amazing magic or superhuman skills, but had merely backtracked the spriggans with common sense and a little sorcery, and there would also be the issue of not actually ensuring the mirror's destruction, so the Guild might well try to wiggle out of paying him the promised youth spell. He would need to have arguments ready, pointing out that he was more than living up to his end of the bargain, and that the Guild would be well-served to see that he continued in his business as their best supplier of exotic ingredients.

Aside from preparing his arguments, there were still a few other loose ends, as well. He would need to see that the mirror was secure, tucked away somewhere no one untrustworthy would meddle with it, and where the spriggans couldn't easily change their minds and steal it. If possible, he wanted to convince the Guild not to destroy it; that would be simpler if he could offer them a way to deal with troublesome existing spriggans. While he wanted the mirror shut away somewhere, it needed to be stored in such a way that if any more spriggans *did* emerge, the Guild would be alerted, and the matter could be dealt with.

Whoever was in charge of the mirror would want to be very sure that if it *did* produce more spriggans, those newly emerged spriggans could not carry the mirror off somewhere and hide it, starting the whole thing over again.

Besides the various aspects of the mirror and the spriggans and the Wizards' Guild, there was one other loose end. He glanced at her.

The reflection of Karanissa's reflection was sitting on a rock in the dimming twilight, watching the spriggans curiously.

She considered herself a person, but Gresh was not at all sure she was right. Presumably she was just as indestructible as the mirror's other creations, just as bound to the mirror's condition. She did not seem hostile or difficult—in fact, she seemed more passive than the original Karanissa—but simply letting her wander off into the mountains did not seem safe or humane.

Karanissa had said she wasn't whole—perhaps something could be done about that. Gresh looked down at his open pack and the box of magical powders in the top.

Javan's Restorative would not do any good; she had never *been* complete. Lirrim's Rectification, though, might turn her into the fully human creature she was meant to be. She would still look just like Karanissa, but that was not really much of a problem. Gresh had met identical twins who seemed to lead individual lives.

Lirrim's Rectification turned things into what they were *meant* to be, more or less. It was not always clear just what that was, since whatever power guided the spell did not always seem to use human logic, but in this case Gresh could see very few possibilities. It might do nothing, as it had on the mirror itself, but he thought it was more likely that it would turn a solidified image into whatever it was an image of. If so, it would turn the copy of Karanissa into a human being, and it would turn an ordinary spriggan into a *real* spriggan.

If it worked that way, then the Guild could use Lirrim's Rectification on troublesome spriggans. They would become *real* spriggans, which were presumably mortal and could be harmed, imprisoned, or killed. Such a transformation would surely be an adequate threat and appropriate penalty for misbehaving reflections.

It would also mean there would be no need to destroy the mirror, though doing so would probably be far, far easier than casting Lirrim's Rectification half a million times.

Of course, no one knew just what real spriggans were like. They were presumably somewhat larger than their images, but there might be other differences, as well. Gresh was not about to try the Rectification on any spriggans. Let some wizard make the experiment.

Gresh was not going to rush into using the spell on the image of Karanissa, either. For the present he just wanted to get the mirror safely stashed away somewhere such as Dwomor Keep. Once that was done...

"There," Karanissa said. "It's returned to normal."

"Ah, good," Gresh said. He lifted the pack off the mirror and quickly wrapped the glass in soft cloth, then tucked it away in the pack, below the box of powders.

Dozens of spriggans watched him do this; none moved to intervene. Apparently his partisans had convinced the rest.

He hoped his message had gotten through and been acted on—if not, he was going to have spriggans appearing in his backpack, which would be inconvenient, and he would need to find some other way to render the mirror harmless.

"You'll let us go back to Dwomor now?" he asked the spriggans.

"Make promise! Make promise!"

"Yes, of course—but then we can go and take the mirror with us?"

"Take spriggans with you," a large one said as solemnly as an eight-inch pop-eyed creature with a squeaky voice could.

Gresh stopped. "What?"

"Take spriggans!" several voices chorused.

Gresh considered for a moment.

They couldn't mean they wanted to jam all half a million onto the carpet, or even just the thousand or two guarding the cave; even spriggans weren't that stupid.

"You want to have a few spriggans there to make sure we take good care of the mirror?"

"Yes! Yes!"

"How many?" he asked.

"Five?"

"Four?"

"Six?"

"Lots!"

"I'll take four," Gresh announced. "That should be enough."

There was some squeaking and muttering in response to that, but the objections did not seem very serious, so Gresh ignored them and started for the mouth of the cave.

The sun was well down now, the sky darkening. Clambering over the rocks was not particularly enjoyable in the fading light. Gresh had to watch his footing. Once he emerged onto the meadow, though, he looked up and found a pair of huge red eyes staring at him.

"Has anyone ever mentioned to you," Tobas said

conversationally, "that dragons have exceptionally good hearing?"

Gresh blinked. "I can't say I knew that," he replied warily.

"I hadn't known it myself until I became a dragon," Tobas said. "But I've found it's quite true. Remarkably so. I heard *every word* you said to the spriggans."

"Ah," Gresh said, noticing just how large the dragon's fangs were and that he could see a faint smoldering glow coming from somewhere behind those fangs.

"Tobas..." Karanissa began, from behind Gresh.

"*Fortunately*," the dragon said, interrupting her, "I think it's a reasonable agreement. Still, I would appreciate it if in the future you would at least *try* to obtain my consent before casting spells on me."

"I was planning to," Gresh said, trying to hide just how relieved he was. "I just wanted to get the hard part out of the way first, and I was fairly sure it would be easier to talk sense to you than to a horde of spriggans."

"Hmph," said Tobas, producing a faint shower of sparks. Gresh quickly brushed off one that landed on the shoulder of his tunic. "Shall we get on with it, then?"

"Keep the Spell of the Revealed Power handy, in case the spriggans change their minds," Karanissa urged.

Gresh glanced at her, trying to assess whether she was genuinely just trying to offer a helpful suggestion, or if there was some other reason she might want her husband turned into a dragon *again*, or if she was being sarcastic.

He couldn't tell. He liked to think he was fairly good

at figuring women out, after growing up among twelve sisters, but he could read nothing from Karanissa's expression. He decided not to worry about it as he readied the jar of orange powder that would cast Javan's Restorative.

"You might want to tell Ali what's happening," Karanissa suggested.

"She's feeding the baby," Tobas said.

"All the more reason to avoid any big surprises."

"Um," Tobas said. He lifted his head and called, "Ali, Gresh is about to turn me back!"

"Good!" Alorria shouted back. "Your clothes are...well, I did my best."

Gresh grimaced.

The dragon's immense head swung back around and lowered down toward Gresh as he raised a generous pinch of orange powder. He flung it at the dragon and shouted, "*Esku!*"

The transformation was not quite as spectacular in this direction; rather than a golden flash and extensive reshaping, there was merely a flicker of blue, an odd shrinking, and then Tobas was standing in the meadow in human form, naked and blinking.

"*Hai*," he said. "That was odd." His voice was faint and unsteady. He turned his head to one side, then to the other. "It's so *stiff*," he said. "And everything's so dim and warm and quiet."

"What's stiff?" Gresh asked.

"My neck." The wizard stretched, rolling his head from side to side. "That long neck was really rather convenient."

"You'll have to tell us about it sometime," Gresh

said. "But first..." He flung a pinch of dark red powder at Tobas and proclaimed, "Never give anyone the spriggan mirror—*esku*!"

The powder flashed and vanished.

Another pinch followed before Tobas had even finished blinking.

"Never harm the spriggan mirror in any way—*esku*!"

Several nearby spriggans applauded at that.

Tobas raised an arm to shield his eyes as Gresh flung a third dose and announced, "Never take the spriggan mirror to a place where wizardry does not work—*esku*!"

The spriggans applauded more vigorously as Gresh capped the jars of powder and put them away. Tobas stood, looking around at the hundreds of leaping, cheering creatures.

Then Gresh pulled the wrapped mirror from his pack and ceremoniously handed it to Tobas.

"Your mirror, sir," he said. "I expect my fee will be paid at the first opportunity."

Tobas accepted it gingerly. He partially unwrapped it and peered at it in the gloom as he said, "You might have waited until I had my clothes on. And I can hardly see anything in this light!"

Karanissa stepped forward with a hand raised; a dull orange glow illuminated the glass disk in the wizard's hand.

"That looks like it," Tobas agreed, studying the mirror.

"We saw it produce spriggans," Gresh said. "Unless there are *two* of the confounded things, that's it."

Tobas looked up. "But it's not producing any spriggans now?"

"No. And with luck, it never will again. I can explain it to you later, if you like."

"I heard most of it—dragons really *do* have good ears—but I'll want you to do that." He turned. "Ali, are you all right?"

"I'm fine. Can we go home now?"

"Yes," Tobas said happily. "Yes, we can, as soon as I'm dressed." He trotted toward the carpet holding the mirror triumphantly before him, while the spriggans cleared a path for him.

"Come on," Gresh said, following in the naked wizard's wake.

Karanissa hesitated. "Wait a minute," she said. "What about my duplicate?"

Gresh paused, startled, then looked back.

The other Karanissa was still in the cave, watching events with evident incomprehension.

"Come on," Gresh called to her, beckoning. "We'll take you with us."

The reflection hesitated, then followed.

A moment later, when the mirror was safely tucked away in the wizard's leather valise and Tobas was pulling his rather damaged tunic over his head, Gresh and the two Karanissas arrived at the carpet; Alorria stared up at them in shocked horror.

"*Two* of her! Tobas, what's going on? How can there be *two* of Kara?"

"We had a little magical accident," Gresh explained. "Don't worry about her; she's quite harmless—and she's not *really* another Karanissa. She just looks like her. See, she's two inches shorter?"

"But..." Alorria was plainly not happy, but was having trouble finding the words to express her displeasure. She looked down at baby Alris, who had fallen asleep at the breast and was not helping her mother convey her annoyance.

"Ask her, Ali," Karanissa said. "She'll tell you she isn't me."

"I don't know exactly *who* I am," the reflection said. "I was only created a little over an hour ago."

"Are you married to my husband?" Alorria demanded, pointing at Tobas as he struggled to get his left arm into a badly sewn sleeve. Her motion jiggled Alris, who burped without awakening.

"Not that I know of," the image replied, puzzled. "Wasn't he a dragon originally? You were married to a dragon?"

"Only for a little while," Gresh said. "I turned Tobas into a dragon for a few hours, and now he's back to his proper form."

"Oh," the reflection said, sounding unconvinced. "I'm fairly sure I never married a dragon. Or anyone else, for that matter. Isn't there some sort of ceremony when one gets married?"

"It *is* customary," Gresh agreed. "So if we've established that Tobas has not acquired a third wife, could we please get moving? It's already almost dark, and it's a long way to Dwomor Keep."

"But if she isn't really Karanissa, why is she coming with us?" Alorria asked.

"Because stranding her alone in the mountains at night seems rude," Gresh said. "Now, may we please find seats?"

Alorria did not seem entirely satisfied, but she moved to one side and let the others crowd onto the rug.

"Four spriggans!" a spriggan reminded Gresh, as he pushed several of the little creatures clear of the carpet. "You take four!"

"Right," he said. He pointed to four who happened to be nearby. "You, you, you, and you. The rest of you, clear away."

The chosen four squealed with delight and clambered onto Gresh's lap, pushing at one another to make room. One of them yipped, "Fun!"

"We're taking them *with* us?" Alorria protested, staring at the foursome in horror and clutching her sleeping child to her breast.

"Yes," Tobas and Karanissa said in unison, as they took their own seats. Karanissa took a moment to get her reflection settled onto the fabric; then Tobas turned to look at the others. He gave Alorria an embarrassed glance, then whispered to Gresh, "Could you use the Restorative on my clothes? I know it's waste to use high-level magic for such a thing, and Ali did her best, but she hadn't come prepared, and I'm afraid these breeches are chafing horribly."

"If it will get us airborne," Gresh said, fumbling to find the right jar of powder. Karanissa provided a handful of light, and a moment later a faint blue shimmer suddenly settled Tobas's rumpled garments back into their proper shapes.

Gresh was still tucking the box back into his

shoulder-pack when Tobas settled cross-legged on the fabric and gestured. The carpet rose silently and smoothly.

"Can you see well enough to get us safely back to the castle?" Gresh asked, as he looked around at the blackening sky and shadow-filled landscape. Stars were appearing overhead, and he wondered whether the greater moon would be visible that night, and when the lesser would next rise. He could not see either of them at the moment.

Some of the stars didn't seem to be *staying*; apparently clouds were starting to gather, which would not help matters.

"I hope so," Tobas said, turning the carpet to the southwest. "I'm hoping to navigate by the glow from the castle windows."

"They don't close the shutters?" Gresh asked, startled.

"They usually miss a few," Karanissa reassured him. Tobas was too busy peering into the gloom to respond.

"We *could* stay up here on the mountain until morning," Gresh suggested, as he noticed the carpet drifting closer to a sharp-looking tree than he liked. "It might be safer than flying in the dark."

"*No!*" answered Tobas and both his wives. The carpet picked up speed.

"I wish I knew where we're going," the reflection said plaintively, as she looked around in obvious consternation. "It's *windy* up here."

"We're going to Dwomor Keep, assuming we can find it in the dark," Gresh told her. "It's a big old castle, but reasonably comfortable."

"Is it? Why are we going there?"

Gresh tried to explain, with both the human reflection and the four spriggans listening intently and asking questions, and that kept him and the real Karanissa busy for the better part of an hour. By then the sky was overcast, hiding the stars and moons, so that the carpet seemed to be soaring through nothingness. Alorria was dozing, and Alris was still sound asleep.

Gresh leaned forward and whispered to Tobas, "Do you know where we are?"

"No," Tobas admitted. He explained that he no longer had any idea where they were. He was just looking for a light, any light, that he could aim for. Gresh pointed out a faint orange glow far off to their left, but Tobas shook his head.

"That's not it," he said.

"How do you know?" Gresh demanded.

"Because that's the Tower of Flame," Tobas said. "I've seen it before. It's a good thirty leagues away. It would take hours to get there, and there's nothing there we want."

"Oh," Gresh said, staring at the distant glimmer. He had heard of the legendary Tower of Flame all his life, but he had never seen it before.

From this distance it really didn't look like much.

"*There's* a light," the reflection said, pointing ahead

"Where?" both men asked, turning to see.

"There."

She was right; a faint flicker of orange was visible, and Tobas steered the carpet toward it. He did not know what the light was, but it appeared man-made and was not the Tower of Flame. At this point that was good enough.

They wound up as guests for the night at a small farmhouse where the man of the house had been out with a lantern, checking on a soon-to-calve cow.

When they first arrived and asked the startled and drowsy farmer where they were, they were assured that they were only a mile or two from Dwomor Keep. Upon hearing the castle was close Tobas wanted to continue on and try to find it, despite the now-total darkness, but just then the first drops of rain began to fall, and the others unanimously overruled him. They hastily hoisted their luggage, rolled up the carpet, and hurried into the cottage, Gresh almost banging his forehead on the lintel.

After the wife and teenaged sons were awakened, Gresh paid the family of farmers generously for a late supper and the use of several beds, even though the beds were just piles of straw and some rather malodorous blankets crowded into various corners of house and barn.

Unlike the sleeping accommodations, the meal was entirely satisfactory, as the family had just that day butchered a hog and had a good supply of vegetables and beer to accompany the fresh pork. The entire party ate heartily after their long and weary day, then tottered off to bed with as little conversation as possible.

Gresh had slept on worse bedding on occasion, on various buying trips; he awoke feeling fine. Most of the others had no real problems, but Alorria had not done as well as some and was alternately yawning and complaining as the company gathered in the main room of the farmhouse shortly after dawn.

Gresh was mildly surprised to discover that all four spriggans had stayed the night and not wandered off seeking fun, but there they were when he arose, clustered around Tobas and his luggage, ready to continue their adventure. As their hosts fried up a pound or so of bacon for breakfast, Gresh and Tobas studied the spriggans carefully and concluded that these were, in fact, the same four, and there were no others to be seen, either running loose or in Tobas's valise. The mirror had not produced any more during the night. Presumably the mirror in the spriggans' world was safely shut away in a box and would never again spew unwelcome visitors into the World.

Since they had opened the valise to check for spriggans, Tobas lifted out the mirror for inspection. "You really did it," he said, marveling as he turned carefully wrapped glass over in his hands. "You got me the mirror."

"It's my job," Gresh replied gruffly. "You saw it last night."

"But it seems more real by daylight. Before I'd only just been turned back to my natural form and was surrounded by spriggans. It was hard to be sure just *what* was real under those circumstances!"

Gresh could not argue with that.

An hour later the ten of them—Gresh, Tobas, Alorria, Alris, Karanissa, the reflected Karanissa, and the four spriggans—spilled off the carpet onto the platform outside the tower window at Dwomor Keep.

CHAPTER TWENTY-FOUR

Gresh decided to spend a day or two in Dwomor before heading back to Ethshar of the Rocks to collect his fee; after all, once he was paid he would have all the time in the World. Besides, he had spent more than enough hours crowded onto the flying carpet, and a brief stay would allow him and Tobas to tidy up loose ends, such as making certain no more spriggans were emerging.

That was easy enough to ascertain, since the mirror was wrapped in cloth—so long as the wrappings stayed in place, no spriggans had appeared, since any new arrival would have had to loosen the bindings to fully materialize. They had been too tired to fully appreciate that at the farmhouse, but now it seemed sufficient evidence.

The mirror was carefully placed in Tobas's tower workshop, where the four spriggans were set to watch over it with strict orders not to touch it, or to meddle with anything else. Gresh had some doubts about ordering them not to meddle and considered using Javan's Geas on them, but eventually decided that if Tobas wanted to risk it, that was his problem, and Gresh wasn't going to waste a bunch of valuable magic safeguarding anything. Especially since he still didn't know whether or not Javan's Geas would work on spriggans.

As for the enchanted powders themselves, Gresh had tucked the pack in a corner when they first came in from the flying carpet's landing platform. He saw no need to move them; none of the residents of Dwomor Keep were going to be foolish enough to steal from the wizard's apartments.

Figuring out what to do about the false Karanissa was a little more difficult. By general consent of everyone involved except the image herself—and even she didn't seriously object—she had been locked away in one of the four small bedrooms in the wizard's tower, out of sight of the castle's other inhabitants but with an adequate supply of food and water, until such time as the others had decided how she should be handled.

Karanissa thought she was harmless and should be released; Alorria thought she was a monster that should be destroyed; and the two men did not yet have fixed opinions.

Over breakfast and a subsequent glass of wine, Gresh explained to Tobas exactly what had happened in the cave and detailed his theories of just how the mirror's magic worked, which included a description of the reflection's initial appearance. That did not bring them to any quick agreement on what should be done with her.

Alorria did not stay around to listen to the debate; she had stated her position and had more urgent concerns, such as showing Alris off to the king and queen again. Karanissa stayed, but had little to say; for the most part she left the discussion to the two men.

"She's just an image. We should use Javan's Restorative to make her disappear," Tobas said.

"Would it do that?" Karanissa asked.

"I think it would," Tobas said. "The Restorative turns things into what they were before they were enchanted or broken or transformed, and she wasn't *anything* before she was enchanted."

"If that would work on her, it would work on spriggans," Gresh said thoughtfully. "That might be a way of disposing of them. An expensive one, though. I wonder if it would work?"

"It ought to."

"Then it could be used to make *any* magical creation vanish?"

Tobas hesitated. Gresh suspected he was reconsidering his position. Javan's Restorative was a powerful countercharm, but surely it wasn't *that* powerful!

"I think we should try it on her," Tobas finally said.

"Why?" Gresh demanded. "She hasn't done anything to harm anyone. How sure are you it will make her disappear, anyway?"

"I'm not sure at all," Tobas admitted. "I'm not comfortable having her around, though—she's an imitation of my *wife*, after all!"

Gresh glanced at Karanissa. "One wife, yes," he said. "Which is probably why the other wants her destroyed. She feels outnumbered. And *you* probably find it unsettling, having a copy of one of your wives. If she *weren't* a second Karanissa, but the image of a stranger, would you still want her destroyed?"

"Probably not," Tobas admitted. He frowned thoughtfully. "All right, you've made your point."

Gresh was not at all sure he *had* adequately conveyed his feelings on the subject, partly because he was not entirely certain himself what they were. He had originally been considering finding a way to erase the reflection himself, but the more he thought about it, the more repulsive the idea seemed. He was beginning to suspect it would amount to murder; the reflection certainly considered herself a person, and anyone seeing her would think she was human.

He had already decided that killing half a million spriggans would be wrong; how would killing this one pseudo-human be any different? These magical reflections might not be entirely real, might not be "complete" in some way, but they certainly seemed to have feelings and desires and intelligence—they could speak and act and showed every other sign of being rational beings. Calling it "erasing" or "unmaking" didn't change the fact that it was killing, ending a life.

But turning a reflection loose in the World didn't seem like the best idea, either. Where would she go? What would she do? If she was like the spriggans she didn't really *need* to eat. She couldn't starve to death, but she would get painfully hungry if she didn't get regular meals.

Gresh could easily imagine her winding up as one of the miserable, homeless residents in Soldiers' Field, or as a slave, or as one of the whores in Wargate; he didn't like any of those ideas.

Of course, she was an attractive woman; she might be fortunate enough to find a trustworthy protector. And she might be a witch; no one had yet determined that definitively, one way or the other.

Using Lirrim's Rectification to turn her human might be a good idea—assuming it would work—because at least then she would be no more tempting to abusers than any other homeless and beautiful orphan. Gresh had some unpleasantly lurid thoughts about what might happen if a slaver or a Wargate pimp found out that an indestructible woman was available and unguarded; it would be better to remove that possibility. The Rectification might fill in some of the holes in her memory—assuming they *were* holes. She had been created with a complete working knowledge of the Ethsharitic language and an understanding of such concepts as marriage and dragons, but had not known whether she was a witch, whether she was married, or any number of other things. If she had arrived completely ignorant, like a baby, needing to learn to walk and talk, that would have made sense. If she had started out believing herself to be Karanissa, with all Karanissa's memories, Gresh would have understood. This halfway state, where she had most or all of Karanissa's general knowledge but none of her personal and specific knowledge, was confusing. Lirrim's Rectification might change that.

Or there might be other spells...

"We should ask her," he said, abruptly arriving at a conclusion he now thought he should have reached long ago.

"Ask her if she wants us to erase her?"

"No—or rather, not just that. We should offer her all the options we can think of and ask which she wants."

"Without promising she'll get her first choice," Tobas said. "If she says she wants to marry me, the answer's no—I can barely handle *two* wives, and three is out of the question." He grimaced. "For one thing, Alorria would kill me. Or her, or both of us." He glanced at Karanissa. "I doubt Kara would be pleased, either."

"You know, in her present condition, she *can't* be killed while you're protecting the mirror."

"Ali would find a way."

"Or *I* would," Karanissa interjected.

"One of you just might," Gresh agreed. "So the marriage option is unavailable—but really, we ought to let *her* choose what she wants."

Tobas sighed. "I suppose. Or perhaps we could just deliver her to one of the Guildmasters, and let the Guild decide?"

"No," Gresh said. "She wasn't part of our agreement, and I'm not giving her to Kaligir."

"I was also thinking of Telurinon."

"Nor him."

Tobas gave in. "All right, then—we'll ask her what she wants."

Gresh finished his wine, set the glass on the table, and rose to his feet. "Now?"

"I don't see any reason to wait." Tobas stood, as well, and the two men headed for the stairs. Karanissa gulped the last of her wine, then followed.

In the tower apartment they made their way up the stairs and unlocked the door to the little-used bedroom where the reflection had been confined. They found her seated on the edge of the bed, staring intently at a tapestry she had taken off the wall and now held stretched across her lap.

She looked up at their entry.

"What are you doing with that tapestry?" Tobas asked, puzzled.

"Seeing how it's made," the image replied. "Studying the weave."

Gresh suspected that further inquiry about her activities would be a waste of time, and before Tobas could say anything more he said, "We've come to ask you a few things. Important things."

"I'm not sure I *know* anything important," the reflection replied.

"Actually, we came to ask what you want, not what you know," Tobas told her.

"Oh?" She lowered the tapestry.

"We've been discussing what we should do with you," Gresh explained. "We finally decided that it wasn't really up to us—*you* should decide."

"But you know so much more about the World than I do!"

"But it's *your* life we're discussing."

"Well, *that's* true. So what is it you want me to decide?"

Tobas and Gresh exchanged glances; then Gresh said, "I know you consider yourself a person, but you aren't exactly a human being; you're a magical reflection of one. You were created fully grown, instead of being born and growing up; you have no name; and the witch here says that there are parts missing—it may be that you don't have a soul, she isn't quite sure. If the spriggans are right, you're bound to the mirror that made you in several ways and immune to physical harm as long as the spell is active. You aren't entirely *real*; you're a magically solidified image that *thinks* it's real."

"I am? Is *that* what I am?" She looked fascinated, but not particularly troubled by this revelation.

"We're fairly certain," Tobas said. "But it's possible our theories are wrong."

"As a magical creation of this sort," Gresh said, pressing on, "you may have some difficulties in dealing with human society. In any case, you definitely aren't going to be permitted to stay here in Dwomor Keep; your resemblance to the woman you're reflected from, Karanissa of the Mountains, would make your presence inconvenient and upsetting to several people here."

"Where else *is* there?" the image asked.

"Hundreds of places, from uninhabited wilderness to huge cities," Gresh told her. "You can go wherever you please, so long as it isn't here."

"Then why did you *bring* me here?"

"Because *we* were coming here, and we hadn't yet decided what to do with you. It seemed cruel to leave you alone in the mountains."

"But now you want to send me away?"

"Eventually, yes. But there are a few other matters to resolve first."

"Go on."

"We have some magic powders—they're downstairs, where I left them. We *think* one of them would undo the spell that created you; if you don't care what happens to you, it would be simplest for *us* if we just *un*created you. If we're right about what the spell would do, you'd just cease to exist; there'd be no pain or discomfort of any kind. You'd just be gone. We aren't *sure* it would work, but we think so. Would you...would that be acceptable to you?"

She stared at him. "I don't *think* so," she said. "I'm not suicidal." She frowned. "I thought you were having trouble with an excess of spriggans. Aren't they the same sort of reflection I am? If you have a spell like that, why haven't you uncreated *them*?"

"Two reasons," Gresh said. "First, it's ordinarily a very expensive spell. I only have a supply of the powder form because the Wizards' Guild wanted me to be well equipped for dealing with the magic mirror. Second, up until we actually found the mirror, and saw you come out of it, we had no idea how it worked and didn't think the spell would do anything to spriggans. We didn't *know* they weren't entirely real."

"Oh. I suppose that makes sense. But I still don't want anything to do with it."

Gresh sighed, though he wasn't surprised. "All right, then. We have another spell that transforms things into what they were *meant* to be. We think—again, we aren't absolutely certain—that it would turn you into a real human being. After that you would be free to go wherever you chose, other than this castle, and do what you please."

"Interesting. Do you have any other spells? Perhaps the one that turned him from a dragon to a man?" She gestured at Tobas.

"That's the one that would unmake you," Gresh said. "He was a man *first*."

"Then what about the spell that turned him *into* a dragon?"

"I don't think that would do *anything* to you; it might be interesting to try it and see, though."

"Would it turn me into a dragon?"

"No. I think I can say that much."

"Oh. Are there any others, then?"

Gresh and Tobas looked at one another, then back at the reflection.

"Not really, no," Tobas replied. "That's the lot."

"So my choices are to remain as I am, to cease to exist, or to turn human?"

"Yes. We think."

"If I turned human and didn't like it, could you change me back?"

Tobas and Gresh exchanged glances again. "The Spell of Reversal?" Gresh asked.

"It *ought* to work," Tobas agreed.

Gresh turned back to the reflection. "You'd have about half an hour to decide; after that, I don't think we could turn you back."

"Javan's Restorative might work, too," Tobas suggested.

Gresh frowned. "Maybe," he admitted.

"Well," the reflection said, "if I have a choice of two possible modes of existence, it seems to me that I ought to try them both before deciding which I want."

Gresh nodded. "Very sensible," he said. "Then you want us to turn you human? Or rather, try the spell that we think will turn you human?"

"You aren't *sure*?"

"I'm afraid not. But we both really do *think* it will work."

"Then I'll try it."

Gresh smiled reassuringly. "I'll go fetch the powder." He turned and left the room, bound for the stairs.

Just outside the bedroom door he almost tripped over a spriggan, but caught himself against the wall of the passage. "What are *you* doing here?" he demanded.

"Heard voices," the spriggan said. "Came to see whether voices were bad mirror thieves trying to sneak up on us."

"There aren't any mirror thieves around here," Gresh said, annoyed. "That's why we brought it here, so it would be safe."

"Yes, yes. Sorry sorry." The spriggan scampered back toward the stairs. Gresh watched it bound up a few steps, then pause to catch its breath. Gresh decided not to waste any more time on it. He marched down the passage and down the stairs to the sitting room, then crossed to the corner where he had left his pack.

He considered hauling the whole thing upstairs, but he was afraid that if he did, Tobas and Karanissa might get caught up in the excitement and start throwing spells around, wasting the powders. He had gotten a little carried away himself out on the mountain. It was the first time he'd ever had so much magic right there in his own hands, and he'd been perhaps a bit careless with his powders, but he was calmed down now and didn't see any need to put needless temptation in anyone's path.

He thought he understood now why wizards didn't ordinarily keep many spells around in powder form. It was too easy to use them. The temptation to just fling a powder and say a word was much stronger than Gresh had imagined. Working a spell from scratch every time meant that a wizard had to think about what he was doing, instead of acting on impulse. Gresh knew he had been lucky that none of his enchantments had ended in disaster, and he did not want to push his luck too far. He intended to take the remaining powders and potions back to Ethshar with him and, if the Guild did not reclaim them, sell them for a healthy price. He did not care to let anyone else experiment with them, trying them all out to see what they might do to the reflected Karanissa, or to spriggans.

So he did not bring the whole box. Instead he opened the pack, pulled out the box, and found the jar of white powder, still mostly full—he had used only one pinch from this one so far, less than any of the others. He pulled it out, pushed the pack back in the corner with his foot, and then headed back up to the bedroom. He heard the spriggans squeaking somewhere above him as he climbed the stairs, but ignored them as he marched back up the passage.

He did wonder idly how much damage they were doing to Tobas's laboratory, but did not let it concern him.

Tobas and the two Karanissas were waiting in the bedroom; the two women were seated side-by-side on the edge of the bed, the wizard standing before them. For a moment Gresh was uncertain which woman was which, but then he got close enough to see the height difference.

"Are you ready?" he asked, opening the jar. "You'll have about half an hour to decide which sort of existence you prefer. If you wait any longer than that the Spell of Reversal won't change you back, and we don't know whether Javan's Restorative will work."

"It ought to," Tobas said.

"I'm ready," the image said. The original Karanissa moved down the bed, farther away from her duplicate, to make room.

Gresh flung a generous pinch of white powder at the smaller Karanissa and proclaimed, "*Esku!*!"

There was a blinding silver flash; Gresh blinked, trying to clear his vision. When he did he saw two identical Karanissas sitting on the bed—truly identical; the size difference had vanished.

So had all differences between their facial expressions and even their position. Both were sitting bolt upright, staring at their own hands. Both spoke in perfect unison, saying, "By all the gods, Gresh—what have you *done*?"

CHAPTER TWENTY-FIVE

"I don't understand," Gresh said, looking from one woman to the other. "What happened?"

Both of them looked at him, which was oddly reassuring, because at least it meant they were no longer in exactly the same position. "Don't you see?" they said, still speaking in unison. "It turned the reflection into what it was meant to be—but it wasn't just meant to be human, it was meant to be *me*!"

"What?"

"We're both *me*!" they insisted. "I have two bodies, but they're both *me*! I can still remember everything from the moment I emerged from the mirror—we can *both* remember it—but we're both Karanissa!"

"Gresh, I think we better undo this," Tobas said.

The two women turned to look at one another, moving in perfect synchronization. "Oh, how strange!" they said, as they stared at one another. "Yes, I think we *should* reverse this!"

Gresh stared, fascinated. "But this is...Shouldn't we...What is it *like*?"

Karanissa—both of her—looked at him. "It's very hard to describe," they said. "When I used witchcraft to hear people's thoughts it was...Well, no, it wasn't *anything* like this, really, because there isn't anyone else, there's just me, but I'm in two places at once."

"Do you see things double, then?"

"No, no—I just see *more.*"

"Gresh, I don't think this is the time..." Tobas began.

Gresh turned. "It's *exactly* the time," he said. "We have half an hour before we need to reverse the spell, so why not try to learn more about it while we can?"

"Because we might lose track of time. Could you at least go get the powder for the Spell of Reversal and keep it ready?"

"I think that would be a good idea," the Karanissas said, turning to look at one another again. "I *really* don't think I want to stay like this indefinitely."

Reluctantly, Gresh acknowledged the wisdom of this. "I'll go get it, then—and meanwhile, Karanissa, could you please take note of anything particularly interesting?"

As the two women stared at each other they made an odd noise that Gresh took for agreement. He turned and headed for the stairs.

Something green peeked up over the steps, then squeaked and scampered down. That spriggan was clearly bored with watching the mirror do nothing, Gresh thought, as he reached the head of the staircase and started down.

At the foot of the stairs he turned toward the corner, then froze in horror.

He had shoved his pack into the corner by the door to the platform, but he had not bothered to fasten it.

Now he found himself looking at all four spriggans, each of them holding one of the jars of magical powder—two in the sitting room, one on the sill of the open door to the platform, one on the platform itself.

Even as he stared, readying an angry shout, he mentally cursed his own stupidity. He *knew* spriggans were attracted to magic; he *knew* the spriggans were getting bored guarding the mirror; he *knew* they had been told not to touch anything in the workshop. No one had said anything about not touching the contents of the sitting room.

"*Put those down!*" he bellowed.

All four spriggans immediately dropped their jars.

The two jars in the sitting room landed with a slight thump, undamaged.

The one on the doorsill flew up out of the startled spriggan's hands, came down hard on the stone, and cracked.

The one on the platform was not so much dropped as flung sideways; it landed rolling, and both Gresh and the spriggan watched in helpless dismay as it kept on rolling, right off the edge of the platform. As the label and clear glass alternated Gresh could see dark powder inside, but he could not be completely certain whether it was blue, purple, or dark red.

A few seconds later he heard the distant sound of breaking glass as it shattered on stonework somewhere far below.

"Oops," the spriggan on the platform said. It looked up at Gresh with an embarrassed grin.

Gresh stared at it, wanting to scream at it, but unable to think of any words that were even remotely appropriate. Then he marched forward to collect the jars before any more damage could be done and to see which spells he still had.

The two unharmed jars held Javan's Restorative and the Spell of the Revealed Power.

The cracked jar contained the dark red powder for Javan's Geas.

The jar of purple powder that could produce the Spell of Reversal was gone.

"Oh, blood, pain, and death!" Gresh cursed, as he hurried out on the platform and looked down, hoping that perhaps part of the jar had survived, intact enough to hold a dose of the powder. Perhaps if he used the potion for the Spell of Retarded Time he could climb down and collect enough of the powder and still get back before the half-hour was up...

"Jar broken," the spriggan said sadly, as it stood beside Gresh and looked over the edge with him.

"Could fix it?" another spriggan said, coming up behind them.

"Fix how?" the first spriggan asked.

"With magic powder?"

That was a possibility Gresh had not yet considered; he started to say something, but before he could, the spriggan who had dropped the jar on the platform leaned over the edge and shouted, "*Esku!*" at the top of its squeaky little voice.

There was a red-gold flash, and a suddenly intact jar came sailing up at them; Gresh stepped back, startled, and narrowly missed being hit by it as it flung itself onto the platform and rolled to a stop at the spot where it had been dropped.

Gresh stared at it, astonished. He had not thought of that, and the spriggans had. They had recognized the powder by color and had known how to use it from watching him back in the cave. Furthermore, they had actually *done* it, and it had *worked*! He had not known spriggans could actually work that sort of magic—but then, it was the powder that really did it; all anyone else had to provide, once the powder was flung, was the trigger word.

"Jar fixed!" the spriggan said happily, pointing.

"Yes, it is," Gresh agreed, as a horrible suspicion struck him. He reached down and picked up the jar and held it up to the light.

It was empty.

Words once again failed him; he bit down so hard he thought his teeth might crack. That spell had retrieved the jar, but it had *used up* all the powder! It had all been flung, and it had all been consumed in one flash—enough powder to work the tenth-order Spell of Reversal eight, or nine, or perhaps even ten more times, all of it gone to repair a cheap glass jar.

He stepped quickly in off the platform, before the spriggans could find a way to break any of the *other* jars.

"Don't touch these!" he ordered emphatically, pointing at the three he held. "Ever!"

Then he tucked them all back into the box in his pack, hoping the cracked one wouldn't shatter, put the lid on, pulled the drawstring tight, lifted the pack onto his shoulder, and hurried upstairs, hoping that Tobas was right about Javan's Restorative being sufficient.

He was almost at the top when he heard the sitting

room door open and Alorria's voice call, "Tobas? Are you in here?"

"We're up here," he called over his shoulder as he turned the corner into the short corridor. He did not wait for Alorria to respond, but hurried to the bedroom.

Tobas and the two Karanissas were just as he had left them, save that all three looked worried.

"What was the shouting about?" Tobas asked.

"The spriggans spilled the powder for the Spell of Reversal," Gresh explained. "We'll have to use Javan's Restorative. And Alorria's here." He set the pack on a bedside table and fumbled with the drawstring, which he now found he had pulled so tight it would not loosen.

"Didn't you say you didn't think that would work?" both Karanissas said.

"Tobas is the wizard here, and *he* thought it would—ow!—work," Gresh said, as he struggled with the pack.

"It ought to," Tobas said nervously.

"But what if it *doesn't*?"

"Well, it can't *hurt* you," Tobas said. "It restores anyone or anything to its healthy normal state."

The Karanissas looked at one another. "But what's normal for a magical image?" they asked.

"What's going on in here?" Alorria asked from the doorway, just as Gresh finally managed to unjam the cord and open the pack.

"We're just trying a few things," Gresh said, as he carefully pulled out the jar of orange powder.

"Might she entirely cease to exist?" the Karanissas asked.

Alorria stared at the two women on the bed. "What did you *do*?" she demanded. "I can't tell them apart, and they're both talking at once!"

"It's possible," Tobas told Karanissa.

"Tobas!" Alorria shouted. "I asked you a question!"

"A spell went wrong," Gresh said, as he closed the pack and set it on the floor. "We're trying to fix it, but the spriggans have been making it difficult."

"What *kind* of a spell?"

"Fifth-order," Gresh said unhelpfully, as he opened the jar.

"I'm not sure this is a good idea," the Karanissas said, eyeing Gresh as he approached, orange powder in the palm of his hand.

"I'm not, either," Tobas said. "Gresh, I know what I said earlier, but I've changed my mind."

"We have to do *something*," Gresh said. "What kind of a life can she have like that?"

"How can you tell which one is which?" Alorria asked.

Gresh had been about to fling the powder at the Karanissa on the right, on the assumption that she was the rectified reflection and the spell would restore her to either her former state as a solidified image, or to nonexistence, but he suddenly stopped.

"She might just disappear," Tobas said. "That would be murder."

"She might," Gresh agreed, staring at the right-hand Karanissa.

"She isn't real!" Alorria protested.

"This one *is* the copy, isn't it?" Gresh asked, gesturing at the right-hand woman.

"Yes, it is," Tobas said. "They didn't switch while you were away. But really, Gresh, shouldn't we..."

He stopped as Gresh flung the powder—on the *left-hand* Karanissa.

"It can't hurt *her*," he explained. "*Esku!*"

There was a golden flash.

For a moment, no one moved; then the two Karanissas turned to look at one another, but Gresh could see that it wasn't the same inhumanly synchronized motion they had displayed before. Both were still full-sized, however; the right-hand one had not been shrunk back to her original size.

"That was..." they both began—but their voices were not perfectly matched anymore. They both fell silent; then the right-hand one pointed at the other.

"I think it worked," the left-hand Karanissa said.

"I'm still rectified, still human," the right-hand one said. "But we're separate."

"I'm just me again," the left-hand one—the original—said. "I don't have her memories anymore."

"But I still have hers," the right-hand one said. She frowned. "I suppose that means she's Karanissa and I'm...someone else, a blend of the two."

"Fine," Alorria said. "Then you can go back to Ethshar with Gresh. *One* witch-wife around here is plenty!"

"But I remember—I was married to you," the right-hand witch said to Tobas. "I'm your wife."

"Oh, no," Tobas said. "No, you aren't. Two wives are plenty. I'm married to her, and her, and nobody else." He pointed first at Karanissa, then at Alorria.

The nameless woman looked at Karanissa for a

moment, and Gresh was certain that even if they were no longer the same person in two bodies, they were still both witches capable of communicating silently. He wondered what was passing between them.

"You need a name," he said, before Tobas or Alorria could say anything more. "Any suggestions?"

"You could call yourself Assinarak," Alorria suggested. "That's the mirror image of 'Karanissa.'"

"That's not a name!" Tobas protested.

Gresh caught himself just before he said "Not to mention stupid and ugly" aloud; there was no need to antagonize the king's daughter.

"And I'm *not* just a mirror image any more," the nameless woman protested. "I intend to be my own woman, not just a copy. No, I'll call myself Esmera."

"I like that," Karanissa said. "But then, I would."

Gresh smiled. He recognized the roots of the name—it was a sort of pun and could mean either "from glass" or "a marvel" in Old Ethsharitic, which seemed very appropriate. "Esmera it is, then. It's a pleasure to meet you. I take it you're satisfied with your current condition and don't want Tobas and I to attempt any further magic?"

"Yes, this is fine—there's much more *to* me now than there was before. I can feel what Kara meant about my not being whole before."

Karanissa smiled at that, and in fact the whole party was now smiling happily at one another—except Alorria.

"Now that you have a name, Esmera, could you please do something so that I can tell you apart from my husband's other wife?" she demanded. "We'll need to find you a place to sleep tonight—I'll talk to the chamberlain. And of course, you *will* go to Ethshar with Gresh, won't you? It would be *much* too confusing having you around here. I don't think my parents would like it."

Esmera glanced at Tobas, then at Karanissa, then at Gresh. She turned up an empty palm. "All right," she said. "I could put my hair up, I suppose."

"That would do nicely," Alorria acknowledged.

Esmera started to say something to Karanissa, but before she could say a word Karanissa said, "You can use my things, of course—you know where the combs and ribbons are."

"Thank you." Esmera rose, said, "Excuse me, Ali," to Alorria, then slipped past her and out the door.

"*You* call me *Alorria*!" Alorria called after her. Then she turned and started toward the door, clearly intending to pursue Esmera.

"Ali," Tobas asked. "Where's Alris?"

Alorria paused. "With my parents and Peren and Tinira," she said. Her anger vanished, and she looked down at her hands, looking suddenly shyer and more appealing than Gresh had ever seen her. "I was hoping we might have a little time together, just the two of us. It's been...well, a while. There's the baby, and we were traveling, and everything. I let you and Kara have the tapestry castle to yourselves in Ethshar of the Sands, and I wanted a turn, but you were all here casting spells..."

"Oh." Tobas blushed. He glanced at Gresh and Karanissa.

"I'll go see if I can help Esmera with her hair," Karanissa said.

"Ali, I need to talk to Gresh for just a moment, but if you could wait for me, I'll be right there."

Alorria watched Karanissa leave the room, then looked back at Gresh and Tobas. "Don't be long," she said. Then she, too departed, leaving the two men in the room.

For a moment neither spoke. Then Tobas said, "You and I are leaving for Ethshar first thing in the morning, and we're taking what's-her-name, Esmera, with us, and *not* my wives, and you are going to be sure to never leave Esmera and me alone together for an instant and be ready to swear to that if Ali ever asks. Having the three of them in one place is *much* too complicated."

Gresh understood perfectly, but could not resist asking, "What do you expect Esmera to do with herself in Ethshar?"

"Anything she pleases. She's a grown woman, a witch, with four hundred years of memories, even if they aren't really *her* memories. She can take care of herself."

"I think it would be fair to provide her with a small sum of money—traveling money."

"That seems reasonable. If you insist, I'll do that, but you could equally well give it to her from that down-payment you got and charge it to the Guild as an expense."

"So I could; I'll do that."

"Thank you. We don't have a great deal of cash on hand."

"Will you be bringing the mirror with you?" Gresh asked.

Tobas hesitated, then said, "No, I don't think I will.

Either Telurinon or Kaligir would probably want me to give it to him, and thanks to your spell, I *can't.* Better I leave it here, so that the issue won't come up right away, and we'll have time to explain the situation."

Gresh nodded. "A wise choice, and one I was going to suggest. You do realize, though, that the geas won't do anything to stop anyone from *taking* the mirror from you? You're only forbidden to *give* it. You aren't required to keep it, or retrieve it if it's lost."

"Yes, I know—but it really is my mirror, and I think I want to hold on to it, at least until I get my new tapestry."

"Good for you. If I might make a suggestion, though, perhaps you might tell them, with the Spell of Invaded Dreams or something of that sort, that you're coming and that you aren't bringing the mirror? You'll want to make absolutely sure of its safety here, too."

"That's a good point," Tobas conceded. "I'll send a message tonight, and I'll put Karanissa in charge of the mirror."

"You could even ask the king to post guards, or at the very least to watch out for spriggans in the vicinity."

"I'll consider that."

Gresh realized he was nearing the end of Tobas's willingness to listen to advice. "We'll meet here first thing in the morning, then?" he asked.

"First thing. I'll pack and see to the rest of it this evening, and ready the carpet. Now, if you don't mind..."

"Your wife is waiting. Go."

Tobas went.

CHAPTER TWENTY-SIX

Gresh arrived at the tower door while the sky was still gray. The dawn was not yet broken. He knocked gently; no one answered. Presumably they were all still asleep. While Tobas had said "first thing," Gresh knew he had probably not expected anyone to take it quite so literally. Gresh had kept a book at the top of his bottomless bag for such an eventuality; he lit the lamp above the stair, settled himself on the staircase, and began reading.

He had not yet finished the second page when Esmera appeared below him, at the curve of the stair; she still wore the same red dress, and it occurred to him that she probably had no other clothes—Karanissa had provided her with combs and hairpins, but so far as he knew, nothing more than that. She certainly had no luggage with her beyond a small purse on her belt.

Her hair was still up, as she had arranged it the night before—tied into a long braid and coiled on the back of her head. He did not think it an especially flattering style, but it did distinguish her from Karanissa, and apparently it was easy to maintain—it either hadn't come undone overnight, or she had been able to restore it unaided. He wondered which it was—wouldn't it have been uncomfortable to sleep on it like that? Perhaps if her bed had been soft enough that wasn't an issue; he wondered what accommodations the chamberlain had been able to provide. Gresh had not accompanied her while those arrangements were made. He had been busy double-checking on the spriggans and the magic mirror, using up the remaining supply of Javan's Geas to order the spriggans never to move the mirror, and re-packing his bottomless bag, and making sure that the packet of Lord Peren's hair was secure.

He hoped that Javan's Geas *worked* on spriggans; he was not at all sure of it. He had tried it anyway, but there was no obvious way to test it.

The mirror was no longer his responsibility, though. He had delivered it as agreed. Now all he had to do was get home and collect his fee—and perhaps help Esmera find a home.

She was looking hesitantly up the stair at him. Gresh closed the book and smiled at her. "Good morning," he said. "I see you rose early, as well."

"I didn't want to keep anyone waiting."

"That doesn't appear to be a problem," he replied. "No one answered my knock."

"So I see. May I join you?"

"Of course." He moved over on the step, making room for her, and pushed his bag further back, out of the way.

She climbed the stair and seated herself beside him, tucking her skirt carefully. "Thank you," she said.

He nodded, and said, "It occurs to me that this must seem very unfair to you."

She looked up at him, startled. "Oh?"

"Well, yes. After all, you remember being Tobas's wife, you must surely think of yourself as the woman he married six years ago, and now he says you aren't. You remember owning an entire wardrobe and all you have now is this one dress, which still has dirt from the cave on it and snagged threads where thorns or spriggans caught at it, while the other pretty clothes all belong to the *other* Karanissa. That can hardly seem just."

"But I'm *not* Karanissa," Esmera replied. "I know that. I'm an exact copy—and I wasn't even that until you cast Lirrim's Rectification on me. You and the enchanted mirror *created* me; Karanissa didn't, so why should she have to give up any of her belongings, or share her husband with me?"

"But don't you think of yourself as her, still?"

"Sometimes. I know I'm *not*, though, however much I might feel otherwise. What I try to do is think of it as if I *was* her, but now I'm someone else. I'm trying to think of it as an *adventure*, starting a new life on my own."

"That's probably a wise attitude." Gresh considered her for a moment, and then said, "I suppose I *did* more or less create you, didn't I?"

"Not deliberately."

Gresh grimaced. "And how many children are created without that being their parents' intent? That doesn't reduce the parents' responsibility, and I don't see why it should reduce mine."

"But you didn't *know* the mirror could produce something like me."

"Well, that's true, and perhaps that *does* lessen my burden somewhat, but all the same, now that you've pointed your parentage out to me, I feel I must assume some of the responsibility for your well-being. I have already spoken to Tobas, and we've agreed that I should provide you with funds until you can make a place for yourself, in Ethshar or elsewhere. This money should be considered part of my expenses in obtaining the spriggan mirror—after all, I would not have figured out how it worked if you hadn't climbed out of it. But beyond that, I think I should also offer you the hospitality of my home, such as it is, and perhaps one of my sisters can see to your education and find you employment. One of them, Tira of Eastgate, is a witch—she ought to be able to provide some guidance. Ekava the Seamstress may be able to help with clothes."

"Thank you," Esmera said, lowering her eyes.

"You're quite welcome—and I would like to make something clear; I'm doing this not as a father, but as a friend who feels responsible for your situation. I am *not* your father; we share no blood." He was fairly certain that as a witch, able to sense his emotions, Esmera would know exactly why he was making this point. She had Karanissa's memories; she would recall his reaction to that white dress she had worn a few days ago. And Esmera, unlike Karanissa, was not married.

He also thought she would be tactful enough not to say anything about it directly.

She raised her gaze and smiled up at him. "I'm glad of that," she said. Then she turned and looked at the door. "Karanissa is awake," she said. "I can sense it. She slept better than I did—her bed was familiar, and her hair didn't get in the way."

"Ah," Gresh said. "Shall I knock?"

"She's on her way," Esmera replied.

Indeed, a moment later the door opened without further action on Gresh's part.

Half an hour later the flying carpet rose from the platform, bearing Tobas, Gresh, and Esmera, as well as Gresh's bottomless bag and a small chest holding a few of Tobas's things. It sailed upward, circled the castle towers once, and then headed westward, gathering speed as it went.

They once again ate lunch at the Dragon's Tail, in Ethshar of the Spices, but since they had so little baggage they rolled up the carpet and took it inside with them, rather than leaving it hovering.

They reached Ethshar of the Sands while the sun was still a hand's breadth above the western horizon and spent the night in Tobas's little house near Grandgate. All three slept in the upstairs rear; no mention was made of the tapestry hidden behind the draperies just the other side of the stairs.

While they ate a simple breakfast the next morning, Tobas reported that he had dreamed a reply—his own message about having the mirror secure in Dwomor had been received, and they were to proceed onward to Ethshar of the Rocks without talking to Telurinon. Kaligir would be meeting them at Gresh's shop to discuss the matter.

"Why did they send a new dream?" Gresh asked. "Didn't you talk it out in the one *you* sent?"

"No," Tobas said. "I used the Lesser Spell of Invaded Dreams, which only sends. It doesn't receive."

Gresh blinked. "Why?"

"Because that's how the spell works."

"No, I *know* how it works. I mean why didn't you use the *Greater* Spell of Invaded Dreams?"

"To save time and because I didn't have all the ingredients for the Greater," Tobas said defensively.

Gresh started to argue further, intending to point out that the only additional ingredients the more powerful spell required were blood and silver. Tobas had certainly had blood available if he bothered to prick his finger, and he *ought* to have access to a silver bit or two given he was the court wizard and the castle presumably had a treasury or at least a petty cash fund somewhere, but then he caught himself.

It didn't really matter why; it was over and done. Tobas was right that the Greater Spell took about half an hour longer to prepare than the Lesser, and if he chose to devote that saved half-hour to getting more sleep or saying goodbye to his wives, that was his business. If he didn't want to cut anyone for a few drops of blood, nor borrow a coin, that was his prerogative, as well.

If the real reason was that he hadn't felt comfortable using a fourth-order spell when a second-order one would serve, as Gresh suspected, there was nothing to be gained by forcing him to admit it.

They finished breakfast in silence and were soon on their way west and north, toward Ethshar of the Rocks.

It was very nearly noon when the carpet soared between the towers of Eastgate and descended toward Gresh's shop. The trip had been far more comfortable than the eastward journey, owing to the lack of crowding, greater familiarity with the hazards of flight, and the absence of a baby, but there had still been relatively little conversation, and Gresh was very glad to stretch his legs after sitting for so long.

Twilfa was standing in the open door of the shop, waiting for them. She waved and called a greeting as the three of them climbed off the carpet onto the street.

"Did you find the mirror?" she called as they approached.

"We did," Gresh replied. "Have you heard from Kaligir?"

"No; should I have?"

"Not necessarily, but it seemed likely, since you seemed to be expecting us."

"Oh, Dina told me you'd be home about now. I suppose *she* heard from Kaligir. So you really found the mirror? May I see it?"

"It's safe in Dwomor; we didn't bring it with us."

"You didn't? But why...?"

"I'll be happy to explain everything once we've had some food, rest, and beer," Gresh told her.

"Oh!" Twilfa realized she was blocking the doorway and stepped aside. Gresh and Esmera moved past her into the shop; Tobas was rolling up the carpet. Twilfa looked at him, then at the pair inside, and asked, "Where's the other one, and the baby?"

"I left my wives in Dwomor," Tobas said, as he hoisted the carpet on one shoulder, picked up his case, and strode to the door. "Both of them."

"But that's..." Twilfa turned.

"That's Karanissa's sister," Gresh told her. "Esmera. She'll be staying with us for a few days."

"Sister?" Twilfa stared.

"I'm told the resemblance is strong," Esmera said, smiling.

"Esmé, I have eleven sisters, and no two of them come *close* to that strong a resemblance!" Twilfa said. "Are you twins?"

"No, Karanissa is older," Esmera replied, her smile widening. "Quite a bit older, actually."

"About that food?" Gresh asked.

"Oh! Yes, of course." Twilfa hurried toward the kitchen, leaving the three of them in the shop's front room. Tobas looked around for a convenient spot to put down the rolled-up carpet. Gresh closed the front door.

That gave the three of them a little privacy. "It occurs to me—do you want your origins kept secret, or would you just as soon let everyone know you're only a few days old?" Gresh asked Esmera, as she headed toward the chairs in the corner.

"I think I'd prefer to keep it to myself," she answered.

"We'll probably have to tell Kaligir," Tobas remarked, as he thumped the rug down in front of a large brass-bound chest.

"If you must," Esmera replied. She sat down in one of the velvet chairs and began undoing her braid.

"What are you *doing*?" Tobas protested.

"I'm letting my hair down, now that I won't be flying anywhere, and I don't need to worry about you confusing me with Karanissa." She had the braid uncoiled and was untying the ribbons that held it together.

"But I'm still...I mean, people will think you're her!"

"Tobas, I am not going to keep my hair up forever; I've braided it for traveling often enough, but I've *never* worn it coiled up that way before, not in four...I mean, *Karanissa* never wore it that way, in four hundred years, and I don't like it any better than she did. I'm done traveling, so I don't need the braid, either."

"But everyone..."

"Tobas." She stopped unraveling the braid and put a hand on his. "I am going to be living here, in this city. People are going to see my face, sooner or later, and whether my hair is up or down, they'll notice the resemblance to your wife. There's no point in trying to hide it, or pretending I *don't* look exactly like her—of *course* I do, because I'm her reflection made flesh. You know that, I know that, and Gresh knows that. I'll be happy to use the twin-sister excuse instead of the truth, just to save a lot of tedious explanation, but I'm not going to ignore the fact that I'm physically identical to her. It would be silly to try. I *will* try to hide that I have all her memories, to save on explanation, but even that is *my* business, not yours. Now, calm down, sit down, and wait for Kaligir."

Tobas looked down, remembered that she was not who she appeared to be, and snatched his hand away. Then, reluctantly, he settled onto the other velvet chair.

Gresh hesitated; he wanted to give Twilfa some help in the kitchen and start getting caught up on business matters, but he had promised Tobas he would never leave him alone with Esmera.

"Will you two be all right here if I go give Twilfa a hand?" he asked.

Tobas threw Esmera a quick glance, then said, "I would really prefer..."

"Could I come with you?" Esmera interrupted. "I'd

like to meet all your sisters and get to know them, if I'm going to be staying around here."

Tobas looked relieved. "I'll stay here, to let Kaligir in," he said.

That was not exactly what Gresh had wanted, but it was close enough—and it really would be a good idea for Esmera to get to know Twilfa. "As you please," he said.

Together, Gresh and Esmera made their way down the passage to the kitchen, where Twilfa was filling beer mugs from the keg in the pantry. A tray of black bread and hard cheese stood ready on the table.

"I thought you'd want something simple and filling," Twilfa explained, with an uncertain glance at Esmera.

"Excellent," Gresh said, not mentioning how similar it was to the breakfast they had eaten in Ethshar of the Sands. "Esmé, could you fetch that big jar of apricots?" He pointed, and then picked up the prepared tray.

As Esmera lifted the heavy jar down from the shelf, Twilfa leaned over and whispered, "Are you *sure* she isn't Karanissa?"

"Quite sure."

"But she isn't really a sister, is she? Isn't Karanissa four hundred years old?"

"Yes."

"So she's, what, a homunculus of some sort? A shapeshifter?"

"More of a magical accident—and a witch, just like the original, so she can hear everything we're saying."

Twilfa threw her a quick, guilty look. "Oh."

"That's all right," Esmera said, as she turned,

holding the jar. "Of course you're curious; anyone would be. As Gresh says, I'm an accident—remember, he went to find a magical mirror? Well, he found it, and it *is* a mirror, as well as the source of the spriggans. I'm a reflection turned human."

"Oh." Twilfa's voice was noncommittal, but her expression was frankly baffled.

"But I really *am* human now and would prefer to be treated as such." There was a faint tone of warning in Esmera's voice.

Twilfa did not miss it. "Oh, of course," she said. "I'm sorry; I didn't mean to be rude."

"You weren't," Esmera assured her, relaxing again. "And as a guest here, I'm sorry if I've made you uncomfortable."

"It's nothing..."

Just then the doorbell jingled.

"That will be Kaligir," Esmera said. "Shall we go?" She hoisted the jar of pickled apricots and led the way back to the front room.

CHAPTER TWENTY-SEVEN

Kaligir stood in the doorway, looking around distastefully. He wore the same red-and-black formal robes and black cap he had worn for his first visit, a couple of sixnights earlier.

Tobas was already on his feet, saying, "Welcome, Guildmaster," when Esmera, Gresh, and Twilfa emerged into the room bearing food and beer. Gresh set the tray of bread and cheese on a table, while Esmera opened the jar of fruit, and Twilfa distributed beer.

"A pleasure to see you, Guildmaster," Gresh said, wiping his hands on his breeches.

"I'll go get more beer," Twilfa said. She had brought only three mugs.

"Don't hurry," Kaligir said.

Twilfa glanced at Gresh, who nodded; they both understood that Kaligir did not want a mere supplier's assistant listening to Wizards' Guild business.

"Shall I give her a hand?" Esmera asked.

"I think we want you here," Gresh said, before either of the other men could respond. "Here, take my beer; I'll wait for another." He took a mug from Twilfa and handed it to Esmera.

Twilfa had already provided Kaligir and Tobas with their drinks; thus unencumbered, she hurried away.

The others watched her go; then Gresh, Tobas, and Esmera turned expectantly to Kaligir and waited for him to speak.

The Guildmaster did not waste time on pleasantries. "I understand from my communications with Tobas that you have found and obtained the magic mirror, but have not destroyed it," Kaligir said, looking directly at Gresh.

"I was not engaged to destroy it," Gresh replied mildly. "I delivered it to Tobas, as our agreement specified."

"Don't play the fool with me, Gresh. You know what the Guild wanted."

"You said that you wanted to ensure the mirror would stop producing spriggans. It *has* stopped producing spriggans, and it's safely in Tobas's possession. That was the full extent of my agreement; I never promised to do anything more than deliver it, and I've done that. If you aren't happy that *he* isn't delivering it to *you* immediately, well, yes, in order to obtain it without undue difficulty I placed Javan's Geas on Tobas, ensuring that he will never give the mirror to anyone else. But the Guild can *take* it from him, should you choose. There's nothing to prevent it, whatever the spriggans may think."

"Nothing to prevent it? So anyone can take it? And what if the *spriggans* take it from him?"

"I don't mean it's unguarded; I mean that Tobas can make it possible for the Guild to take it, should you want to. As for the spriggans, they have agreed not to retrieve it—and even if they do, it's no longer generating spriggans. It's harmless, regardless of who has it."

Kaligir glanced at Tobas, who gulped beer; then he turned his attention back to Gresh. "The spriggans have *agreed* to this? And you believe them?"

"I do," Gresh said quietly. "Seriously, have you ever known a spriggan to break a promise?"

"I have never been in a position to hear one of the little pests *make* a promise!"

Gresh turned up a palm. "Well, there you are, then," he said. "That's why you couldn't find the mirror, and I could. Because I thought to ask the spriggans where it was. Because I took the time to talk to them and made an effort to understand them, instead of simply chasing them away. I negotiated terms with them, as one speaking creature to another. I treated them, annoying as they are, with a trace of respect."

Kaligir blinked at him. "Is *that* how you found it? You *asked* them?"

"Well, that, and some careful questioning, and a little sorcery."

"So you talked to spriggans who led you to the mirror and who promised not to take it back—but what makes you think they spoke for all the half-million of the creatures who are roaming the World? Why shouldn't some other bunch of spriggans snatch the mirror away?"

"I have reason to believe the ones I spoke to represent the majority and that many of the others don't concern themselves with the mirror at all."

Kaligir frowned. Gresh met his gaze calmly.

"I promised only to deliver the mirror," Gresh said.

"Holding on to it is not my problem. I would have thought that the Wizards' Guild could manage that without my assistance."

Kaligir said nothing more for a long moment, but finally demanded, "And once you had the mirror, why did you and Tobas not see to its destruction? You say that it's no longer producing spriggans, but destroying it would seem a far more certain way to ensure that no more spriggans would be produced than whatever you *did* do."

"Well, Tobas *cannot* destroy it—I placed a geas on him to that effect."

"Why did you do that? Having done it, why did you not destroy it yourself? Tobas could not destroy it or give it back to you, but surely you, more than anyone else, could just *take* it. Why didn't you?"

"There are three reasons, each of them sufficient," Gresh said. He raised a finger. "First: We conducted a test where we broke the mirror into four pieces and discovered that this resulted in multiplying that half-million spriggans to two million. Using Javan's Restorative to repair the mirror reduced that number back to the original. This leads me to suspect that destroying the mirror may have unanticipated and unfortunate results, and until we know much more about it, it would be unwise to risk doing anything that might multiply the number of spriggans, rather than reducing it."

"Ah," Kaligir said, stroking his beard with one hand, while the other still held his untasted beer. "Is *that* what that was about? We did notice a very brief increase in the number of spriggans."

"Yes. Shattering it is a very bad idea. I doubt other obvious methods would be better."

"I see your point. Go on."

Gresh raised another finger. "Second: I gave my word to the spriggans who had possession of the mirror, and who allowed us to take it, that neither I nor Tobas would attempt to destroy the mirror. We did not say anything to bind the Guild, but I *did* give my word about my own actions and Tobas's. My word is good."

"Fair enough, if somewhat inconvenient," Kaligir agreed. He looked down, as if just now noticing he held a mug, and took a sip.

"And finally," Gresh said, holding up three fingers. "I refuse to participate in the murder of half a million speaking beings. Aren't we taught that what made humans more than mere animals was that the gods taught us to speak? Well, spriggans can speak, too. They can make and keep promises. They can understand far more than you might think. They were bright enough to figure out things about the mirror that we might never have guessed. If they hadn't told me what they knew, I might not have guessed as much of the mirror's true nature as I have. I don't say they're human—they're stupid and annoying and troublesome, and I don't want them in my house—but they are thinking, speaking creatures, and killing them indiscriminately is wrong. I won't be a part of it. Destroying the mirror *might* kill them—so I won't do that. I know better than to think I can stop the Wizards' Guild from doing whatever it pleases, but I will do what I can to keep you from exterminating the spriggans. I'm sure you can find ways to kill individuals who are especially troublesome or dangerous, if you must—I could even suggest a few spells that might help. I'll do nothing to stop that, any more than I'll stop a magistrate from hanging a murderer. But I won't help you to wipe them *all* out, guilty and innocent alike."

Kaligir took a long, thoughtful swig of beer before replying, "It seems to me that your first and third reasons contradict each other. Destroying the mirror cannot both multiply and exterminate the little pests."

"There's a contradiction, yes. That's because I don't know which is true. Destroying the mirror might kill them, or it might multiply them infinitely. I don't know. And neither do you."

"Not yet," Kaligir admitted.

Gresh nodded. "Well, then—I've explained my position. I delivered the mirror. I ensured it would not produce more spriggans. I have fulfilled my end of our contract; I expect the Guild to honor its end. I trust my shop will be permitted to resume normal business operations immediately? And my fee will be paid promptly? And that my bill for expenses will be honored, when I have prepared it?"

"The shop can re-open, of course, and your expenses will be paid. We will expect the return of all remaining powders and potions. When we have verified that the mirror is truly in Tobas's possession, and that it really is the correct mirror, Enral's Eternal Youth will be cast on you."

Gresh smiled. Returning the powders and potions was not ideal, but otherwise he appeared to have won on all points. "Excellent!" he said. "Thank you!" He lifted a hand in salute, regretting that he had given Esmera his mug.

Tobas, Esmera, and Kaligir all drank in response. Kaligir wiped foam from his beard and said, "I do have a few questions, though. You said you have ensured the mirror would not produce any more spriggans. How did you do that?"

"That's a long story."

"And Tobas, you said in your message that you were not bringing your wives—it's of no consequence, but in that case, why is Karanissa here?"

Tobas had been caught with his mug to his lips; he spluttered. "That's not Karanissa," he said.

"It's not?" He turned to Esmera.

"My name is Esmera," she said, and curtsied.

Kaligir stared at her for a moment. Then he looked at Gresh. "Is she part of your long story?"

"Yes, she is," Gresh said.

"Then I think I would like to hear the tale now."

"Of course; if you would join me?" He gestured at the velvet chairs.

There were not enough seats for all four of them. Esmera said, "Shall I go help Twilfa?"

"If you would," Gresh agreed.

Then he sat down with the two wizards and began explaining everything that had happened over the past several days.

By the time he finished, all three of them had consumed a mug or two of beer, as well as a modest amount of the bread, cheese, and fruit the two women had delivered. From what Gresh saw of them, Twilfa and Esmera appeared to be becoming fast friends—they were laughing happily at each other's jokes as they brought out the food and drink.

He also noticed that a spriggan had slipped into the shop and was listening from a nearby shelf.

"So you believe that there is a corresponding mirror in another reality," Kaligir said thoughtfully. "And you've convinced the inhabitants to seal it away in a box."

"Yes."

"And what happens if it is taken *out* of that box?"

"Then we would once again have reflected spriggans emerging into the World," Gresh said. "Which is why I did not leave the mirror in the spriggans' possession—I wanted it somewhere we could keep a watch on it."

Kaligir nodded. "You would send messages by writing them on spriggans, and using the Spell of Reversal, reflect those into the spriggans' realm."

"That's one approach," Gresh said. "After seeing what happened to Esmera, though, I can suggest another—cast Lirrim's Rectification on a spriggan, and it should become a part of its original in that other realm, providing a direct and more efficient means of communication. This would also, incidentally, render the spriggan vulnerable to ordinary weapons and magic; it might be a suitable punishment for troublemakers." He looked up at the spriggan on the shelf. "You might want to spread the word about that."

The spriggan squealed and ducked out of sight behind a stuffed owl.

"That's a very interesting possibility," Kaligir remarked, as he glanced at the now-empty bit of shelf.

"There are a good many other possibilities here, as well," Gresh said. "It seems to me that it should be possible to put the spriggans to use—yes, they're stupid and clumsy and absent-minded, but they *can* be made to cooperate. I think they might be very handy as messengers, for example."

"Or spies," Kaligir murmured thoughtfully.

Gresh did not comment on that; he had thought of it himself, but had doubts about how well it would work.

"Then the outcome is satisfactory?" Tobas asked. "Even though there are still half a million spriggans in the World?"

"We've survived them this long," Kaligir said. "Now that we know more of their true nature—assuming that Gresh is correct—I think we ought to be able to manage them."

"Then might I ask about *my* fee, for services rendered? The tapestry?"

Kaligir blinked. "Oh, that's between you and Telurinon. I don't see any reason that it shouldn't be started, though."

"Oh." Tobas looked annoyed, but said nothing more.

"And Esmera?" Gresh asked. "Does the Guild have any interest in her?"

"The reflection of Tobas's wife? No—as far as I can see, she's just another animation, like Lady Nuvielle's miniature dragon, or those teapots so many people like. She's none of the Guild's concern unless she starts casting spells herself."

"She's a witch," Gresh pointed out. "She does cast spells."

"But not wizardry. Witchcraft is the Sisterhood's problem, not the Guild's." He stood and held out a hand. "I believe we're done here, then."

Gresh rose, as well, and took the wizard's hand.

"Thank you for your services," Kaligir said. "Send me the bill for expenses at your earliest convenience, and I'll see that it's paid. Give me the unused powders and potions; I'll take those with me. Then I'll see about having Enral's Eternal Youth cast."

Gresh nodded. He crossed to the bottomless bag to retrieve the rather battered box that held the remaining jars.

Five minutes later the doorbell jingled as Kaligir departed, box in hand.

"That went more smoothly than I feared it might," Gresh remarked.

"Yes, it did," Tobas agreed, picking up the flying carpet. "I suspect that there's been discussion within the Guild we weren't privy to, and that worked out in our favor. If you don't mind, though, I'd like to go now and see if I can get back to Ethshar of the Sands before dark. I want to get that tapestry started!"

"Of course," Gresh said. "Shall I call Esmera, so you can say goodbye?"

Tobas glanced uneasily at the passage to the kitchen; soft feminine laughter could be heard from it.

"No," he said, grabbing the handle of his case. "She's not my wife, after all—just someone I met a few days ago."

"As you please," Gresh said. He did not offer to shake hands; Tobas's hands were full. He did hold the door for the wizard, though, and watch as he unrolled the carpet and set his chest and himself securely aboard it.

Gresh waved a farewell as the carpet rose. Tobas waved back as it glided away with a faint whoosh, rising as it went.

Gresh stood in the familiar street for a moment, watching as the people of Ethshar went about their everyday business. Then he turned and walked back into his shop. He paused there, as well, taking in the tidy but heavily laden shelves, the locked cabinets, the vault door, the velvet chairs, and all the rest of it.

This comfortable and familiar shop was his and would be his as long as it lasted. He had just earned himself a way out of aging and eventual inevitable death. Oh, he could still die, certainly, but it was no longer guaranteed.

That was a very pleasant thought.

And all in all, the errand had not been so very difficult or time-consuming.

And there might be other benefits, besides his official pay. He ambled down the passage to the kitchen.

"Oh, there you are!" Twilfa said, looking up at his entrance. "We were just discussing where Esmera would sleep."

"Anywhere she likes, I suppose," Gresh said. He smiled. "She's certainly welcome in *my* bed!"

Twilfa made a disgusted noise, but before she could say anything more, Esmera said, "Then I won't be needing that cot made up after all."

Twilfa stopped and stared at her, then turned her astonished gaze on Gresh.

He was struggling to hide his own pleased surprise. He hadn't expected it to be quite *that* easy. He turned up an empty palm.

Twilfa's astonishment turned to disgust. "Oh, you two are just hopeless," she said, as she stamped away.

Esmera and Gresh looked at one another, smiling.

Then they were in each other's arms and using their mouths for something a little more intimate than smiling.

CHAPTER TWENTY-EIGHT

"I had thought better of Tobas," Esmera said, as she stretched in the morning sun. "Abandoning me here without even a farewell." She was standing naked by the window of Gresh's bedroom.

"He already *has* his Karanissa," Gresh said, as he watched her admiringly from his bed. "I think he was afraid that if he allowed himself to have anything to do with you, he'd wind up with *three* wives, and Alorria would never forgive him."

"I suppose—but it still isn't very considerate of my feelings! I was married to him for six years, after all—or at least, that's how *I* remember it."

"But it's not what *he* remembers."

"Hmph." She stepped away from the window and returned to the bedside.

"Is your very enjoyable presence here a sort of retaliation for how he mistreated you, then?" Gresh asked.

"Not exactly—but being cast aside so very definitely certainly made it *easier* to be here. There's no lingering regret." She turned and looked at him intently. "If Tobas has managed to avoid making any comparison between Alorria and myself for six years, I would hope I can do the same after a single night."

"I didn't say a word!" He grimaced. "I can see that being married to a witch could have its drawbacks."

She stared at him silently for a moment, then said, "I won't hold you to whatever might be implied by that mention of marriage."

"And I won't rush you," Gresh said. "I haven't offered; you haven't accepted. Marrying a witch might not be the best idea for keeping peace in my family and business, in any case. All of my sisters except Tira might consider it inappropriate favoritism, and my customers, almost all wizards, might think it odd. I've been happily unmarried all my life, though a few women have clearly been willing, so why should I change? All that said, though, right now, looking at you and listening to your voice, I think it might be worth it."

"That's very sweet—and I have no intention of rushing into anything." She turned to the window. "For one thing, I think I might like to travel before settling down. I've seen so little of the modern World! When I *did* travel, it was always with Tobas and Alorria—Alorria would not allow me to go much of anywhere without her."

"You aren't Karanissa anymore," Gresh reminded her. "*She* was the one Alorria insisted on accompanying."

"But it's hard to stop talking of myself as if I were. I *am* her, in so many ways!"

"Of course. I expect you'll grow apart in time, though, as you each have your own experiences."

"I suppose we will." She sighed. "I might want to go back to Dwomor briefly, to visit her."

"Really? Alorria wouldn't like that."

"Really. Who cares what Alorria wants? She isn't family anymore."

"But her father is still king of Dwomor. Was living with her so very difficult?"

"Sometimes. Not always. Not even usually. She was generally pleasant when she wasn't being jealous." She sighed. "She was much better before the baby came."

"Then perhaps you're the lucky one, abandoned outcast that you are, being free of her. It almost makes me feel sorry for Karanissa."

Esmera did not answer; she stood, still looking out the window.

"But you miss Tobas," Gresh said.

"I'm sure I'll get over it in time," Esmera said. "But yes, these last few days have not been pleasant, having him shun me."

"If you go back to visit Karanissa and see him again?"

She turned up an empty palm.

Gresh was no witch nor seer, but he was fairly sure he could guess what Esmera was planning. "You're thinking of trading places with her for a while, aren't you?"

"Possibly. No one would ever know, not even Tobas." She turned. "Not even you."

"You may be underestimating us."

"I suppose I might be." She did not say aloud that she doubted it, but Gresh could almost hear the words, all the same.

"And which of you would come back to me, here in Ethshar?"

"What makes you think either of us would?" She turned to glare at him.

"My high opinion of myself."

She smiled. "Well, you might be right. One of us might come back. Karanissa would probably be curious about you, if nothing else."

"Karanissa is married to someone else. That doesn't bother you?"

"Tobas has two wives. Would it really be so terrible for Karanissa and I to share two husbands?"

"I thought you weren't ready to marry me."

"I'm not. I'm just considering possibilities."

"Ah, I see. Would it bother *you* if Karanissa shared my bed for a time?"

"I've never been the jealous type—not with Derry, not with Tobas, not with you. Would it matter to *you* if it were Karanissa here, instead of me?"

Gresh hesitated.

"I hope so," he said. "You *aren't* the same person anymore. You're the one I want here."

She laughed. "You couldn't tell the difference!"

"I don't know. I think I might."

She laughed again—and then her laughter changed, and she was crying. He leapt from the bed and took her in his arms.

As he stood there, holding her and trying to comfort her for the loss of her husband and her past life, he kissed the top of her head and wondered whether he *would* know if she traded places.

He hoped he would never have occasion to find out. He wanted *this* one to stay. He wanted her to stay for a long, long time.

Thanks to Enral's Eternal Youth, it might prove to be a *very* long time.

EPILOGUE

Piffle slipped into the room as silently as it could—and as it was a wiry young spriggan, that was very silently indeed. It looked around.

There was the black box, just as the stories said, atop the giants' table. Piffle looked up at the looming structure, then grabbed one of the table legs at head height and began pulling itself up.

It was perhaps halfway up the table-leg when a gigantic hand closed around it, pulling Piffle off its perch. It found itself swept up in the air and turned to face the immense hairy face of a He-Giant.

"Now, what do you think *you're* doing?" the giant demanded, in its impossibly deep, rumbling voice.

"Nothing!" Piffle said. "Do nothing, really!"

A She-Giant appeared beside the He-Giant, looking at Piffle. Her incredibly long, lush hair spilled down around her. Piffle had never before seen a She-Giant's hair so close up, and he was impressed.

"It just looks like an ordinary mirror," she said. "You don't need to see it. There's nothing special about it—except when giants are climbing out of it. If you look at it, that might just happen."

"I would think you'd consider eight of us to be quite enough," the He-Giant said. "Especially after we smashed up those shops when we first appeared."

"Yes, yes!" Piffle said, nodding wildly. "Enough giants!"

"Then *don't open the box*!" the He-Giant bellowed.

"Yes yes yes! Put Piffle down now? Please?"

With a snort, the He-Giant set Piffle back on the floor. Piffle turned and scampered away. The He-Giant watched it go.

"Silly spriggan," he said.

"They're just curious," the She-Giant told him.

"And attracted to magic."

"That, too."

The He-Giant glanced at the box. "Do you think more giants would *really* come out of it? Or did our mysterious message-writer have some other motive?"

She spread empty hands. "Who knows?"

"If more giants appeared—well, it might be nice to have more company."

"Female company, you mean? I'm not enough for you?"

"Of course you are! I didn't mean that. But where we're all so much alike, the four of you sisters and my three brothers and me—aren't there any *different* people wherever it is we came from? It might be nice to talk to someone who isn't just like us."

"Just talk? So you aren't hoping that someday a beautiful woman might come climbing out of the magic mirror, so you'd have a choice, and not just the four of us with the same boring face?"

"You're more than beautiful enough! Besides, now

that I think about it, it's just as likely to be another man, and I'm not interested in sharing you. Better we keep everything balanced, four and four."

"Or maybe we'd get worse monsters next time," the She-Giant mused. "Remember, we got those funny false spriggans before. We could get anything—it's not as if we have any idea how the magic works, or where we actually came from."

"Right." He glanced at the black box, still securely sealed.

He wondered who had sent that message, sixnights ago, not much more than an hour after their own arrival—"SHUT THE MIRROR IN A SOLID BOX, AND NOTHING ELSE WILL COME OUT OF IT." Why had it been written across a false spriggan's belly? Why hadn't the mysterious magician sent a piece of paper?

He shook his head.

They would probably never know—but they would do their best to see that the mirror stayed safely locked away. It was just too dangerous to let out.

They didn't really need any more giants. The fact was, the He-Giant rather *liked* being one of only four men in a world of spriggans, an object of awe to all the millions of little green creatures. It was really quite enjoyable—so long as there were four women, as well!

Lawrence Watt-Evans has been a full-time writer of fantasy and science fiction since 1979. He has authored more than three dozen novels, and over a hundred short stories. He lives in Gaithersburg, Maryland with his wife and Chanel, the obligatory writer's cat.

THE SPRIGGAN MIRROR is the ninth novel in the "Legends of Ethshar" series, which began in 1985 with THE MISENCHANTED SWORD. THE SPRIGGAN MIRROR originated as a serial on the author's website at Ethshar.com, and additional notes about it can be found there at http://www.ethshar.com/thespigganmirrornotes.html

Readers may also be interested in the short story "Sirinita's Dragon," at http://www.ethshar.com/sirinitasdragon1.html

MARJORIE M. LIU

SOUL SONG

Against her will, Kitala Bell foresees the future. Now her own future is in peril. From the ocean's depths rises an impossible blend of fantasy and danger, a creature whose voice is seduction incarnate, whose song can manipulate lives the way that Kitala herself manipulates the strings of her violin...even to the point of breaking. He is a prince of the sea, an enigma—a captive stretched to the limit of his endurance by a woman intent on using him for the purest evil. And when survival requires he and Kitala form a closer partnership than either has ever known, the price of their bond will threaten not just their lives, but the essence of their very souls.

ISBN 10: 0-8439-5766-2
ISBN 13: 978-0-8439-5766-2 $6.99 US/$8.99 CAN